A *[...]*
A hus*[...]*
Stirring t*[...]*

THE STEEPWOOD

Scandals

VOLUME THREE

When the debauched Marquis of Sywell won Steepwood Abbey years ago at cards, it led to the death of the Earl of Yardley. Now he's caused scandal again by marrying a girl out of his class – and young enough to be his granddaughter! After being married only a short time, the Marchioness has disappeared, leaving no trace of her whereabouts. There is every expectation that yet more scandals will emerge, though no one yet knows just how shocking they will be.

The four villages surrounding the Steepwood Abbey estate are in turmoil, not only with the dire goings-on at the Abbey, but also with their own affairs. Each of the eight volumes in THE STEEPWOOD SCANDALS contain two full novels that follow the mystery behind the disappearance of the young woman, and the individual romances of lovers connected in some way with the intrigue.

THE STEEPWOOD
Scandals

Regency drama, intrigue, mischief...
and marriage

Volume 1 – November 2006
Lord Ravensden's Marriage by Anne Herries
An Innocent Miss by Elizabeth Bailey

Volume 2 – December 2006
The Reluctant Bride by Meg Alexander
A Companion of Quality by Nicola Cornick

Volume 3 – January 2007
A Most Improper Proposal by Gail Whitiker
A Noble Man by Anne Ashley

Volume 4 – February 2007
An Unreasonable Match by Sylvia Andrew
An Unconventional Duenna by Paula Marshall

Volume 5 – March 2007
Counterfeit Earl by Anne Herries
The Captain's Return by Elizabeth Bailey

Volume 6 – April 2007
The Guardian's Dilemma by Gail Whitiker
Lord Exmouth's Intentions by Anne Ashley

Volume 7 – May 2007
Mr Rushford's Honour by Meg Alexander
An Unlikely Suitor by Nicola Cornick

Volume 8 – June 2007
An Inescapable Match by Sylvia Andrew
The Missing Marchioness by Paula Marshall

THE STEEPWOOD
Scandals

Volume 3

Gail Whitiker & Anne Ashley

*M&B™ and M&B™ with the Rose Device
are trademarks of the publisher.*

*Harlequin Mills & Boon Limited, Eton House,
18-24 Paradise Road, Richmond, Surrey TW9 1SR*

First published in Great Britain in 2001

THE STEEPWOOD SCANDALS © Harlequin Books S.A. 2007

A Most Improper Proposal © Harlequin Books S.A. 2001
A Noble Man © Harlequin Books S.A. 2001

*Special thanks and acknowledgement are given to
Gail Whitiker and Anne Ashley for their contribution to
The Steepwood Scandals series.*

ISBN-13: 978 0 263 85497 8
ISBN-10: 0 263 85497 3

052-0107

*Printed and bound in Spain
by Litografía Rosés S.A., Barcelona*

A Most Improper Proposal
by
Gail Whitiker

Originally hailing from Pembrokeshire, **Gail Whitiker** now lives on beautiful Vancouver Island on the west coast of Canada. When she isn't indulging her love of writing, you'll find her enjoying brisk walks along the Island's many fine beaches, or trying to catch up on her second love – reading. She wrote her first novel when she was in her teens, and still blesses her English teacher for not telling her how bad it really was.

Chapter One

July, 1811

'*Ut sementem feceris, ita metes,*' Miss Desirée Nash recited for the benefit of the twelve young ladies sitting in front of her. 'Or as the saying is more commonly known, as you sow, so shall you reap. Now girls, you will notice that—yes, Miss Melburry?'

'My grandmama used to say that to me all the time, Miss Nash, but she never told me what it meant.'

Desirée smiled at the nine-year-old's confusion. 'It simply means that everyone is responsible for the way their lives turn out, Jane. For example, if you are kind and considerate to the people you meet, it is likely that you will be treated with the same kindness and consideration in return. After all, if a farmer planted only stones in his field, what could he expect to harvest *but* stones? Now, girls, you will notice that in the pronunciation of the word *feceris,* we put the emphasis on—'

'Miss Nash, why must we trouble ourselves to learn

a language that was spoken by fusty old men over a thousand years ago? Surely it cannot be relevant in today's society?'

This question too originated from the back of the room, but unlike Miss Melbury's, Desirée knew that it had not been raised to clarify a point. The Honourable Elizabeth Perry had made no secret of the fact that she disliked the ancient languages and that she resented the time spent in the learning of them. So there was no doubt in Desirée's mind that the question had been asked not just to express the girl's boredom with the subject, but in an attempt to disrupt the class as well.

'Latin, Miss Perry, is at the root of all civilized language,' Desirée began patiently. 'It provides the very foundations upon which English is based. So it only follows that to have a better understanding of Latin is to have a better understanding of the way we speak.'

'And I am sure that is all very well, Miss Nash, but how is that to help us in our search for a *husband*? My father says that all a lady need concern herself with is how to appear charming and attractive to a gentleman. Surely our time would be better spent in those pursuits than in the memorization of words and phrases typically reserved for barristers and the clergy.'

There was a faint titter of amusement from the tall girl seated next to Elizabeth, but Desirée paid it no mind. Isabel Hewton worshipped Elizabeth Perry and had since the first day of class, but she was not in herself a troublemaker. She simply needed someone of a more domineering nature to follow.

No, it was the rest of the girls Desirée was concerned with, and for whatever reason, they seemed unwilling to take up Elizabeth's cry—for which Desirée could only be thankful. She had no wish to antagonize her young charges. Most of their fathers were wealthy and influential men and Mrs Guarding, the founder and headmistress of the Guarding Academy for Girls, was dependent upon their largesse for her living. For that reason alone, it was accepted by all that in difficult situations it was best to avoid confrontation and to move on in as amiable and tactful a manner as possible.

That particular edict did not always sit well with Desirée, however, especially when it came to the likes of Elizabeth Perry. Desirée found it exceedingly difficult to have her authority undermined by a spoiled young woman who would never utter a single word of Latin—or possibly anything else of intelligence— once she passed beyond these walls.

'I would venture to say that you are correct, Miss Perry,' Desirée replied finally. 'In all likelihood, you will not be required to sprinkle your everyday speech with Latin quotes, or to impress your future husband with your knowledge of their meanings and subtleties. However, *because* of the antiquity of the language and the insight it gives us into the nuances of our own, we feel that the inclusion of Latin in the Guarding curriculum is not only necessary, but vital. Therefore, I suggest that if you do not appreciate the opportunity you have been given to learn the language, you might at least have the good manners to remain silent so that the other young ladies can.'

Desirée had not raised her voice. She knew from experience that to lose one's temper was to lose the advantage and that, upon occasion, a well-delivered reprimand could be just as effective as a scold. But when Elizabeth Perry abruptly got to her feet and glared at her, Desirée knew that the outcome had been much the same. Obviously the viscount's daughter was not used to being spoken to in such a manner and certainly not by a person she deemed to be beneath her in every way.

'I shall not stay here and be treated like this,' the young woman cried. 'I shall speak to my father about you this very day, Miss Nash. Just see if I do not!'

With that, she gathered up her things and stormed out of the room.

A shocked silence followed her departure. The eleven remaining girls glanced at each other while Desirée patiently waited for the sound of Miss Perry's footsteps to fade into the distance. When they had, she slowly began to smile.

'The great philosopher Ovid once said, *rident stolidi verba Latina.* Do any of you know what that means?' At the tentative smiles which appeared on the faces of some of the older girls, Desirée nodded. 'Precisely. Only fools laugh at the Latin language. Now, Miss Chisham, perhaps you would be good enough to translate the phrase, patience is a virtue.'

The class soon settled back into its normal routine and the outburst by Miss Perry was forgotten. But Desirée was not so naïve as to believe that she had heard the last of it. She had no doubt that Miss Perry *would* speak to her father about what had happened today. Or that he in turn would speak to Mrs Guarding; a conversation which would result in a meeting between Desirée and the headmistress, at which time she would be gently reminded of the importance of tact and diplomacy when dealing with some of the school's more difficult students. But since Mrs Guarding had also complimented her on her skills as a teacher and upon her unwavering dedication to the Academy, Desirée could not bring herself to feel unduly concerned about it.

It was an acknowledged fact that the Honourable Elizabeth Perry was a thorn in many of the teachers' sides. Ghislaine de Champlain, the French mistress, had encountered the same resistance when it came to the conjugation of verbs. And poor Henriette Mason, who gave instruction in history and geography, had nearly been reduced to tears by the girl's repeated threats to invoke her father's wrath if she was forced to memorize the names of any more than five of the British colonies.

Personally, Desirée wondered why Lord Perry and his wife had enrolled their daughter in the Guarding Academy for Girls in the first place. The school had a well-deserved reputation for academia and its teachers for attempting to break down the intellectual barriers which faced women in society. Its students were encouraged to speak out against the generally accepted norms and to stand up for their rights and freedoms. Indeed, the school's founder and headmistress, Mrs Eleanor Guarding, was an acknowledged emancipationist, as well as being a noted poet and historian.

That was not to say that the social niceties were not also part of the daily curriculum. Miss Jane Emerson guided the young ladies very nicely through the intricacies of the dance, as well as in the proper way to acquit themselves in polite society. And Miss Helen de Coverdale instructed them in watercolours and Italian. But at the Guarding Academy, it was generally accepted that the more important subjects were those which stretched the limits of a young woman's mind; subjects which, hitherto, had been deemed the exclusive domain of men.

At length, the handbell rang in the hall to signal the end of the session.

'Thank you, ladies, that will be all,' Desirée said. 'Tomorrow, we shall begin to study the writings of Euripedes. Perhaps Miss Perry will deign to join us to hear what words of wisdom *that* fusty old man had to share.'

There was a smattering of giggles as the girls filed out and Desirée knew that she had won the day—at least in the eyes of her pupils. And for now, that was all that mattered. The life of a teacher was seldom easy, and she knew there would always be an Elizabeth Perry waiting to make things difficult. But as long as she could instill the required knowledge in the minds of the pupils who truly did wish to learn, Desirée was content. Some might think that a formidable task, but it was not an impossible one. Certainly her mother had managed to imbue her own teachings with insight and humour. And Papa, bless his soul, had been a clergyman of unusual wit and vivacity. He had made the learning of Latin and Greek an adventure rather than the dull, dry undertaking it could have been.

It was because of her parents that Desirée had never found her studies tedious. She had risen to meet the educational challenges they had set forward and had taken great satisfaction in seeing a language come alive. Unlike Lord Perry, they did not adhere to the belief that all a young lady needed to know was the best way to attract a wealthy husband. Before their untimely deaths, they had impressed upon Desirée the value of understanding other cultures and the importance of exploring the philosophies behind them. They had instilled in her an appreciation for the early societies which had formed the models upon which all other civilizations were based, and she had learned to recognize the wisdom of Pythagoras and Euclid.

'Fusty old men indeed,' Desirée muttered as she walked around the room collecting books and papers. Had Elizabeth Perry but troubled herself to find out, she would have been *shocked* at some of the things those fusty old men did.

Of course, there would never be any need for Miss Perry to actually *use* her education, Desirée reflected wryly. Her immediate challenge upon leaving Guarding's would be to find an eligible gentleman and to marry him as quickly as possible. Unlike Desirée, she would never be called upon to make her own way in the world. And while it was true that Desirée might have been more pleasantly situated had she spent time developing the skills which would have allowed her to go to London and find a husband, it was the education her parents had given her which had proved to be her ultimate salvation.

When both of them had succumbed to illness and Desirée had found herself alone in the world at eighteen, it was not the nicety of her manners which had enabled her to apply for a position at the Guarding Academy for Girls, but rather her extensive knowledge of Greek, Latin and philosophy. It was education, not charm, which had spared her the humiliation of having to appeal to her own family for charity when no such offers had been forthcoming.

Even her late grandfather, a man whom Desirée had barely known, but who had had the wherewithal to help her, had refused to reach out his hand. And all because of some silly argument arising from her mother's insistence on falling in love with a penniless clergyman and then on her marrying him against her father's wishes...

'Have I caught you day-dreaming again, Miss Nash?' came a teasing enquiry from the doorway.

Recognizing the voice, Desirée's features relaxed into a smile. Helen de Coverdale was a fairly recent addition to the staff at the Guarding Academy for Girls, but time notwithstanding, she and Desirée had already become good friends. She was six years older than Desirée, and with her soft brown eyes and long dark hair she was one of the loveliest young women Desirée had ever met. Certainly, she was the only teacher at the Guarding Academy who turned heads wherever she went.

And yet, for all that, Desirée had never seen Helen

so much as *glance* at a passing gentleman. Nor did she talk about her past, except to say that she had come from a good home and that she had once been a pupil at the very institution at which she now taught.

But what had caused her to return to the school at the advanced age of thirty, and to apply to Mrs Guarding for a teaching position, was something that Desirée could only wonder at. She turned now and offered her friend an apologetic glance. 'Helen, forgive me, I had no idea you were there. I was, as you say, quite lost in my thoughts.'

'Yes, I noticed as much, but given the way you were beginning to frown, I thought you might have been grateful for the interruption,' Helen said with a smile. 'Have you been having problems with the Honourable Elizabeth again?'

Desirée glanced at her in surprise. 'How did you know?'

'I saw her heading in the direction of Mrs Guarding's study and she had that *look* in her eye. I think you know the one to which I refer.'

Desirée grimaced. 'All too well. I daresay I shall be called to Mrs Guarding's rooms and taken to task once again for the less than diplomatic way I dealt with her reluctance to participate in class today.'

'Let me guess? Was she once again questioning the usefulness of Latin in everyday life?'

'That, and insinuating that the only subjects that *were* worth studying were those which dealt directly with the arts of attracting and securing an eligible *parti*. You can imagine my response.'

'I can indeed.' An attractive dimple appeared at the

corner of Helen's mouth. 'No wonder Miss Perry was looking so put out.'

'Aggravating child,' Desirée muttered. 'I have often wondered *why* Lord and Lady Perry chose to send her here. If all they required of a school was that it teach their daughter how to dance and manage a gentleman's household, they could easily have sent her to any one of a number of exclusive lady's seminaries in London. Goodness knows, they could well have afforded to.'

'Yes, but perhaps they sent her here *because* they did not wish Elizabeth to be so close,' Helen suggested. 'I seem to recall Mrs Guarding saying that there were some problems between Lady Perry and her daughter. Perhaps it was she who suggested Steep Abbot in the first place.'

'I do not find that in the least surprising,' Desirée commented. 'If the Honourable Elizabeth were my daughter, I would have suggested a school in the wilds of Scotland. Still, I suppose it is no concern of mine. And on such a lovely day, I refuse to let thoughts of her weigh me down. I think that I shall go down to the river and amuse myself there for a while.'

At the mention of the river, Helen's eyes widened in dismay. 'Desirée, never say you are going *swimming* again. You know how Mrs Guarding feels about that.'

'Yes, but I have only been down three times this summer, given the dismal weather we've had, and once autumn is upon us, I shall have no inclination to go at all. And on a warm day like this, what could be better than immersing oneself in the cool, clear waters of a secluded woodland pool?'

'Any number of things to my way of thinking,' Helen murmured. 'And you should think better of it too. You know that Elizabeth Perry will take great pleasure in informing Mrs Guarding of your transgressions if she is lucky enough to catch you at them.'

'No one knows that better than I, Helen dear, but you need have no fear that I shall be discovered. Mrs Guarding has given me extra time in exchange for some work I did at the beginning of the week. And since the girls are still in class, I intend to make good use of it. *Sedit qui timuit ne non seccederat.*'

'Which means?'

'He who feared he would not succeed, sat still.'

Helen tilted her head to one side and said in rapid Italian, *Ella che e impigliata deve essere costretta ad soffrire le conseguenze.*'

This time, it was Desirée who smiled. 'And that means?'

'She who is caught must be made to suffer the consequences. Be careful, Desirée. Sometimes, even the most carefully laid plans go awry,' Helen warned softly. 'And when they do, the consequences can come back to haunt us in the most unexpected of ways.'

The River Steep meandered pleasantly through the pastoral countryside south of the small village of Steep Ride before flowing quietly into the densely forested area known as Steep Wood. It changed course once inside the trees, heading north at a point just past Bredington, the hunting-lodge owned by Viscount Wyndham, and took another turn before exiting the woods south of the village of Steep Abbot. There, it formed in its bend a natural pool that measured some sixty feet across and some ten feet deep.

Desirée had stumbled upon the secluded bathing spot quite by chance when she had been out walking earlier in the spring. She had taken a different path into Steep Wood that day and had wandered further into the forest than she'd intended. But when she had found the tranquil glade and the shimmering waters of its pool, she felt as though she had discovered a pot of gold at the end of the rainbow. She had quickly glanced around to make sure that she was completely alone, and then, confident that no one else was likely to intrude, had stripped down to her shift and dived in.

Oh, how blissfully cool and refreshing the water had felt—and how liberating to swim without having to worry about anyone watching her! It was much better than going to the seaside, where there were all manner of people milling about and one had to put up with those dreadful bathing-boxes for getting in and out of the water.

Desirée had splashed about and swum for the better part of thirty minutes.

Unfortunately, Mrs Guarding had been considerably less pleased when Desirée had finally returned to the school with her hair dripping wet and damp spots showing through her clothes. She had told Desirée exactly what she'd thought of her little escapade. And while she had not forbidden Desirée to swim in the river, she had certainly left her in no doubt as to what would happen the next time she was caught doing so!

Unfortunately, the lure of the forbidden pool continued to beckon, and Desirée did indeed make several more trips to it. But with each visit she grew more circumspect. She only ventured there when she knew she had time enough to get down and back, *and* when she knew the whereabouts of certain students. She also made sure she kept her hair dry and that she brought extra clothing to wear back to school.

Reaching the edge of the pool now, Desirée stood for a moment to enjoy the special feeling of peace and tranquillity that permeated the glade. She could hear the birds singing in the branches overhead, and smell the delicate perfume of wildflowers and grass all around her. It was such a pleasure to escape from the confines of her everyday life. To break free from the confines of a world where there was always someone watching her; waiting to pronounce her guilty for the slightest breach of propriety. And that really was not fair. Whereas men were allowed every freedom imaginable, women were constrained almost from the moment of birth. Even those who endeavoured to enrich their minds by the study of books were labelled bluestockings and looked down upon by their peers.

Still, there was little she could do to change society as a whole, and, unwilling to harbour such dismal thoughts on such a wonderful day, Desirée blithely cast them—and her clothes—aside. Dressed only in her shift, she made her way towards the edge of the pool. She took care not to lose her footing on the slippery grass and slowly made her way in until she stood about waist-deep in the water. Then, putting her arms together, she pushed off with her legs and competently began to swim across the widest part. Her slender arms cut cleanly through the water, her long legs kicking effortlessly behind.

When she reached the far side of the pool, Desirée gracefully turned and started back. Most of the glade was in shadow, but even so, she was not cold. However, when she spotted a sunny patch of grass close to where she had entered the pool, she decided to head that way, knowing it would help to dry her body more quickly.

As soon as her feet touched the bottom, Desirée stood up and slowly began to emerge from the water. Water poured off her body in silver rivulets, her sodden shift clinging to her breasts and hips like a diaphanous veil. The sun felt gloriously warm on her face and the gentle whisper of the breeze against her bare arms and legs was like a soft caress. She closed her eyes and reached her arms up over her head, stretching her fingers to the sun.

'What vision is this?' a deep voice said suddenly. 'A young Aphrodite rising from the waves? For surely, the goddess herself could not have looked more magnificent.'

The teasing yet undeniably masculine voice shattered the peaceful silence of the glade and caused Desirée to utter a sharp gasp. 'Oh!' Dropping her arms protectively over her chest, she anxiously looked around for the source of the voice. 'Where are you, sir? I demand that you show yourself at once!'

The gentleman did—and as soon as he moved, Desirée realised why she had not seen him. He was sitting in the deep grass no more than thirty feet away from her, but he was hidden in the shadows at the base of a huge oak. And it was immediately evident from his appearance that he too had been enjoying the refreshing waters of the pool. His black hair glistened like polished jet against his head, and his wet shirt clung to a chest and shoulders that were altogether too large for her liking.

Thinking only to conceal her nakedness, Desirée quickly stumbled back into the pool. 'You are no gentleman, sir, to sit and watch a lady in such a state of undress!'

'Perhaps not a gentleman, but a man nonetheless. And one not so foolish as to turn away from the sight of a beautiful woman as God intended her to be seen.'

The fact that the man did not even attempt to hide his enjoyment of her scantily clad body brought the blood rushing to Desirée's cheeks. 'Who are you, sir, and what is your business here?'

'The same as yours. The day is fine, the air is warm, and the waters of the river are refreshingly cool. I succumbed to its pleasures the same as you.'

'But…why did you not speak out when first you saw me?'

'I think I must have been asleep,' he admitted sheepishly. 'The first awareness I had of you was when I awoke to the sound of splashing and looked up to see you halfway across the pool. Then I was afraid to speak out lest I startle you and cause you to drown.'

Desirée snorted. 'I am hardly like to drown, sir.'

'How was I to know that?'

'By watching me swim,' she said in a tone that indicated he must either be blind or simple. 'However, that is no longer of import. What is, is that you remove yourself from my glade at once!'

'*Your* glade?' The man chuckled softly. 'Forgive me, Aphrodite, I was not aware that I was trespassing on *private* property.'

'Well, it isn't private…precisely, but I have every right to ask you to leave.'

'Oh? And why would you think so?' he challenged. 'You are obviously enjoying your day, and I am certainly enjoying mine.'

'I *was* enjoying it until you came along to spoil things,' Desirée told him curtly. 'As to why I am asking you to leave, you must realise that, dressed as I am, I cannot get out of the water.'

The man sat forward and locked his arms around his knees. 'Let me be the first to assure you that I have no objection to the manner of your dress, my dear. As for asking me to leave, surely you would not wish me to endanger my safety by pushing me beyond the limits of my endurance?'

Desirée frowned. 'The limits of your endurance have nothing to do with me, sir, and I am hard pressed to understand why you would bring them up. You look fit enough to me. Surely it would be no great effort to rise, turn and walk away.'

'Ah, but unlike you, fair Aphrodite, I did not walk to this tranquil spot. I swam here from Bredington.'

Desirée gasped. 'From *Bredington*?'

'Yes. And once having reached this peaceful glade, I thought to take the opportunity of both enjoying its beauty, and of catching my breath.'

'You *swam* all the way from the lodge?' Desirée repeated in surprise. Mercy, no wonder he was tired. Viscount Wyndham's hunting-box was more than half a mile away and, as fit as this fellow looked, it was a considerable distance for any man to swim. 'I apologise, sir. I can understand your wish to catch your breath before setting off again. However, it does not excuse your conduct in remaining silent. You should have made yourself known to me as soon as you saw me in the water.'

'If it makes me seem any less of a cad, I did think to say something when you began to emerge, but soon after that, I was lost in such wonder that I was robbed of the ability to speak. I could do naught but watch in reverent silence as a lovely water sprite rose from the woodland pool to dry her tender limbs in the golden warmth of the sun.'

Desirée rolled her eyes. 'That, sir, is the most ridiculous thing I have ever heard, and a true gentleman would not have said it.'

'Ah, but I have already told you that I am not a true gentleman, Aphrodite. And I am beginning to think that you are not a true lady either.'

'I *beg* your pardon!'

'No lady of *my* acquaintance would see fit to divest herself of her clothes in a public place and swim in a manner that would make an Amazon proud.'

Desirée blushed hotly. 'I do *not* swim like an Amazon! And this is hardly a public place.'

'But it is not wholly private either. Therefore it is not impossible that someone might have passed by, as you or I have done today.'

'But in all the times I have come here, I have never—'

'Good Lord, do you mean to tell me that you have been here before and that I have missed the pleasure of your loveliness? Dear me, had I but known, I would have left Wyndham to his sport and gone for a swim to see to mine.'

The insinuation that she had suddenly become his 'sport' was the final straw for Desirée. 'I resent you speaking to me in such a manner, sir, and I demand that you leave here at once!'

The man deliberated upon the idea for a moment, but when at length he spoke, his answer was hardly encouraging. 'Well, I suppose I should be heading back. No doubt Wyndham will be wondering where I am. But tell me, fair Aphrodite, how is it that I have not seen you before? Do you live in one of the quaint little villages hereabouts?'

'I do.'

'And have you a handsome husband and several children at home?'

'I am…not married, sir,' Desirée said stiffly, wondering why was she was even bothering to answer his questions.

'Really?' He sat up a little straighter in the grass. 'You live with your family then? A mother and father perhaps.'

She swallowed hard and glanced away. 'No, my parents are…both gone.'

'Are they indeed? Then…what holds you here, sweetness?'

Desirée had not expected the question, nor the sudden softening of his voice. She might even have told him had not the fear of reprisal kept her silent. For in spite of what she accused him of being—or more correctly of *not* being, Desirée had no doubt that the man sitting opposite her *was* a gentleman. His tone of voice and the manner of his speech left her in no doubt as to his position in life. And the fact that he might well have a wife and children, perhaps even a daughter who was, or might some day be, in attendance at the very school at which she taught, made her think twice about revealing her identity.

Unfortunately, by the time she had formed an evasive answer, the gentleman had reached his own. 'So, there is nothing and no one keeping you here. What a shame. To be so young and so lovely and with no one to appreciate it, is a waste indeed.'

'I do not see it as a waste, sir,' Desirée said, lifting her chin in defiance. 'I have no need of a gentleman's appreciation to make my life worthwhile. I am content with it just as it is.'

'But there is so much more than just contentment to be had from life, Aphrodite,' he told her softly. 'So very much more.' Then, with an alacrity that left Desirée gasping, the man stood up—treating her to a brief glimpse of muscular legs clad in buff-coloured breeches—and dived into the water. He disappeared for a few moments, and then surfaced no more than two feet in front of her.

Dear heavens, what a giant of a man he was! The

width of his shoulders was striking from a distance, but up close, Desirée could see just how ruggedly developed his chest and arms were. There was no doubt that, should he wish it, he would have the advantage of her on land *or* in the water.

Desirée gasped and stumbled backwards, struggling to get out of the pool.

'No, wait!' he urged, quickly reaching for her arm.

The hand that closed around her wrist was like iron. 'Let me go, sir!' Desirée cried, trying not to sound as alarmed as she felt.

'If I do, will you stop floundering about like a freshly landed fish and listen to what I have to say?'

The less than flattering description did nothing to lessen the colour in Desirée's cheeks, but it did serve to bring her struggles to a halt. 'I make no promises, sir. How do I know that you do not intend to take advantage of the situation?'

'Because I give you my word as a gentleman that I will not. You have nothing to fear from me, Aphrodite,' the man said softly. 'All I wish from you is a moment's conversation.'

For some reason, Desirée believed him. Though she was woefully inexperienced when it came to men, she did not see the darkness of lust in his eye. But she knew that he was studying her. She saw his eyes drop down below the waterline and knew that she might as well have been wearing nothing at all for what little protection the shift was giving her.

'By God, you're a beauty,' he whispered huskily. 'You have a body that was made to be loved. Come, Aphrodite, let me take you back to London with me.

I shall show you a life unlike any you have ever known. You will have a comfortable house with a maid to attend you and servants to do your bidding. I shall dress you in fine clothes and give you pretty jewels to wear. And all I ask in return is a few hours of sweet pleasure for us both.'

Desirée stared at him, speechless with shock. *Take her back to London with him?* But...surely he was not suggesting...that is, was it possible that he was saying...

'Are you asking me to be...your *mistress*?' she finally gasped out.

A decidedly sensuous smile curved his lips. 'Would that be so terrible? I would never hurt you, sweetness. Indeed, I would be exceedingly gentle and give you all that a woman could ask for.'

His hand moved slowly through the water towards her and Desirée gasped as the tips of his fingers brushed lightly across her breast. 'You forget yourself, sir!' she cried, thrusting his hand away. 'And not only in your conduct! How dare you speak to me in such an inappropriate manner!'

'Why? Do you truly find the idea of being my mistress so *very* objectionable?'

'I do indeed! You are sadly mistaken if you think that the lure of fine clothes and jewels would be enough to tempt me into becoming your courtesan. Did Cleopatra go with Caesar merely because of his wealth? Did Isolde spurn her beloved Tristan for a king's gold?'

The man quirked one dark eyebrow in surprise.

'What's this? My beautiful water sprite possessed of a learned mind as well as an enchanting body?'

'I am no more your beautiful water sprite than I am your sweet Aphrodite,' Desirée snapped. 'And I would thank you to refrain from addressing me in such ridiculous terms. I am not one to be moved by such empty words of flattery. Much to your disappointment, I am sure.'

'On the contrary, I am delighted to find a questioning mind behind so beautiful a face.' He paused for a moment to assess this new piece of information. 'But perhaps I was wrong to try to tempt you with the promise of pretty jewels and fine clothes. Perhaps I should have mentioned the abundance of fine museums and libraries which are to be found in London, all of which are filled with books and artefacts from all over the world. I should have piqued your curiosity with the promise of lectures from learned historians, and teased you with talk of political assemblies held in the homes of some of London's most entertaining hostesses, all of which I could make available to you.'

His hands had stilled but his words were evoking a different kind of excitement in Desirée's breast all together. Oh, how she had longed to visit the cultural centres of London; to see the British Museum, and Westminster Abbey where the tombs of the former kings and queens of England were on display for all to see. To view centuries-old sculptures and priceless collections of Greek and Roman artefacts.

And surely the political hostess he referred to was Lady Holland; a woman who was well known for hosting scintillating parties attended by some of

London's most interesting people. Desirée knew that some of the sharpest minds in England took part in the lively discussions to be had at her home, and though Lady Holland might not be deemed quite acceptable to the highest levels of society, she was, nevertheless, a fascinating woman.

'Come, Aphrodite, what do you say?' he whispered persuasively. 'Come live with me and be my love, and we will all the pleasures prove.'

The misuse of the Marlowe poem, originally intended for a passionate shepherd to the lady he wished to court, brought sparks of anger to Desirée's eyes. 'I do not doubt that you expect me to be flattered by your estimable offer, sir, but I am not a simple shepherdess to be so persuaded, nor some willing lightskirt who exists only to pander to your pleasures.'

'Pleasures for us both,' he reminded her smoothly. 'For I assure you, I enjoy both the giving *and* the taking in love.'

It was suddenly too much for Desirée. She was submersed to her neck in a woodland pool, wearing a shift that was as transparent as a fairy's wing, and she was having a conversation with a stranger in the most normal of tones about going to London and becoming his mistress!

Truly, he was no better than the old Marquis of Sywell himself, for he, too, had believed that any girl in the neighbourhood was ripe for the picking.

'I have no desire to become your mistress, sir, nor that of any man,' Desirée said in a voice not unlike that which she had used to chastise Elizabeth Perry earlier in the day. 'I am an intelligent woman and one who thinks too highly of my own worth to debase myself in such a manner. But do not fear. I am sure there are many who would be only too eager to accept your offer. And now, if you will kindly turn your back and allow me a few moments of privacy, I shall be on my way.'

After a moment's hesitation, the man reluctantly inclined his head. 'Very well. Never let it be said that Sebastian Moore would force a lady to do anything she did not wish to. For there must be mutual respect and affection for a liaison to achieve any level of satisfaction—even in one such as this.'

Then, without warning, he bent his head and kissed Desirée full on the mouth. His lips were warm and possessive over hers as his arm closed firmly around her waist and drew her against the long hard length of his body.

'Farewell, Aphrodite,' he murmured against her mouth. 'I shall not soon forget you or our chance encounter here.'

Then the man called Sebastian Moore turned and began to swim back in the direction from whence he had come.

In the quiet of the woodland pool, Desirée stood and gazed after him long after he had disappeared from view. She knew that she should dress and make haste to return to school, but somehow, thoughts of duty and obligation were far from uppermost in her mind. She kept thinking about the way his fingers had brushed ever so lightly against her breast. She had never been touched like that before; never been made to feel as though her body was burning hot yet icy cold at the same time.

Then she thought about the way he had kissed her, remembering how incredibly soft yet firm his mouth had felt against hers. The heat of his lips against the coolness of hers had evoked the strangest feelings of excitement and breathlessness.

But who was this Sebastian Moore whose touch had sparked such a traitorous response from her body? Why did the sound of his voice yet linger in her mind? He had asked her to be his mistress! He had treated her with a complete lack of respect, speaking to her in a way that no gentleman would ever speak to a lady. He had even kissed her—without so much as a by your leave! Surely she should be repulsed by a man who took such liberties, and who clearly thought so little of her as an individual.

Yes, of course she should. And she would go back to Guarding's and laugh about this with Helen. She would tell herself that she was glad she would never have cause to see such a reprehensible gentleman again.

'And maybe in time, I might even come to believe it,' Desirée whispered as she slowly climbed out of the pool and started to dress.

Chapter Two

14 May, 1812

The occasion of Desirée's twenty-fifth birthday was not a cause for celebration. All it signified to Desirée was the passing of another year and one which had been difficult for any number of reasons, not the least of which was Miss Elizabeth Perry—or more specifically her father, Viscount Perry. Desirée had been introduced to Lord Perry at the time of Elizabeth's enrolment at Guarding's, as were all of the teachers to the parents of every new student. On first acquaintance, she had thought him to be a handsome man with pleasant manners and was not surprised when some of the other teachers had professed themselves quite taken with his charm.

But Desirée had soon come to realise that beneath the guise of the gentleman lay a man who was both disreputable and untrustworthy. He seemed to have a knack for appearing in a room when she was in the presence of only the younger girls and more than once she had felt his eyes upon her, only to see him glance away when she turned to look at him.

But lately, he had stopped troubling himself to look away. Now when Desirée looked up, it was to find him watching her with a boldness she found both disconcerting and frightening. For that reason, she had begun taking pains not to be in the same room with him. When she knew that he was visiting Elizabeth—which he seemed to be doing with increasing regularity—Desirée kept to her room. If he arrived prior to the dinner hour, she made sure that she was in the company of one of the other teachers, most often Helen de Coverdale, with whom she finally shared her concerns.

'But *why* will you not speak to Mrs Guarding about it?' Helen whispered as they stood together in Desirée's classroom at the end of the day. 'I am sure she would be most upset if she knew that Lord Perry was making improper advances towards you.'

'But that is just the problem, Helen, he hasn't made any advances towards me yet,' Desirée admitted. 'It is simply the way he *looks* at me. Besides, who is to say that Mrs Guarding would believe me if I were to tell her?'

'Why would she not?'

'She might believe that I was imagining it. Or worse, that I had somehow encouraged his attentions myself.'

Helen glanced at her in astonishment. 'How can you even suggest such a thing, Desirée? You have been here for over six years and in all that time there has never been a whisper of scandal about you. Why do you think Mrs Guarding would suddenly believe that you were encouraging a gentleman's attentions?'

Desirée smiled sadly. 'Perhaps *because* I have been here for six years and there has never been a whisper of scandal about me. Perhaps she thinks that as another birthday approaches, I might decide to cast aside discretion for one reckless taste of impropriety.'

'Tosh, I do not believe that for a moment,' Helen asserted. 'You are a model of propriety, Desirée. You would never do such a thing, and we both know that you have had opportunity to.'

At Helen's words, a memory flashed into Desirée's mind; the memory of a handsome face, a masculine voice, and the most improper suggestion it had whispered. It was a memory which had come to her more than once during the past year, and it was one which—Desirée was embarrassed to admit—had caused her more than a fleeting moment of regret.

Helen was the only person in the world to whom she had confided the details of her meeting with the handsome stranger. And it was from Helen that Desirée had learned that Sebastian Moore was actually Viscount Buckworth, a noted rake and man about town. From her friend, Desirée had learned that Lord Buckworth was a wealthy gentleman with a fine house in London and a large estate in the south of Kent.

But she had also learned that he was a man who enjoyed the company of women. It seemed that he had never been seriously attached to any one woman, but that he had kept a string of beautiful young mistresses, all of whom had enjoyed his generosity both during *and* after their association. And while Helen had been astonished to learn that Lord Buckworth had made Desirée such a proposal, she had been equally practical in her assessment of it.

'It is only natural that your first reaction would have been shock—and that your immediate response would have been to turn it down,' Helen had said at the time. 'After all, we have been raised to believe that marriage is the ultimate goal of any well-bred young woman, and that to be a courtesan is the worst possible thing which could befall us. And yet, I wonder if in truth it would really have been all that bad.'

At Desirée's shocked exclamation, Helen had smiled her lovely smile and lifted her shoulders in a graceful shrug. 'Only think of the freedom you would have enjoyed, Desirée. Especially when compared to the life you live now. You would have had a fine house to live in and servants to attend you. You would have had beautiful clothes and jewels to wear, and you would have been seen on the arm of a handsome and charming gentleman. You would have been able to go to the opera and masquerade balls, and even to the museums and libraries you love so much.'

'But I would have been his…whore!' Desirée had cried, blushing as she had stumbled over the word. 'I would have been forced to…give him my body in exchange for an opulent lifestyle that might end at any time. Indeed, I should think that with a man like Lord Buckworth, the future would be very precarious indeed. He likely changes his mistresses as frequently as he changes his cravat.'

'Ah, but think of the pleasures you would have

enjoyed whilst you were under his protection, Desirée,' Helen had said, surprising Desirée with the note of envy in her voice. 'You would have had the freedom to walk about town during the day, and to visit the pleasure gardens by night. You would have had shops to browse in and amusements to exclaim over. You might even have been able to go riding with him, had he thought to provide you with a suitable mount.'

Desirée had thrown up her hands in despair. 'Yes, but I would have been...a fallen woman, Helen. A creature despised by society.'

'And are we as teachers thought of so very highly by society now?'

The question had stopped Desirée dead. She hadn't had an answer then, nor did she have one now. It had been an extremely disturbing revelation to say the least.

'Speaking of your birthday—' Helen said softly now, 'I have something for you.' She dug into a hidden pocket in her gown and pulled out a small box. 'Happy birthday, dear Desirée.'

Desirée looked down at the gift in Helen's hand and felt her eyes fill with tears. 'Oh, Helen, there was no need—'

'Of course there was,' Helen whispered. 'But it is not so very much. Just a little something I made for you, so there is no need to cry. Oh dear, and there is the bell for dinner.'

Desirée sighed. When Mrs Guarding rang the bell, woe betide anyone who did not heed its calling. But because of the time she and Helen had spent talking, there was not enough time for her to go up to her room and safely tuck her present away. Nor had she pockets in her gown like Helen.

'Why don't you put it in the slate cupboard?' Helen suggested. 'You can always come back for it after dinner.'

'Yes, of course,' Desirée said with relief. 'No one will be likely to look for it there.'

So saying, she carefully tucked the precious box at the back of the cupboard and closed the door. 'Thank you, Helen. I really do not know what I should do without you!'

Dinner at the Guarding Academy for Girls was not the unpalatable meal so often to be had at English boarding schools. In fact, Mrs Guarding prided herself on the quality and the variety of food served at the Academy. She was often heard to say that a body starved was a mind starved, and if there was one thing the headmistress demanded from her girls, it was the constant use of their brains. Fortunately, she employed a cook who was somewhat feared by the local tradespeople, and who had, on more than one occasion, taken a supplier to task for trying to sell her inferior goods.

Dinner that night, for example, consisted of a savoury chicken pie, served with bread and boiled potatoes, followed by custard and fruit. The girls sat at two long wooden tables with one teacher sitting at the head, and one at the foot. Conversation was not forbidden, but it was to be kept to a polite level. Mrs Guarding appeared at the beginning of the evening meal to lead them in grace, and if she was not otherwise engaged, generally sat down to eat with them. If she did retire to her private dining-room, it usually meant that she was entertaining a visitor, either a local person of some importance, or one of the girls' parents.

Mrs Guarding had retired to her dining-room tonight, but Desirée had no need to guess at the identity of the visitor. She had already seen Lord Perry's carriage in the courtyard and knew that after dining with Mrs Guarding, he would spend some time with Elizabeth before heading back to Town.

Desirée's own relationship with Elizabeth had not improved during the past year. In fact, the girl seemed to have made it her mission to make Desirée's life as miserable as possible. She continued to disrupt the class whenever possible, and was disrespectful almost to the point of rudeness. Of course, Desirée knew that *she* would be the one made to suffer if she did lose her temper, and for that reason alone she endeavoured to ignore Miss Perry's outbursts and to carry on with the class. But it did not make for amiable working conditions, nor for a congenial relationship.

At the conclusion of the meal, the girls rose and quietly left the tables. Desirée rose too, intending to head directly back to her room, when she suddenly remembered the gift Helen had given her. She hesitated for a moment, wondering where Lord Perry might be, and then realised that he must still be with Mrs Guarding. The headmistress usually made a point of being there to bid the girls a good evening. The fact that she had been absent tonight meant that she must still be entertaining her guest—which left the way clear for Desirée to return to her classroom.

Desirée seldom went back to her room after dark. The wing was totally removed from the rest of the school, situated as it was at the far end of the building, and although she had never been one given to flights of fancy, neither did she relish being alone in the deserted corridors. Even now, her footsteps made a hollow, empty sound on the wooden floor. And apart from the eerie glow of the full moon and the rather feeble light cast by her candle, Desirée was surrounded by the night.

She was heartily relieved when she finally reached her room. Opening the door, she hesitated for a moment in the doorway. She knew the layout of the desks and where the cupboard was located, but it felt strange to be moving around in total darkness. She held the candle aloft and carefully moved forward.

She finally found the cupboard she was looking for, and setting the candle on the corner of the desk, Desirée bent down to open it. She put her hand inside and began to feel around for the small box she had secreted there. It was then she heard the words, spoken in a low, lazy drawl, that frightened her far more than darkened rooms and empty shadows ever could.

'Good evening, Desirée.'

Desirée froze, her pulse beginning to beat an erratic rhythm in her chest. Lord Perry! He must have followed her here from the dining-room. But she had not heard his footsteps. Which meant that he had trailed her stealthily, not wishing her—or anyone else—to know.

Desirée rose slowly, forcing herself to remain calm. 'Good evening, Lord Perry.'

He was standing just inside the doorway, the light from the candle in his hand shedding a soft glow on his handsome face. 'What a pleasant surprise to find you here all alone, Desirée. I have been hoping to do so for some time now.'

Desirée only just managed to repress a shiver. Even in the dim light, she recognised the look in his eyes. 'I cannot imagine why, my lord.'

'Can you not?' His mouth curled upwards in a mocking smile. 'I thought that would have been quite obvious to you by now.'

A chill, black silence surrounded them. 'I think it would be best if you were to leave, Lord Perry,' Desirée said quietly. 'It is not seemly that we be alone together.'

'But I have waited so long for just such an occasion, my dear. Surely you would not deprive me of a few moments of conversation now that we are here.'

A weak flutter of hope arose in her breast. 'Do you wish to speak to me about Elizabeth?'

'Elizabeth? Good God, no. I have quite enough conversation with my daughter as it is. She is an impertinent child at the best of times. But then, I am sure I have no need of telling you that.'

Desirée swallowed tightly. 'My lord?'

'Oh, come, Miss Nash, you need not mince words with me. Elizabeth is a cold little bitch who probably enjoys making your life hell. You can blame her mother for that. She raised her in her own image.'

The cold, impersonal manner with which he spoke

of his wife and daughter did nothing to endear him to Desirée. 'Then what would you wish to speak to me about, if not Elizabeth's progress?'

He took a step forward and closed the door behind him. 'I wish to speak to you, Desirée. About the possibility of our achieving...a much warmer relationship than the one we have now.'

A shudder rippled through Desirée's body. 'We do not have a relationship.'

'That is precisely my point.'

Icy fear twisted around Desirée's heart. She had not mistaken the look in Lord Perry's eye. He had followed her down here with one purpose in mind, and unless she did something to prevent it, he was going to attempt to force himself on her right here in the darkness of the deserted classroom.

In spite of her fear, Desirée felt anger and loathing rise in her breast. What right had he to think he could treat her in such a manner! Did he think that because she was a woman and a teacher that she had no feelings? How dare he treat her with such a blatant lack of respect?

Desirée glanced quickly about the room, peering into the darkness for a possible means of escape. Had there been more light, she might have been able to make a dash for the door, but in the darkness, she knew she was likely to stumble over a chair or fall upon a table. Besides which, Lord Perry stood between her and the door. Which left her only one alternative.

'I shall scream,' Desirée threatened in a low voice. 'I swear if you touch me—'

'Oh, I do intend to touch you,' Lord Perry whispered. 'But I do not think you will scream. Because I know that in the deepest recesses of your heart, you don't really want to fight me, Desirée.'

'My name is Miss Nash.'

'Oh yes, I've seen that look in your eyes, Desirée. And I know what it means.'

'Stay away from me!'

'They won't believe you if you say you fought me,' Lord Perry murmured as he took another step closer and set his candle on the desk. 'They'll believe that you encouraged my advances. And why would you not? I can make your life very pleasant, Desirée. I'm a very wealthy man. I can give you anything you ask for. But if you fight me—'

It happened so fast that Desirée had no time to prepare herself. Lord Perry covered the ground between them in a single stride. He reached for the bodice of her gown and ripped it open.

'No!'

'I will have you,' he ground out, his voice thick with desire as he locked his hand around her waist and pulled her against him. 'Come, let me taste the sweetness of your lips.'

Incensed beyond reason, Desirée began to fight. She twisted and writhed in his arms, trying to strike him as she fought to get away, but she was no match for his strength.

'Yes, my little hellcat, a fight only adds to the pleasure,' Lord Perry breathed darkly. 'But I won't have you mark me.'

Pushing her backwards, he pinned her body against

the wall and captured both of her hands in one of his. Shoving them behind her back, he held them there in a punishing grip while his free hand moved aside the fabric of her blouse. 'Beautiful,' he murmured huskily. 'So…beautiful.'

For Desirée, time ceased to have any kind of meaning. She had never felt so humiliated, so utterly degraded, in her entire life. She felt Lord Perry's mouth on her throat and shuddered in revulsion. But when she felt him begin to fumble with the fastenings of his breeches, she opened her mouth to scream, only to have the sound swallowed by his mouth as it hungrily fastened on hers.

Then, from somewhere in the dim recesses of her mind, she heard the sound of the door opening…

'*Miss…Nash!*'

The shocked and horrified voice of the headmistress reverberated around the dark room like a clap of thunder. As Lord Perry took his mouth from hers, Desirée turned in horror to stare at the cluster of women who were gathered in the doorway. A group which included Mrs Guarding and Helen de Coverdale, and behind them, Elizabeth Perry and Isabel Hewton.

'It would seem that we have been discovered, my dear,' Lord Perry observed, seemingly unconcerned by the interruption. With no outward show of haste, he let go of Desirée's hands and stepped away from her. 'I told you that your room would have been a more appropriate place for a rendezvous, but you would not wait.'

Desirée choked back a cry as shock drained the

blood from her face. 'How can you suggest—I never said—'

'Miss Nash, attend to your clothing!' Mrs Guarding interrupted sharply. 'I will speak to you later.' She turned to the two young girls behind her. 'Back to your rooms, both of you!'

Reluctantly, the girls scampered away. Desirée raised her hands to the torn bodice of her gown as the gravity of her situation began to sink in. 'Mrs Guarding, please—'

'Lord Perry, if you would be so good as to wait for me in my office,' Mrs Guarding said tonelessly.

Straightening the folds of his cravat, Lord Perry offered them a thin smile. 'I am, of course, at your service.' Then, as a final humiliation, he turned back to Desirée and bowed. 'Your servant, Miss Nash.'

Desirée closed her eyes in disgust. She turned away from Lord Perry and prayed that she would not be physically ill.

As soon as the man left, Mrs Guarding breathed a heavy sigh. 'Go to your room, Miss Nash,' she said quietly. 'I will expect you in my sitting-room in half an hour. Kindly do not be late.'

'Mrs Guarding—'

'Miss de Coverdale, be so good as to assist Miss Nash.'

It was clear from the tone of the headmistress's voice that she would brook no argument, and Desirée hung her head in shame. She could only imagine how this must look. She had been caught in a darkened room, locked in a passionate embrace with the father of one of her students. It would not matter that it had been nothing short of an attempted rape. Because he was a nobleman, and she a teacher, there would be no quarter given. She alone would be held up for blame and censure.

Worse, the fact that the episode had been witnessed by two of the Academy girls made any hope of salvation impossible. Desirée knew how Elizabeth Perry would make it sound in front of the rest of the school. Her reputation would be in shreds.

Her life at Guarding's was over.

Desirée felt the softness of a shawl being draped around her shoulders, and looked up to see tears shimmering in Helen's eyes. 'Are you all right?' Helen asked, looking decidedly shaken by the night's tragic events.

Desirée nodded but her eyes were haunted. 'It wasn't what it seemed,' she whispered wretchedly.

'On the contrary, Desirée, it was *exactly* what it seemed,' Helen said. 'But I fear that is not how it will be made out to be. Come, my dear, we must get you ready to see Mrs Guarding.'

The interview conducted in the privacy of Mrs Guarding's sitting-room proceeded much as Desirée had expected it would. It was evident from the way the older woman spoke that she was deeply regretful of the circumstances which had precipitated the meeting, but nevertheless, the conclusion was inescapable.

'I am very sorry to have to do this, Miss Nash,' she said quietly, 'but under the circumstances, I have no choice but to dismiss you.'

Sitting on the faded chintz sofa across from her,

Desirée raised her eyes to the level of the headmistress's. 'But I did not encourage Lord Perry's advances, Mrs Guarding. Please, you must believe me. I had…gone back to my classroom after dinner to collect a birthday present Miss de Coverdale had given me. He—Lord Perry—must have followed me. I did not hear his footsteps, but when I turned around, he was standing in the doorway. On my honour, I *swear* that is what happened.'

Mrs Guarding sighed, but it seemed to Desirée, a heavy sound filled with regret. 'Whether you are guilty or not does not signify, Miss Nash. What does, is that you were caught in an extremely compromising position by myself, another teacher, and two of our students.'

'One of whom is a young lady who makes no secret of the fact that she has no affection for me,' Desirée pointed out.

'I cannot deny that that is so, Miss Nash. But surely you can see that because of the rancour which exists between you and Miss Perry, what happened tonight will be used to destroy you.'

The words rang like a death knell in Desirée's head. 'Is there nothing I can say to convince you?'

Mrs Guarding rose slowly to her feet. She was a handsome woman still, her youthful beauty having been mellowed by the passage of the years. But her eyes were as sharp and as discerning as they had ever been. 'I am afraid there is nothing that anyone can say,' she said regretfully. 'Lord Perry's character is not unlike that of many of his peers. And as much as I might resent it, the word of a woman against a man

such as that counts for little in this world. Young
ladies will gossip, Miss Nash, and therein lies our
problem. I do not expect for one minute that Elizabeth
or Isabel will keep this to themselves, and once word
gets back—as it inevitably will—to the parents of the
other girls, questions will be raised and fingers will
most certainly be pointed. For me to keep you here
now would be to condone what happened.' Mrs
Guarding paused. 'I have to think of the reputation of
the school, my dear. I hope you can understand that.
I have been longer in this world than you, and I know
how unkind people can be. News of this will get
about soon enough, and I have no doubt that it will
be embellished and enhanced until it will rival the
goings-on up at the Abbey.'

'Mrs Guarding,' Desirée began desperately, 'the
last six years have been very special to me. To have
had an opportunity to work with educated and intelligent women like yourself, and to try to foster that
knowledge in other young women, has been more ful-
filling than anything else I might have done with my
life.'

Mrs Guarding nodded, and in the soft light of the
candles, the grey strands in her hair glowed like silver. 'And you have been an excellent teacher, Miss
Nash, which makes this all the more difficult for me
to do. But I hope that under the circumstances you
can understand why your tenure here must end. And
why I cannot provide you with a reference.'

Desirée clasped her hands together in her lap to
keep them from trembling. No, she could not understand. She could not understand or accept that the six

years she had been a teacher here suddenly counted for nothing. That in the blink of an eye, her reputation and her future had been ruined by the thoughtless actions of an arrogant man.

'Have you anywhere to go, Miss Nash?' Mrs Guarding asked quietly. 'Any family with whom you can find a home until you manage to secure other employment?'

Like one awaking from a dream, Desirée slowly looked up at the headmistress and shook her head. 'No. There is…no one.'

Mrs Guarding sighed. 'I feared that might be the case. That is why I always like to keep a little aside for emergencies.' Turning towards the sideboard, the headmistress removed a small key from the ring at her waist and opened the bottom drawer. From within, she drew out a small velvet pouch and placed it in Desirée's hand. 'It is not a lot, but it should help tide you over. And I do not expect you to pay it back.'

Desirée glanced down at the bag in the palm of her hand, and felt her eyes fill with tears. There was so much she wanted to say, and yet, what could she say that would make any difference?

'You have been…more than kind, Mrs Guarding,' she said at last. 'Thank you.'

Then, knowing that it was time, she got up and turned to go.

'Miss Nash,' the older woman said abruptly, 'you are welcome to stay for a few days while you make enquiries into a new position.'

Desirée managed a feeble smile. 'Thank you, Mrs Guarding, but I think it is best that I leave as soon as possible. Word of this will get out soon enough and as you say, you have the reputation of the school to consider. And…while I know it won't change anything now, I do want you to know that…what happened tonight truly was not my fault.'

Sadness glowed in the warm blue eyes that looked back at her. 'If it is of any consolation at all, Miss Nash, I never believed that it was.'

In her tiny room on the top floor of the building, many things went through Desirée's mind that night, not the least of which were the extremely dim prospects for her immediate future. She had been dismissed in disgrace. Turned off without a reference. And without a reference, she could not hope to approach a reputable school or a respectable family for work. Even as a governess she would be expected to provide a letter from her past employer. The problem was, Mrs Guarding was the only employer Desirée had ever had, and she was coming away from her with nothing.

Stifling a groan, Desirée rolled over on to her back and stared up at the ceiling. What would it be like to leave Mrs Guarding's after all these years? This tiny room had become her home, and Mrs Guarding and the staff her friends and family. All of them had played an important part in her life. A part which, as of tonight, had come to an abrupt end.

So what were her choices now? Desirée's thoughts turned briefly to the likelihood of employment in the immediate area. There were several shops in Abbot Quincey, along with the post office and the coaching inn. And while she had no desire to work as a tavern maid at the Angel, perhaps she might apply to Mrs Hammond for a position in either the general store or the linen-drapers. Or even to Mr Westcott at the bakery.

But close on the heels of that came the realisation that she would be no more likely to find a job in the village than she would anywhere else. Word would soon spread that Miss Desirée Nash had been found in a compromising position with the father of one of her students, and what respectable doors would be opened to her then?

All right, then what other options did that leave her? Where would her tarnished reputation not work against her? Desirée thought hard for a moment. She might be able to get a job on one of the farms. There was always plenty of work to be had, and farmers generally didn't ask too many questions as long as the work was done. Nor was Desirée afraid of hard work. But she was afraid of the tedium her days would offer. She would find no intellectual companionship among the loutish farm lads, nor with the young maids who tended the goats or milked the cows. And if she ended up working in the kitchens, she would be at the beck and call of the cook or the housekeeper, both of which could make her existence a nightmare.

Her prospects were looking very dim indeed.

The answer finally came to Desirée about an hour later—and it was an indication of her state of mind that she did not dismiss it out of hand. In truth, it shocked her so very much that she abruptly got out of bed and began to pace back and forth the confines of her room.

Desirée Nash become a *courtesan*?

No, it was quite impossible, she assured herself. It was…too ridiculous for words. She could never lower herself to such an unseemly and disgraceful existence. Indeed, the very thought of it made her shudder, as it would any educated, well-brought-up young lady.

No, there had to be another way. All she had to do was think of it.

Unfortunately, as hard as Desirée put herself to think of an alternative, nothing came to mind. For every good idea she came up with, logic provided twice as many reasons as to why it would not work. But there had to be something she could do. Something other than…throwing herself into the protection of a man who was not her husband—and was never likely to be. But what? She had lost both her reputation and her good name as a result of being found in Lord Perry's embrace tonight.

But that was an accident, a little voice whispered in her head. *A mistake. You know the truth of it and so does Mrs Guarding.*

Yes, she did, Desirée reflected grimly, but what did her own opinion and that of a school headmistress count for in the overall scheme of things? When word of this got out, society would draw its own conclusions as to her conduct, and she doubted they would be kind. Added to which was the undeniable fact that, should Lord Perry be questioned about his part in the proceedings, he would certainly deny any charges of guilt. He would be the first to proclaim that Desirée had lured him to her classroom, and that she had been perfectly amenable to a tumble...until they had been discovered, at which time she had cried foul. Was that not what he had claimed this very evening when Mrs Guarding had questioned him about the matter?

As the first light of dawn stretched its golden fingers across the sky, Desirée made her decision. Crossing to her writing table, she pulled forth paper and ink and sat down to write the letter that would, if accepted, change the course of her life. She did not think too hard or too long about the content or the words, for she knew that if she did, she would surely change her mind. But when the missive was done and dispatched, she returned to her room, sat down upon her bed and closed her eyes in despair.

The deed was done. She could not change her mind now, even if she wanted to.

The response came three days later. The letter, scrawled in a bold, masculine hand on heavy cream vellum, was delivered personally into Desirée's hands by a liveried servant, and the content of it was mercifully brief and to the point.

It informed her that the gentleman in question would be pleased to take the young lady on in the capacity suggested, and that if she could arrange transportation as far as Bredington, he would endeavour to take care of the rest. It was signed with one word.

Buckworth.

Chapter Three

Sebastian Moore stood at ease in front of the long window in the study at Bredington. His hands were clasped lightly behind his back and his posture was relaxed as he surveyed the wooded hills beyond. The hunting-lodge had long been a favourite retreat of his. It belonged to his good friend, George Lyford, Viscount Wyndham, a gentleman whom Sebastian had first encountered at Angelo's Haymarket Room where he regularly went to practise his fencing skills. Although a good deal younger than Sebastian, Wyndham had proved himself a worthy adversary, and the two had soon become friends.

It was Wyndham who had first invited Sebastian to join him for a weekend at the remote country lodge. And ever ready for an excuse to get out of London, Sebastian had accepted with alacrity, knowing that Bredington offered some of the finest shooting and fishing in the land. And hidden as it was in the rich forests around Steepwood Abbey, it offered peace and tranquillity from the frenetic pace of London.

Now, as Sebastian gazed at the woodlands surrounding the lodge, he thought about his reasons for being at Bredington today, and about the meeting he was soon to have. How strange to think that, as a result of a casual swim in the river last summer, he was this very day to acquire a new mistress.

The thought brought a smile of expectation to Sebastian's face, just as it had the day the unusual letter had arrived at his townhouse in London. In fact, he'd had to read it twice before fully comprehending that the lady—who had identified herself only as Miss Nash, and their meeting by a geographical point of reference in her letter—was asking if the offer the gentleman had made to a certain young lady in July of last year was still in good standing?

It had taken only a moment for Sebastian to recall the occasion and even less for him to remember the young woman. The image of her rising out of the water to stand in a bright patch of sunlight, with her arms stretched out towards the sun and her glorious body clad in nothing but a sodden chemise, had lingered in his mind for a very long time. But never in his wildest dreams had he expected to hear from her again.

The fact that the lady had made no reference to *his* name—which Sebastian knew he had given her—lent an element of subterfuge to the correspondence, and had led him to believe that she was not willing to risk discovery. For that reason, he had likewise made no reference to anything in his response, except by the application of his title, which would hardly condemn him if the letter were to fall into the wrong hands. But Sebastian had no concerns that it would. He had given it to one of his own servants with the instructions that it was to be taken to the address the lady had specified in her letter and that it was to be put into none but the lady's own hands.

And very soon, she would be here. He had instructed her to meet him at Bredington, and to arrive early enough in the day that they could set off in time to reach London by nightfall. That way, he would be able to settle her in the house he had rented for her, and possibly to commence their relationship forthwith.

Sebastian smiled in anticipation of the coming night. Yes, it made for a most pleasing prospect altogether.

Desirée had taken a quiet leave of Guarding's. She had said her goodbyes to Helen and Mrs Guarding the night before, knowing that it would be easier than at the actual time of departure. The following morning, she had waited until the girls were at class before slipping out through the back door to the waiting chaise. Now, as she travelled along the road she knew so well, she began to wonder what lay in store for her.

She had refused to think too long or too hard about the upcoming meeting with Lord Buckworth. Indeed, she found that if she thought about it for more than a few minutes, her palms began to grow damp and her heart to beat in a most alarming manner. But she knew that she could not back down. By sending her letter to Lord Buckworth, she had set her course. With his acceptance, she had committed herself to it.

The only bright spot in the proceedings was that since receiving his letter, Desirée had taken her plan one step further. If nothing else, agreeing to become Lord Buckworth's mistress would provide her with a means for getting to London. And once she was there, she intended to look around for alternate employment. She knew there were agencies in London that handled that type of thing.

The main thing now was to get to London as expediently as possible. Thanks to Mrs Guarding, she had a little extra money to look after expenses, but there was no question in her mind that travelling to London with Lord Buckworth would provide the most economical and comfortable way of doing so.

Desirée suffered a brief stab of conscience at the thought of misleading the man, but then decided that her sympathies were surely misplaced. After all, *he* was the one who had mistaken her for a woman of loose morals in the first place. To her mind, providing her with a means of getting to London was the very *least* he could do in the way of an apology!

In all too short a time, Desirée found herself following a liveried manservant through the panelled corridors of Bredington. Eventually he opened the door to a room which appeared to be a study. He then bowed towards the gentleman who was standing by the window watching her. 'Miss Nash, my lord.'

'Thank you, Manson. Have the carriage brought round and readied for departure. We leave within the half hour.'

'Very good, my lord.' The servant bowed and withdrew, leaving Desirée alone with the man she had encountered in such a humiliating way all those months ago.

'I am surprised you told him your name. Your letter led me to believe that discretion was of the utmost importance.'

Desirée inclined her head. 'Had the servant been connected to one of the local families hereabouts, I would not have vouchsafed it, even now.'

'So you are confident that he is not?'

'I know most of the families in the villages,' Desirée replied, 'and I know which sons and daughters work at the big houses. Your man has the look of a gentleman's valet, not of a household servant.'

Sebastian Moore leaned back against the edge of his desk and crossed his arms over his chest. 'Your assessment is quite correct, Miss Nash. Manson has been with me for some time and has travelled with me from London.'

Desirée again inclined her head and allowed herself a few minutes to study the man standing opposite. He had changed little since the occasion of their first meeting. He was every bit as large and as intimidating as she remembered. In the polished Hessians, he stood well over six feet and his long legs were clad in buckskins that fitted like a second skin. His beautifully tailored jacket had been made to accommodate the width of his massive shoulders and although the musculature of his chest was hidden now behind a silk shirt and cravat of impeccable whiteness, Desirée remembered how it had looked with a wet shirt clinging to its every ripple.

His face, too, was as she remembered it. Handsome enough to make any young girl's heart beat faster, but with a devil-may-care look in his eyes that warned anxious mamas to be wary. His lips were full and sensuous, his mouth curving upwards in a disturbing smile.

Desirée sighed. He was all that she remembered. His ease of manner and the quality of his clothes proclaimed him for the gentleman she'd known him to be. And despite the fact that this was their second meeting, she felt more than ever that she was standing in the presence of a complete stranger.

'Am I as you remembered, Aphrodite?'

The familiar term of endearment brought a flood of embarrassed colour to Desirée's cheeks. 'To be honest, I find that I remember…very little of our first encounter, Lord Buckworth,' she lied, hoping that it sounded more convincing to his ears that it did to hers. 'But I am moved to comment that you do look somewhat…different with your clothes on.'

His smile broadened and turned sensual. 'As do you, my dear, for I have carried the memory of what you looked like with your clothes *off* close to my heart since last July.'

The comment was meant to put her off stride—and it did. 'A gentleman would not remind a lady that he had seen her…*en déshabille*,' Desirée said, struggling to recover her composure.

'And as I told you last year, Miss Nash, I am no gentleman. That has not changed.'

Desirée was grateful that he did not repeat the other

assertion he had made last year. Namely, that *she* was not a lady.

'But never mind that,' Sebastian continued. 'I think it is time that we made some proper introductions. And in the absence of anyone to do it for us, I shall take the liberty of doing it myself. I am, as I think you already know, Sebastian Moore, Viscount Buckworth. And you are…?'

Desirée took a deep breath and clasped her reticule a little tighter. 'Miss Desirée Nash.'

She saw his eyes widen in amusement. 'Desirée. From the Latin, *Desirata*. She who is desired.' A devilish look came into his eyes. 'How appropriate.'

His knowledge of Latin took her completely by surprise, and in spite of herself, Desirée smiled. 'Sebastian. From the Greek, *Sebestyen*. To be…revered.' Her eyes took on a decided sparkle of their own. 'How decidedly less so.'

'Oh-ho! I think that I shall have to mind my words around you, Miss Nash. At least until I have found out, and can use to my advantage, some of your own…weaknesses.'

There was a distinctly sensual undertone to his words, and it served to remind Desirée of the reason she was here. For all their bandying about of words, Lord Buckworth was not looking at her as a social or intellectual equal. He was looking at her as the woman who would soon warm his bed. 'Lord Buckworth, I—'

'Sebastian.'

Desirée stared at him in dismay. 'My lord, our acquaintance is not—'

'Of the kind that makes it necessary for us to engage in formal language,' Sebastian interrupted smoothly. 'At least, not in the intimacy of our chambers…Desirée.'

Her name was the softest whisper on his lips, and the words Desirée had been about to utter completely deserted her. Oh yes, he certainly had a way with women. He had likely only to speak their names in that honeyed way to have them melt into his waiting arms. Well, she did not intend to melt. In fact, as soon as she got to London, she was going to…

Abruptly, Desirée stopped. She was not going to be doing anything for herself when she got to London. Because the moment she did, she would be occupied with duties of a different kind entirely. She had applied to this man for his protection. And liking what he had seen in the forest all those months ago, he had agreed to take her to London and to establish her there as his mistress.

As soon as she got to London, *that* was what she was going to be doing.

Desirée hung her head, fighting back a wave of shame and embarrassment. Dear Lord, what had she done? What had she sentenced herself to? She could not even take pleasure from the fact that Lord Buckworth had remembered her, or that his response to her query had come so swiftly. Indeed, she almost wished now that he had retained no memory of her at all and that she had been left to find some other means of employment. At least as a servant she might have aspired to some level of dignity. What had she left of any worth now?

'Your carriage awaits, my dear,' Sebastian asked softly. 'Shall we go?'

Desirée could not meet his eyes. She was heartsick at being unable to think of an answer to her dilemma. Truly, she was no better off here than she had been at the pool last summer. For just as he had there, Sebastian Moore had the advantage of her here as well.

The first half hour of their journey passed in silence. Desirée kept her face turned towards the window as they drove the half mile to the tiny hamlet of Steep Ride, and then on to Abbot Giles. In her heart, she bid a silent farewell to the countryside that was as familiar to her as her own name. They passed by the church where Mr Hartwell delivered his sermons every Sunday, and then past the tiny cottage where Lucinda Beattie, the former vicar's spinster sister lived.

Desirée knew them all. She had met them at Lady Perceval's annual summer fête, held on the grounds of Perceval Hall. It was one of the few times in the year when everyone from servant to master met to play games and enjoy the day—even teachers from Mrs Guarding's Academy. From there they passed through the southern tip of Giles Wood before connecting with the road which, three miles on, would put them on the main Northampton to London road. From there, it was on to London and her new home.

As if sensing her need for time, Sebastian did not press her for conversation. He seemed content to let her stare through the window, letting her thoughts take her where they would. But she knew that in the closed confines of the carriage he watched her. She could feel his eyes on her, inspecting every inch of her appearance from the tip of her light brown hair to the toes of her serviceable brown boots.

Finally, as they left the Abbey villages behind, Desirée drew a long, deep breath. Her past was precisely that now. Something she was leaving behind in the dust raised by the carriage wheels.

'You claimed there was nothing holding you to the area,' Sebastian said quietly, 'and yet, I cannot help but remark on the regret and unhappiness I see in your face at leaving it, Desirée.'

His comment was perceptive, and the tone in which he offered it surprisingly gentle. Desirée sighed and drew her eyes away from the window. 'When one has lived and worked in a place for so many years, my lord, one develops a certain attachment to it, even if it is only for the comfort of the routine it has provided.'

'Are you fond of routine?'

'I am comfortable with it,' she repeated. 'There is a difference.'

'Yes, I suppose there is. But as a woman who would cast off her clothes and swim in the river, you do not strike me as the type who would be comfortable with routine.'

A fierce blush suffused Desirée's cheeks. 'I hope you do not intend to keep reminding me of that occasion at every opportunity, my lord?'

Sebastian smiled at her irritation. 'Not at every opportunity, no. But it did leave a lasting impression upon my mind.'

Desirée studiously avoided his gaze.

'You mentioned that you worked in the area,' he commented as the silence lengthened again. 'What manner of employment did you leave?'

Desirée's first inclination was to remain silent. After all, what need was there for him to know anything about her past life or what she had done in it?

'I am not trying to pry, Desirée,' he said, as if reading her thoughts. 'But the hours will pass more quickly if we endeavour to fill them with amiable conversation. Or at least with the exchange of useful information.'

Realising that it served no useful purpose to prevaricate, Desirée took another deep breath and raised her eyes to his. 'I was...a teacher at Mrs Guarding's Academy for Girls.'

He smiled his mercurial smile. 'A teacher?'

'Yes. Of Latin, Greek, and philosophy.'

This time he stared at her in astonishment. 'Good Lord, it would seem that I have indeed taken up the company of a bluestocking.'

Desirée blushed. The term was not generally flattering, but it was hard to tell from Sebastian's tone what his true feelings on the subject were. 'Does that bother you?' she asked, almost hoping to hear him say that it would.

Unfortunately, it seemed that she was mistaken in her assessment of him.

'Surprised? Yes. Bothered? On the contrary, it will

no doubt provide us with ample subjects upon which to converse when we are not otherwise engaged.'

His meaning was perfectly clear, and once again, Desirée felt her cheeks grow warm. Heavens, would she never be able to stop blushing in the man's presence?

'Mrs Guarding's Academy has a reputation for being somewhat forward-thinking, as I recall,' Sebastian said conversationally. 'Did you enjoy being a teacher there?'

It was Desirée's turn to be surprised. She had not expected a London rake to be familiar with the reputation of a country school, no matter how illustrious some might consider it to be. 'I always enjoyed the subjects I taught,' she said carefully, 'perhaps more than I enjoyed the teaching of them.'

'I take that to mean that not all of your students were as anxious to receive instruction in the ancient languages and philosophies as you were to provide it?' he ventured.

Despite her feelings of awkwardness, Desirée was able to dredge up a smile. 'Most of them were. In fact, I believe that some of the girls asked to be sent to Guarding's *because* of the opportunity it allowed them to study subjects which most other girls' schools viewed as strictly male-oriented. The philosophies of Aristotle, for example, are not generally discussed among ladies of a certain social class.'

'Pity,' Sebastian observed. 'It might make for more enjoyable time spent in their company if they were.'

Desirée flicked him a look of surprise. 'You are familiar with the teachings of Aristotle?'

'Not as familiar as you, perhaps, but I am acquainted with some of his more common precepts. But tell me, Miss Desirée Nash,' Sebastian said, 'if you enjoyed being a teacher at Mrs Guarding's excellent academy and were comfortable with the routine it provided, why did you apply to me?'

Desirée hesitated. She had prepared herself for this question. Anticipated it, in fact. But now that she had been asked and was faced with having to tell him an outright lie, she found that the words of deception would not come so easily to her lips.

'I felt the need for a…change in my life,' she said, stumbling a little over the words. 'I wanted to see something of the world, and I could not imagine doing that from the confines of a girls' school.'

He regarded her in silence for a moment with those piercing blue eyes. 'So you applied to a man you had met on the bank of a river and asked him if he would take you on as his mistress.'

His words were blunt and Desirée had no doubt he meant them to be. But it was too late to change her story now. 'I saw in your offer a chance to…broaden my horizons,' she replied softly.

Thankfully, this time his reply came in the form of a throaty chuckle. 'Well, it's been called many things, Desirée, but I doubt it's ever been called an opportunity to broaden one's horizons.' His eyes caught and held hers. 'So there was no reason other than this sudden lust for adventure which prompted your writing a letter to me and asking me to take you to London as my mistress.'

Again, Desirée flinched. She wished she could

think of something else to say, but there was nothing. Besides, what was the point in telling him the truth? Would he think any better of her for having been told that she had been caught in a compromising position with one of the girl's fathers? More importantly, would he believe her?

Of course he wouldn't—why should he? He had seen nothing in her behaviour thus far to lead him to believe that she was a fine upstanding young woman. He had already accused her of being less than a lady by swimming half-naked in a public place. Now she was sitting in his carriage on the way to London to become his mistress. What kind of credibility did that lend her?

'Desirée?' he prompted.

'I told you...I was simply looking for a change,' Desirée repeated stubbornly. 'Is it so out of the realm of possibility to think that a five-and-twenty-year-old spinster might wish to have a change at this time in her life?'

The bitterness in her voice astonished her—as did the fact that hot tears of dismay were welling up in her eyes. What did this fine London gentleman know of humiliation? What manner of social injustice had the lofty Viscount Buckworth ever been forced to endure? Certainly nothing that would have induced him to turn his back on everything he knew to cast himself into the path of destruction.

Desirée quickly averted her face, blinking hard to keep the hot tears from disgracing her—and then caught her breath when she felt the warmth of Sebastian's large hand on her arm.

'No one is forcing you to do this, Desirée,' he said in his deep, quiet voice. 'You have only to say the word and I shall turn the carriage around and take you back to Steep Abbot. I have no wish to force myself upon you. But when I received your letter, I thought it was your desire to become my mistress. If that is not the case, tell me now and let that be an end to it. No wrong has been committed and I will not be offended. And I am sure Mrs Guarding will be happy to take you back. After all, how many young ladies with a background in Greek, Latin and philosophy is she likely to have encountered within the space of a few days?'

The sentiments, which were expressly intended to offer her comfort, were the last things Desirée expected from Lord Buckworth. She had not expected compassion or understanding from a man who was well known to be a rake and womanizer. He was giving her an opportunity to turn around; to go back before her reputation was well and truly lost.

And for a moment, just for a moment, she was tempted to do it. But what had she to gain by it? What possible good could be achieved by her returning to Mrs Guarding's Academy now?

Sadly, the question provided its own answer.

'My lord—'

'Sebastian.'

Desirée offered him a faint smile. 'Sebastian. It is…very good of you to be so…understanding of my circumstances and I thank you for your consideration. But I…do not wish to change my mind. I have made my decision and I must stand by it.'

Besides, it was already too late, Desirée reminded herself. She could not turn back now even if she wanted to. The damage to her reputation had already been done. Lord Perry had seen to that. The gates to her past were closed and locked.

Sebastian sat back against the squabs and studied her. 'All human actions have one or more of these seven causes,' he recited quietly. 'Chance, nature, compulsion, habit, reason, passion, desire.'

Desirée smiled. 'Aristotle knew much of men and their actions, but it was Sophocles who said, fortune is not on the side of the faint-hearted.'

'So you go to London to seek your fortune, Miss Desirée Nash?' Sebastian enquired.

'I go to London to seek my *future*.' Desirée met his gaze straight on. 'Only time will tell what manner of fortune it holds.'

They stopped for lunch at a roadside inn. Sebastian secured a private room in which they might dine, and while it was a pleasant enough place, it was there Desirée experienced first-hand what life as Sebastian's mistress would be like—both the good and the bad of it.

To the good, Sebastian was a perfect gentleman. He was kind and attentive to her needs, and ensured that she had everything she required. But while her clothing was respectable, the fact that she was travelling with a gentleman who was clearly a member of the aristocracy, and that she did so without benefit of a maid or chaperone, proclaimed her to be either a family member or his mistress.

Had she been a better actress, Desirée might have been able to convince those around her that she was indeed, Sebastian's sister or niece. Unfortunately, the lack of ease with which she moved in his company soon put paid to those circumstances. And judging by the way the innkeeper and his wife kept looking at her, and then at each other, Desirée knew that they had made their own assessment of the situation.

She was exceedingly grateful when they got on the road again.

Thankfully, the weather was clement and they made good time. Sebastian dozed for an hour or so in the afternoon, allowing Desirée to relax a little and enjoy the passing scenery. It had been a long time since she had travelled through this part of the country, and it was exciting to see how, or if, it had changed. But in truth, Desirée did not find the countryside nearly as interesting as the man who was sitting across from her.

For the first time, she was able to take a good look at this man with whom her immediate future was now irrevocably entwined. She observed that his hair was not black as she had first thought, but a very dark shade of brown into which a few stray streaks of grey had found their way. His eyelashes were surprisingly long and of the same dark shade as his hair and brows. In sleep, his face was as relaxed as that of a child. Desirée found herself able to admire the shape of his wide brow and the fine, aristocratic nose.

His fingers were laced together across his chest and he had unbuttoned his jacket for greater comfort. Yes, his clothes would certainly proclaim him for the gen-

tleman that he was, Desirée acknowledged. His
Hessians shone with a gleam indicative of an attentive
valet, and the superb manner in which his clothes fitted his large body gave evidence of a tailor worthy
of his craft. But beneath all the trappings of wealth
and class, what was this man called Sebastian Moore
really like?

As was his habit, Sebastian woke quickly, rising
from the depths of slumber to instant consciousness.
His eyes snapped open and he found the soft green
eyes of his companion fixed upon him. Seconds later,
he saw the colour rise to her cheeks—and watched
her eyes dart quickly away. 'Too late, Aphrodite,' he
murmured in a throaty voice. 'I caught you looking.
Do you approve of what you see?'

'You are…mistaken, my lord,' Desirée assured him
hastily. 'I merely…chanced to look in your direction
as your eyes were opening. I was actually engaged in
a study of the scenery beyond.'

Smiling, Sebastian drew himself into a sitting position and stretched. 'You know, there is something
which has been niggling at me ever since I received
your note. A bit of information which I would like to
have clarified.'

Desirée glanced at him warily. 'What information
is that?'

'Just before we parted last summer, I told you that
my name was Sebastian Moore. At the time, you evidenced no knowledge as to who I was and I assumed
that you would have no reason to. And yet, the letter
I received in London was addressed to Sebastian
Moore, Viscount Buckworth. How did you learn of

my identity? And this time, I will have the truth, Desirée,' Sebastian warned her. 'You do not have the face to lie. Your pretty green eyes give you away.'

A dark shadow of lashes dropped down over those enchanting eyes, but a few moments later when they lifted again, Sebastian could see that they were clear. 'Well?'

'One of the teachers at the Academy...knew who you were,' Desirée said hesitantly.

'Good Lord. You actually *spoke* of our interlude to someone at the school? You continue to surprise me, Desirée.'

'I only told her because I knew that I could trust her implicitly,' Desirée explained in her own defence. 'When I explained what had happened and...mentioned your name, Helen told me who you were.'

'I see. And was it...Helen's idea that you apply to me for protection?'

Desirée gasped. 'Certainly not! The idea was mine and mine alone.'

'I'm glad to hear it. But what else did she tell you about me, other than my title?'

By the blush which appeared in Desirée's cheeks, Sebastian knew that it must have been quite a lot. 'Ah, let me guess.'

'My lord, I—'

'No, please, Desirée, you would be amazed at how good I have become at this. Let me see. She probably would have started off by saying that Viscount Buckworth is a gentleman of good family, not to be found lacking in either money or property, but that he has, upon numerous occasions, shown himself to be something of a rake and a ne'er-do-well,' he recited thoughtfully. 'He likes to gamble, both at cards and at horses, and has been known to lose a fortune in a single night's sitting—only to claim it all back again through a fortunate turn in luck the next.'

'Lord Buckworth—'

'No, wait, there is more,' Sebastian continued cheerfully. 'I have no doubt that my reputation with the fair sex precedes me. So I must assume that you are aware that I play with the affections of many of the young ladies who are presented to me, but that I continue in my bachelor ways and find pleasure instead with a string of beautiful young mistresses.' He glanced at her quickly to gauge her reaction. 'I see I have the right of it.'

'Well, yes, you do, more or less.'

'Was there anything I left out?'

'No, not really.'

'You are not being truthful with me, Aphrodite.'

Desirée fidgeted in her seat. 'It is…not the type of thing to be discussed—'

'Ah, but it is, my dear. Because there is nothing that we cannot discuss together, and I should like to know what advice she gave you. Did she tell you that I was a drunk and a reprobate—'

'Of course not.'

'Or that I was foolhardy and reckless—'

'Not at all!'

'Perhaps she intimated that I was a cruel beast with a vicious temper who beat my mistresses on a regular basis?'

Desirée uttered another gasp. 'She said nothing of the kind! In fact, she told me that you treat your mistresses with the utmost kindness, and that you continue to do so even after you have—' She broke off in dismay, her eyes wide. 'Oh, dear! I never should have said—that is, I didn't mean to suggest—why are you laughing?'

'Why am I laughing? Dear me, I should have thought *that* would have been very obvious,' Sebastian said when his laughter finally subsided. 'Your friend obviously had a good source of information indeed. Even I was not aware that I was possessed of such benevolence of spirit. Is that why you wrote to me, Aphrodite? Because you knew that if I agreed to offer you my protection, I would treat you well, both during our liaison and afterwards?'

Desirée opened her mouth to speak and then abruptly closed it again. How could she tell him that he was her last resort? That she had applied to him because she had no other choice?

Her silence was its own response. 'Well, you shall soon have opportunity to see if they are right,' Sebastian said softly. 'For as of tonight, you shall have a comfortable house in which to live, beautiful clothes in which to dress, and a big, soft bed in which to express your pleasure and gratitude. Not a bad way, I think, to start…how did you put it? Broadening your horizons?'

Chapter Four

The house that Sebastian had chosen for Desirée was of modest though pleasing proportions and was located in a discreet though respectable area of town.

Sebastian was looking forward to reaching it. He was anxious to see Desirée settled, and then to return home to his own bed. He had no intention of spending the night with her. As anxious as he was to see her lovely young body again, he knew there was more to the young woman's story than she was telling him, and he sensed she needed some time alone to work things out in her mind.

Sebastian had been totally in earnest when he had asked her if she wished to back out of their arrangement. He had never forced a woman in his life, and he certainly had no intention of starting now. But when she had declined, albeit with some hesitation, he had concluded that the part she was not telling him counted for a good deal. She was obviously of good though not high birth, and had been educated in more than just the ancient languages. So it was only natural for him to conclude that the life upon which Desirée had embarked would be as alien to her as it would be to any other well-brought-up young lady.

For that reason, it occurred to Sebastian that if she would not tell him details of her most recent life, perhaps he could encourage her to speak of her earlier one.

'When were you last in London, Desirée?' he asked as they reached the outskirts of the metropolis.

Desirée had been eagerly glancing out of the carriage window, but at his question, a shutter dropped down over her eyes. 'A very long time ago, sir. I was born in London, but we…moved to the country when I was very young. My parents occasionally brought me back to visit relatives, but that was all.'

Sebastian glanced at her quickly, surprised to hear that she had any relatives in London at all. 'Do you still see these relations?'

Desirée shook her head. 'No. My grandfather was very angry when my mother went against his wishes and married my father. He told her that…she was marrying beneath herself and that if she went ahead with the marriage he would have nothing more to do with her.'

'And she went ahead with it?'

'Of course. My parents were in love,' Desirée said, as if that explained everything.

Sebastian smiled at her naïveté. 'I see. And your grandfather never forgave her?'

'Never. Even when I wrote to tell him of her passing, he did not reply. Nor did he come to her funeral.' Desirée glanced at him earnestly. 'Could you imagine not attending your own child's funeral, my lord?'

Sebastian shrugged. 'No, but then such things seldom do to people who are not of such a nature, Desirée. Your grandfather may have thought that he was acting in your mother's best interests by forbidding her to marry a man whom he perceived to be unworthy of her.'

'But how could he not have seen how much in love they were?' Desirée cried. 'Surely a father would wish to see his only daughter married to someone she loved, rather than to someone she did not, even if he was possessed of a title or a great fortune.'

'Perhaps her father was hoping that by providing her with one, she might, in time, come to feel the other. It is not unheard of for love to develop within the confines of an arranged marriage.'

Desirée sighed. 'I know, but for all that, I could never find it in my heart to feel charitable towards him. He came to see me when I was very young and he frowned at me the entire time. I thought him quite dreadful.'

'I daresay you would,' Sebastian said, hiding a smile. 'Have you any desire to see your grandfather now?'

'The possibility no longer exists,' Desirée said regretfully. 'I received a letter from his solicitor last year, informing me that Sir George Owens had died and that I had been left nothing.'

'I beg your pardon!' Sebastian glanced at her in shock. 'Did you say...Sir George Owens was your *grandfather*?'

'Yes, why? Did you know him?'

'I certainly knew *of* him,' Sebastian muttered, not

adding that what he had known of the crusty old ter-
magant would not have endeared him to anyone.
Good Lord, what a cock up this was turning out to
be. It was bad enough finding out that his beautiful
water nymph was an erudite young lady who taught
Latin and Greek at a well-known girls' school. But to
discover that Miss Desirée Nash from Steep Abbot
was also the granddaughter of the late Sir George
Bartholomew Owens cast an entirely different light
on the situation.

How could he possibly make a baronet's granddaughter his mistress?

Close on the heels of that dilemma came another.
Namely, if he wasn't going to make her his mistress,
and she had no desire to return to Steep Abbot, what
in God's name *was* he to do with her?

Sebastian thought hard for a moment, thankful that
their destination was still some miles off. He had no
intention of taking her to the house on Green Street
now, but where else *could* he take her? Not to his
own home, that went without saying. And if he put
her at an hotel, there was a distinct possibility that
someone might see them together and begin to ask
questions. So where—

And then the answer came to him. Of course! Why
hadn't he thought of it before? Aunt Hannah would
help him. She had done so more than once in the past.

Sebastian thumped his cane on the roof of the carriage and instructed the driver to take them to an address in Mayfair.

The abrupt change had Desirée glancing at him in

alarm. 'Are we not going to our original destination, my lord?'

'No. I suddenly remembered that…repairs are still being carried out in one of the rooms upstairs,' Sebastian told her. 'I had forgotten about that when I gave John the directions. I think it best that you stay with my aunt until the house is ready for occupation.'

Mistaking his hesitation at having had his plans disrupted for annoyance, Desirée nodded. In truth, she was relieved at having been spared—if only for a night or two—the reality of entering her new life. But the idea of having to stay with Sebastian's aunt was not an entirely comforting prospect either. The lady would no doubt be a pattern card of propriety and one easily able to discern the nature of the relationship which existed between her nephew and the young woman travelling with him.

After all, she reflected grimly, well-to-do gentlemen simply did not bring single, unattended ladies to London with them for any purpose—but one.

On first appearance, Sebastian's aunt was everything Desirée had expected her to be. A handsome rather than pretty woman, Hannah, Lady Charlton looked to be in her mid to late forties and conducted herself with all the grace and dignity of her position. Her hair was a rich, dark brown, elegantly styled, and her face was smooth and unlined. She was quite tall for a woman, standing a good head taller than Desirée, but her height lent her an elegance and stature that a shorter woman could never hope to achieve.

'Sebastian, what a delightful surprise,' Lady

Charlton said when her nephew and his guest had been shown into the comfortable drawing-room. 'I was only thinking the other day that I had not seen you this age. How are you, my dear?'

'Very well, thank you, Aunt,' Sebastian said. He smiled as he bent forward to kiss her cheek. 'I hope you will forgive my stopping by so late—'

'My dear, you know that you need never make apologies to me.' Lady Charlton's bright blue eyes flickered towards the young lady who was standing quietly in the background. 'But come, will you not introduce me to your companion?'

'Aunt Hannah, may I present Miss Desirée Nash. Desirée, my aunt, Lady Charlton.'

Silently drawing a breath, Desirée stepped forward and gracefully curtseyed. 'My lady.'

'Desirée. What an unusual name. From the French, is it not?' Lady Charlton asked, glancing at her nephew.

Sebastian shrugged his shoulders in a charmingly cavalier fashion. 'I thought it was Latin.'

'Well, never mind, it is uncommon to say the least.' Lady Charlton looked at Desirée and did not even attempt to disguise her curiosity. 'How do you and my nephew come to be acquainted, Miss Nash?'

'Actually—' Sebastian began.

'I asked Miss Nash the question, Sebastian,' Lady Charlton said pleasantly. 'Can she not speak for herself?'

'Lord Buckworth and I met in the vicinity of Steep Abbot, my lady,' Desirée said quickly. 'The small village where I was living.'

'Yes. We were both enjoying the pleasures of a warm summer's day,' Sebastian piped up.

'Really. And dare I ask *how* you were enjoying the pleasures of the day?'

Aware that Sebastian had phrased his answer poorly, Desirée hastened to explain. 'We were swimming, my lady.'

'Swimming?'

'Yes. In the River Steep.'

'Good gracious! Not in public view, I hope?'

'On the contrary, the pool was located deep within the forest and was very private,' Desirée assured her.

To her credit, Sebastian's aunt evidenced little of the shock she must have been feeling at the news. 'I see.' She turned to direct an amused glance at her nephew. 'And how did you happen to be in the area of a private pool in the woods near Steep Abbot, Sebastian?'

'I was staying with Wyndham at Bredington for a few days and decided to go for a swim.' Sebastian's smile flashed briefly. 'Purely by chance, I happened to arrive at the pool the same time as Miss Nash did.'

'And the two of you swam in it...together?'

The word conveyed a wealth of meaning and brought a hot flush of embarrassment to Desirée's cheeks. 'Y-yes, my lady, but only for a very brief time. I was not aware of...Lord Buckworth's presence when I first arrived. I have never encountered anyone in the glade before, and was astonished and alarmed when I discovered that I was not alone.'

'You may not have been aware of *his* presence, Miss Nash, but I find it difficult to believe that my nephew was not aware of *yours*,' Lady Charlton drawled.

'Lord Buckworth informed me that he was asleep when I arrived, ma'am, and that he was not aware of my presence until my splashing woke him. He left shortly thereafter.' Desirée did not intend to tell her of the argument which had ensued before Sebastian had reluctantly agreed to leave.

'I see.'

Desirée felt the lady's eyes upon her and knew that she was assessing everything about her, from the colour of her hair to the unstylish cut of her clothes. She wished that Sebastian would say something, but he seemed content merely to watch the two ladies study each other. Finally, Lady Charlton walked back towards the bellpull and said in a voice that gave no indication as to her feelings, 'Have you dined, Sebastian?'

'Not since lunch, Aunt Hannah.'

'Good. Then you would not object to partaking of some light refreshment?'

Sebastian inclined his head. 'I'm sure we would both be most grateful for the opportunity.'

The door opened shortly to admit the butler. 'Yes, my lady?'

'Grant, would you be so kind as to ask Cook to prepare a light supper for my nephew and his guest. Then perhaps you would show Miss Nash to the Green Room. I think she might like to freshen up before dinner.'

Desirée glanced at Lady Charlton in surprise. 'Thank you, Lady Charlton, I would indeed.'

'Travelling is a dusty occupation, but a necessary one,' Lady Charlton observed kindly. 'Grant will show you the way.'

Desirée inclined her head and followed the ramrod-straight figure of the butler from the room.

Lady Charlton waited for the door to close behind them before turning an inquisitive eye on her nephew. 'Now, Sebastian, would you care to explain what all this is all about—and tell me why you have brought your mistress to my house?'

Sebastian winced. For all her grace and refinement, his aunt could be painfully blunt when she chose to be. 'Desirée is not precisely my mistress.'

'Then what precisely is she?'

He thought for a moment, wondering whether it would be judicious to temper truth with fiction, or whether he should just blurt it all out. He decided on the latter. He had learned long ago that when dealing with his aunt, honesty was always the best policy.

'Miss Nash is a young woman I was bringing to London to *become* my mistress, but one who, on the way here, disclosed certain facts to me which made me think better of my decision.'

Lady Charlton's eyebrows rose. 'Indeed. I think that before the young lady returns, Sebastian, you had best tell me all about Miss Nash. Brandy?'

'Yes, thank you.' Sebastian waited while his aunt filled two glasses and then handed one to him. That was yet another of the things he loved about her. She did not adhere to the custom of polite social drinking at the prescribed times. When she wanted a brandy, she had one. But then, Hannah Charlton had long been considered something of an Original.

'Miss Nash is, or rather was, a teacher at a private girls' school in the village of Steep Abbot,' Sebastian began. 'We met, as she said, one afternoon last summer when she had slipped away to enjoy a swim in the River Steep. I had swum up from Bredington and was taking a brief respite on the bank, well hidden from view, when Miss Nash appeared out of the woods and started to undress.'

Lady Charlton smiled. 'So you were not asleep?'

He offered her a sheepish grin. 'No. I merely said that in an effort to allay her feelings of embarrassment. But I did wait until she had enjoyed her swim and had climbed back out on the bank again before making her aware of my presence.'

'How gracious of you, Sebastian,' came the laconic reply. 'I will spare us both the embarrassment of asking you if the young lady was wearing any manner of clothing—'

'As a matter of fact, she was—'

'By asking you how you came to discover that she was a teacher.'

'Actually, that was one of the things I learned today.' Sebastian had the grace to look contrite. 'At the time, I was not particularly interested in what Miss Nash did for a living.'

Lady Charlton shook her head. 'Really, Sebastian. You saw a beautiful young woman and immediately dismissed her intellectual standing to think only about her potential as your bed partner. How typical of you and your sex. So, Miss Nash was employed as a teacher. Where?'

'At Mrs Guarding's Academy for Girls in Steep Abbot.'

'Mrs Guarding?' Lady Charlton stared at him in shock. 'Good Lord, could that be...Eleanor Guarding?'

'I have no idea, Aunt. I did not think to delve into the identity of the headmistress either.'

'What subjects did Miss Nash give instruction in?'

'Greek, Latin, and philosophy.'

Lady Charlton began to smile. 'Then it would have to be Eleanor Guarding's school. I am aware of no other establishment that would offer such advanced subjects to women.'

'Are you acquainted with the venerable Mrs Guarding?' Sebastian asked, not even attempting to conceal his surprise.

'Not acquainted, but certainly familiar. I chanced to read one of her papers a few years ago. It gave a rather chilling depiction of female slavery and its effect upon society as a whole.' Lady Charlton glanced at her nephew shrewdly. 'As a teacher at Mrs Guarding's Academy, Miss Nash is not your usual type of ladybird, Sebastian.'

'No, that much I discovered today, Aunt,' he agreed ruefully. 'But that is nothing compared to what I learned about her as we were arriving on the outskirts of town.'

Lady Charlton gazed at him expectantly. 'Well?'

'Miss Desirée Nash is the estranged granddaughter of the late Sir George Owens. What do you think of that?'

The look of astonishment on Lady Charlton's face told him exactly what she thought, and more. 'Good heavens, that comes as something of a shock indeed. I knew that Sir George had one daughter and that he had disowned her as a result of her marrying a man of whom he did not approve. But I had not heard news of a child resulting from that union.'

'Well, one did,' Sebastian told her. 'And once I realised what Miss Nash's connections were, I could not, in all good conscience, set her up as my mistress. Word travels too fast in this town and I could only imagine what Sir George's family would say if they were to discover that I had taken his only grand-daughter as my *fille de joie*.'

Lady Charlton laughed softly. 'Yes, I have no doubt that such a diverting piece of news would make its way around town very quickly indeed.' She studied her nephew's handsome face in silence for a moment. 'So, what do you intend to do now? Take Miss Nash back to Steep Abbot?'

Sebastian sighed and stood up in a gracefully rest-less motion. 'I can't. I gave her the option of returning to Steep Abbot today and she told me that she could not.'

'Could not, or did not wish to?'

'She led me to believe that she did not wish to, but I tend to think there is more to it than that.'

Lady Charlton rose and poured herself another glass of brandy. 'I am quite sure there is, Sebastian. I have trouble believing that a well-born young lady who gave instruction in the ancient languages and philosophy, and who was accepted by a woman like Eleanor Guarding, would suddenly decide to turn her life upside down and become a courtesan. Tell me, what exactly did Miss Nash say her reasons for coming to London with you were?'

'She said that she felt it was time for a change in her life,' Sebastian said, repeating the words he himself had spent considerable time reviewing on the way here. 'When I said that it was *quite* a change, she informed me, rather bluntly, that at five-and-twenty, she had every right to do so.'

'Sebastian, did you *ask* this young lady to become your mistress?'

'No. Well, that is to say, not *recently*. I did allude to the idea last summer when I met her, but at the time, Desirée told me exactly what she thought of my suggestion. So you can imagine my surprise when I received a letter from her just last week, addressed to me here in London and asking me if the offer I extended to her last summer was still open. I wrote back saying that it was…and here we are.'

Lady Charlton nodded thoughtfully. 'Well, I suspect you are right about one thing, my dear. There is certainly more to Miss Nash's story than the little she has shared with you. For an educated young woman to do what she has done is unthinkable. I can only conclude that something desperate must have happened to her to bring about this astonishing change.'

'I tend to agree, Aunt Hannah, but the question remains, what I am to do with her now? I feel responsible for having brought her here, but I cannot in all good conscience set her up in the house on Green Street,' Sebastian said quietly. 'The news will surely get back to Sir George's family and I am just as like to be called out as to be left to go about my business.'

Lady Charlton nodded. 'Yes. Families can be funny things. Sir George might have disowned his daughter and ignored his grandchild, but there is nothing to say that his heir will not suddenly feel his responsibilities. Especially when he learns that a not so distant family member is now the mistress of a man whom Sir George referred to on more than one occasion as a rakehell and scoundrel.'

Sebastian tossed back the rest of his brandy. 'Yes, I am well aware of what Sir George's feelings about me were.'

There was a moment of silence as they both contemplated the situation.

'Look, why don't you leave Miss Nash here with me for a few days?' Lady Charlton offered unexpectedly.

Sebastian glanced at his aunt with hope. 'Are you sure?'

'Why not? I have no plans to go out of town, and she seems a pleasant enough young woman. And to be honest, I would welcome the opportunity of talking to someone who has more than dress patterns and gossip on her mind. I have not had occasion to enjoy a good philosophical discussion in some time. I think I would enjoy it.'

Impulsively, Sebastian bent down and kissed her cheek. 'You are a godsend, Aunt Hannah. If you would agree to keep Miss Nash here for a few days,

I can spend the time trying to find her suitable employment elsewhere. In fact, Jeremy and Regina Stewart have just had another child, and their eldest daughter is now five. Perhaps they would consider employing Miss Nash as a governess.'

'It is worth a try, Sebastian, but that is not to say that Miss Nash will welcome the opportunity.' Lady Charlton's eyes sparkled. 'If I had the choice of becoming the mistress of one of London's most handsome and eligible bachelors, or governess to a five-year-old child, I wonder which I should choose.'

Sebastian threw back his head and laughed. 'Dear Aunt Hannah. I should like to think that as my aunt, you would do what was socially and morally correct. However, *because* you are my aunt, I tend to think you would do the other and say to hell with what everyone thought.'

'Pray do not tell our young guest that.' Rising to her feet, Lady Charlton tucked her hand in her nephew's arm and winked at him. 'I should like to retain some pretence of dignity for a little while at least!'

For Desirée, Lady Charlton's suggestion that she freshen up before dinner had been a most welcome one. The trip had been long and emotionally draining, and notwithstanding the comfort of Sebastian's carriage, Desirée was weary. She was also extremely apprehensive about going back downstairs and facing Lady Charlton again. She knew that the lady suspected the nature of her relationship with Sebastian.

To believe otherwise was to pretend an ignorance of the most simple of facts.

Respectable unmarried ladies simply did not arrive with single gentlemen, unescorted and unattended, in the early hours of the evening. And knowing that, Desirée could not help but wonder what opinion the lady had taken of her. She knew that during her brief absence the situation would have been made clear, so it was quite likely that Lady Charlton would refuse to allow her to take a meal with them, let alone stay in her home for a few days!

It was that certainty which accounted for the shock Desirée felt when, upon re-entering the drawing room, she discovered that not only was she to stay for a meal and for the night, but that she was to remain at the house as Lady Charlton's guest for a few days.

'But...I don't understand,' Desirée said with a confused glance at Sebastian.

'It is really quite simple, Miss Nash,' Lady Charlton said. 'My nephew has explained that the establishment in which you were to reside is in need of repairs. That being the case, I have offered to put you up here until they are finished.'

'That is...most kind of you, Lady Charlton, but given the circumstances of my being here, I would understand perfectly if you did not wish me to stay. I am sure I could find lodgings elsewhere.'

'There is no need for you to go elsewhere, Miss Nash,' Lady Charlton assured her. 'I have plenty of room, and as I was telling Sebastian, I am looking forward to the opportunity of engaging in conversation with an educated young woman. I understand that you were employed as a teacher at Mrs Guarding's Academy for Girls?'

Desirée blushed, certain now that the conversation during her absence had been about her. 'Yes, I was.'

'Eleanor Guarding is a remarkable woman,' Lady Charlton commented. 'Would that more gentlemen paid heed to her teachings. If they did, I feel certain that the cause of women would be greatly improved.'

'You are acquainted with Mrs Guarding, my lady?' Desirée asked in surprise.

'Not personally, I regret to say, but I am very familiar with her work. What woman of intellect could not be?'

Inordinately pleased that Sebastian's aunt was in sympathy with Mrs Guarding's philosophies, Desirée felt some of her apprehension ease. 'She is a remarkable woman indeed, Lady Charlton, and the school is a reflection of all that she is. I consider myself extremely fortunate to have had the benefit of her employ for the past six years.'

Desirée would have said more, but the drawing-room door opened and the butler announced that a light collation had been laid in the dining-room.

'Splendid. We shall continue our conversation there.'

'*We?*' Sebastian enquired in amusement. 'But surely you have already eaten, Aunt?'

'Of course I have, Sebastian, but I am eager to talk to Miss Nash about Mrs Guarding's school and to learn what it was like to be a teacher there.'

At that, Desirée only just managed to keep the smile on her face. She was pleased that Lady Charlton was familiar with the school and with the formidable woman who ran it. Nor was she surprised that she would wish to know more about what went on within its walls. But as to how she had come to be a teacher there, Desirée knew that if she answered that question, it would only be a matter of time before Lady Charlton asked her why she had left it.

And that troubled her sorely. For while she had been able to fool Sebastian as to her reasons for leaving, she was not at all sure that she would be able to do as convincing a job on Lady Charlton.

To Desirée's relief, there was no inquisition over dinner. Rather, the meal—which consisted of a delicious consommé, followed by slices of cold ham, a selection of cheeses and a creamy custard for sweet—provided an excellent opportunity for Lady Charlton to discuss Mrs Guarding's beliefs in general, and to ask how she had incorporated them into the running of the school.

The subject of Desirée's life there and why she had left did not arise at all.

Desirée also enjoyed watching the exchange of conversation between Sebastian and his aunt. It was clear that a great depth of feeling and respect existed between the two. Their shared laughter over people and events known only to them evidenced a like sense of humour and Desirée could see that they were completely at ease with one another. It brought home to her how much she missed her own family, and the comfort of being with people she loved.

'You look tired, Miss Nash,' Lady Charlton said suddenly. 'Would you perhaps like to retire?'

Desirée touched the fine linen napkin to her lips. 'Thank you, Lady Charlton. I admit, I am weary. It has been…a long day.'

'Yes, and a rather momentous one, I should think. Sleep well.'

As Desirée rose, Sebastian did, too. 'I shall call to see you in the morning. Good night, Desirée.'

Desirée felt the colour rise to her cheeks. For a little while this evening, she had been able to forget that the reason she had come to London was to become this man's mistress. Until she saw the look in Lord Buckworth's eye. Then the memory of it all came rushing back. But to be fair, Desirée knew that she could no longer reproach Sebastian for the direction her life was taking. The gentleman had been kindness itself. He had offered her a graceful escape from her promise and when she had turned him down, he had tried to make the rest of her day as comfortable as possible.

Truly, if there was any blame to be assumed for the position she now found herself in, Desirée knew at whose door it would have to be laid.

'Good night, Lord Buckworth. And I would like to thank both of you—for the kindnesses you have shown me today.' With that, she walked across the room—very conscious of the two pairs of eyes that followed her—and quietly closed the door. Taking one of the candles that had been left at the bottom of the stairs, she went up to her room and once there, sat down on the bed and gazed at her surroundings.

Certainly the luxurious bedroom was a far cry from her humble lodgings at the Guarding Academy. The walls here were covered in the palest green fabric, with window hangings and bed linens to match. There was a large, comfortable bed, a small mahogany desk and a roomy armoire.

Of course, it was only a temporary accommodation, Desirée reminded herself. The house where she was to stay was currently being repaired. It was only a matter of time before she was ensconced there, and that her role as Sebastian's latest mistress would commence.

Refusing to think about that any longer than she had to, Desirée started to get ready for bed. Someone—possibly Lady Charlton's maid—had already unpacked what few meagre belongings she had brought with her, and had laid out her old cotton nightgown. Desirée frowned when she saw that it was wearing thin in a few places, and wondered if she might take some of Mrs Guarding's money to buy herself a new one.

Then, remembering that it was highly unlikely that she would *need* night-clothes, Desirée buried her face in the well-worn fabric, and quietly began to cry.

Chapter Five

As she had been accustomed to doing at Guarding's, Desirée awoke early. She had passed a restful night, no doubt due to the fact that she had been emotionally drained when she had gone to bed, and had slept without interruption until the first light of dawn had edged over the horizon. She yawned and stretched, and then rising, tiptoed across to the window.

The day was a fine one, with the sun shining brightly from a cloudless blue sky. In the street below, flower-girls and milkmaids were selling their wares, along with the countless other merchants who took to the streets in the early hours of the morning.

Desirée leaned against the windowframe and watched the bustle of activity below her. It was hard to believe that she was actually here in London. It brought home to her how much her life had changed in the course of a single day. But it also impressed upon her how far she had fallen. The young women in the streets below were doing an honest day's work for the money that would keep bread on their tables and a roof over their heads.

What was she going to be doing to earn hers?

Feeling some of her pleasure in the day evaporate, Desirée turned away from the window and walked towards the armoire. Her spirits plummeted even further when she realised that she had only two dresses in which to go downstairs, both of a serviceable grey fabric. Her clothes had been fine at school, where all of the teachers had dressed alike, but here in fashionable London, her drab gowns seemed even drabber by comparison.

Still, they were clean and, unlike her nightgown, they sported no holes. Most importantly, they were hers. She had paid for them with her own hard-earned money. A sobering thought when she realised that within a few days, nothing she owned would be earned in such a way.

Lady Charlton eschewed the popular pastime of staying in bed until noon and was already seated in the breakfast-room when Desirée came down. She looked up from her coffee as Desirée entered and greeted her with a smile. 'Good morning, Miss Nash, did you sleep well?'

'Very well indeed, thank you, Lady Charlton.'

'Splendid. You may help yourself to anything on the sideboard. I shall have Grant bring fresh eggs if you wish. To my mind, eggs are one food which do not improve with standing.'

'Thank you, Lady Charlton, but I am sure I will have no need of anything more than is here,' Desirée said. Indeed, after the good but plain fare she had partaken of at the school, the vast array of silver dishes arranged on the sideboard before her promised a veritable feast.

'Dear me,' Lady Charlton said. 'Is that the manner of dress you wore at school?' At Desirée's reluctant nod, she tutted. 'Well, we shall certainly have to do something about that. It does nothing for your colouring or for your figure.'

Desirée glanced down at the gown and blushed uncomfortably. 'I had thought to order some new clothes when I arrived, but I did not know...what I would need.'

'Well, you will certainly need better than what you have on. I think our first order of business will be to take you to my modiste. Mrs Abernathy does excellent work and her prices are very reasonable. Besides, Sebastian is very particular about a lady's attire, and I am sure you will wish to look nice for him.'

It was the first mention Lady Charlton had made of her role in her nephew's life, and it was more distressful to Desirée than she could have imagined. She dropped her fork onto her plate and winced as it clattered against the fine china. 'Forgive me, Lady Charlton, that was clumsy of me,' she said wretchedly.

Lady Charlton studied her in silence for a moment. 'There is no need to apologise, my dear. I tend to be something of a butter-fingers myself at times.' She hesitated a moment longer and then obviously decided that it was time for plain speaking.

'Miss Nash, I will not try to pretend an ignorance of why you are here. We are both intelligent women, and I see nothing to be gained by indulging in deception. But what I do not understand is *why*. Why would a beautiful and educated young woman like you wish to become a courtesan?'

Desirée did not think it was possible for her to feel any worse, but truly at that moment, she did. 'Lady Charlton, I—I—'

'Please do not dissemble, Miss Nash. Sebastian told me that you wrote to him of your own free will *and* that you refused his offer to return you to Steep Abbot. But judging from what little I have seen, I find it hard to believe that this is truly what you want from life. So I shall ask you here and now. Was this what you meant when you wrote to my nephew and told him that you wanted to…broaden your horizons?'

Desirée raised her eyes to those of her hostess and shook her head. 'Not at all.'

'Then why did you say it? Surely this is not really what you truly wish to become?'

Desirée closed her eyes and felt utterly wretched. 'Of course it isn't. But there were no other options left open to me.'

'Good Lord, child, there are always other options. Becoming a courtesan because you *wish* to is one thing, but becoming one because you perceive there are no other avenues of opportunity—'

'But there were no other avenues, Lady Charlton,' Desirée insisted. 'Please do not ask me to tell you why, but you must believe me when I say that my…choices were exceedingly limited. Had there been anything else that I could have done—'

'You would have done it. Yes, I can see that. But I also see that you are very disturbed about this whole affair and I know in my heart that there must be a reason for it,' Lady Charlton said gently. 'Will you not tell me what happened, my dear?'

The offer was more tempting than Desirée cared to admit, but she knew she had to resist. She barely knew Lady Charlton. And while there was compassion in her eyes now, what would happen once she discovered what had taken place in Steep Abbot on that fateful night? How was Desirée to know that the lady would not misunderstand what had happened, and that she would not lay the blame for Lord Perry's seduction attempts squarely at her door?

'I really would prefer not to discuss it, Lady Charlton,' Desirée said quietly, but firmly. 'You have been...very kind to me, and I am more grateful than I can tell you. But it is best that I say nothing. It can have no bearing on the matter.'

'On the contrary, my dear, it can have a considerable bearing on it. Once you enter into the life you have chosen, there will be nothing anyone will be able to do for you. You will be forever lost to respectable society.'

Desirée gazed at her hostess in despair. 'I am already lost to a portion of it, my lady. This will simply remove me from the rest.'

It was clear from the expression on Lady Charlton's face that she wanted to help. But Desirée also knew there was nothing the lady could do. What she was doing right now by giving her a temporary home was consideration enough.

'Well, I shall not push you for a confidence,' Lady Charlton said finally. 'I know there is a great deal more to this story than you are telling me, and I hate to think that nothing *can* be done about it. But you are not a stupid girl, Miss Nash, nor an impulsive one. I am sure you have given this a great deal of thought and I respect the right of any young woman to make up her own mind. But I want you to know that if you ever feel the need to talk, you have only to ask.' Lady Charlton leaned forward to place her hand over Desirée's. 'I give you my word that nothing you say shall leave the confines of this house, or reach my nephew's ears, if you should not wish it to.'

It was a sincere offer genuinely made, and it touched Desirée deeply. She would not have expected such kindness from a woman who was all but a stranger to her. 'Thank you, Lady Charlton. My gratitude for the compassion you have shown goes beyond what I am able to express in words.'

'Well, never mind,' Lady Charlton said brusquely. 'You're a sweet child and I hate to see you throw your life away. Though I suppose if you have to throw it away, you could do a great deal worse than Sebastian. He's a bit of a rogue but he has a good heart and he would never hurt you, which is more than I can say for some of his acquaintances. Speaking of Sebastian,' she said, pressing the napkin to her mouth, 'he told me to tell you that he would call for you around eleven. I have an appointment at half past ten, so I will not be able to keep you company until he arrives, but please feel free to remain downstairs until he does. If you have nothing else with which to pass your time, there are magazines and a small collection of books in the drawing-room.

Then, this afternoon, I think we shall pay a call on Mrs Abernathy to see about some clothes for you, and perhaps this evening, enjoy a little conversation over dinner.'

'Thank you, Lady Charlton, you are being very kind.'

'Nonsense. To tell the truth, Miss Nash, I'm looking forward to the pleasure of some company for a change. My husband has been gone these twelve years and sometimes I find time grows heavy on my hands.'

Surprised to hear a woman like Lady Charlton admit to feeling lonely, Desirée said softly, 'Have you never thought about remarrying?'

'Oh, the thought crosses my mind every now and then, but the plain truth is, I cannot think of anyone who would have me. I am far too independent for my own good,' Lady Charlton admitted with a chuckle. 'I like being able to come and go as I please, and, since I am wealthy enough to look after myself, I have no need of a man to do it for me. But that is not to say that I would not *enjoy* a gentleman's companionship from time to time. Perhaps to go to the theatre with, or to ride out with on a fine afternoon. Speaking of which, do you ride, Miss Nash?'

'I do, though it has been years since I have had the opportunity to do so.'

'Well then, you may ride my mare whenever you wish. Sebastian is a fine horseman and I am sure he will wish to take you riding in the park. I have a lovely little mare, but I don't get out very often, so

I'm sure she would be glad of the exercise. Now, Miss Nash, eat up. You've a busy day ahead.'

At the conclusion of breakfast, Lady Charlton left to prepare for her outing. Not wishing to return to the solitude of her room, Desirée made her way to the drawing-room, where there were indeed an interesting selection of books and magazines to peruse. Taking one from the top of the pile, she sat down upon the blue velvet settee to wait for Sebastian.

It had been a long time since Desirée had had the opportunity to study any fashion magazines, and as she flipped through the pages of a recent copy of *La Belle Assemblie*, she was alarmed to see how dreadfully out of fashion she was. Indeed, she was so engrossed in her study that she did not even hear Sebastian come in.

'Now, here is something new for Miss Desirée Nash,' he teased softly from the doorway. 'The erudite teacher of Greek, Latin and philosophy at Mrs Guarding's excellent academy studying fashion plates at eleven o'clock in the morning. How terribly decadent.'

Startled, Desirée lifted her eyes from the page—and then started to laugh. 'I fear you have caught me out, my lord. I must confess myself guilty. But I would not be telling a lie if I said it is years since I have had time for such idle pastimes.'

'You refer to the study of fashion as an idle pastime?'

'Of course.' Desirée's eyes twinkled. 'You and I both know that my time would be much better spent reviewing the words of Sophocles, for what is education but the constant learning and re-learning of that which we already know? Seneca was right when he said that diligence is a very great help, even to a mediocre intelligence.'

'Hmm, somehow I doubt you possess a mediocre intelligence, Desirée,' Sebastian observed dryly. 'But we all decide for ourselves what is important. I venture to say that most of your pupils are far more conversant with the pages of the magazine you hold in your hands now than they were with any of Seneca's wisdom.'

Desirée sighed and set the magazine aside. 'I daresay you are right, my lord.' She looked up into his eyes, and then away again. 'Have you been to see…the house?'

'The house?' he repeated blankly.

'Yes. Where we were to have gone…last night.'

'Ah, yes, the house. Actually, no, I haven't,' Sebastian admitted. 'I have been engaged in other pursuits entirely.'

'I see. So you have no idea how long the repairs will take?'

'It is hard to say. Sometimes these things can drag on for weeks.'

'Weeks!'

'You sound alarmed, Desirée. Does the idea of staying here for that length of time bother you? To be honest, I had a feeling you might prefer it.'

'Well, yes, I do. That is to say, your aunt is a most charming lady and I am enjoying her company very much,' Desirée said quickly. 'But in all fairness, I cannot continue to impose upon her. Surely you understand?'

'It is my understanding that she is very pleased to have you. Did she not tell you as much this morning?'

'Yes, but she is a polite and gracious woman. She would hardly be so rude as to ask me to leave.'

'She would if she did not like you,' Sebastian said briefly. 'Aunt Hannah is not one to suffer fools gladly. I have seen her send more than one foppish dandy off with a flea in his ear. But she does get lonely, and I know she is delighted at having someone in the house with whom she can discuss matters of intellectual diversity.'

'But she *knows* why I am here with you, Lord Buckworth,' Desirée said, not so easily convinced. 'And knowing that, how can she feel easy about having me under her roof? Her friends in society will surely begin to wonder. I think it would be best if I were to go to the…place you have chosen for me and live there as best I can until the repairs are finished.'

Seemingly at a loss, Sebastian sighed and sat down on the settee beside her. He had not wished to go into it at length, but since she seemed to be pushing him to move things along, he had no choice. 'Desirée, I may as well tell you, I have been giving… considerable thought to our situation.'

'Our situation?'

'Yes. About that of you becoming my mistress.'

Desirée started. 'But I thought we had already settled the matter.'

'Yes, we had, but given the information I am now in possession of—and which I was not at the time I made my offer—I wonder if you might be interested in employing your services…elsewhere.'

'Elsewhere! Lord Buckworth, I am *not* prepared to go as mistress to anyone else, if that is what you are suggesting!' Desirée cried.

'Good God, that's not what I'm suggesting at all. I was talking about finding you employment of a more respectable nature altogether.'

Desirée blinked. 'You were?'

'Of course. In fact, some very good friends of mine have just had another child, and they are interested in speaking to you about the position of governess to their eldest one, who is now five.'

'A governess?'

'Yes. I think it would be an excellent position for you. I know you would get on very well with the family. Jeremy is a fine fellow, and his wife, Regina, is equally good-tempered. And Mary is possibly the most well mannered five-year-old I have ever had the pleasure of meeting.'

Not wanting him to see her despair, Desirée quickly rose. 'My lord, I thank you for your efforts, but I fear I cannot possibly entertain such an offer.'

'But why not? It is not unlike what you were doing in the past, Desirée,' Sebastian pointed out. 'You will once again have an opportunity to instruct young ladies, albeit not in the areas with which you are most familiar. Given their ages, I doubt they are ready for the complexities of Latin, though they might find Greek mythology amusing.'

Desirée bit her lip in dismay. This was all so very difficult. It would be so much easier if she could just tell Sebastian the truth, for without doing so, how could she tell him that she could not be employed by any honourable people for fear of the scandal that might arise?

'My lord, I cannot, in all good conscience, accept such a position,' she told him regretfully. 'For one thing, I have no letter of reference, and it goes without saying that they will ask for one.'

Sebastian's surprise was genuine. 'Mrs Guarding did not provide you with one?'

Desirée hung her head. 'No.'

'I see.' He was silent for a moment, thinking. 'Well, that should not present a problem. Either myself or my aunt would be willing to vouch for you, and that will be good enough for Jeremy.'

'My lord, I repeat, I am most appreciative of your offer, but I'm afraid I must decline.'

'But why?'

'For reasons that I…cannot make known to you, at this time,' Desirée answered, turning away from him.

His frustration evident, Sebastian walked towards the fireplace. 'Desirée, I find myself at something of a loss here. I am of the opinion that you do not truly wish to become my mistress, and yet when I endeavour to find something else for you to do, you persist in turning it down. Why?'

'Because there is little else I am qualified for—any more.'

Sebastian groaned in exasperation. 'Damn it, woman, you cannot keep throwing out statements like that and not expect me to ask questions.'

'Yes, my lord, I can.' Desirée turned back to face

him. 'I have told you all that you need to know about me, and if I choose to keep certain facts to myself, that is my right. You cannot condemn me for that. But if you have changed your mind and do not wish me to be your mistress, you have only to say so.'

'I beg your pardon?' he said in bewilderment. 'What did I say to make you believe that?'

'The fact that you are looking so hard to find alternate employment for me.'

'The reason I am looking for alternate employment is because you are the granddaughter of the late Sir George Owens,' Sebastian pointed out bluntly. 'It has nothing to do with whether or not I want you to be my mistress. You have family in London. How would it look were we to encounter one of them at the theatre one evening?'

Desirée shrugged her shoulders. 'I have no idea how it would look. I have no reason to believe that any of them would recognize me. I have not been presented to society, so how would they know who I am?'

'Trust me, Desirée, they will know,' Sebastian told her. 'If they are anything like your late grandfather, they will make it their business to.'

'Well, whatever the case, the fact remains that there is really no reason for me to trespass on your aunt's hospitality any longer,' Desirée said quietly. 'And with that in mind, I shall begin to make enquiries into alternate accommodations, and then make my preparations to leave.' She rose and gave him a tremulous smile. 'It goes without saying, of course, that there is really no reason for you and I to have anything further to do with one another. But I did want you to know how…grateful I am for everything you have done.'

'Desirée, please, I wish you would reconsider my offer to place you in the home of my friends,' Sebastian said. 'And if you are adamant that you cannot, then at least tell me what manner of position you *did* have in mind, and I am sure that in time I will be able to find something suitable.'

She glanced up at him and quickly shook her head. 'Thank you, Lord Buckworth, but the answer is still no. You and your aunt have already done far more than was necessary. I think it best if I just say…goodbye and be on my way.'

And Desirée did just that. Before she—or Sebastian—had a chance to change her mind.

After the awkwardness of her meeting with Sebastian, Desirée was forced into an even more embarrassing situation in the afternoon, when Lady Charlton insisted on taking her to see the modiste. Desirée had fully intended to tell Sebastian's aunt of the discussion she had had with her nephew that morning, of course, *and* that she would shortly be leaving her home. But Lady Charlton did not arrive back until shortly before they were ready to leave, and she then spent the entire way there telling Desirée about the new furniture she was having made.

And once they reached the modiste's, of course, it was too late. Mrs Abernathy was at her most attentive from the moment they entered the shop until she quickly ushered them both into the private salon in the back. 'Now, Lady Charlton, how can I be of service to you today?' the woman enquired.

'Miss Nash is the daughter of an old acquaintance of mine, Mrs Abernathy,' Lady Charlton said without preamble. 'Unfortunately, we have not had occasion to see one another since her mother died, but now that she is out of mourning and back in London, I am delighted that she has come to spend some time with me. And naturally, when she expressed a desire to have some new clothes made, I thought of you at once.'

'Well, I think we can make the young lady look very nice indeed, ma'am,' Mrs Abernathy said, obviously satisfied with the young lady's credentials. She studied Desirée's drab outfit for a moment, and then snapped her fingers in a way that had her assistants scurrying in all directions. 'I think an apricot sarsenet would go very nicely with the young lady's complexion, as would an apple-green silk.'

And so Desirée spent the next two hours being measured, fitted, turned and draped with every colour, shade and texture of fabric available. She was not given a single opportunity to speak to Lady Charlton alone, and that in itself caused Desirée great concern. She knew that at the rate the bill for the clothes was mounting, the money Mrs Guarding had so kindly given her would be gone before the day was out.

It was not until they had left the shop with two dresses for immediate use and the rest promised for later in the week, that Desirée finally had an opportunity to express her misgivings.

'Lady Charlton, it was very good of you to say that I was the daughter of a friend, and I am exceedingly grateful for everything you have done. But please, you must cancel the order for the other things. These dresses will be fine, and I do not have enough money to—'

'Do not worry about money, Miss Nash, that is no longer an area with which you need concern yourself,' Lady Charlton told her candidly. 'My nephew will wish to see you well and fashionably attired and he is the one paying the bills now. And you certainly cannot go abroad in London society dressed like a schoolmistress—'

'But that is just it, Lady Charlton,' Desirée interrupted, feeling worse with every word the woman spoke. 'I shall not be going about in society. Lord Buckworth has thought better of his decision and we will not be proceeding with our…relationship. As such, I think it would be best if I were to leave your house at the earliest opportunity.'

'What?' Lady Charlton glanced at her in bewilderment. 'But…when did all this come about?'

'This morning when Lord Buckworth called to see me. He explained his feelings of reluctance with regard to his original plan, and he presented me with the offer of another position,' Desirée told her carefully. 'One as governess to some friends of his.'

'And did you not accept the offer?'

Desirée stared into the distance, seeing neither the bustle of people nor the crowded shops around them.

'I did not, for reasons that I could not explain to him, or to you.'

A thoughtful expression descended on Lady Charlton's face. 'Miss Nash, as I told you this morning, I am well aware that there are things you have not told us. I consider myself to be a very good judge of character and I believe that you left Mrs Guarding's employ for reasons that were disturbing and perhaps even embarrassing to you.'

'Lady Charlton, I—'

'Hear me out, Miss Nash. I can well understand my nephew's reasons for changing his mind about you and the relationship the two of you were to have, and I for one, am glad. I do not think you will be surprised to learn that he and I spoke of you last night, and it was then that he informed me of your connection with the late Sir George Owens. I also knew that Sebastian was going to approach you about the position of governess to Lord Jeremy and his wife and I thought it an excellent idea. But now to hear that you have declined it again leads me to believe that it has something to do with your reasons for leaving Guarding's. Because it is evident that it has nothing to do with looking after children, which I assume you enjoy doing.'

'Yes, I do, Lady Charlton, very much.'

'As I thought. And is it also necessary that you secure employment of some kind in the very near future?'

'Yes, my lady.'

'Very well. In that case, I should like to put forward an offer of my own.' Lady Charlton leaned forward in the carriage and looked straight into Desirée's eyes. 'I wish you to consider allowing me to employ you as my companion.'

Desirée gasped. 'Your *companion*! But, my lady, I could not possibly—'

'Listen to what I have to say before you answer, Miss Nash,' Lady Charlton advised. 'As I told you, my husband has been gone this many years, and as a widow, I have the freedom to move about as I wish. But I have in recent years been feeling the loneliness of my life, and I freely admit that the thought of having a companion has crossed my mind more than once. However, I was not sure what kind of person I wished to employ in that regard. I could not see myself spending time with a silly, missish young woman, or one with little more than a simple education to recommend her,' Lady Charlton said plainly. 'You, however, are neither missish nor stupid. Indeed, I believe your company would provide me with a great deal of satisfaction.'

'Lady Charlton, you do me a great honour, but I could not possibly accept.'

'Why not? I am offering you both a home and a means of employment, Miss Nash. And one which I think would be preferable to becoming either a mistress or a servant. Would you not agree?'

Two spots of colour stood out on Desirée's cheeks. 'Most definitely, my lady.'

'Then why do you hesitate? By accepting my offer,

surely you would have an answer to all of your problems?'

Desirée bit her lip in consternation. The position Lady Charlton was suggesting was something she would dearly love to do, but going about as a companion would expose her to a great many people, including those who might have heard of her past. And she would not risk embarrassing Lady Charlton for all the tea in China!

'Lady Charlton, the offer is a generous one, indeed more so than I can say. But my skills are in teaching young ladies subjects of an educational nature. I have not been taught the niceties of being a companion to an elegant lady of society.'

Lady Charlton snorted. 'Gracious, girl, you have all the training necessary. You were raised by a woman of good birth, were you not?'

Desirée did not even attempt to hide her surprise. 'Yes, I was, but—'

'And your father was…?'

'A clergyman.'

'Then your upbringing is as genteel as it needs to be. I have watched you, Miss Nash. In the very brief time you have been with me, I have observed your manners and have found them to be most pleasing. You conduct yourself with grace and dignity, and you speak well and in a most pleasing manner. I see nothing at all in your behaviour or conduct to preclude you from being a most suitable companion to myself. Or anyone else for that matter.'

'But…what would be the nature of my job?'

Desirée enquired, hardly daring to hope that this might come to pass.

'To accompany me to whatever society outings I choose to attend,' Lady Charlton said. 'To visit whatever shops and places I choose to frequent, and to be at my beck and call when I desire. And I warn you, Miss Nash, I can be very demanding at times.'

Desirée carefully hid her smile. 'You paint an intimidating picture indeed, my lady.'

'I would also expect you to play cards with me and to entertain me on the pianoforte after dinner. I do enjoy music but cannot play a note. Tone deaf, as my father used to say. I would also expect you to converse with me, and to discuss matters which are of interest to us both. Do you think you can do that?'

'I think I probably could, my lady.'

'Good. In return, you will be given room and board, a clothing allowance, and one free afternoon a week. Does that suit?'

'Most adequately, my lady.'

'Good. Oh, and one last thing, Miss Nash. You will not be permitted to question which events I ask you to accompany me to. I will also not allow you to question how I introduce you about in society.'

Desirée hesitated, aware of her first vague stirrings of doubt. 'You are within your rights to ask me to attend whatever manner of entertainments you choose, Lady Charlton, but I hope that if I were to express some…reservations about accompanying you on a particular outing, you would consider my feelings.'

Lady Charlton narrowed her eyes thoughtfully. 'I would be willing to listen, Miss Nash. That is only fair. But the final decision must be mine. Do you agree?'

Desirée thought about it. It was hard to believe that a woman she had met only last night was now offering her both a home and a paying position. And one which, in all honesty, hardly seemed like work at all.

'I think I would have to be a very foolish young woman to refuse such an offer, my lady,' Desirée said quietly. 'Thank you, yes, I would be most grateful to accept.'

'Splendid,' Lady Charlton said with obvious satisfaction. 'Well, now that that is settled, we must work out a few of the details. I think that we shall continue with the story I gave Mrs Abernathy, and which is close enough to the truth that it need not be considered a lie. You are the daughter of a friend of mine, and you are staying with me following the death of your parents and a lengthy sojourn in the country. Your presence and intellect will do the rest. And once you are outfitted in the type of clothes suitable to your station, no one will be any the wiser.'

'But...am I not to wear the clothes of a companion?'

'Yes, such as I believe them to be,' Lady Charlton said. 'I will not have you look like a shabby little wren, Miss Nash. You are too lovely for that. Besides, it will give me great pleasure to dress you. I was never blessed with a daughter of my own, so you will have to do.'

The thought that this great lady would treat her in such a way when she knew perfectly well the reasons for her coming to London in the first place all but brought tears to Desirée's eyes. 'I shall endeavour not to disappoint you, Lady Charlton,' she said quietly.

A smile curved the older woman's lips. 'It never occurred to me that you would, Miss Nash.'

Chapter Six

And so began the next phase of Desirée's life. The house in Mayfair became her permanent home and the charming bedroom on the third floor, her own private domain.

Lady Charlton took her to see Mrs Abernathy again and promptly ordered a whole new wardrobe for her. She justified the expenditure by saying that, as Desirée would be accompanying her on a wide variety of visits and excursions throughout the day, it was imperative that she have the proper type of garments to wear on each and every occasion.

Desirée noticed that Lady Charlton did not cancel any of the lovely evening gowns that were already on order for her, but when she asked about it she was told that she would still need those for the more formal functions the two of them would attend in the evening.

All in all, it helped raise Desirée's confidence immensely. She quickly regained her sense of self-worth, secure in the knowledge that she was once again earning her keep. Certainly it was a much more appealing prospect than being kept by Lord Buckworth, Desirée assured herself.

As to that gentleman, she had seen nothing of him at all since the morning five days ago when they had spoken together in the drawing-room. Perhaps that was why she felt a little nervous as she stood in the hall waiting for Lady Charlton to come down. Sebastian had suggested a carriage ride through the park, and while Desirée was looking forward to it, she could not deny to feeling a considerable degree of apprehension as well. She was no longer his intended mistress, but the companion of his own dear aunt. She wondered how he would feel about her in such a familiar role.

'Ah, Miss Nash, prompt as always,' Lady Charlton said as she descended the staircase a few minutes later. 'Excellent. I deplore tardiness.'

'As do I, my lady,' Desirée informed her with a smile. 'It was one thing Mrs Guarding would not tolerate from either her staff or her students.'

'You must tell me more about Mrs Guarding and her school,' Lady Charlton commented as she pulled on her soft kid leather gloves. 'I am fascinated by her ability to successfully operate an establishment dedicated to the furthering of academic excellence in young women. It is truly a remarkable achievement, and she, a remarkable woman.'

Recalling her conversation with Mrs Guarding on the night of Lord Perry's attack, and the kindness that lady had shown her, Desirée smiled wistfully. 'She is indeed, my lady.'

Soon after, Sebastian arrived at the front door,

looking all the crack in a dark blue jacket over buff-coloured breeches. Desirée had almost forgotten how handsome and dashing he was, and was surprised to feel her heart begin to beat a little faster at the sight of him.

'Good afternoon, ladies. What a delightful day we have for a drive,' he said, bowing to them both. 'Aunt Hannah, you are looking as elegant as ever. And Miss Nash, upon my word, I must remark on the change which has come over you. You look like a breath of spring in that most charming gown.'

In spite of her determination to remain distant, Desirée's breath quickened at his compliment. She was wearing one of her new gowns today and she knew that the soft lemon shade became her very well. Certainly it made a delightful change from the drab grey gowns she had worn at school.

'Your aunt has been kind enough to provide me with clothes more suitable to my new position,' she explained. 'Though to my mind, she has been more than generous.'

'Tosh, I have given you no more than is necessary,' Lady Charlton assured her. 'I was not about to have you accompanying me all around London wearing dreary outfits in grey and brown, but I have not been at all extravagant. That outfit, for example, is in a pretty enough shade, but the quality of the fabric is inferior to what I would have purchased for myself. However, I felt that for a companion it would suffice.'

Desirée tactfully hid her amusement. Lady Charlton constantly tried to downplay her role as benefactor but the truth of it was, Desirée knew she would never be able to thank the woman enough for all that she had done. Her wage was exceedingly generous, and the work Desirée did was more a pleasure than anything else. She enjoyed talking to Lady Charlton and had discovered that her employer was possessed of an agile mind and a quick wit. As far as Desirée was concerned, time spent in her company was a delight rather than a duty. Now if she could just come to terms with her past, all would be well.

Unfortunately, as Desirée sat next to Lady Charlton in the elegant barouche on the way to the park, she knew it was unlikely that she would. The memory of her humiliation at Lord Perry's hands was still too fresh in her mind, and she had a feeling it would stay that way for some time.

'You look very deep in thought, Miss Nash,' Sebastian observed suddenly. 'Are you lost in the words of some ancient Greek philosopher or just musing about your next social engagement?'

Desirée laughed softly. 'Indeed, my lord, on such a lovely afternoon as this, I can assure you that my thoughts were not on academic matters of any kind.'

'I am glad to hear it,' Lady Charlton commented. 'A well-rounded mind is all very well, but to have nothing of a more frivolous nature to contemplate would make life decidedly dull. Young people must have their diversions. For that reason, I have decided that we will attend Lady Rumsden's ball on Thursday evening. She is celebrating the engagement of her eldest daughter, and there will be plenty of young people about. Sebastian, if you are not otherwise engaged, I should be pleased for your escort.'

'I am, as ever, at your service, Aunt Hannah,' Sebastian replied urbanely. 'And I should be more than pleased to accompany you both.'

Both? Desirée felt a quick stab of alarm. 'But surely you will not require my presence at such a grand occasion, Lady Charlton? You will have Lord Buckworth to keep you company, as well as many of your friends.'

'Yes, all of whom will be far too eager to talk about the same boring old things, Miss Nash. Society lives for gossip, I do not. No, I shall require your company even more on an occasion such as that. Which reminds me, we must call on Madame Félice as soon as possible. You will need a gown.'

'Madame Félice?' Desirée looked confused. 'But I thought the modiste's name was Mrs Abernathy.'

'Mrs Abernathy is all very well for day dresses and more simple gowns, Miss Nash, but a lady goes to Madame Félice when she wants something truly superb. The woman is a sensation in London. She creates the most marvellous gowns, and in the most sumptuous of fabrics. She is, however, very selective of her clientele and does not accept just anyone.'

'But I already have more than enough gowns, my lady,' Desirée objected. 'And I certainly have no need for anything elaborate. The blue silk or the pale green sarsenet will do very well, I am sure.'

But Lady Charlton would brook no argument. 'Those are pretty enough for a musicale or a soirée, Miss Nash, but they are not appropriate for a ball, and certainly not for one given by Lady Rumsden.'

Sebastian glanced at Desirée with interest. 'Do you

not wish to attend an elegant ball dressed in a gown created by one of the finest dressmakers in London, Desirée? You might find yourself being heralded as a diamond of the first water.'

For a moment, Desirée felt a mindless rush of panic. She had no wish to be noticed, let alone fêted. What if she were to bump into someone who knew of her?

'I have never sought attention, Lord Buckworth,' she said anxiously, 'and as your aunt's companion, I seek it even less.'

'Rest easy, Miss Nash, we shall not stay long,' Lady Charlton assured her. 'But Lady Rumsden is a good friend and I should enjoy the chance for a coze. And I dare say it will make a pleasant change for you. You must be tired of sitting at home talking to me all the time.'

Her assurances did little to calm Desirée's worries. The lady had no idea how much she dreaded the prospect of moving about at a society ball. The more people that were there, the greater her chances of being recognized, and ultimately exposed.

And as far as the offer of a new gown went, it was very flattering to be told that she was to visit one of London's foremost modistes, and that she was possibly to receive a gown which would put everything else she owned to shame, but what would be the cost of such an elaborate creation? Lady Charlton had already bought her an extensive wardrobe which consisted of more clothes than she could possibly wear. And she always did so with the justification that the gowns and the riding habits, the carriage dresses and the morning gowns, not to mention the fans, gloves, shoes and reticules were all a necessary part of any companion's wardrobe.

The problem in Desirée's mind was, where did necessity end—and charity begin?

The Gown, as Desirée came to think of it, was nothing short of magnificent. The renowned Madame Félice had created it herself from a length of rich, amethyst velvet, saying that the vibrant hue toned perfectly with Desirée's delicate complexion. Silk gloves of a matching hue covered her slender arms, while dainty amethyst slippers trimmed with lace encased her feet.

On the evening of Lady Rumsden's ball, Lady Charlton sent her own maid to dress Desirée's hair, and the result was nothing short of astonishing. She had taken Desirée's soft, honey-brown hair and swept it up on top of her head, then wound a ribbon of amethyst silk through the richly glowing curls. As a finishing touch, she had secured the style with a glittering amethyst comb; an unexpected gift from Lady Charlton.

To Sebastian, standing at the bottom of the stairs and watching Desirée come towards him, she looked even more like a goddess than she had upon the occasion of their first meeting. The ripe fullness of her breasts rose above the bodice of the low-cut gown, bringing back vivid memories of her standing in the patch of sunlight beside the Steep Wood pool. Her bare arms and shoulders glowed like cream against the richness of the amethyst velvet and her lips, softly parted in anticipation of the evening, seemed to offer a sweet invitation.

And for an instant, just for an instant, Sebastian regretted the impulse which had compelled him to let Desirée go. He was startled at the unexpected rush of desire he felt for her, and at the longing he felt to hold her in his arms. It was a long time since he had been moved by the beauty of a woman to such a degree.

But when she smiled at him in that sweet, breathless way of hers, Sebastian knew he could never have made her his mistress. Desirée Nash was too much a lady in far too many ways.

'You look stunning,' he said as she drew level with him. 'Truly, you will be the belle of the ball this evening.'

'Sebastian, I must ask you to stop putting such ideas in the young lady's head,' Lady Charlton said sharply. She had emerged from her sitting-room, elegantly gowned and ready to go, and now surveyed her companion's appearance with a discerning eye. 'Miss Nash is my companion and quite content to be so.'

'Of course,' Sebastian said smoothly. 'But she is an exceptionally beautiful companion all the same, and people will talk.'

'Of course they will, I would not expect them to do otherwise.' Lady Charlton's eyes softened slightly. 'You look very well, my dear. I vow, Madame Félice has a skill beyond that of any modiste I have ever encountered.'

Desirée dropped her employer a graceful curtsey.

'I have you to thank for my appearance, Lady Charlton. And for the most unexpected gift of this lovely comb,' she said, touching her hand to the back of her head.

'Well, I thought someone might as well wear it,' Lady Charlton said in an offhand manner. 'The style is far too delicate for me. I cannot think what possessed me to buy it in the first place. I never have been partial to amethysts.'

'Your momentary weakness was Miss Nash's gain, Aunt,' Sebastian said gallantly. Then, holding out his arm to both ladies, he smiled and said, 'Shall we go?'

Desirée had never been invited to such a fine house before, nor had she ever been part of such an elegant assembly. Ladies dressed in finery equal to her own drifted about the room, while dashing gentlemen resplendent in formal black attire moved among them. Thousands of candles placed in overhead chandeliers and wall sconces bathed the room in a warm, golden light, and the sweet perfume of flowers hung in the air.

To Desirée, standing in the shadow of Lady Charlton and her nephew, it was truly a magical sight. 'It is almost too breathtaking for words,' she murmured.

'As are you, Desirée,' Sebastian whispered in her ear. 'I daresay there will be many people wondering at your identity tonight.'

Desirée nibbled anxiously at her bottom lip. She had already noticed the curious glances being sent her way, and began to think she should have insisted on staying at home. But it was too late for that now. She was here as Lady Charlton's companion, and the least she could do was act the part.

'As I told you, I have no desire for such recognition,' Desirée said, trying to ignore the nervous flutterings in her stomach.

'Perhaps not, but I fear it will come regardless.'

After passing through the receiving line, Lady Charlton and her party moved slowly through the crowded room, stopping here and there to have a word with a friend, or to nod a greeting to an acquaintance.

'Before you are besieged by fawning young gentlemen intent on discovering your identity, might I beg the pleasure of a dance?'

Desirée glanced at Sebastian in alarm. 'I do not think that would be appropriate, my lord. I am not here as a guest.'

'No, you are here as the companion of a guest, and one who really has no need of your services this evening. And it would be foolish to stand idle along the wall when that is the case. See there, even now Aunt Hannah is engaged with Lord and Lady Merton, and I can assure you that once she and Lady Rumsden get together, they will be chatting for some time. So, I shall ask you once again. Will you grant me the honour of a dance?'

Desirée sighed. She wanted to dance with Sebastian very much, but did she dare? What would society think of a lady's companion dancing with a lord?

'No, I am sorry, Lord Buckworth,' Desirée said reluctantly. 'I do not think it would be correct.'

Sebastian frowned in annoyance. 'I am not at all pleased with your answer, Desirée. Nor by this insistence of yours at addressing me by my title. I thought we had agreed that when we were alone, you would call me Sebastian and I would call you Desirée.'

'That was true when our relationship was to have been of a different nature, my lord,' Desirée informed him. 'But now that our circumstances have changed, it is not fitting that I address you by your Christian name. Nor that you address me by mine.'

'Ah, Desirée,' Sebastian murmured close to her ear. 'I do not think I shall ever be able to think of you as plain Miss Nash, whatever the circumstances we happen to find ourselves in. You will forever be Aphrodite to me. And I would like to think that because of the nature of our first meeting, you would have felt at ease calling me by my name. Come say it, Desirée. Let me hear my name whispered upon your lips.'

A curious swooping sensation in the pit of Desirée's stomach halted her words and brought the blood rushing to her cheeks. His voice was so sweetly persuasive—but the smile playing about his sensuous lips so decidedly wicked, that Desirée frowned at him in mock annoyance. 'Now you are trying to discomfort me, Lord Buckworth, and I will not have it. You must call me Miss Nash and I shall call you Lord Buckworth. Any other form of address is quite unacceptable.'

'To the ears of polite society, perhaps, but I am not concerned with such things. Neither, I thought, would be a lady who was willing to shed her clothes and swim in the River Steep in the middle of the afternoon.'

Suddenly, Desirée's lips trembled with an urge to laugh. 'Lord Buckworth, I *wish* you would not keep reminding me of the folly of our first meeting.'

'I will as long as it continues to bring such a lovely pink flush to your cheeks.'

'I should have remained at school that afternoon.'

'Then you would not be standing here flirting with me.'

'I am not flirting with you, sir!'

'There, that is better,' Sebastian said with satisfaction. 'I prefer to see you with a sparkle in your eyes and defiance in your tone, than to hear you going about meek and mild and in fear of what society has to say. You are not like other women, Desirée. You never will be. You have passion in your heart and adventure in your soul. Who else would have agreed to be my mistress simply in order to change her life? You should celebrate that uniqueness as much as I do. Now come and dance with me.'

As much as she wanted to ignore his teasing remarks, Desirée knew that she could not. Just being around Sebastian set her pulse to racing. His conversation was so stimulating, and certainly, his appreciation of her was flattering in the extreme.

'My lord. Whatever the nature of our…past relationship, and however much you might feel I have qualities which other ladies do not, I would ask you to be mindful of the circumstances in which we find ourselves now. You are Lady Charlton's nephew and I am her companion. And in the eyes of society, you will be seen as paying too much attention to a servant.'

'Bother society!'

'All very well to say, my lord, but do you see the faces of the ladies around us? Look closely. Even now, they are watching us from behind the cover of their fans.'

Sebastian did not bother to look. 'I care little enough for what society thinks about me, Desirée. But I do care about *your* feelings, and for that reason alone, I shall leave you. But I shall be back, and I will ask you again for the pleasure of a dance. You shall not escape me so easily, Aphrodite.'

With that, he offered her a formal bow, a mischievous smile, and then moved off to seek other acquaintances.

In spite of herself, Desirée had to smile. Lady Charlton was right. Sebastian Moore was a terribly likeable rogue—and a devastatingly handsome one at that. His massive shoulders strained at the seams of the tailored black coat he wore and he carried himself with such commanding presence that people invariably moved aside to let him pass.

But it was truly more the character of the man which had her senses spinning. Sebastian possessed a gentle heart and a depth of sincerity seldom to be found among the dandies and fops of London society. He was exactly who he appeared to be. And Desirée knew she would have been lying if she'd said she wasn't grateful for a job that caused her frequently to be in his company.

She turned with a smile of bemusement on her

lips—only to feel it freeze solid when she saw the man standing before her.

'Well, this is a most pleasant surprise,' Lord Perry said smoothly. 'We meet again, Miss Nash.'

For Desirée, time suddenly seemed to stop—and go tumbling backwards. In that instant, she was once again trapped in the darkness with a man intent on her ruination. She felt the oppressive weight of Lord Perry's body against hers, heard the sound of her gown ripping, and remembered the loathsome touch of his hands on the softness of her skin.

Desirée felt the trembling begin deep in the pit of her stomach and prayed that she would not faint. 'Lord…Perry.'

'My daughter informed me that you were no longer at Guarding's, but I was not aware you had removed to Town.'

The peer's smile was as confident as it had always been; his manner that of a man completely in control. Desirée had to fight back the urge to run as far away from him as she could. 'No. Very few people did.' She knew that Lord Perry was waiting for an explanation, but she would see him in hell before he would have one from her. As far as she was concerned, the less this repulsive man knew about her and her life, the better. 'Now if you will excuse me—'

'I do not believe you have met my wife, Miss Nash,' Lord Perry cut in smoothly. 'Permit me to make you known to her.'

Desirée's composure was little more than a fragile shell around her. In her agitation, she had not noticed the tall, slender woman who was standing just behind Lord Perry. A woman as beautiful as any in the room, but one whose dark eyes were filled with suspicion as her husband turned to draw her forward. 'Lydia, my dear, this is Miss Nash. One of Elizabeth's teachers at the Guarding Academy. Miss Nash, my lovely wife, Lydia.'

Because she had no choice, Desirée curtseyed gracefully. 'Lady Perry.'

'Miss Nash.' The lady's greeting was as reserved as her manner. 'How can it be that a schoolmistress from Steep Abbot should come to be a guest at a London ball? Should you not be at school?'

There was a note of accusation in the woman's voice, and Desirée stiffened. 'I am no longer employed by Mrs Guarding, Lady Perry. I reside in London now.'

Lady Perry's eyes widened in surprise. 'Do you indeed? My, my, quite a change in circumstances for a woman of your position.' She glanced coldly at her husband. 'I wonder how such a thing came to pass?'

It was an agonizing and humiliating moment for Desirée. She had no way of knowing whether Lady Perry suspected the nature of her husband's conduct towards her, for while she doubted that Lord Perry would have told her, she was not at all sure that Elizabeth would not.

Thankfully, Lady Charlton chose that moment to make a most timely entrance.

'Ah, Miss Nash, there you are. I have been looking for you.' She glanced at the couple standing beside

Desirée and the expression in her eyes cooled. 'Good evening, Lord Perry, Lady Perry.'

'Lady Charlton, a pleasure to see you again.' Lord Perry bowed formally. 'You are acquainted with Miss Nash, I see.'

'I am indeed.' Lady Charlton's glance at Desirée was so quick, and her smile so warm, that none could have perceived the depth of concern behind it. 'I do apologise for leaving you on your own, my dear, but Lady Rumsden was of a mood to chat. However, she has expressed a desire to speak with you about the Oracle at Delphi.' Lady Charlton turned to smile in a rather condescending manner at the other two. 'If you will excuse us, Lord Perry, Lady Perry.'

His wife managed a cool smile, but Lord Perry was all gracious humility. 'But of course.' He bowed politely towards Desirée. 'I hope you enjoy your evening, Miss Nash.'

Desirée inclined her head, but offered no reply. She could not bring herself to utter the empty words that were usually expected at such a time. Because she was *not* pleased to see Lord Perry again, nor was she happy to have made the acquaintance of his wife.

It seemed that Lady Perry too, felt no need of social politeness. She moved away without speaking, her expression no warmer than it had been at the onset.

'Are you well acquainted with Lord Perry and his wife?' Lady Charlton enquired as they themselves moved away.

'Not at all, Lady Charlton,' Desirée said stiffly. 'I was introduced to Lord Perry at Mrs Guarding's, where his daughter, Elizabeth, is a student. I made the acquaintance of Lady Perry only this evening.'

'I see.' Lady Charlton was silent for a moment. 'And...would I be correct in assuming that you do not hold either of them in esteem?'

Desirée walked quietly at Lady Charlton's side, but her formerly white cheeks were now ablaze with colour. 'You would be very correct in your assumption indeed, Lady Charlton.'

The lady nodded in understanding. 'Yes. I thought perhaps I was.'

Sebastian too had observed the meeting between Desirée and Viscount Perry and his wife, and while he had not been able to hear any of the conversation which had taken place, he could tell from Desirée's expression that she was extremely ill at ease. Her lovely face had gone deathly pale, and then reddened with angry colour. She was clearly uncomfortable with the situation and had his aunt not appeared upon the scene when she had, Sebastian would have intervened himself.

Nevertheless, when half an hour had passed and he spied Desirée once again standing on her own, he casually walked across the room to talk with her. 'So, Desirée, how are you enjoying your first London ball?'

Initially startled, Desirée glanced up into his familiar face and slowly felt herself begin to relax. She had been horribly on edge ever since her encounter with Lord Perry and all but flinched when anyone came near. Thankfully, she suffered no such worries with Sebastian. Indeed, she was astonished at how comfortable she was beginning to feel in his presence. 'It has been an interesting experience, my lord, but I will be glad when it is over,' she admitted. 'I am anxious to get home.'

Sebastian saw the frown creasing her forehead and wondered what had put it there. Lord Perry perhaps? He wished he could have asked, almost as much as he wished he could have smoothed his fingers over her brow and erased the lines of worry and concern he saw there. The knowledge that he had no right to do either disturbed him.

'I shall ask Aunt Hannah if she is ready to leave,' Sebastian said softly, 'and then I shall return with your wrap.'

'Oh, yes, thank you, Lord Buckworth, I should be most grateful.'

Desirée watched him stride away, more affected by the concern in his voice than she wanted to admit. It would do her no good to develop feelings of affection for Sebastian. They were worlds apart in so many ways and it would be foolish of her to harbour hopes that he might some day think of her with anything more but the most passing of interest. But it was so easy to like him. He was truly a good and admirable man. There was no arrogance in his manner and no mockery in his speech. When he smiled he did so honestly, and when he frowned he left no one in any doubt as to his displeasure. Desirée hoped that his displeasure would never have cause to be directed towards her.

'Miss Nash?'

She turned to see a young footman standing at her side. 'Yes?'

'Lady Perry asks if she might have a word with you on the terrace.'

Lady Perry? A cold knot formed in the pit of Desirée's stomach. There was only one reason why the woman would have requested a meeting. Elizabeth must have told her what had happened in the classroom that night—and Desirée could just imagine what a horrid picture she would have painted.

For a moment, Desirée considered refusing. Why should she subject herself to the unfounded accusations of an angry and suspicious woman? But then, knowing that Lady Perry would only continue to harbour such beliefs if she did not meet with her and try to set the record straight, Desirée relented. Did she not owe it to herself to try to make the woman understand? For surely, as a woman, Lady Perry would understand what it was to be put upon by a man.

Not holding out much hope that she could, Desirée nevertheless followed the footman into the darkness of the warm summer evening. He led her to the far end of the terrace and then bowed politely before turning and walking away.

Desirée glanced around. At the moment, she seemed to be the only one here. 'Lady Perry? It is I, Miss Nash. You wished to see me.'

'Lady Perry is not coming, Miss Nash,' came a familiar voice. 'It was I who requested this meeting.'

Desirée whirled to see Lord Perry standing behind her and once again felt anger rise in her breast. 'How dare you trick me like this,' she said in a low, tremulous voice. 'What do you want?'

'You do not seem pleased to see me, Desirée.'

'My name is Miss Nash. And I am not pleased to see you. How could you expect me to be after what happened at the Academy?'

'Ah, yes. A most regrettable incident our being discovered like that,' he said in a voice which evidenced no signs of regret at all. 'But how fortunate to have discovered you here in London.'

'The discovery bears no pleasure for me, Lord Perry. Now if you will excuse me, I must return to the ballroom. Lady Charlton will be looking for me.'

'Lady Charlton can wait.' Lord Perry's fingers closed around her wrist. 'We have much to talk about, Desirée.'

'I told you, my name is Miss Nash. And we have nothing to talk about.' She glared down at his hand. 'Unhand me, sir.'

'All in good time, my dear. All in good time. Right now we have a few things to settle.'

Desirée tried to pull free, but Lord Perry only tightened his grip.

'You're hurting me!'

'And I shall continue to hurt you until you stop fighting and listen to what I have to say.' His eyes turned hard and unyielding. 'You have a very slender wrist, my dear. It would be a pity to snap it.'

Desirée paled, recognising the very real threat behind his words. She reluctantly stopped struggling, but remained purposely cold and distant. The man might have the physical advantage of her, but she refused to give him the emotional one as well. 'Very well, I shall listen to what you have to say. But not until you release me.'

'I would advise you not to run.'

'I give you my word that I shall not.'

The silence grew tight with tension. Lord Perry gazed down into her face, and then reluctantly released her. Desirée drew back her hand and prayed it would not bear evidence of bruises in the morning. 'Why did you trick me into coming out here?'

'Because I wanted to talk to you. And because I knew that if I made you think my wife had asked to see you, you would not refuse.'

'You sound very sure of yourself.'

Lord Perry began to smile. 'On the contrary, it was *you* I was sure of. I knew that you would agree to see her, if only to try to convince her of your innocence. Which, I might add, would be a waste of time. She already suspects that you are, or were, my mistress. But that is of no concern to me. What is, is how you came to be in London, and where you are residing now.'

'And *that* is none of your business.'

'On the contrary, my dear, it is because I choose to make it so.'

'Lord Perry, I agreed to listen to what you had to say but I refuse to engage in conversation with you,' Desirée said coldly. 'I despise the sight of you and if you asked me here for a specific purpose, then state it and be done. I am anxious to return to the ballroom.'

Lord Perry studied her in silence for a moment, and

then slowly began to smile. 'Do you know, I never realised how truly beautiful you are, Desirée—'

'Miss Nash.'

'Such glorious eyes, such tempting flesh.' His eyes dropped lower, lingering darkly on the swell of her breasts. 'You make my blood boil, Desirée. You always have.'

Desirée slowly began to back away. 'I will not stay here and be spoken to in such a manner.'

'It is difficult to keep a rational head when you are around me,' he continued as though she hadn't spoken. 'When I remember how warm and soft you felt in my arms—'

'Leave me *alone*.'

'I want you, Desirée,' Lord Perry whispered. 'I want you in my bed.'

Desirée turned her face away in revulsion. 'No!'

'Take care before you answer, my dear. As I told you before, I can make life very pleasant for you. I have the wherewithal to set you up very nicely—'

'I will not listen!'

'Clothes, jewels, carriages, you have only to say the word and they will all be placed at your disposal.'

Desirée wanted to clap her hands over her ears to shut out the words. 'There is nothing you can say that would tempt me to consider such an offer. You are a vile and hateful man and—' Abruptly, Desirée broke off. She heard the sound of voices drifting towards them. Thank heavens, someone was coming!

Lord Perry must have heard them too, for he glanced towards the door and his face darkened in anger. 'This is not over, Desirée. I will have you. It is only a matter of time.'

He looked over his shoulder to see who was coming—and Desirée saw her chance. She picked up her skirts and flew past him, running down the flagstone terrace until she reached the French doors. Only then did she stop to risk a look back over her shoulder.

But Lord Perry was gone. The terrace was deserted.

She turned back around and walked straight into Sebastian's chest. 'Lord Buckworth!'

'You seem out of breath, Miss Nash,' Sebastian observed quietly. 'Were you running?'

'Yes. That is, I did not wish…to keep you or…Lady Charlton waiting,' she gasped.

Sebastian glanced towards the darkened terrace, and then back at her. 'Who were you out there with, Desirée?'

'No one, my lord. I simply went out when I grew…overly warm. Unfortunately, I lingered longer than I should have, and when I realised that I was probably keeping you waiting, I ran back.'

Sebastian watched her in silence for a moment, and then said, 'My aunt is waiting for you at the door. Go to her.'

Desirée hesitated. 'Are you not coming?'

He glanced towards the terrace again. 'I shall be there directly.'

Desirée felt her stomach clench tight. There was nothing she could do to stop him from going out on to the terrace. If she tried, she would only succeed in arousing his suspicions further. But what if he were to encounter Lord Perry? If Sebastian had witnessed her meeting with Perry earlier in the evening, and now discovered him out on the terrace—after she had told him that she had been alone—what would he think?

'Very well, I shall wait with Lady Charlton,' Desirée said, knowing she could do nothing else. She pressed her gloved hand to the pulse beating at her throat and walked as calmly as she could back into the ballroom.

Sebastian waited but a moment before turning and walking out on to the terrace. But what he saw there did nothing to arouse his suspicions. A young couple were seated on a stone bench engaged in polite conversation, Lord Rumsden was enjoying a cheroot at the far end of the stone walk where his wife was unlikely to find him, and a turbaned matron was fanning herself down by the palms. There was no one else in sight.

Frowning, Sebastian walked back into the ballroom. He had fully expected to find Lord Perry on the terrace. Because one thing had been very clear just now. Desirée *had* been in a hurry to leave the terrace, but not because she was anxious to join himself or Lady Charlton. She had been running *away* from someone. The look in her eyes hadn't been one of embarrassment.

It had been one of fear.

Chapter Seven

To Desirée's relief, Sebastian did not comment upon her flight from the terrace during their ride home. Nor did he allude to it as he bid her goodnight at Lady Charlton's door. Nevertheless, the memory of it stayed with her through the long hours of the night and caused her an uneasy sleep from which she awoke feeling troubled and little refreshed.

'Well, Miss Nash, did you enjoy yourself at the ball?' Lady Charlton enquired at breakfast the following morning. 'I daresay it made quite a change from the social life offered at Mrs Guarding's excellent Academy.'

'I cannot even speak of it in the same breath,' Desirée said, forcing a smile to her lips for the benefit of her employer. 'The opportunity for a schoolmistress to mingle with elegant society was usually reserved to the Christmas ball at the Angel or the annual summer picnic on the grounds of Lord Perceval's estate near Abbot Quincey.'

Lady Charlton, who had been perusing her copy of the *Morning Post*, suddenly sat back in her chair.

'Abbot Quincey. Is that not in the area of Steepwood Abbey?'

'It is.'

'And were there not some rather bizarre goings on up there last year?'

'My lady?'

'It seems to me I recall hearing rumours about the Marquis of Sywell's young wife running off and leaving him after less than a year of marriage.'

'Oh, that. Yes, you did.'

'There was a considerable age difference between them, was there not?'

'Some forty years.'

'And…was there not also some speculation that the Marquis himself might have murdered her? Or are you at all acquainted with the story?'

Desirée bit back a smile. For a woman who professed to have little interest in gossip, Lady Charlton seemed particularly well informed about an event which had taken place in a small village at quite some distance from London. Not that she would have appreciated anyone pointing that out to her, of course.

'It would have been impossible to live in Steep Abbot and not be familiar with the story,' was all Desirée said. 'Louise Hanslope was actually the ward of the Marquis's bailiff, Mr John Hanslope. Many believed she was his daughter, but as nothing was ever proven, I cannot comment upon the validity of the rumour. Louise left home at the age of fourteen, when Mrs Hanslope died, and then returned seven years later to find her guardian on his deathbed. The Marquis, having also gone to pay a final visit to Mr

Hanslope, met her there. By all acounts, he was so smitten by her appearance that he proposed to her on the spot.'

'Good Lord! And she accepted him?'

'Indeed. They were married at her guardian's bedside.'

'What, as the poor man lay there dying?'

'So I have been told. Needless to say, the haste of the marriage took many people by surprise.'

'Yes, I should rather think it would,' Lady Charlton remarked with a frown. 'But why would such an eligible young woman agree to marry such a reprehensible man? And one so very much older than herself?'

'I have no idea, my lady,' Desirée admitted. 'Some said Louise was so distraught at finding her guardian at death's door, that she hardly knew *what* she was doing when she accepted the Marquis's offer. Others believed she married him *because* he was old, and because she knew she would soon be a very wealthy young widow.'

Lady Charlton shook her head. 'Goodness, what fodder *that* must have provided for the prattle-boxes.'

'To be sure.' Desirée smiled. 'Of course, gossip has always been rife about the goings on up at the Abbey. Especially as regards the Marquis himself.'

'Yes, a most unsavoury character altogether,' Lady Charlton commented as she returned her attention to the paper. 'I remember hearing tales of Sywell's disgraceful behaviour in town when he was but a young man. He and his rapscallion friends were forever losing money at the tables or on horses, and Sywell himself was reputed to have a vile temper. I am not surprised his wife ran off and left him. Serve him right, the old reprobate.' She signalled to the footman for more coffee. 'Now, on a more positive note, I thought we might visit Hatchard's this afternoon, Miss Nash, and after that, pay a call on the modiste. Lady Rumsden advised me that Mrs Abernathy has received a shipment of new shawls and I am of a mind to have one. I would like you to accompany me.'

'Yes, of course,' Desirée said, though her thoughts were elsewhere.

'As for this evening, I have accepted an invitation to a soirée at Lady Appleby's in Portman Square. Letitia is a most amiable woman, something of an Original like myself, and her receptions are always well attended. There will be dancing and conversation and it should make for a pleasant evening.' Lady Charlton turned the page of her newspaper and sent Desirée a probing glance. 'Do you play whist, Miss Nash?'

Desirée slowly put down her cup. 'Yes, I do. My parents and I passed many a winter evening so engaged. I found it to be a most enjoyable pastime.'

'And were you skilled at the game?'

'I seem to recall that I acquitted myself tolerably well.'

'Good, then you shall be my partner,' Lady Charlton announced with satisfaction. 'Lady Appleby always sets up tables for whist and I cannot abide lacklustre play. I once had the misfortune to be paired with a gentleman who kept forgetting which suit was trump. It made for an abysmal evening. We were trounced every hand.'

'I think I can safely say that I remember which cards to play,' Desirée assured her with a smile. Then, picking up her cup again, added in as casual a voice as she could effect, 'Will your nephew be escorting us as usual?'

'Sebastian? I think not. I seem to recall him saying that he was engaged to dine with Lord Mackenzie this evening, and I cannot imagine him crying off from that to attend a card party. Lord Mackenzie has two daughters and the eldest, Lady Alice, is quite a beauty. I suspect she has more to do with Sebastian's visit than her father.'

Desirée stirred uneasily in her chair. 'Really? I was not aware Lord Buckworth was looking for a wife.'

'I doubt he is, my dear,' Lady Charlton said ruefully. 'But it is long past time he gave thought to marrying and settling down. I lecture him on the subject every few months. You see, he is in possession of a considerable fortune and he must have an heir. Thankfully, for all his apparent recklessness, Sebastian does take his responsibilities seriously. So when I mentioned to him that Lady Alice seemed a very pleasant sort of girl, he obviously took my words to heart.'

Desirée made no reply, but she continued to mull over Lady Charlton's words well into the morning. In fact, she was still thinking about them as she followed her employer into Mrs Abernathy's shop later that afternoon. Strange that she had never given any thought to the idea of Sebastian marrying, when it was only natural that he would. He owed it to his family and to himself to secure the line. But perhaps it was *because* Sebastian had shown absolutely no signs of a man bent on duty that Desirée had not thought him so inclined. Certainly, his *laissez-faire* attitude towards life in general made it hard to imagine him settling down with Lady Alice Mackenzie to the staidness of married life.

Or was it just the thought of him settling down with *any* woman that Desirée found so hard to accept?

'Miss Nash, a moment if you will,' Lady Charlton called from the other side of the shop. 'I require your assistance.'

Grateful for the distraction, Desirée hastened to her employer's side. 'Yes, my lady?'

'I am hard pressed to make a decision between these two shawls. Which one do you prefer?'

Desirée glanced at the exquisite lengths of fabric draped over the counter and resolutely bit back a sigh. Woven of the softest wool, either would have been a pleasure to own, but the price put them well beyond the means of someone like her. 'I suppose that would depend upon what you intended to wear them with.'

'I did not ask for a discussion, Miss Nash, I asked for your opinion.'

'In that case, I would choose the white with the green border.'

Lady Charlton's eyes narrowed. 'You prefer it to the cream one with the blue?'

'I do.'

'Very well, we shall take both shawls, Mrs Abernathy,' Lady Charlton said to the waiting modiste. 'The cream and blue for myself, and the white and green for Miss Nash.'

Desirée gasped. 'But...Lady Charlton, I thought the shawl was for you!'

'It was, but I had already decided upon the cream one, so your preference of the white made everything that much easier. Now, come along, Miss Nash. The library awaits.'

Hatchard's on Piccadilly was both a bookseller and a circulating library, and on this particular afternoon it was very well attended. Ladies perused the shelves for the latest offerings by the Minerva Press or for books of an improving nature, while the gentlemen leaned towards those offering intellectual variety and stimulation. Shakespeare happened to be Lady Charlton's particular favourite, and while she headed towards that section of the shop Desirée moved to the shelves stocked with translations of Greek and Roman history. It was a long time since she had found time to indulge her natural love of reading. Her father had kept a notable library, of course, but much of his material had been old. Here, Desirée was able to find more recent treatises, along with opinions of the learned men of the day.

What she had not expected to find was Sebastian standing in the aisle next to her.

'Lord Buckworth!' she exclaimed.

'Miss Nash.' He gallantly doffed his gleaming black beaver. 'What a pleasure to find you here among the dusty tomes. Does my aunt accompany you?'

'Strictly speaking, I accompany her, but yes, she is over there by the window.'

'Ah yes. Perusing Shakespeare. I might have known. She is a voracious reader of the man's work. Along with Niccolò Machiavelli.' A mischievous light came into Sebastian's eyes. 'Are you familiar with Machiavelli's work?'

An answering twinkle appeared in Desirée's. 'Wise men say, and not without reason, that whoever wished to foresee the future might consult the past,' she quoted knowledgeably.

Sebastian grimaced. 'I might have known. I was informed some time ago that you were not of simple mind.'

'Ah, but if I could not claim familiarity with the work of such a statesman and writer as that, how could I profess to know my subject?' Desirée teased him. 'And what brings you here on such a fine day?'

'The opportunity to secure a rare book by Pierre François Galliard,' Sebastian told her. 'John Hatchard knew that I had been looking for it, and when he chanced to stumble upon a copy of it in Dublin, he was good enough to pick it up for me. I came by today to collect it.'

'I see.' Desirée glanced up at him, and then just as quickly away. His proximity was disturbing, as was the way he kept looking at her. 'How fortunate.'

'Yes, I thought so. So, has my aunt been keeping you busy?'

'We do seem to fill our days. So far this week, we have been to the modiste's three times and the man-tua-maker twice, we have ordered new china from Mr Wedgwood's showroom, and a set of matching tables from Waring & Gillow. Oh, and yesterday we spent a few hours at the British Museum so that I might see Mr Towneley's collection of classical sculptures.'

'Dear me, all that on top of Lady Rumsden's ball and Mrs Taylor's musicale,' Sebastian observed. 'I wonder that you have energy enough to last the week. Tell me, Miss Nash, do you look forward to a quiet sojourn at home this evening or are you engaged on yet another social outing?'

Desirée sighed. 'We are expected for cards at Lady Appleby's. Lady Charlton has asked me to be her partner.'

'Has she, by Jove? Then you must be a very good player indeed, for my aunt cannot abide people who are not.'

'Fortunately, my mother taught me the rudiments of the game and she had a very good head for cards,' Desirée said with a smile. 'I expect to acquit myself reasonably well.'

'I have no doubt that you will.' Sebastian's gaze travelled over her face, lingering for a moment on the soft curve of her lips. 'As you do...so many other things.'

His voice was disturbingly low and it affected Desirée deeply. But then, everything about Sebastian had begun to affect her of late. Even now, her heart was beating like a breathless young débutante's.

The problem was, she wasn't a breathless young girl any more. She was a mature woman of five-and-twenty, and one far too sensible to be swept away by pretty words and flattering sentiments. 'You are... very kind to say so, my lord, but I assure you there are many things I do poorly. However, I understand that...you are also engaged for the evening,' Desirée said, anxious to change the subject.

'You seem to be well informed of my activities, Miss Nash. Am I to conclude that my aunt has been speaking about me behind my back again?'

A stain of scarlet appeared on Desirée's cheeks. 'She does occasionally mention your name, my lord, but always with the utmost affection and respect.'

'Now you are bamming *me*,' Sebastian said ruefully. 'Actually, I *was* to have dined with Lord Mackenzie but a wretched toothache has forced him to cry off.'

'Oh, what a shame. Your aunt will be most disappointed.'

He frowned at her comment. 'And why should she be?'

'Because I understand that Lord Mackenzie is Lady Alice's father.'

'And Lady Alice is?'

'A young woman Lady Charlton seems to think would make you an admirable wife,' Desirée said as she reached for a dictionary on Greek mythology. She was pleased with the steadiness of her voice as she delivered the message. She was *not* pleased with the way her hands suddenly began to tremble as she flipped back the cover of the book and pretended to read the first page.

'Lady Alice. I might have known,' Sebastian said in exasperation. 'Would that people minded their own business as keenly as they seem to mind mine. Well, what do you say, Miss Nash? Do you agree that I should cast myself into the matrimonial nets?'

'It is really no business of mine, my lord,' Desirée said, running her finger down the column of Greek characters whose names began with the letter A. 'Whether you choose to marry or remain single is surely your own decision to make.'

'I have always thought so, but it seems to be a topic of great interest to everyone else. Still, I suppose we all get there in time. Even you.'

'Me?' Desirée repeated in surprise.

'Yes, you. Well, surely it is your hope to eventually marry and settle down. Perhaps raise a family?'

The nature of the question alarmed her, but not as much as did the sudden and very disturbing awareness of *who* she wanted to marry and settle down with.

'I…really have not given it a lot of thought, my lord.' Desirée abruptly closed the book and placed it back on the shelf, aware that she suddenly had no interest in Abaris, Achilles or any other mythological Greek character. 'My situation in life has not made it necessary that I do.'

'But your position in life has changed now,' Sebastian reminded her. 'And by virtue of the fact that you *are* the granddaughter of a baronet, you have every right to expect that you shall marry, and marry well.'

'Lord Buckworth, I am the granddaughter of a man who chose to ignore my existence almost from the moment of my birth. That and certain other realities of my life have necessitated my following a practical, rather than a romantic course.'

'And that is a great pity, Desirée.' Sebastian raised his gloved hand and brushed it gently against her cheek. 'Because I believe that beneath that very prim and intellectual exterior beats the heart of a young woman who would very much like to indulge in romantic, rather than practical thoughts. Am I right?'

'Sebastian? Is that you?' Lady Charlton enquired behind them.

'Damn,' he swore softly, though without heat. He sighed as he dropped his hand and took a step backwards. 'It is, Aunt Hannah.'

'What excellent timing, my dear. I was just thinking about stopping at Gunter's for refreshments. Will you join us?'

'Thank you, but I'm afraid I cannot. I have an appointment at Angelo's.'

'What's this? Have you traded your fists for a foil, Sebastian?'

A smile ruffled his mouth. 'Not entirely. I still enjoy a match with the Gentleman when he has time, but I have always found the skill and finesse of fencing more satisfying. And of late, I have found Signor Angelo's rooms to be far less congested than Mr Jackson's.'

Lady Charlton sighed in disappointment. 'Well, we shall miss the pleasure of your company, my dear, but gentlemen must have their sport. Come along, Miss Nash, you and I shall go and enjoy the confections ourselves.'

Not sure whether to be relieved or disappointed that he was not to join them, Desirée offered Sebastian a tremulous smile and then quickly followed Lady Charlton out. The temptation to turn around and see if he was watching her was very strong.

She was thankful that she had learned long ago, how *not* to give in to temptation.

The diminutive Lady Appleby was not at all what Desirée had been expecting. Garbed in a fantastic gown that must surely have belonged to her grandmother, she wore her grizzled white hair in an elaborate pompadour, insisted on wearing buckled shoes, and even sported a tiny black patch on her left cheek. And she stood no higher than Desirée's shoulder.

'My dear, I am so very delighted to see you again. And Miss Nash, you are most welcome,' Lady Appleby said in a voice that was surprisingly robust for her size. 'Now, I have reserved the Yellow Saloon upstairs for cards and we already have quite a few games under way. Lady Fortescue particularly requested the honour of your first set, Hannah, so I kept one table in reserve. I hope you do not mind.'

'I do not mind so long as I am not expected to pass the entire evening in her company,' Lady Charlton replied. 'Lady Fortescue is a formidable opponent but I find her conversation boring at the best of times. And I do not care for her niece at all.'

'Miss Gregory is a milk-and-water miss, to be sure,' Lady Appleby agreed, the mound of hair upon her head suddenly tilting precariously to the right. 'But you need spend only as much time in their company as you wish. And I doubt you will find her conversation lacking this evening. There has been considerable talk of *The Wicked Marquis* of late, and with Miss Nash hailing from the area in which the main character resides, no doubt mention will be made of it again.'

'*The Wicked Marquis*?' Desirée glanced at the older woman in bewilderment. 'Forgive me, Lady Appleby, but I am not familiar with the name. Is that a play?'

'Oh, no, my dear, it is a most highly entertaining book. It came out a little while ago from the Minerva Press, and while no one knows who the author is, most agree that it is very well done. It pokes fun at some of the most illustrious gentlemen of the Ton. Certainly there can be no doubt as to the real identity of Beau Broombrain. Or that Sir Hugely Perfect was actually a young Hugo Perceval.'

'Be that as it may, there is no reason to think Miss Nash would be familiar with the work simply because she lived near Steepwood Abbey, Letty,' Lady Charlton pointed out. 'Certainly no ladies of *my* acquaintance have admitted to reading it.'

'Nor have any of mine, but it is remarkable how many are familiar with it regardless,' Lady Appleby said with a smile as she turned to lead the way upstairs.

'You said one of the characters lived near the Abbey,' Desirée said. 'Does the book come right out and say who it is?'

'Not in so many words, but there is no question it is the Marquis of Sywell. The conduct and mannerisms of the fictitious Marquis of Rapeall can leave no doubt in anyone's mind.'

Recognising the similarity between the character's name and the real Marquis's propensity for womanising, Desirée gasped. 'Oh my! Are all of his descriptions so...uncomplimentary?'

'For the most part,' Lady Charlton said. 'Sebastian himself was made sport of as Lord Baconwit, though I tried to assure him the author must have been speaking of someone else, and his good friend Wyndham was characterised as Viscount Windyhead. And I am sure Lord Dungarren was not at all pleased at being referred to as Lord Dunthinkin. The author has taken considerable liberties, and I daresay he shall be taken to task for it once his identity is revealed.'

'Which is likely why he is taking such pains to *keep* it concealed,' Lady Appleby said, chuckling in amusement. 'Especially since he eventually murders the Marquis with rather bloodthirsty glee. Well, here we are.'

The room they entered was quite spacious and Desirée could see why it was called the Yellow Saloon. The walls were covered in strips of pale yellow silk and the drapings and brocade upholstery throughout were of varying shades of yellow and gold. Paintings with ornately gilded frames covered nearly every inch of wall and there were knick-knacks and statuary everywhere. At least, everywhere there was not a card table and chairs set up.

In a matter of minutes, Desirée found herself seated across from Lady Charlton at one of the tables, with the famed Lady Fortescue and her niece sitting on either side of them. Lady Fortescue was a masculine-looking woman in her late forties, while her niece was a pale and meek-looking thing of perhaps two-and-twenty. Desirée soon found herself in agreement with her employer as to the brilliance of their opponents' conversation. It was monotonous at best, and Desirée almost wished for some mention of the scandalous book all London was talking about.

Unfortunately, it seemed that no discussion of *The Wicked Marquis* was to be allowed to distract play at *this* table. Lady Fortescue was clearly determined to win, and after only a few moments, Desirée found herself immersed in the game and exceedingly grateful for the skills her mother had taught her.

For all their single-minded determination, however, Lady Fortescue and her niece were not equal to the challenge. Desirée and Lady Charlton handily took the first rubber, and were well on their way to claiming the second when Lady Fortescue abruptly brought the proceedings to a halt by claiming a slight indisposition of the stomach. At that point, Lady Charlton smiled, rose and thanked them for a most enjoyable game. Desirée rose too and dutifully accompanied Lady Charlton back downstairs.

'Thank you, Miss Nash, that was excellent,' Lady Charlton said in a voice of obvious satisfaction. 'I have not thrashed Lady Fortescue that soundly in a long time. I have no doubt her slight indisposition was merely an excuse to bring the rubber to a halt. You play exceedingly well.'

Desirée inclined her head as they stepped into a high-ceilinged room where a series of couples were already engaged in the lively steps of a country dance. 'Thank you, Lady Charlton, but you are a formidable player yourself. Indeed, had you and I played against my mother and father, I am not sure who would have won, though I dare say it would have made for an excellent match.'

They soon found chairs along the wall and sat for a little while watching the dancers.

'Oh, dash it all,' Lady Charlton exclaimed suddenly. 'I have left my shawl in the card room. Would you be so good as to fetch it for me, my dear? I seem to be feeling a draught.'

'Yes, of course, Lady Charlton.' Desirée rose and quickly made her way back to the Yellow Saloon. She was not particularly surprised to see that Lady Fortescue had recovered from her indisposition and that she and her niece were back at a table with another pair of ladies. But she was very surprised when she looked up a few moments later and saw Sebastian standing in the opposite doorway.

'Miss Nash,' he said, crossing the floor as soon as he saw her. 'How disappointing. I had hoped to arrive in time to see you and my aunt engaged in a battle of wits with Lady Fortescue and her niece, but I fear I have come too late.'

'I'm afraid you have, Lord Buckworth. Lady Fortescue was compelled to bring the set to an early close,' Desirée whispered, 'but I think Lady Charlton had already decided that we had made a sufficient mark at the tables.'

'You mean you won?'

'Every game.'

'My word, Aunt Hannah must be as merry as a grig.'

Desirée laughed and was astonished at how light-hearted she suddenly felt. Just seeing Sebastian's handsome face was enough to make her senses spin. 'Yes, I believe she was. But surely the opportunity of seeing us play was not your only purpose in coming?'

'To tell the truth, it wasn't. I came to collect a debt from Lady Appleby,' Sebastian informed her with a grin. 'She owes me a small matter of some thirty pounds.'

Desirée's eyes opened wide. 'Gracious, Lord Buckworth, never say that you would actually take that sweet old lady's money?'

'For your information, Miss Nash, that sweet old lady is as cunning as they come. I have seen her relieve swaggering young greenhorns of their allowances and unwitting ladies of their pin-money. You would do well to keep your distance from her,' he cautioned.

The thought of Lady Appleby being a scheming trickster caused Desirée to burst out laughing—and several pairs of eyes to turn and glare in her direction. Sebastian himself was hard pressed to keep a straight face. 'Come, Miss Nash, I think it is time we left,' he advised, observing the expressions all around them. 'We seem to be disturbing the level of concentration in the room.'

Desirée dutifully retrieved Lady Charlton's shawl and then accompanied Lord Buckworth back downstairs.

As expected, Lady Charlton was thoroughly delighted to see her nephew. 'But what are you doing here, Sebastian? I thought you were to have dined with Lord Mackenzie this evening.'

'Lord Mackenzie is stricken with toothache, so I

came here thinking to witness your supremacy at cards,' he told her. 'But alas, I arrived too late.'

At that, Lady Charlton's expression grew decidedly smug. 'That is the best rubber of whist I have played in months. Indeed, if Miss Nash were a gentleman, I should accuse her of being a gamester.'

'Lady Charlton!' Desirée exclaimed. 'I have never resorted to cheating in my life. I simply apply my mind and remember which cards have been played.'

'And you do it very well, my dear,' her employer said, patting her hand. 'I vow it will be a long time before Hortense challenges me again. Well, I suppose we had best get something to eat before it is all gone. Sebastian, take Miss Nash and find somewhere for the three of us to sit, and preferably not in a draught. I'm going to have a word with Lady Appleby. By the by, has she paid you your thirty pounds yet?'

'Not yet, but I intend to collect it before I leave.'

'Then I shall be sure to warn her of your intentions. No doubt she will find some excuse to make herself scarce.' With a knowing smile, Lady Charlton headed off to find their hostess—and Desirée found herself once again alone in Sebastian's company.

'Your aunt is truly a remarkable lady, Lord Buckworth,' she said as she followed him to a quiet table. 'I wonder that she has remained a widow all these years.'

'I would venture to say it is only because she does not choose to seek the company of any particular gentleman.'

'But surely some gentleman has sought hers? She

is such entertaining company, and under that brusque exterior, she is possessed of a very kind heart.'

'She is indeed, Desirée. Much like the young lady she has employed to be her companion,' Sebastian said softly as he bent over her.

His words caused Desirée's breath to catch in her throat. She looked up at him, standing so close that she could see the dark flecks in his eyes, and felt a pulse begin to beat in her throat.

'Ride with me tomorrow,' Sebastian said in a husky whisper. 'My aunt tells me that you enjoy the sport and I long to see you on horseback. We could go for a gallop through the park early in the morning, before there are many about.'

'A l-lady does not gallop,' Desirée said, stumbling over the words.

'A lady might not, but Artemis would.'

Desirée started. Artemis, the great virgin goddess of fertility, wild animals and the chase. She was not at all sure how to take his comparison.

'Lord Buckworth, I cannot just *leave* Lady Charlton to go off riding with you. Whatever would she say?'

'Does my aunt not give you time off during the week?'

'Yes, but only in the afternoon.'

'Then I shall speak to her about switching your afternoon for a morning. I cannot believe that she would be unwilling to forgo a trip to the shops for a few hours. But I want to hear your answer, Desirée. Is it to be yes, or no?'

No, shouted the voice in her head. *This path will*

bring you heartache and despair. It can do nothing else.

'Yes. I should like that...very much,' Desirée said, blissfully ignoring the voice. Because there was no point in listening to it now. The heartache was already here and she had no doubt that despair would surely follow.

She had fallen in love with Sebastian Moore. And nothing she did now—including a ride in the park—was going to make any difference!

Chapter Eight

The following day dawned clear and bright. There was nary a cloud in the sky and the breeze was warm with the promise of approaching summer. In short, a perfect morning for a ride.

Unable to sleep past seven o'clock, Desirée rose and donned one of her new riding habits: an elegant ensemble in royal-blue broadcloth with black frogging on the jacket and matching black trim around the edge of the full skirt. Her hat—a dashing confection of blue and black—sat prettily on her upswept hair. Sebastian had told her that he would call for her at half past eight and Desirée knew he would not be late. He wanted to arrive at the park while it was still relatively quiet, a plan with which Desirée had been in complete accord. If they hoped to enjoy a good gallop, it would have to be well before the crowds descended and made the paths impassable.

Desirée's only concern was the length of time since she had been on horseback and the chance that she might not acquit herself well in the saddle. She needn't have worried, however. As soon as she was

comfortably settled in the saddle atop Lady
Charlton's sprightly chestnut mare, she knew that everything was going to be all right. She felt the familiar
movement of the horse beneath her and immediately
relaxed into it.

'I thought as much,' Sebastian commented with a
nod of approval. 'You have the look of a seasoned
equestrienne, Desirée.'

Desirée smiled as she gathered the reins in her
hands. 'I do not know about my being a seasoned
equestrienne, my lord, but at least I do not feel in
danger of falling off as I feared might be the case.'

'You look very comfortable and pretty indeed,'
Sebastian complimented her. 'Nor do I think you will
be reluctant to gallop once we reach our destination.'

And Desirée wasn't. As soon as they reached the
park and beheld the verdant green fields rolling out
before them, they put their horses to a canter and then
spurred them on to a gallop. Desirée felt like laughing
out loud for the sheer joy of it. She had been confined
for such a long time; forced to put up with the re-
strictions of her life so that even the most simple of
youthful pleasures had been denied. But now to be
riding a spirited horse again, with the open fields
ahead of them and the man she loved by her side, her
happiness knew no bounds.

Sebastian, of course, was a superb rider. He and
the black stallion moved as one, his gloved hands
lightly holding the reins yet controlling the big horse
with ease. The wind had blown the dark hair back
from his face, and against the warm brown of his skin

his teeth flashed a brilliant white. Truly, he made her feel as breathless as the ride!

When she sensed that her mount was finally beginning to tire, Desirée conscientiously drew her in. She had no wish to tire the mare and gently pulled back on the reins, already knowing how responsive the mare's mouth was. Sebastian, however, was hard pressed to bring the stallion to as graceful a halt. The animal was obviously reluctant to curtail his gallop and put on a great show of snorting and head-tossing as he finally came to a prancing stop.

'Your aunt's mare is positively delightful,' Desirée said, observing with amusement the stallion's performance. 'Indeed, she is almost as fleet of foot as your own big brute, and she is certainly better behaved.'

'Big brute? Have a care, Aphrodite, Trojan does not take kindly to being unfavourably compared to a mare,' Sebastian told her. 'He is merely in high spirits and feeling his oats. As for being as fleet of foot, the mare would not have stood a chance had I let Trojan have his head. In truth, I held him in check so that you might not lag too far behind.'

'Ah, then I fear I owe him—and his owner—an apology,' Desirée said, sending him what could only be deemed a flirtatious glance. 'For certainly it was not my intent to injure either with my observation.'

After the exhilaration of the gallop, the two walked their horses in silence for a while, content to enjoy the freshness of the morning and to savour the peace and quiet of the park at this early hour of the day.

'How ironic to think that in only a few hours, we should be hard pressed to find room to walk our horses, let alone gallop them,' Desirée commented with a smile.

'That is why morning has always been my favourite time of day. When the mist is still on the lake and the grass is heavy with dew, everything seems so fresh and clean. And it is the *only* time one can truly enjoy a gallop.'

'I am so glad you suggested it, my lord, thank you.'

Sebastian turned his head, and his eyes moved slowly over her face. 'You have no need to thank me with words, Desirée, for the look I saw on your face when you were galloping across that field was all I needed.' He drew the stallion to a halt. 'You are a remarkably beautiful woman, Desirée Nash. Have I ever told you that?'

'Not in...such a way,' Desirée admitted as she likewise drew the mare to a halt. 'As I recall, your comments to me at the pool last year were somewhat more...direct in nature.'

Sebastian's eyes brimmed with tenderness. 'My comments to you then were as honest as they are today. Though, I admit, they were not as tempered by my feelings. I did not know you then, but I do now. Indeed, I like to think I have come to know...a great deal about you in the short time we have been acquainted.' He suddenly sent her a look so intense that it sent a shiver up her spine. 'Desirée, I—'

'Well, well, what have we here?' a voice cut in unexpectedly. 'The rake and the schoolmistress enjoying a quiet coze in the park. How charming. I hope I am not interrupting anything.'

Desirée felt her entire body go icy cold. *Lord*

Perry! But…what was he doing here? Was it just a coincidence that he was in the park this morning?

Sebastian didn't seem to think so. He turned to regard the newcomer with eyes that glinted like slivers of black ice. 'There is nothing to interrupt, Lord Perry. Miss Nash and I were simply enjoying a morning ride and some quiet conversation. But I take exception to your terms of address and would advise you not to use them again.'

'Of course.' Lord Perry inclined his head. 'I meant no offence. It is just that the morning air seems to agree with you, Miss Nash. It has raised a most becoming colour in your cheeks. But then, I have always said that riding is best done first thing in the day.'

Desirée steeled herself to look at him. There was nothing she could take exception to in his appearance. He was seated astride a fine grey stallion and was, as always, impeccably dressed. But it was the unpleasant curl of his lip and the mocking expression in his eyes that made her shudder. 'I take it Lady Perry does not share your enjoyment of the morning air?' she asked, compelled by good manners to respond.

'Lady Perry does not rise until noon and does so then only to take herself to the shops,' Lord Perry remarked distantly. 'We keep very different hours.'

'A pity for you,' Sebastian said mockingly.

Lord Perry shrugged. 'I find other ways to amuse myself.' His smile widened as he looked at Desirée. 'A man always can.'

His mocking tone brought an uncomfortable flush to Desirée's cheeks, and she quickly looked away.

She knew what he was alluding to; as did Sebastian, judging by the way his hands suddenly tightened on his reins. 'Come, Miss Nash, it is time we were returning home. My aunt will be expecting you. Good day, Perry,' he said coldly.

Lord Perry smiled and touched the brim of his beaver. 'Always a pleasure, Miss Nash. Buckworth.'

Anxious to escape his leering eyes, Desirée pulled the mare's head around and lightly flicked the crop against her flanks. Dear God, would she never be free of the hateful man? The memory of his words burned in her heart and brought tears of anger and humiliation to her eyes. She could not bear the way he looked at her or the way he made her feel. Indeed, whatever pleasure she had taken in Sebastian's company had been effectively destroyed by his unwelcome presence and suggestive remarks.

'Desirée!' Sebastian called. 'Wait!'

Reluctantly, Desirée drew the mare to a halt. She turned her head away and quickly dashed the back of her hand across her eyes. 'I am sorry, Lord Buckworth, it was rude of me not to wait.'

'Don't be silly, you had every right to leave. The man is a thoughtless boor and I am more sorry than I can say that our ride had to come to such an end,' Sebastian said as he drew level with her. 'Had I but known he would be here—'

'You could not, my lord, so you certainly owe me no apology,' Desirée interrupted. 'But I, too, am exceedingly sorry that he was here all the same.'

'Desirée, I must ask, how do you come to know Lord Perry?' Sebastian enquired urgently. 'And please do not tell me that you first met at Lady Rumsden's ball, because I know that is not the case. You were already acquainted with the man when he came up to you at the ball, were you not?'

'Yes.' Desirée briefly closed her eyes. 'Lord Perry's daughter, Elizabeth, was one of the pupils I taught at Mrs Guarding's Academy. I was introduced to him, as I was to the parents of all the girls, at the time Elizabeth was enrolled.'

'Did you and Lord Perry have much occasion to speak to each other?'

Desirée swallowed hard. 'I saw Lord Perry... several times at the Academy, but I spoke to him... only once.'

'And you do not like him.'

It was not a question, but a statement of fact, and Desirée acknowledged it as such. 'No, I do not.'

'Was he aware of your feelings towards him?'

'I have no reason to suspect that he was not.'

'Then why did he seek you out at Lady Rumsden's ball?'

Desirée faltered. 'He... wished to make me known to his wife.'

'I see.' Sebastian's blue eyes pierced the distance between them. 'Does it not seem strange to you that a man who knew of your enmity would wish to introduce you to his wife?'

'In all honesty, I did not stop to think about it at the time,' Desirée told him distantly. 'I turned around to find him standing behind me and realised moments later that Lady Perry was with him. I suppose it would have been rude had he not introduced her, given that he and I were obviously acquainted. But now, I think you are correct, Lord Buckworth, we should be returning home,' Desirée said, abruptly gathering the reins. 'Your aunt will surely be wondering where I am.'

With that, she pressed her heel into the mare's side and set her off at a brisk trot.

Sebastian sighed and fell in behind her. He knew that Desirée was hiding something about her relationship with Lord Perry, but he also knew that badgering her would do no good. Whatever had happened between them was obviously a source of pain, and he sensed that it was something she would not talk about easily. Which meant that he would have to find out for himself what had happened.

With that grim thought in mind, he turned and headed back to Mayfair.

The next few days seemed interminable for Desirée. She accompanied Lady Charlton to a Venetian breakfast the next day and to a musicale the following evening, but her thoughts were too much on Sebastian to allow her any kind of enjoyment of either event.

He had said little to her on the ride home from the park. Had he been wondering, perhaps, at the nature of the relationship between herself and Lord Perry? She could not blame him if he had. Her disgust of the man had been all too evident, and it would only have been natural for Sebastian to question what had caused it to be so in the first place. Especially when she had not offered any logical explanation for her dislike.

'Miss Nash, you are remarkably quiet this evening,' Lady Charlton commented with a frown. 'It is not like you to be so distracted when I am speaking to you.'

Desirée flushed in embarrassment. 'Lady Charlton, forgive me. I fear I have been rather preoccupied of late.'

'Yes, but the question, my dear, is why—or by whom,' she said wryly. 'I am beginning to wonder if some handsome gentleman has not captured your heart.'

The words were so close to the truth that Desirée hardly knew where to look. Had Lady Charlton guessed her secret? She could not bear to think that she had. What would the lady think if she were to learn that her companion had fallen in love with her nephew?

'Lady Charlton, I think I shall go and fetch some punch,' Desirée said, abruptly rising to her feet. 'I find it…exceedingly warm of a sudden. Do you not agree?'

'Well, I am comfortable enough,' the lady said, 'though the temperature has risen to be sure. But I would not turn down a glass of punch regardless, my dear. Thank you for offering.'

Desirée quickly turned and headed into the next room, where a number of couples were gathering to dance. She smiled at a lady she remembered having been introduced to at Lady Rumsden's ball, and then made her way to the large silver punch-bowl. Her cheeks were still burning from Lady Charlton's untimely comment about the likelihood of a gentleman stealing her heart, and in the absence of a cool cloth to press against them, she picked up a gleaming silver cup and placed that against her cheek instead.

'Well, fortune seems to be smiling upon me yet again,' Lord Perry said from behind her. 'She has a way of putting you in my path at the most convenient of times.'

The cup slipped from Desirée's fingers. It landed on the edge of the table and clattered to the floor, drawing the attention of every eye in the room. Desirée groaned as she bent to pick it up.

'Lord Perry. I am beginning to think that you are following me.' She set the cup on the table and smiled apologetically at her audience.

Lord Perry smiled too, but with superiority rather than apology in his air. 'Nothing so evil as that, I can assure you. Your role as companion to Lady Charlton simply affords us the opportunity of attending the same social gatherings. If it *was* in my mind to pursue you, however, the outcome would be much the same. I can be very persistent when I feel it is worth my while. And you, my dear, are very much worth my while.'

'Lord Perry, what will it take to convince you that I have no wish to become involved with you?' Desirée said coldly.

His thin smile flashed. 'You cannot, my dear, because while serving as a lady's companion must be eminently preferable to being a teacher at a girls' school, it will not allow you the kind of privileges I can give you if you consent to be my mistress.'

'You are sadly mistaken if you think I long for such privileges.'

'But they could be yours nevertheless. All it would take is one word from you.'

Desirée shuddered at the thought. 'Lord Perry, let me be very clear. There is nothing you can say that would induce me to become your mistress. I am very happy with the circumstances of my life and I have no wish to change them. Lady Charlton is a kind and generous employer and I am provided with all that I require.'

'But what about pleasure, Desirée? Lady Charlton cannot give you the type of pleasure to be found in the arms of an experienced lover.'

'Neither can you, Lord Perry. And now I would thank you to leave me *alone*.'

Lord Perry smiled and let his gaze roam absently around the room. 'I wonder, Miss Nash, if your reticence to become my mistress has anything to do with a certain gentleman I found you riding with in the park the other morning. Perhaps you are hoping to receive a similar offer from him?'

Desirée's heart skipped a beat. 'You are quite mistaken, sir. My relationship with Lord Buckworth is nothing of the kind.'

'But you admit that you do *have* a relationship with him. Or perhaps, that you would like to.'

'My *acquaintance* with Lord Buckworth is no concern of yours,' Desirée said stiffly. 'Nor is any other aspect of my life.'

'Of course not. But I should tell you, my dear, that if you are hoping to receive a respectable offer from

Buckworth, or from any other gentleman for that matter, you would do well to think again.'

'Is that a threat, Lord Perry?'

He shrugged with deceptive nonchalance. 'Not at all. I am simply stating the facts as I see them.'

Desirée sighed, all too aware of where this was going. 'Lord Perry, I know that it is within your power to destroy whatever reputation I have left in London, just as you destroyed the one I had at Guarding's—'

'Oh no, my dear, I did nothing to ruin your reputation at Guarding's. That was done long before I appeared on the scene.'

Desirée frowned. 'What are you talking about?'

Lord Perry slowly began to smile. 'Desirée, you are a beautiful and desirable woman, but I would hardly have gone to the trouble of travelling all the way to Steep Abbot if I did not think it would be worth my while.'

'Now you are not making sense,' she said in annoyance. 'Surely your only reason for going to Steep Abbot was to visit your daughter.'

'That was my *excuse* for going to Steep Abbot. It was not my *reason* for doing so.'

A shadow of alarm touched her face. 'I have…no idea what you're talking about,' she whispered.

'I am talking about Lord Buckworth and the story he told as to how he found you swimming naked in a secluded woodland pool.'

'W-what?'

'And about what happened *after* he joined you in the water.'

Desirée felt the colour slowly drain from her face. 'You are *lying*!'

'Am I?' Lord Perry laughed softly. 'Then why don't you ask him for yourself?'

Desirée quickly looked away from him, aware of a roaring in her ears that drowned out every other sound. *No. Not Sebastian. Surely he would not have done this...*

'I see that my news has startled you,' Lord Perry murmured. 'Forgive me, I did not mean to destroy whatever illusions you might have of the fellow. But neither was I willing to have you think that I alone was responsible for bringing you to your current situation.'

Desirée stared up at him with a mixture of horror and disbelief. 'When did...Lord Buckworth tell you about this?'

'I believe it was towards the end of last summer. And he didn't tell me. I had it from another chap who'd heard Buckworth talking about it at his club. Apparently he related the story with considerable enjoyment.'

'But Lord Buckworth didn't know who I was,' Desirée said, grasping at straws. 'I never told him my name. So why would you or anyone else assume that I was the young woman about whom he was speaking?'

'Desirée, do you really think a man like Buckworth would find it difficult to discover the identity of a beautiful young woman who lived in a tiny place like Steep Abbot? Especially if he was of a *mind* to. After all, I *myself* knew that you liked swimming in the

river and if *I* am able to discover such things, why
would you think Buckworth could not?'

Desirée shuddered as she stared down at the silver
punch-bowl. 'Who else...knows about this?' she
asked in a hoarse voice.

'Oh, a number of the gentlemen here tonight, I
should think,' Lord Perry said as he glanced around
the room. 'Which is why I say that you may as well
accept my offer, Desirée, because you will not receive
a better one.'

Desirée's heart began to beat with alarming force.
She was speechless with shock; her world turned upside down by the horrifying news she had just received. *Sebastian had betrayed her.* He had come
back to London and told several of his friends about
his encounter with her in the pool at Steep Wood.
Worse, he had *lied* about it, making it sound—according to Lord Perry—far less innocent than it had
really been.

And knowing that, how could she possibly go
about in society now? How could she hold her head
up when she knew what people were thinking? What
dignity had he left her?

'You could of course, leave London and begin life
elsewhere,' Lord Perry continued pleasantly. 'Perhaps
you might meet a shopkeeper or a prosperous farmer
in some small country village. They would certainly
not be familiar with the details of your background
and they would, I am sure, be happy to offer you
marriage. But they could not give you the type of
lifestyle I am offering you, Desirée. And I should
think a beautiful young woman like you would prefer

not to have the rough, callused hands of a tradesman or farm worker all over her.'

Desirée closed her eyes to shut out the hateful sight of him. 'Please leave me, Lord Perry.'

'Yes, perhaps I shall,' Lord Perry said smugly. 'I have given you enough to think about for one night. And I am prepared to give you a few more to mull over what I have said. Then we will meet again. You can give me your answer at that time.'

Desirée was not aware of Lord Perry moving away from her. She stared down at the floor, feeling nothing but the pain of Sebastian's betrayal stabbing at her heart. *How could he have done this to her? How could he have lied about her in such a cruel and heartless manner?*

Aware that her knees were dangerously close to giving way, Desirée turned and stumbled towards the door. She had to get out. She had to leave before she saw anyone else. Even now, she imagined that all of the men in the room were looking at her, watching her, as they recalled Sebastian's lurid descriptions of how she had looked in the woodland pool. How she had been sport for a gentleman. Well, she would be sport no longer.

She was halfway across the hall when Sebastian walked in. She saw him at precisely the same moment he saw her—and watched his smile fade as he drew closer.

'Desirée, what in God's name is wrong? Your face is deathly pale.'

Desirée stood and gazed at him with haunted eyes. Oh, how she longed to hurt him. To fling angry words at him and to wound him as deeply as he had wounded her. But what good would it do? The damage to her reputation was already done. There was nothing she could say to regain that which she had lost. She could not change what had happened that day in the pool, any more than she could change what had resulted from it.

'I am…fine, Lord Buckworth,' Desirée said finally. 'I was on my way back to Lady Charlton.' *And to beg her to let me go home.*

'But you look ill,' Sebastian repeated, his concern for her evident. 'Shall I take you home?'

'Yes. No! That is, yes, I should…like to go home,' Desirée said wretchedly. *But not with you. Never again with you.*

'Shall I fetch my aunt?' Sebastian suggested.

'Yes. T-thank you.'

'Desirée, you are not well,' he repeated urgently. 'Let me fetch a doctor.'

'No, I said I am…well. I have no need of…attention. I should simply like to go home.'

Sebastian left her then to go and find Lady Charlton. Desirée took advantage of the time to gather her scattered thoughts and to try to regain some semblance of composure. Her initial shock was rapidly giving way to anger and hurt. She would hold those emotions close to her heart, knowing that she would need them to get her through this. Anger would allow her to survive. Despair would bring her to her knees.

'I told my aunt that I am taking you home,' Sebastian said when he returned to her side, 'and that I shall come back for her directly.'

It was not what Desirée had been hoping to hear. She had no wish to be alone with Sebastian, but she was grateful that they were leaving. And perhaps it was just as well that she did not have to face Lady Charlton right now. That good lady saw too much, and Desirée had no wish to go into any kind of explanation while her pain was so fresh.

She managed to say a quick goodbye to Lady Appleby but she avoided all others. And she resolutely kept her eyes down as she accompanied Sebastian outside.

'Desirée, will you not tell me what is wrong?' he said when they were finally settled in the carriage. 'I cannot help but feel that there is more to this than just a touch of illness.'

Desirée pointedly averted her face. 'I have told you, my lord, there is nothing wrong.'

'But you were shaking like a leaf when I came upon you. Indeed, you looked for all the world as though you had seen a ghost.

I had, Desirée thought sadly. *The ghost of the man I thought I knew...*

'Will you not tell me what happened tonight?'

Desirée stirred uneasily on the bench. She would have to tell him something, otherwise he would never let her rest. But what was she to say? She needed time to be alone; time to think about what all this meant.

'I received some...very disturbing news just before you arrived,' she said woodenly.

'News?' Sebastian frowned. 'Concerning what?'

'Concerning...someone that I know. A friend.'

'And what was the nature of this news? Is your friend ill? Have they been injured in some way?'

Oh yes, they have been injured, Desirée felt like saying. Indeed, they have, but in a way that can never be healed.

'Lord Buckworth, please, I wish you would cease questioning me. I cannot reveal the nature of the injury nor the name of the person upon whom it was inflicted. Suffice it to say that it has caused me...great pain.'

Sebastian sat back against the squabs and his face was lost in the shadows. 'Yes, I can see that it has. But it pains me to see you suffer like this, Desirée.'

How ironic, Desirée thought, since *you* are the one who has caused it to be so.

'Is there nothing I can do to make you feel better?' he asked. 'No help that I can offer?'

Desirée finally raised her eyes to his. 'There is nothing you can say and nothing you can do. Please accept that as the truth and leave me to myself. I shall deal with this in my own way.'

The rest of the drive home was completed in silence.

Not surprisingly, Desirée found little solace in sleep that night. She lay in her bed and stared up at the ceiling as she relived every painful moment of her meeting with Lord Perry that evening—and, in turn, of her very first meeting with Sebastian in Steep Wood.

Oh yes, she remembered in detail what had happened. How she must have looked to him that day in the pool, and how he had treated her as a result. And she closed her eyes in humiliation as she thought of him telling his friends.

Had he really thought so little of her at the time? He must have, or he would not have spoken of their encounter, let alone have embellished it in such a way. To him, she had obviously been a young woman of questionable morals, who had been bold enough to shed her clothes and swim in a woodland pool. He must have thought of her in such a way, for he had made her a proposition because of it. One he would never have made to a proper young lady.

What a pity that she had not told him the truth of her identity sooner, Desirée reflected bitterly. She could have thrown that in his face and watched his smile disappear. For as matters turned out, that was all that had been required to change his mind. They had barely reached the outskirts of London, and all she had said was that she was a baronet's granddaughter, and suddenly, everything had changed.

Desirée realised the truth of that now. The house Sebastian had rented for her hadn't been undergoing any kind of repairs. He had simply told her that to give himself time to find a way out of his predicament. Once he had discovered that she had connections in town, it was obvious that his conscience would not allow him to set her up as his mistress. So he had diverted the carriage to his aunt's house, and once there, had asked Lady Charlton if she would be willing to entertain her until he managed to secure some manner of alternate employment. Unfortunately, when he had offered her a good position with some friends of his, Desirée had felt compelled to turn it down *because* of what had happened with Lord Perry and the potential damage it could have caused.

How would it have looked, for example, if word had got back to his good friends that the lady Sebastian had recommended to look after their children was a woman of loose morals? Because Desirée could not be sure that such information would *not* get back to them—and that the source would not be Lord Perry himself. Certainly the man was not above using blackmail if he felt it could achieve his ends. Desirée knew that he was well connected, and even if he was not well liked, he would nevertheless be listened to. Had Mrs Guarding not done precisely that when faced with a similar dilemma? Which meant there was only one thing Desirée could do.

She would have to leave London. She would have to leave Lady Charlton's house as soon as possible and look for a position in the north or the far west of England. It was vital that she remove herself from that good lady's home before Lady Charlton had cause to regret all of the kindness she had shown her.

And that would hurt so very much, Desirée reflected as the tears began to well in her eyes. Because Lady Charlton had been kindness itself, and to repay her in such a manner seemed shabby treatment indeed. But Desirée knew that she would rather do that than subject Lady Charlton to any kind of humiliation or disgrace as a result of the company she kept.

At half past four in the morning, Desirée finally drifted into a fitful sleep. But she had made her decision. As soon as she rose in the morning, she would begin making her preparations to leave.

In his house across town, Sebastian sat at his desk holding a half-filled glass of brandy, and wondered what the hell had happened tonight.

To say that he was confused was putting it mildly. Desirée had been in a great deal of pain. He had seen it in her eyes and heard it in her voice. But according to her, there was nothing he could do or say to help ease her suffering.

'Damn it all!' Sebastian swore softly. 'Why won't she talk to me?' Had their relationship not developed far enough that she trusted him with such confidences? He had begun to think, perhaps to hope, that she held him in some affection. But after tonight, he wasn't so sure any more. She had shut him out at a time when she most desperately needed someone to talk to.

Well, he had no doubt that she would talk to his aunt. The two had become very close in the short time Desirée had been there and he knew that she would not be able to hide her feelings from her. He would just have to wait until Desirée had shared the details of her unhappiness, and then perhaps, once he understood its nature, ask his aunt if she would be willing to share it with him.

Sebastian had to know what was bothering Desirée. Because it went without saying that if he did not find out the source of *her* unhappiness, he could not know happiness himself.

* * *

Desirée found a copy of *The Times* in the drawing-room the next morning. Lady Charlton had not yet appeared and, grateful for the time alone, Desirée opened the paper and quickly found what she was looking for. She jotted down the information on a piece of paper and tucked it into the pocket of her gown. By the time Lady Charlton finally walked into the room, she was sitting on the chintz love-seat with her embroidery in her lap.

'Ah, there you are, Miss Nash,' Lady Charlton said, her usual vivacity noticeably lacking. 'Are you feeling better this morning?'

Desirée made an effort to smile. 'Yes, thank you, Lady Charlton.'

'Good. Though I would wonder, given the dark circles under your eyes. Still, if you tell me you feel well, I shall believe it. I myself have a touch of the megrim this morning and was wondering if you would be kind enough to pick up these few things for me.'

'Of course,' Desirée said, immediately setting aside her tambour. She took the list, neatly written in Lady Charlton's hand, and glanced at it. For once, luck seemed to be with her. Lady Charlton's errands would take her quite close to the servant registry she wished to visit. She could conduct her business there and attend to Lady Charlton's errands without arousing anyone's suspicions.

A small sigh escaped Desirée's lips as she tucked it into the pocket in her gown and headed to her room. Perhaps this was the Lord's way of telling her that this was truly the way things were meant to be.

* * *

Over the next few days, Desirée endeavoured to spend as little time as possible in Sebastian's company. She took to pleading illness when it came to attending functions at which she knew he would be present, and she avoided all opportunities to be alone with him. When he did call upon his aunt of an afternoon, Desirée made sure that she was otherwise engaged. If he stumbled upon her by chance, she was polite but reserved. To anyone observing them together, it looked as though Desirée was not only uncomfortable in the gentleman's presence, but that she did not even care for him.

And the sad part was, nothing could have been further from the truth. She loved him as much now as she ever had. Indeed, the intensity of her feelings startled her. And yet, how could that be? She had tried to convince herself that the treachery she had discovered within him should have changed her feelings towards him—but she knew that it had not. She had been angry and hurt by what he had done, but his actions in themselves were not enough to stop her loving him.

And the knowledge that in a very short time she would never see him again made any time spent in his company sweet torture.

It was for that reason alone that Desirée did everything she could to avoid him. She knew that Sebastian was aware of the change in her demeanour, as was Lady Charlton. But nothing either of them could say would arrest a response. Desirée continued to be polite but distant. And every day she prayed that an answer would come to her aid.

The only person to whom she had confided her dilemma was Helen de Coverdale. The two had kept up a close correspondence throughout Desirée's stay in London, and it was to Helen that Desirée confessed the details of her unfortunate meetings with Lord Perry, and of his subsequent proposition.

And as expected, Helen's letters back to her were filled with genuine expressions of affection and concern. When she learned of Desirée's intention to leave London and seek employment elsewhere, she even offered to speak to Mrs Guarding to see if anything had changed.

Desirée had asked her not to, of course, because while she appreciated Helen's concern, she knew it would be to no avail. Mrs Guarding could not change her mind even if she wanted to. Nor did Desirée wish to go back to Steep Abbot, where she knew she would be recognised by the people she had worked with and possibly made to suffer their condemnation.

No, what she wanted to do was to go far away, to a place where no one knew who she was or anything about her background. And it was that longing which prompted Desirée to do something she had never done in her life. When the letter came from the service registry saying that there had been a reply to her advertisement and would she please provide a letter of reference that could be forwarded to the prospective employers, Desirée contacted Helen and asked her to write one. Because she knew that without it, her chances of being considered for the post were non-existent.

Helen, of course, had been more than willing to comply. She had written a glowing letter of recommendation, signing herself as the Signora Helene de Grazziano, Comtesse de Coverdale, and giving *her dear Miss Nash* a recommendation that would have stood her in good stead had she applied to the Regent himself.

Desirée had shed a few tears at the lengths to which her friend had been willing to go, but beyond that, she had little time for emotion. This phase of her life was coming to an end. The next one was about to begin. She had no time to grieve over what she had lost.

And so, enclosing Helen's letter with one of her own, she posted her letter to the registry, accepting the position as governess to Mr and Mrs Bertrand Clyde, of Banksburgh House, Yorkshire.

Chapter Nine

By the end of the week Sebastian had had enough.
Desirée had avoided him, ignored him, or just plain
looked through him ever since the night of the musicale. And he didn't like it one bit. There had to be
some way of spending time alone with her so that he
could find out what was wrong. And knowing of only
one way that had any chance of succeeding, he sent
a letter to his aunt and asked her to join him for dinner
the following evening. He specifically asked that she
come alone and said that the explanation for his request would be given at the time.

Naturally, Lady Charlton had agreed. But as she
sat across from him at the table and listened to what
he had to say, her eyes opened very wide at finally
being told the reason behind the unexpected invitation.

'You invited me here to tell me that you wished to
speak to *Desirée*? Good Lord, Sebastian, you speak
to her every time you come to visit me,' Lady
Charlton said in astonishment.

'Yes, but you cannot have failed to notice that our

conversations of late have been noticeably lacking in depth, Aunt. All Desirée is willing to talk to me about is the nature of the weather and the likelihood of rain.'

'Well, yes, of course, I had noticed a certain diffidence on her part, but I did not think it evidenced a problem between the two of you.'

'Well, it does,' Sebastian said darkly. 'And I have no idea why. All I know is that Desirée was given some information on the night of the musicale and she has been distant with me ever since.'

'And you don't like it.'

'No, Aunt, I do not.' Sebastian signalled for more wine. 'I do not see that I have done anything to warrant such treatment on her part.'

'Sebastian, what precisely did Desirée tell you?'

'That the news she had been given concerned a friend of hers, and that she was both surprised and pained by it.'

'But she did not give you any indication as to who this friend might be?'

'No.'

'Did it ever occur to you that the friend she was talking about was herself?'

Sebastian stared at her in bewilderment. 'Not for a moment. Why would she refer to herself as someone else?'

'Because ladies often refer to someone else as having a problem when it is they themselves who are looking for an answer.' Lady Charlton picked up her knife and cut into a tender slice of roast beef. 'I have done so myself on numerous occasions.'

Sebastian frowned. 'But what news could Desirée

possibly have received that would have caused her so
much pain? And who could have delivered it?'

'That I cannot say, Sebastian, for I did not spend
the entire evening in her company. In fact, I did not
see Desirée again after she went to procure two
glasses of punch.'

Sebastian thought for a moment. 'How long was it
before I came to tell you that I was taking Desirée
home?'

'It must have been going on for fifteen minutes.'

'So it is possible that she spoke to someone between the time she left you, and the time I found her.'

'Oh yes, most certainly. There were a lot of people
at the house that night. She could have spoken to any
number of them.'

'But think about it, Aunt Hannah,' Sebastian said
slowly. 'On the occasions where you and Desirée
have been out in society together, how many people
have actually *spoken* to her? Everyone knows you, of
course, and they know that Desirée is your companion. But of the people you have introduced Desirée
to, how many would actually go up to her and engage
her in conversation? Especially conversation of a disturbing nature regarding a friend of hers?'

Lady Charlton slowly nodded her head. 'Yes,
Sebastian, I see what you are getting at. The only
people who might have spoken to Desirée would have
been people she'd met since coming to London. And
the chances of any of them saying something that
would have upset her to such a degree is very small.'
She glanced at her nephew in dismay. 'Then who else
could it have been?'

'Did you happen to notice if Lord Perry was at the musicale?'

'Oh dear. Now that you mention it, I do believe he was,' Lady Charlton admitted with concern. 'He came in late; after the tenor had sung, as I recall, and I do not think he mingled much. But I think you could be right about him being the one to have upset Desirée. I came upon her speaking to Lord Perry and his wife at Lady Rumsden's ball and it was evident that she was uncomfortable in his presence.' Lady Charlton glanced at her nephew sharply. 'Had they met before that night?'

'Yes. Desirée informed me while we were out riding that she had been introduced to Lord Perry at the Guarding Academy. Apparently, all the schoolmistresses were introduced to the parents of the students at the time of their enrolment. She told me that she had only spoken to him once, but I could tell that she held him in disfavour.'

'Well, I know that Desirée was upset by his presence at the ball. And when I asked, she told me outright that she did not like the man. So it seems very likely that he was the one to have upset her on the night of the musicale. But what might he have said that would have troubled her to such an extent?'

Sebastian's face took on a grim aspect. 'I don't know, Aunt, and unless I am given an opportunity to speak to Desirée, we may never know. That is why I would like you to invite me to have dinner with you, and to make sure that Desirée is present as well.'

'I shall invite her if that is what you wish, but that

is not to say she will accept when she learns you are to be there, Sebastian.'

'She will if she believes the reason for the dinner is to celebrate your birthday.'

'But it is not—ah, I see,' Lady Charlton said, suddenly beginning to smile. 'You wish me to *pretend* that it is my birthday because you know that she will feel obligated to stay for such an occasion.'

'That is precisely what I am hoping, Aunt. And in truth, it is not such an outlandish plan. After all, your birthday is in three weeks' time, and I think it only right that we do something special to celebrate the occasion of your—'

'Thank you, Sebastian, that will do. There is no need to inform the entire house of my age.' Lady Charlton abruptly signalled to the footman. 'Grey, you may tell Mrs Clarke that her dinner was excellent. As for you, Sebastian, you shall have your opportunity to speak with Desirée. But I warn you it may all be for naught. If she has been as reluctant to speak to you as you say, I cannot conceive that a birthday celebration will encourage her to say a great deal more!'

'It is your birthday, Lady Charlton?' Desirée's face brightened. 'Oh, but how splendid. And we are to have a special dinner to celebrate it.'

'Yes. Well, that was Sebastian's idea, actually,' Lady Charlton admitted. 'He generally plans little surprises for my birthday, and this year, he thought it might be nice to have a formal dinner at home, just the three of us.'

Desirée's face fell. 'The *three* of us?'

'Well, surely you did not think that I would exclude you, Desirée,' Lady Charlton said, trying to sound as though inviting a companion to partake of a family dinner was the most natural thing in the world. 'I could not conceive of celebrating my birthday without you.'

'But my lady—'

'In fact, I would be most unhappy if you did not agree to join us.'

Desirée stirred uneasily in her chair. What was she to do? She dreaded the thought of spending an entire evening in Sebastian's company, but the thought of disappointing Lady Charlton was almost as bad. It was her birthday, after all, and Desirée was honoured to have been invited. Surely she could put up with Sebastian's presence for one night?

After all, how many more would there be before she left for Yorkshire for good?

Sebastian pulled the set of high-stepping matched blacks to a halt in front of his aunt's house on the evening of her supposed birthday, and tossed the reins to the groom with the instructions to 'keep 'em warm'. Then, jumping down from the high seat, he climbed the four steps leading to the front door and rapped his cane smartly upon it.

He had dressed formally for the occasion, wearing a superbly cut black jacket over white satin knee-breeches, white stockings, and black shoes. His jewellery was simple yet elegant, his cravat well but not fussily tied. And as the door swung open to admit

him, Sebastian was aware of a state of nerves unlike
any he had ever suffered before, because he had no
idea whether his plan to encourage Desirée to talk to
him would work or not.

She was already seated in the drawing-room when
he arrived, and Sebastian felt his heart turn over at
the sight of her. For indeed, she was all that was beautiful. Her gown of pure white India muslin was decorated with delicate gold beadwork around the square
neck and hem, and was slightly raised in the front to
display a pair of delicate gold and white slippers. The
sleeves were short puffs of fabric that left her lovely
arms bare, and her hair had been braided and wound
in a regal coronet atop her head. But he could sense
her dismay as she rose and said, 'My lord, you are
early. Lady Charlton is not yet down.'

'In all truth, I cannot say that I am sorry, Desirée,'
Sebastian said as he crossed the room to stand in front
of her. 'For I cannot think of anyone with whom I
would rather wait.'

Desirée blushed deeply. 'It was...good of you to
plan this for your aunt. I think she is looking forward
to the occasion.'

'I am glad to hear it.' Sebastian moved towards the
love-seat and indicated that Desirée should join him.
When she sat down in the chair next to the fireplace,
he stifled a sigh and sat on the love-seat himself.
'Truth is, my aunt enjoys occasions which allow her
to drink champagne and her birthday is one of them.'
He smiled at her warmly. 'Do you like champagne,
Desirée?'

'To tell the truth, my lord, I have never had it. My

parents did not drink, and there has not been much to celebrate in the last six years.'

The words were not spoken in an attempt to secure sympathy, but rather to set forward a statement of truth, and Sebastian recognised them as such. He saw her glance around the room, and then watched her rise in agitation.

'Perhaps I should go and see what is keeping Lady Charlton—' she said hesitantly.

'Desirée, wait.' Sebastian was on his feet and at her side before she was halfway to the door. 'Please, I wish you would stay. There is much I wish to say to you.'

'There is nothing that needs to be said.'

'But there is. You have scarce talked to me since the night of the musicale. And although you told me at the time that...you had received news of a disturbing nature about a friend of yours, I have since come to believe that the news was not about someone else, but about you. And even more than that, that *I* might have something to do with it.'

Desirée quickly dropped her eyes. 'Why would you think that?'

'Because since the night of the musicale, you have taken pains to avoid me,' Sebastian said bluntly. 'You refuse to ride with me, and our conversation, when you are forced to engage in it, is faultlessly polite and absolutely colourless.'

Indignation brought a flush to her cheeks. 'Colourless?'

'Yes. Something that you are not, Desirée. Something you have never been.'

'Something I have never been,' Desirée repeated slowly. 'An opinion formed, no doubt, upon the occasion of our first meeting when you saw me swimming in the pool at Steep Wood.'

Sebastian's brows drifted upward in surprise. 'What has that to do with this? I thought you resented my bringing that up.'

'I always have, but now I think that perhaps we should discuss it.' Desirée walked towards the fireplace and stood with her head held high and her hands clasped together in front of her. 'Lord Buckworth, what did you think of me that first day you saw me in the woods?'

'What do you mean, what did I *think* of you?'

'I thought the question simple enough. Did you believe me to be a household servant or a dairy-maid? Perhaps the wayward daughter of a gentleman or the bored sister of a bootmaker?' Desirée tilted her head to one side. 'What did you think was the manner of my upbringing?'

Sebastian frowned. 'I admit, I thought little enough about it at the time. I remember thinking that you were a beautiful young woman whom I wanted to know better.'

'You mean who you wanted to bed.'

Her bluntness startled him. 'It is not like you to be vulgar, Desirée.'

'And it is not like you to be deceitful, Lord Buckworth. You may have thought I was a beautiful young lady, but did you not also think that I had the morals of a tavern wench?'

'Of course not!'

'Then why did you feel no compunction about asking me to be your mistress? For surely such a question suggests a truer perception of my character?'

Sebastian's dark eyebrows drew together in a frown. 'All right, I admit that at the time I did not know you were the granddaughter of a baronet—'

'The fact is that you knew *nothing* about me, Lord Buckworth, other than that I was a young woman who chose to swim in a public place. And based upon that, you drew your own conclusions as to the moral strength of my character.'

'I drew no conclusions about anything.'

'Did you not? Then why did you tell all and sundry upon your return to London that you had had the good fortune to dally with a comely young wench whom you found swimming naked in the River Steep?'

The question was so totally unexpected that for a moment Sebastian found himself at a complete loss for words. *Why had he told all and sundry?* What on earth was the girl talking about? He had told no one what had happened that day in the pool at Steep Wood. And he certainly had not intimated that he had *dallied* with her.

'Desirée, I have no idea what you're talking about.'

'Are you denying that you spoke to anyone of our encounter in the river?' she challenged.

'Yes, that's exactly what I'm—' And then, belatedly, Sebastian remembered. Damn, he *had* told one person. Lord Hutchings, whom he'd always considered a good friend and someone with whom he could entrust details of a personal nature.

But now, judging by what Desirée was telling him, it seemed that his trust had been misplaced.

'Yes, Desirée, I did tell someone. But it was a very brief recounting of the events and there was never any mention of—'

'Pray spare me the details, Lord Buckworth,' Desirée interrupted in a cold, quiet voice. 'You have told me all I needed to hear. Now perhaps you will understand why I have been avoiding you. For obvious reasons, the subject is one I prefer not to discuss. And now, if you do not mind, I shall make my apologies to Lady Charlton and go to my—'

'Sebastian, I thought I heard your voice,' Lady Charlton said as she walked into the room. 'Forgive me for not being here to greet you, my dear, but you came a touch earlier than I expected.' She brushed his cheeks with her lips and gave him a knowing glance. 'I hope Miss Nash has been keeping you suitably entertained.'

'Oh she has, Aunt,' Sebastian said darkly. 'Very entertained indeed.'

'Good. And Miss Nash, you look absolutely charming this evening,' Lady Charlton said. 'I vow Mrs Abernathy does an excellent job. While she may not have Madame Félice's flair, she certainly has an eye for what works best for you.'

It seemed to Sebastian that his aunt was trying to move past the tension she could sense in the room and he silently blessed her for trying. At the moment, Desirée looked as if she was ready to bolt. It was only the arrival of Grant, to announce that dinner was served, which prevented her from doing so.

'Splendid,' Lady Charlton said in relief. 'Shall we all go in?'

From almost every standpoint, the dinner was a success. The table setting was exquisite, the five course meal—complete with wines and iced champagne—perfectly cooked and beautifully presented, and the appearance of the three people sitting down to enjoy it elegant and refined.

The only thing wrong was the noticeable lack of conversation between two of the three guests.

Desirée was thoroughly discomforted by her earlier conversation with Sebastian and had all but retreated into silence. She refused to meet his eyes and spoke to him only when called upon by good manners to do so. She had so desperately wanted to believe him innocent of Lord Perry's charges. Although it was difficult to imagine how, she had clung to the slim hope that someone else had taken news of her escapades in the River Steep back to London. Perhaps even Lord Perry himself, for she certainly believed him capable of lying to get what he wanted.

But she realised now that it had been a foolish hope at best. Because when Sebastian had been faced with the accusation, he had been unable to deny it. He admitted that he had spoken to someone of their meeting, and it was then that Desirée had truly felt the humiliation. She had attempted to conceal it, of course, acting in as natural a manner as it was possible for her to do, for she had no wish to cast a damper on Lady Charlton's birthday celebration. But she could not help but feel that the tension which existed between herself and Sebastian did precisely that.

The only good piece of news she received was that Sebastian was going away. But when she found out where, she was hard pressed not to show her dismay over that as well.

'I'm sorry I won't be able to escort you to Lady Chambray's ball, Aunt Hannah,' Sebastian said in answer to her request, 'but I shall be in Hertfordshire. Lord Mackenzie has organised a shooting party. I leave tomorrow and shall be gone the better part of a week.'

'A week? Goodness, Sebastian, however will Miss Nash and I manage without you?'

'Quite well, I should imagine,' Sebastian drawled. 'Especially Miss Nash.'

'Nonsense, we shall both miss you, dear boy,' Lady Charlton said. 'But I would venture to say it will be a very pleasant time for you, as I suspect Lady Alice and a number of other young ladies will be present.'

Sebastian touched the napkin to his lips. 'I have no idea whether Lord Mackenzie is inviting ladies or not, Aunt. Given that this is to be a shooting party, I would doubt it.'

'But you cannot shoot all day *and* all night, Sebastian,' Lady Charlton reminded him. 'And I am sure that some of the single gentlemen will be happy for the pleasure of female companionship.'

'I cannot speak for the desires of the other gentlemen, Aunt, but I know that *I* am looking forward to the opportunity of male companionship and conversation. In general I find it far less confusing to that of women.'

His comment seemed to bring the subject to a close, and in a somewhat subdued manner the dinner came to an end. He did not stay to linger over port, but accompanied the ladies to the drawing-room, and then took his leave of them. Before he did, however, he briefly drew Desirée aside. 'Desirée, I need to talk to you.'

'There is nothing to say.'

'On the contrary, there is a great deal to say,' he whispered urgently. 'I have no idea where you came by the ridiculous notion that I told half of London I found you swimming in the river, for it is certainly not true. You never even told me your name—'

'Lord Buckworth, please,' Desirée said in an anguished voice. 'I have said that it is of no consequence, and it is not. The damage is done. There is nothing you can say to change that now.'

Sebastian clamped his lips together in frustration. Damn it, why would she not listen to him? They needed to talk about this. He needed to find out exactly what had happened so that he could have some idea as to how to go about repairing the damage. Unfortunately, he also knew that now was not the time. He could tell from the look on Desirée's face that she had shut him out, and he knew that his aunt was watching them from the corner of the room. But he would have his answers.

'Very well. We will speak of this upon my return, Miss Nash,' Sebastian said firmly. 'It is far too important a matter to leave unresolved. For now, I bid you good evening.'

The heaviness that had been weighing on Desirée's heart all evening seemed to spread to the rest of her body. It was the last time she would ever see him, and no matter what had happened between them, she still loved him. Which was why she wanted to hold on to this last sight of him, to press it like a flower between the pages of a book where she might look at it for all the rest of her days.

'I hope that…all goes well for you in Hertfordshire, Lord Buckworth.'

'I am sure it will. I doubt anything untoward happens in the country. It seems that there is a great deal more to worry about in the city. Good evening, Miss Nash, Aunt Hannah.'

'Good night, Sebastian, dear,' Lady Charlton called. She waited until the door closed behind him before saying, 'Thank goodness he is planning to spend the week with Lord Mackenzie. He has been noticeably withdrawn of late, and he was certainly not happy this evening. Indeed, I am beginning to think there is more on Sebastian's mind than he is telling me.' She sent a casual glance in Desirée's direction. 'Are you retiring, my dear?'

'Yes, I am rather tired this evening, Lady Charlton,' Desirée said, avoiding her eyes. 'It must have been the champagne.'

Lady Charlton sent her an amused glance. 'You had but half a glass, my dear. Still, I suppose if one is not used to imbibing, it would take little more than that to have an effect. Well, good night, Desirée. Sleep well.'

Desirée nodded and quietly left the room. As she listlessly climbed the stairs, she thought how ironic it was that Lady Charlton had finally called her Desirée, when Sebastian had made a point of addressing her as Miss Nash.

In his carriage on the way home, Sebastian thought about what Desirée had told him and shook his head in anger and disbelief. To think that something so small had come back to haunt him in such a way. When he had returned to London last summer after his brief stay at Bredington, and had told Lord Hutchings about the young woman he had encountered there, he had never thought that a year later he would be regretting that confidence.

Sebastian cast his mind back to the evening in question and tried to remember exactly what he had said to Hutchings. Certainly, it would have been nothing damaging to Desirée's reputation. After all, what had he known of her, other than that her parents were dead and that she was single? She hadn't even told him her name. She had simply been a beautiful, intelligent young woman whom he'd had the pleasure of talking to while they had both enjoyed a brief dip in the crystal clear waters of a secluded pool.

Well, perhaps that wasn't entirely true, Sebastian admitted ruefully. He had likely enjoyed it a good deal more than Desirée had. Knowing what he did of her now, he could just imagine how embarrassed she would have felt at being discovered by a man in such a state of undress. Her chemise had given her precious little protection from his eyes, and he had made no secret of his enjoyment of her body. But had he truly spoken of her in as lewd a manner as Desirée seemed to think?

No, he was convinced he had not. Even then, Sebastian had felt a certain amount of affection for her. Something about her had touched him even at that early stage in their relationship. So if the tale which had made the rounds of the gentlemen's clubs in London had been of a damning nature, it was Hutchings who must be held accountable. For whatever reason, he had seen fit to take a story—which had been told to him in confidence—and had embellished it in the hopes of making it a more interesting tale to tell. And for that, Sebastian would never forgive him. Hutchings had violated his trust, and an innocent young woman had been made to suffer the consequences.

But there was still a question which needed to be answered. A question that Sebastian couldn't help but think was key to the issue. And that was, how had Hutchings come to learn Desirée's name? Sebastian himself hadn't known it the night he'd spoken to Hutchings, so how could anything he'd said have ended up being attributed to Desirée?

Was it possible that he wasn't the *only* gentleman who was familiar with the lovely Desirée Nash from Steep Abbot?

Desirée broke the news of her impending departure to Lady Charlton two days later.

'You wish to leave?' that lady repeated in dismayed surprise. 'But why, my dear? I thought you were happy here.'

'I am, but it is partially because of you that I must go. I do not wish to take advantage of your kindness any longer.'

'My kindness? What nonsense, Desirée. You do a job for me and I pay you for your services. That is not kindness. It is simple economics.'

'You do much more than that and we both know it,' Desirée said softly. 'You gave me a home when your nephew suddenly found himself in an awkward situation. And when he realised that he had made a mistake, you offered me a position which prevented me from having to go elsewhere. You call me your companion and pay me to act the part, yet you neither treat me as a servant, nor outfit me as one. And when it comes down to it, Lady Charlton, we both know that you really do not lack for companionship. You have an abundance of friends, and were you to show even the slightest inclination towards marriage, you would have any number of eligible gentlemen dancing attendance upon you. So you see, you really have no need of a companion.'

Lady Charlton sighed. 'While the truth is that I do not *need* a companion, Desirée, it is also true that I have become very fond of you these last few weeks. And when I say that I wish you would stay, I say it in all sincerity. You are a pleasure to have around, my dear.'

'Thank you, Lady Charlton. I have enjoyed being here more than I can tell you. But it is not fair to you that I continue to do so. Besides, I am quite sure that you will soon have...another young lady in the family with whom to become friends,' she said, hesitating a little over the words. 'Lord Buckworth may very well return from Hertfordshire with news of an engagement.'

Lady Charlton glanced at her shrewdly. 'Desirée, I cannot help but feel that your sudden wish to leave has something to do with my nephew. And if that is the case, I hope you would tell me.'

'It has nothing to do with Lord Buckworth,' Desirée said, hoping that she would be forgiven for the lie. 'But I think we both know that I am here under false pretences. And in all good conscience, I cannot stay here knowing that you are paying me for doing something which, had I a choice, I would be willing to do for free. Well, that is all I wished to tell you, other than that I shall be leaving first thing in the morning.'

Lady Charlton's face fell. 'So soon?'

'I'm afraid so. I am expected at my new post by the end of the week.'

Lady Charlton seemed at a loss to know what to say. 'Well, will you at least tell me where you are going, Desirée? Is it perhaps somewhere we might still have a chance to visit?'

Not wishing to give too much away, Desirée said simply, 'The position is in Yorkshire, my lady, as governess to a family with two young daughters.'

'A governess?' Lady Charlton glanced at her in surprise. 'But I thought you were reluctant to accept such a post?'

'The circumstances surrounding the family I am going to are somewhat different from those pertaining to the friends Lord Buckworth told me about.'

'Are they a titled family?'

'No, but I understand they are quite wealthy.'

'Hmm, no doubt as a result of having made their money in trade,' Lady Charlton said disparagingly. 'Well, if there is nothing I can say to make you stay, I suppose I shall just have to say goodbye and wish you well.' She got to her feet and pressed a kiss to Desirée's cheek. 'But I shall miss you very much, my dear.'

'I shall miss you, Lady Charlton.'

'Mind you dress warmly. Winters can be very harsh in that part of the country and I would not wish to hear that you had taken ill.'

'I shall be careful, my lady.'

'And I want you to take *all* of your belongings. There is no point in leaving them here, for the servants will not be able to wear them. Nor would I wish to see you go to your new position less than suitably attired. And you shall have your full wages for the month, being that it is so close to the end anyway.'

Desirée felt a lump rise in her throat. 'It is too much, Lady Charlton. I could not possibly take full wages *and* all the clothes. Surely there is someone who can wear them.'

'There is no one,' Lady Charlton said briefly. 'Take them, Desirée. Please. Your new post may be that of a governess, but there is no reason for your new employers to think that your last ones did not provide for you. And I shall, of course, prepare a letter of recommendation for you to give them.'

The woman's kindness nearly left Desirée speechless. 'Thank you, my lady. For…everything.'

'And if you need anything else, you have only to write,' Lady Charlton said finally. 'If you find that you are unhappy, you can always come back.'

It was a comforting thing to hear, but Desirée knew that she would never be back. Because when all was said and done, it wasn't Lady Charlton she was trying to get away from.

Chapter Ten

Sebastian returned to London in a foul humour, though not for any reason he could put a name to. He had enjoyed a reasonably good week with Lord Mackenzie, partaking of the fine shooting and hunting to be had at his Hertfordshire estate, and had enjoyed the company of several amiable gentlemen with whom he was well acquainted. He had even passed a pleasant evening in the company of Lady Alice and a few of the lady friends she had invited to join her for the week.

Then why was he feeling so damned blue-devilled about life in general?

Perhaps *because* of the time he had spent in Lady Alice's company, Sebastian acknowledged as he climbed the steps to White's. And the fact that it had been a complete waste of time. In truth, none of the elegant young ladies with whom he had spent time had moved him in the least. Instead, he kept seeing a pair of sparkling green eyes that smiled up at him from a woodland pool and a sweet gentle voice that quoted Aristotle and Machiavelli...

'Sebastian,' a voice hailed him. 'What a grand surprise. I hadn't thought to see you here tonight.'

Sebastian turned to see his good friend Thomas Burton walking towards him. 'Thomas, you're a sight for sore eyes. I haven't seen you around the place in weeks.'

'As a matter of fact, I've been away in the country. Just got back to London this week and was saying hello to a few of the chaps when I saw you come in. Are you engaged for dinner?'

Sebastian hesitated. He had thought to stop only for a drink before continuing on to Mayfair, but the more he thought about it, the more he realised it was probably best that he didn't call at his aunt's tonight. He wasn't in the best mood to see Desirée, nor to play the part of the genial nephew. Perhaps it was better all round that he delay his visit until the morning.

'I am not engaged,' he said as a result. 'I am only just returned from Hertfordshire myself and thought to break my journey before heading home. But I think now that I shall stop and have dinner with you.'

'Splendid. Because I have some wonderful news to share with you.'

Sebastian gave his friend a lazy smile. 'Has this anything to do with the young lady you have been keeping company with so much of late?'

'Actually, it does,' Thomas said as they settled themselves at a table. 'The thing of it is, I have just this afternoon asked Miss Dean to marry me, and she has accepted!'

'Has she indeed? And has her father given his consent?'

'Yes, *and* his blessing. We are to be married in a month's time and you, my friend, are the first to know.'

'Then let me also be the first to congratulate you,' Sebastian said with all sincerity. 'Miss Dean is a lucky young woman.'

'On the contrary, I cannot help but feel that I am the lucky one,' the younger man said. 'I only wish that *you* might find a young lady who would make you half as happy as Miss Dean has made me.'

Sebastian's mouth curved in a smile that didn't quite reach his eyes. 'Yes. Would that we all had such good fortune.'

'Well, what of it? Is there no one who has captured your heart? I have been hearing rumours about you and the charming Lady Alice. Was that what prompted the visit to Hertfordshire?'

Sebastian shook his head. 'My visit to Hertfordshire had nothing to do with a lady, Thomas. I went for the shooting. I will admit that I briefly entertained the thought of paying court to Lady Alice, but after having spent time in her company, I realise that we should not suit.'

'Not suit? Good Lord, Sebastian, the lady is all that is amiable. She is lovely as any man could wish and she is an heiress in her own right. What more could you want?'

Love, Sebastian thought as they got up from their table after dinner and went in search of more comfortable chairs. Love and respect, both from the woman he chose to marry, and to her in return. He wanted someone who could turn his house into a home; a lady he could go to bed with every night and wake up loving even more in the morning. A woman with fire in her eyes and passion in her soul.

A woman like the one who seemed to have taken possession of his heart in a way that he was helpless to ignore and powerless to stop...

'Well, Buckworth, I see that you are returned from your sojourn in the country,' a mocking voice taunted from a table nearby. 'Did you find the air and the company to your liking?'

Sebastian had stiffened at the sound of the man's voice and did not smile as he turned to address him. 'More to my liking than I find the present company. But then, that will hardly come as any surprise to you.'

Lord Perry smiled as he reached for his glass. He was sitting with a few of his friends, and while it was obvious that all of the men had been imbibing, Perry himself seemed to be relatively sober. 'You know, I have never been able to understand why the ladies find you so charming, Buckworth. Personally, I have never found *anything* in you to like.'

'You have no idea how relieved I am to hear you say so,' Sebastian drawled, 'but at the same time, it makes me wonder what prompted you to speak to me in the first place.'

'As a matter of fact, it was Jackson's idea,' Lord Perry said. 'We were just discussing the merits of certain desirable young ladies and he thought you might like to lend an opinion.'

'Sorry. I prefer to keep my opinions to myself.'

'Even about Miss Desirée Nash?'

There was an ominous silence before Sebastian said quietly, 'I cannot imagine why you would include Miss Nash in such a discussion. She is a fine young woman who is presently engaged as my aunt's companion. If you are referring to anything else—'

'In point of fact, I was referring to your initial meeting with her in Steep Abbot last summer.' Lord Perry sat back in his chair and smiled. 'I was just sharing with my friends the details of your charming interlude with her in a secluded woodland pool. And I am surprised to hear you refer to her as a fine young woman. From what Hutchings said, you were openly admiring of her charms. Why do you think I troubled myself to go to Steep Abbot as often as I did?'

The line of Sebastian's mouth tightened. 'I do not intend to comment on anything Hutchings might have said, since it seems he has concocted his own version of the story. As to any visits which *you* might have made to the area, I assume they were for the purpose of visiting your daughter, whom I know is presently at school there. But I am curious, Perry. How did *you* know that the lady I spoke to Hutchings about *was* Miss Nash?' he asked in a deceptively quiet voice. 'Because while I do not remember everything I said to him, I do know that I did not provide him with a name.'

'As I said, Buckworth, I had been visiting Mrs Guarding's Academy in Steep Abbot for some time and was aware of Miss Nash all along. My daughter also acquainted me with the fact that she liked to slip away to the river to swim, so it was not difficult to make the connection between the two. But I have *you* to thank for passing along details of your encounter with her.' Lord Perry shot him a meaningful glance. 'After all, I had no reason to think that a young woman who swam naked in the river on a summer's day might not also be fit for a tumble in the grass alongside.'

'Have a care, Sebastian,' Thomas said as Sebastian took a threatening step forward. 'I would not wish to see you come to blows with a man unworthy of your time.'

Lord Perry's eyes swivelled to the younger man. 'I would advise you to keep out of this, Burton. Unless you are acquainted with the young woman and have an opinion of your own to put forward.'

'I am not acquainted with her, but the fact that she is Lord Buckworth's acquaintance is reason enough to defend her,' Thomas said stiffly.

Perry snorted. 'What a pity not all of your friends are as loyal, Buckworth. If they were, you might not now be having to defend Miss Nash's honour all over London. Speaking of which, is it still your intention to set Desirée up as your mistress? Because if it is not, I thought perhaps I might give some consideration to establishing her as mine.'

It took all of Burton's considerable strength to prevent Sebastian from charging the man then and there. 'Come away, Sebastian!' he urged desperately. 'You'll do yourself no good getting into a fight here.'

'Stay away from her, Perry!' Sebastian warned in a low, throaty growl. 'Miss Nash will never be any man's mistress and certainly not yours. Do I make myself clear?'

Lord Perry steepled his fingers in front of his face and laughed. 'I do not wonder that you show such emotion about her. Indeed, after having the pleasure of spending some time alone in Desirée's company, I am well able to understand why any man would go to such lengths to keep her for himself.'

This time, not even Burton was able to restrain Sebastian. He was across the table and had Perry by the throat before anyone had chance to stop him.

'Now you listen to me, you arrogant bastard,' Sebastian ground out. 'If I hear so much as a whisper that you have attempted to get in touch with Miss Nash, you'll regret ever leaving London. But if I find out that you've touched her in any way, I'll kill you with my bare hands.'

Sebastian knew that he had made his point. For all his posturing, Perry had gone deathly white, and no one else at the table moved.

Satisfied, Sebastian shoved the man back in his seat and turned on his heel in disgust.

Once they were far enough away, Thomas put his hand on Sebastian's arm. 'Sebastian, think carefully on what you said tonight. I do not know this Miss Nash, but if she is a woman of loose virtue—'

'Damn your eyes, Thomas. She is as fine a lady as your own Miss Dean! It is merely a set of unfortunate circumstances which have placed her in her current predicament.'

'That being the case, unless you wish to be seen as the lady's champion, you might like to have a care for what you say,' Thomas persisted gently. 'Listening to the way you defended her would almost lead one to believe that—'

'Believe what?' Sebastian growled.

'That you…cared for the young woman.'

It was too close to the truth for Sebastian's liking. As was the fact that he couldn't say a damn thing to refute it.

Shortly after the confrontation with Lord Perry, Sebastian left White's and headed for his aunt's house. He needed to speak to Desirée. It was time for them to clear the air once and for all. A number of things had become clear to him while he was in Hertfordshire and the rest had fallen into place tonight. Not the least of which was that he was in love with Desirée Nash.

Oh yes, he loved her, Sebastian admitted. It might be the first time he had admitted it in so many words, but he knew it to be the truth. As he did the fact that he'd been feeling this way for a long time. He wasn't sure when he'd fallen in love with Desirée, but he suspected it was last summer when she'd told him to his face that she was too good to be his mistress. And everything that had happened between now and then had only caused him to love her more.

And now it was time to tell her that. He wondered for a moment how his aunt would take the news, but in all honesty, he did not think she would be unhappy. She liked Desirée, and after all, she was Sir George Owens's granddaughter.

Unfortunately, as it turned out, Sebastian was to be

denied the pleasure of telling the woman he loved how he felt about her. Upon arriving at his aunt's house, he was informed that the lady who had become such an important part of his life—the woman who meant more to him than anyone in the world—had packed her bags and left London for good!

Desirée did not settle well into her new position in Yorkshire. Banksburgh House was located on the side of a remote, windswept hill in the northern dales, and was about an hour by carriage from the nearest village. The prospect from the front window was mildly pleasing, but the house itself was not. Desirée found the dark ugly mansion extremely depressing after the airy brightness of Lady Charlton's elegant town house. As she did the personalities of the brooding Mr Clyde and his wife.

To be sure, there was precious little laughter to be heard in the halls of Banksburgh House. The only bright spot in an otherwise gloomy picture was the younger of the two girls Desirée had been engaged to look after. Miss Sarah Clyde was four years old and was as sweet as any child Desirée had ever had the pleasure to meet. Her thirteen-year-old sister, Caroline, however, was a different matter altogether. She was sorely in need of discipline as a result of having been spoiled by her mother, and was now used to getting whatever she wanted. Unfortunately, when Desirée tried to chastise her, the child inevitably ran to her mama, who then informed Desirée that it was her job to *teach* her children, *not* to discipline them.

Hence, it was not long after her arrival that Desirée knew she had made a dreadful mistake.

Still, there was nothing she could do about it now. She could hardly turn around and ask Lady Charlton to take her back. Nor *would* she go back if she'd been given the choice. Because the problem which had caused her to leave would be the same. Sebastian would still be there. He would still call at the house whenever he felt so inclined, and he would continue to smile at her in that special way that set Desirée's heart to racing.

And foolishly, she would continue to hope that one day he might see her as something other than the young woman he had discovered swimming in the Steep Wood pool. A woman he had brought to London to be his mistress, only to think better of it once he had discovered her connections.

But she knew it was unlikely that he would. He might even now be engaged to the Lady Alice Mackenzie. Lady Charlton might have already forgotten about her and be busy making wedding preparations, excited at the prospect of her beloved nephew finally settling down to married life.

It was that thought more than any that made life tolerable for Desirée at Banksburgh House. Because the thought of the alternative, of having to see Sebastian every day, and to hear him talk about the woman he loved and was soon to marry, would have been far more destructive to her happiness than anything the parsimonious Mr Clyde and his family could do.

* * *

'But did she give you no indication as to *where* she was going?' Sebastian dragged his hand through his hair again, sending it even further into disarray, as he turned to face his aunt. 'She *must* have said something!'

'Sebastian, I told you, Desirée did not tell me anything about where she was going, other than to say that it was to a wealthy family in Yorkshire where she would be employed as their governess. I did not wish to interrogate her on the subject.'

'But did she say that she would write?'

'No, my dear, she did not. I hope that she will keep in touch, of course, but I do not expect to hear from her for some time. Sebastian, you do seem unusually disturbed by Desirée's departure.' Lady Charlton's eyes narrowed thoughtfully. 'Why should her leaving London to secure other employment bother you so much?'

'Because *I* am the one who let her down,' Sebastian said heavily. 'After all, it was my idea to bring her to London in the first place, and now she has left it *because* of me.'

'What do you mean she's left because of you? Desirée told me that she was leaving because of *me*. She told me she felt she wasn't earning her way and that I was treating her more like a friend than a companion. Which I suppose I was,' Lady Charlton acknowledged ruefully. 'But I really couldn't help myself. I liked Desirée and I wanted to help her.'

And I love her, Sebastian thought desperately. And now because of him and the things he had said, she was gone.

But what was he to do? How in God's name was he to find a young woman who clearly didn't want to be found? She could have gone to any one of hundreds of small villages dotted throughout the dales. Or she could have gone to a wealthy family in one of the towns: Sheffield or Wakefield in the south; Middlesborough or Northallerton in the north. She might even have gone to the cathedral city of York. How was he to find her then?

Where did he start his search for what could turn out to be the proverbial needle in a haystack?

Chapter Eleven

Sebastian set out for Yorkshire the following day. He did not tell anyone where he was going, though he had a feeling his aunt suspected. She seemed to have a funny, knowing look in her eyes since he'd returned from Hertfordshire. But Sebastian didn't care. He wouldn't have bothered to deny his feelings for Desirée even if his aunt had asked. The fact that she hadn't simply allowed him to keep the knowledge to himself until the time was right to share it.

If, he reminded himself, the time would ever be right.

Not surprisingly, the trip north seemed endless. Sebastian had mapped out the route he intended to take, and stayed at coaching inns he knew along the way. And at every one, he asked the same questions. Even so, by the time he arrived in Kettlewell, near Skipton, Sebastian was weary of the road. He walked into the local inn and then headed for the bar, casually pulling out his purse as he did. 'I am looking to make enquiries,' he said in a voice loud enough for the innkeeper to hear.

The burly, red-faced man looked at Sebastian's heavy purse and all but licked his lips. 'Aye, my lord, and what kind of information would you be looking for?'

'I am looking for a young woman. She would have arrived about a week or so ago.' Sebastian made a show of opening up the neck of the bag and removing a coin. 'She has light brown hair and green eyes, and she is exceedingly lovely. Do you recall having seen anyone like that?'

The innkeeper's eyes turned shrewd. 'I don't *recall* seeing any young lady like that, my lord, though there's plenty of them come through here. Maybe I need a bit more reminding.'

Knowing the game, Sebastian drew another coin from the bag. 'She was going to a big house to be a governess. Apparently the family is quite wealthy.'

'Now, I could be remembering a young lady who came about a job,' the innkeeper said slowly. He tapped his finger against his cheek. 'But I'm just not too clear about which family she was going to.'

'No? Pity.' Sebastian began to close his purse. 'I was willing to pay well for the information.'

'Oh, now wait a minute, my lord, I—'

'Would you be willing to pay anyone for the information, my lord?' a young woman asked suddenly. 'Because I remember seeing a young lady who looked like the one you're referring to come through here last week.'

Sebastian turned to see a girl of about eighteen standing behind him. She was remarkably pretty and there was a gentleness about her that seemed strangely out of place in this rough and tumble place. But her face was already beginning to show signs of age and her hands were rough and reddened from hard work. 'You saw her?'

'Aye, m'lord.'

The landlord frowned darkly. 'Nobody was talking to you, Jenny, my girl. Go on back to the kitchen. There'll be plenty o' pots waiting.'

'No, just a minute,' Sebastian said, stopping her as she went to turn away. 'My money goes to anyone who can supply me with the information I need.' He reached for her hand and put the two coins into her palm. 'Now, Jenny, what did you see?'

Jenny glanced nervously at the man standing behind the counter, then at the money in her palm, and then anxiously bit her lip. 'A young lady like you described came through here late last week, m'lord. But she wasn't here long. They came to fetch her.'

'They?'

'Aye. One of t'lads from Banksburgh House. They came with the trap.'

Sebastian pulled another coin from the bag. 'And where is Banksburgh House, Jenny?'

'Now, my lord, I can supply you with that bit of information,' the innkeeper said hastily. 'You've given our Jenny more money than she's seen in her entire life. No need to be giving her more than she'll have need of.'

'Are you her father?'

The man shook his head. 'Nay, I'll not say that I am. But she's worked for me for nigh on four years now, so I tend to think of myself that way.'

Sebastian ignored him and placed the coin in Jenny's palm. 'Jenny?'

Hardly able to believe her good fortune, Jenny's eyes widened. 'It's on down t'road, m'lord, then left at Miller's Cross. It's a big place, is Banksburgh House. You can't miss it from t'road.'

'And the owner is?'

'Mr Clyde. They have two daughters, a Miss Caroline and young Sarah. It's for them that Mrs Clyde was wanting a governess.'

It was all Sebastian needed to know. He put away his purse and, drawing out one of his cards, pressed it into her hand. 'Thank you, Jenny. The information you have given me is very important and I am forever in your debt. If you ever find yourself in any kind of trouble—' Sebastian glanced pointedly at the inn-keeper, 'I want you to get in touch with me at that address. Do you understand?'

Jenny took the card and her eyes grew even wider as she read the name printed upon it. 'Aye, m'lord.'

'Good. And I shall stop by whenever I am passing through the area to enquire after your health,' he added, again with a look for the burly man standing beside her. Then, satisfied that he had done all he could for her, Sebastian turned and left the coaching inn, heading for Banksburgh House.

The afternoon had turned uncommonly warm and Desirée decided to take her two young charges out-side to enjoy it. The grounds around Banksburgh House were surprisingly well tended, given the rela-tive barrenness of the surrounding area, and Desirée had walked more than once to the farthest reaches of the property. At least there she was able to escape the overbearing presence of Mrs Clyde.

Fortunately, Desirée got on reasonably well with the rest of the staff. The housekeeper, a stern-faced woman by the name of Mrs Hagerty, was accom-

modating if not friendly, and life on the whole was
tolerable. But her spartan room was a far cry from
the comfort and charm of the Green Room at Lady
Charlton's. Nor were her lovely clothes of any use to
her here. Mrs Clyde insisted on Desirée wearing the
drabbest of garments and had provided her with two
highly serviceable gowns, one in grey and the other
in a dull shade of brown.

Desirée almost felt as if she was back at the
Guarding Academy again.

It was wearing her unbecoming grey gown that
Sebastian came upon her that afternoon. Quite by
chance, he spotted Desirée and her two young charges
as he was making his way up the long drive. Rather
than announce himself to the lady of the house and
formally ask permission to see the governess, however, he stopped the carriage at the side of the drive
and made his way across the field to where she was
standing.

'Good afternoon, Desirée,' Sebastian said, removing his shining black beaver as he swept her a bow.
'I don't expect you ever thought to see me again.'

Desirée, who had indeed been rendered speechless
by the sight of the man walking across the field towards her, now struggled to find her voice.
'Lord...Buckworth! Yes, I confess, I am...astonished
at seeing you here.'

'Miss Nash, who is this gentleman?' Miss Caroline
Clyde asked imperiously.

This is the man I love, Desirée wanted to tell her.
*The man who has come all the way to Yorkshire to
find me, and hopefully to take me back to London.*
All she said, however, was, 'This is a...friend of mine
from London, Caroline. Lord Buckworth, may I pre-

sent Miss Caroline Clyde and her sister, Miss Sarah Clyde. Girls, this is Lord Buckworth.'

The elder Miss Clyde seemed suitably impressed that a titled gentleman had come to call, and she bobbed a pretty curtsey. Sarah, bless her heart, merely smiled her winsome smile and held out her hand to him. 'Have you come to see our governess?' she asked sweetly.

Sebastian grinned at the colour which suddenly bloomed in Desirée's cheeks. 'As a matter of fact, I have, Sarah. Is that all right with you?'

Sarah thought about it for a moment, and then nodded, setting her blonde curls dancing. 'Yeth.'

'Good. Now, Miss Caroline,' Sebastian said to the elder girl, 'perhaps you would be so good as to take your sister back to the house. Miss Nash will be along…directly.'

'But Mama says that Miss Nash is to stay with us at all times,' Caroline told him stubbornly. 'Isn't that right, Miss Nash?'

'Well, yes it is—'

'But I am sure that your mama will not mind if you walk back alone just this once,' Sebastian interposed smoothly. 'We are in clear sight of the house and you have only to follow the path back through the gate there.'

Surprisingly, it was Sarah who took her sister by the hand and started dragging her back in the direction of the house. 'Come along, Cawoline. I think we should go.'

To Desirée's astonishment, Caroline actually went. 'Oh, very well,' she grumbled. 'It was very nice meeting you, Lord Buckworth.'

Sebastian offered her his most charming smile. 'The pleasure was all mine, Miss Clyde.'

Desirée bit her lip as she watched the two young figures retreat. 'I really shouldn't let them walk back alone, Lord Buckworth,' she said anxiously. 'Mrs Clyde is most particular—'

'They will be fine, Desirée. We are well within sight of the house.'

'Yes, I know. Which is why I should not have let them go back alone. Mrs Clyde may see them walking on their own and she has made it very clear that the girls are to be accompanied at all times.'

Sebastian took her by the shoulders and gently turned her to face him. 'Desirée, I want to talk to you. And I could hardly do that with two young girls listening to every word I said, now could I?'

Dismayed both by the touch of his hands and by the softness of his voice, Desirée reluctantly inclined her head. The thought of having to talk with him in the presence of the Misses Clyde was decidedly unwelcome, but the thought of being alone with him was not much better—especially given that she had thought never to see him again.

She watched her two young charges until they reached the safety of the house and felt marginally better once she saw them go inside. Now it was time to face her other problem.

'To say that I am…surprised to see you would be something of an understatement, my lord,' Desirée began carefully. 'You must have gone to considerable trouble to discover my whereabouts.'

'I hardly knew where to begin,' Sebastian admitted. 'But once I arrived in Yorkshire I happened upon a bit of luck. A young lady at the coaching inn in

Kettlewell remembered seeing you and was good enough to point me in the right direction.' He glanced at the scenery all around them, and then turned back to gaze deeply into her eyes. 'Are you happy here, Desirée?'

'I find the work...satisfying.' *How can I be happy when you are so far away?* 'Caroline can be somewhat trying at times, but her sister more than makes up for it.' Desirée's mouth curved in an affectionate smile. 'You saw for yourself what a delight Sarah is.'

'I did indeed. And your employers?' Sebastian enquired, his eyes turning to the nearby bulk of a house. 'Are they as delightful as their youngest daughter?'

The thought nearly made Desirée laugh. She doubted anyone who knew the Clydes would have called them delightful. 'I do not see a great deal of Mr Clyde, as he is mostly occupied on business in the north. Mrs Clyde, however, is typical of her kind. She does not put up with nonsense from her children or her staff, and I think most of the maids go in fear of her.'

'And you?'

'I know what my job is and I do it,' Desirée said, careful not to allow the slightest inflection into her voice. *Why had he come?* There had to be more to his visit than a desire for polite conversation? Surely he would not have troubled himself to travel all this way if that was all he had in mind...would he?

'My lord, I must be returning to the house—'

'Desirée, forgive me for interrupting, but there is something I must ask you,' Sebastian said abruptly. 'Something which has been on my mind ever since I left London. Indeed it was part of my reason for coming.'

Desirée found that her hands were suddenly trembling. She clasped them together in front of her and strove for a casual tone. 'And what is that, my lord?'

'Before I left, I had occasion to speak to...Lord Perry,' Sebastian said quietly. 'It was not a pleasant meeting and he told me things which I found most disturbing. Things which, quite frankly, I did not know how to take.'

At the mention of Lord Perry's name, the trembling in Desirée's hands grew worse. 'And what has your...disturbing conversation with Lord Perry to do with me?'

'It has everything to do with you.' Sebastian stopped walking and turned to face her. 'He led me to believe that the two of you had spent some time together while you were at Guarding's. He said that...after having done so, he could understand my fascination and desire for you. And he said, in front of others, that if it was not my intention to set you up as my mistress, that he would very probably do so himself.'

Desirée listened with growing dismay, until in the end, the depth of her grief went far beyond tears. Truly, it was worse than she had imagined. They had been discussing her as though she were little more than a used piece of baggage; something to be picked up by one when carelessly cast off by another.

She stared into the distance and felt a sudden chill in the afternoon air. 'And what did you tell Lord Perry in answer to his question, Lord Buckworth?'

'Damn it, Desirée, what do you think I told him?'

'I have no idea.' She turned to face him with eyes that were curiously devoid of expression. 'Because the fact that you came here today and told me what you have leads me to believe that *you* doubt my integrity as well. The fact that you would even *consider* Lord Perry's story to be the truth tells me what you really think of me.'

'The fact that he was known to you in Steep Abbot, and that you hold him in such abhorrence makes all manner of things possible, Desirée,' Sebastian said harshly. 'Because I now believe that whatever happened between you and Lord Perry was the cause of your leaving the Guarding Academy. The reason you were…asked to leave.'

Desirée closed her eyes. 'And you think that I…brought this on myself? That I invited Lord Perry's attentions?'

'That is not what I said. I am *asking* you to tell me what happened, and to explain why you left London so abruptly. God knows, I hold Perry in no higher esteem than do you. In fact, it was only through the intervention of a good friend that I did not challenge him on the spot. But I am asking you now to tell me what passed between the two of you at Guarding's. Because the manner of what Perry told me led me to believe that the two of you had had…an intimate encounter.'

His words hung heavy in the air between them and Desirée suddenly felt a coldness spread through her body, as though the blood in her veins had turned to ice. So he had not followed her all the way to Yorkshire to declare his love and to take her back with him. He had come on a fool's journey to find out whether or not a rumour told to him by a man he admitted disliking had any truth to it.

'Very well, Lord Buckworth, you shall have your answer,' Desirée said in a voice that was as bleak and as barren as the hills all around them. 'Lord Perry *was* the reason I left the Guarding Academy. He caught me in my classroom at the end of the day and he…he…'

'Tell me, Desirée,' Sebastian said quietly. 'Please.'

'He t-told me that he had been waiting to get me alone for a long time. And he asked me to be his mistress. When I refused, he lunged at me and…tore my gown.' Desirée closed her eyes against the painful memory. 'I tried to resist, but he was too strong.'

A muscle tensed in Sebastian's cheek. 'What happened then?'

'I was fortunate. The door opened and Mrs Guarding walked in. She had one of the other teachers and two of the students with her. But they all…saw me in Lord Perry's arms.'

'How did Mrs Guarding know to come and find you?'

'Apparently Helen had been waiting for me,' Desirée said slowly. 'She knew that I had planned to go back to my classroom after dinner, and when I didn't return to my bedroom, she began to worry. So she went down and got Mrs Guarding. I have no idea how Miss Perry and her friend came to be there—'

'Miss Perry?' Sebastian's dark brows lifted in surprise. 'Lord Perry's daughter?'

'Yes. Perhaps she knew what was afoot, I don't know,' Desirée said wearily. 'All I know is that she was there and that she saw what happened.'

'And you left because of that?'

'I was *asked* to leave because of it,' she said tersely. 'With two of the girls there to witness my ruination, I had no choice. Mrs Guarding had to consider the reputation of the school.'

'So that is why she did not provide you with a reference.'

'Under the circumstances, she could not.'

'And when Lord Perry saw you again at Lady Rumsden's ball in London—'

'He...asked me again to be his mistress.' Desirée took a deep breath. 'He told me that I might as well accept his offer because I could not hope to do better. And when I said that I knew he could ruin my reputation in London just as he had in Steep Abbot, he informed me that...my reputation was already lost because *you* had told all of your friends and acquaintances upon your return to London that we had been...together in the River Steep.'

'Desirée, I swear, I told only one man of our meeting in the woods,' Sebastian said desperately. 'A gentleman I thought of as a friend. But it was he who spread the tale and he who embellished it to make it sound far worse than it really was. Only think, Desirée. Why would I have gone around talking about you? I didn't even know who you were. I had seen you once and knew nothing about you, save that your parents were dead and that you were not married. From your conversation I was able to glean that you were well educated, but I knew nothing else. All I saw was a beautiful young woman who enjoyed swimming in a woodland pool.'

'And whom you suspected of having loose morals.'

'That's not what I said!'

'But you must have thought it, my lord. Why else would you have asked me to be your mistress? In truth, you are no better than Lord Perry. And it does not matter whether you told one or a hundred people,' Desirée cried. 'It was enough that you recounted the details of your escapade in the country to one man, and that you both enjoyed a good laugh at my expense.'

'Desirée, please—'

'Well, I am not laughing, my lord,' Desirée told him angrily. 'When Lord Perry asked me to be his mistress and I turned him down, he told me that he would use every means at his disposal to ensure that I *did* eventually agree. And that's why I left London. I was not willing to endanger Lady Charlton's good name. I did not want to make her look a fool in front of her friends, when it became known that the lady she had chosen to be her companion was a woman of questionable morals. I turned down the position as governess to your friends for exactly the same reason.'

'Desirée, for God's sake, why didn't you tell me any of this?'

'Because it didn't matter. What did, was that I left your aunt's house—and London—as quickly as possible. Lord Perry was waiting for an answer. I knew that I was running out of time. So the morning after Lady Appleby's soirée, I went to one of the service registries in town and applied for a position. Eventually, I was lucky enough to be offered one.'

'But without any letters of reference, how did you secure it?'

Desirée blushed. 'I wrote to my friend Helen at the Academy and asked her to provide me with one.'

'I hardly think the recommendation of a friend and fellow teacher would have accomplished what was required.'

'No, but one signed by the Signora Helene de Grazziano, Comtesse de Coverdale was.'

Sebastian nodded. 'So you lied.'

'I did what I had to do!' Desirée cried in frustration. 'I needed a position, Lord Buckworth. And while this might not be exactly what I would have wished for, it has provided me with a roof over my head and a steady wage. More importantly, it has given me a chance to start again. I came here with my reputation intact and I keep to myself as much as possible. And that is the way it will be from now on because I will not let myself be hurt again. Not by you or anyone else.'

'Desirée, I had to ask,' Sebastian said, praying that she understood. 'Perry made it sound as though—'

'Yes, I know how Lord Perry would have made it sound,' Desirée said bitterly. 'Why would he not? He has no reputation to worry about. I was a lowly teacher at a girl's school; a woman he felt perfectly within his rights to approach with lewd suggestions and improper conduct. He would not have treated a lady in such a way. Indeed, I wonder if he would have attempted such a seduction had he known that I was the granddaughter of the late Sir George Owens. I venture to say he would not.'

'Desirée, let me take you back to London,' Sebastian said earnestly. 'There is no need for you to remain here any longer. My aunt misses you terribly and so do I. Come back with me and everything shall be as it was.'

Desirée looked at him askance. 'But don't you understand what I have been saying, Lord Buckworth? Nothing will *ever* be as it was! How can I go back to London knowing what I do now? How could I...walk into a room and hold my head up, knowing that half the gentlemen in the room are seeing me as

Lord Perry does? Wondering, perhaps, if I would agree to be *their* mistress, if I would not be his—or yours?'

'You will be no man's mistress, Desirée,' Sebastian growled, 'and you will have nothing to fear. When I am around—'

'Yes, when you are around no one is likely to approach me,' Desirée agreed readily enough. 'But when you are not, what shall I do then? How am I to protect myself against the likes of Lord Perry and his friends?'

A sudden movement at the front door of the house drew Desirée's eye, and she abruptly caught her breath. Mrs Clyde was standing in the doorway, with Caroline on one side of her and the housekeeper at the other. And all three were staring directly across the field towards them.

'I have tarried too long,' Desirée said anxiously. 'I must return to the house at once.'

Sebastian glanced in the direction of the house too, and frowned. 'Then I shall come with you. There is more that I would say to you, Desirée, and if necessary, I shall introduce myself to your employer and—'

'No, it is best that you leave now, my lord. Mrs Clyde does not allow the staff to have visitors at the house. I shall go back and make my explanations as best I can.'

'Damn it, Desirée, I am not a visitor and I have no wish to go—'

'But you have no reason to stay either,' Desirée told him, feeling as though her heart was being wrenched in two. 'I...thank you for coming, but now that the question as to why I left London has been answered, there is no reason for you to remain.

Please, go back to London, my lord. Your staying here now can do neither of us any good.'

Desirée whirled around before he had a chance to say anything more and ran all the way back to the house. What a fool she had been. What a silly, ignorant fool to think that Sebastian Moore might have ever truly cared for her. The apprehension she felt over the coming interview with Mrs Clyde was nothing compared to the emptiness she felt at his cruel betrayal.

Oh yes, he had come to Yorkshire looking for her. But only to find out the truth of the matter with regards to Lord Perry. He thought no better of her now than he had on the day he'd met her in the river. If he had, he would *never* have believed what Lord Perry had said. He would not have blamed her for what had happened.

Well, she would not be so foolish in the future, Desirée assured herself. She refused to allow any man to reduce her to such a state again. She had let it happen once by being stupid enough to fall in love with Sebastian Moore.

She would not be so careless a second time.

Chapter Twelve

Mrs Clyde did not waste any time in telling Desirée exactly what she thought of her conduct.

'I am shocked at your behaviour, Miss Nash,' she said after summoning Desirée to her private parlour immediately upon her return to the house. 'I look out of my window to see my governess talking to a strange man in the field, while my daughters are left to make their own way back to the house? What am I to make of such conduct?'

'We were only in the pasture, Mrs Clyde.'

'I don't care if you were in the garden, Miss Nash!' the woman snapped. 'Your responsibility is to my children, not to your fancy gentlemen friends. I will not have my staff behaving in such a disgraceful manner!'

'Do you wish me to leave?' Desirée asked, not at all sure that she wouldn't be relieved if the woman *were* to dismiss her.

But Mrs Clyde only shook her head. 'Unfortunately, my wishes are not the only ones to be considered here. My girls have taken to you and it is *their* wish, Sarah's in particular, that you remain. For their sakes alone, I shall allow it. But you will be confined to the house for the next three weeks, Miss Nash, and I warn you, if anything like this should happen again, you will be turned off immediately and without a reference. Is that understood?'

'Yes, Mrs Clyde.'

'Good. You may go.'

Desirée inclined her head and turned to leave as anger and resentment welled up inside.

'Thank you, Sebastian,' she muttered under her breath as she headed for the nursery. 'It seems that you have brought me to the edge of grief once more.'

Sebastian sat in the bar at the Three Crowns and stared morosely into his glass. It had all gone wrong. Everything he had come here to do had gone abysmally wrong. And he had no one to blame but himself.

Why hadn't he trusted Desirée? Surely he'd known enough of her character to know that she would never have *agreed* to a relationship with Perry. And if she *had* ended up in one, it would only have been because he had coerced her in some way. Desirée was not the type of woman to involve herself in an *affaire de coeur* with such a loathsome man.

And yet, when he had finally caught up with her this afternoon and had been given an opportunity to talk to her, what had he done but let her believe that that was *exactly* what he had thought. Why had he not just asked her to tell him what had happened without imposing any opinions of his own?

And on top of all that, it was very possible that he had cost Desirée her job. He had seen the look on

Mrs Clyde's face when she had stood in the doorway and glared at them. And he knew what Desirée would have had to face when she walked back into that house. But what was he to do now? Go back to London? Leave Desirée to her miserable existence here? Because Sebastian knew that's what it was. Her carefully worded answers hadn't disguised the truth for a minute. She might care for one of the young girls in her care but there was certainly no affection or respect for the master or his wife.

Sebastian signalled for another drink and remembered again Lord Perry's smug complacency. God, when he thought about what the bastard had done, he felt like killing him. He could only imagine how Desirée must have felt at being trapped in a room with such a man and knowing what he intended to do—what he *would* have done had it not been for a most timely interruption.

But then, at the same time, how humiliated Desirée must have felt at being discovered by Mrs Guarding herself; a woman she admired and respected. And then to be dismissed by that same woman for conduct that had nothing to do with her and everything to do with a rich, powerful man who selfishly used others for his own pleasure and amusement.

How can I go back to London, knowing what I do now? Desirée had told him. *How could I…walk into a room with Lady Charlton, and hold my head up, knowing that half the gentlemen in the room are seeing me as Lord Perry does? Wondering, perhaps, if I would agree to be their mistress, if I would not be his—or yours?*

Hearing again the despair in her voice, Sebastian abruptly got up and began to pace. He could not bear the thought of *anyone* thinking of Desirée in such a manner. Making a mockery of all that she was. Ignoring her gentleness and compassion, and seeing her only as a beautiful woman to be used and bedded.

All right, damn it, so that was what he had once thought too, but those were not his feelings any more! Desirée would never be just that to him. Because if he was ever fortunate enough to have her in his bed, it would be because he wanted *all* of her. Not just her body, but her mind, her spirit, and her intellect as well.

Then tell her that, you fool, the voice said in his head. *Tell her and be done with it.*

Sebastian abruptly stopped pacing. Yes, of course that's what he would do. He would go back to that dreadful house tomorrow and he would demand to see her. And when he did, he would get down on his knees and beg her to forgive him.

He hoped to God that it wasn't already too late.

Sebastian called at Banksburgh House at precisely eleven o'clock the following morning. He knew that he was calling in advance of the socially accepted time, but he could not believe that in such a dismal place the niceties would be adhered to. Besides, the wait had already tried his patience sorely enough.

He was met at the door by a dour-faced butler who informed him that the master was not at home. When Sebastian presented his card and told him that he wished to see the lady of the house, he was grudgingly admitted to a chilly, cavernous hall and asked to wait. Moments later, he found himself being led into a large, cheerless drawing-room, where he was greeted by an obsequious Mrs Clyde.

'Lord Buckworth, I am honoured by your call,' she said, visibly flustered by his unexpected arrival. 'Most honoured indeed.'

'I hope I am not calling too early, Mrs Clyde.'

'Not at all, my lord. We do not keep town hours here. We rise very early at Banksburgh House. Can I offer you some refreshment?'

Sebastian politely inclined his head as he removed his leather gloves. 'Thank you, no. This is not entirely a social call. In fact, I have come on another matter altogether.'

'My lord?'

'I wish to see your governess.'

'I...beg your pardon?'

Sebastian smiled at her look of astonishment. 'Yes, you heard me correctly, Mrs Clyde. I wish to speak to Miss Nash. I believe you saw me talking to her in the field yesterday afternoon.'

'Well, yes, I did, but—'

'By the by, I apologize for sending your two lovely daughters back to the house without her,' Sebastian said before the woman had a chance to continue. 'Miss Nash was most upset at my doing so, but what I had to say to her was for her hearing alone. And I thought that with the house being within such easy distance there would be no problem.'

'Well, no, of course not, Lord Buckworth, however—'

'Good. I am relieved to hear it,' Sebastian interrupted smoothly. 'I should not like to think that Miss Nash was reprimanded for something that was not her fault. And now, if you would be so good as to send for the young lady, Mrs Clyde, I will trouble you no more.'

* * *

Desirée was in the nursery when the housekeeper arrived. She frowned at being told that Mrs Clyde wanted to see her in the drawing-room straight away, and wondered what she had done wrong now. Surely her employer had not changed her mind and decided to turn her off as a result of what had happened yesterday?

'Thank you, Mrs Hagerty. I shall go down at once.'

'Can I come too, Miss Nash?' Sarah asked innocently.

In spite of her concerns, Desirée managed a smile for the little girl. 'No, Sarah, not this time. I think your mama wishes to speak with me alone.'

'Don't know about that,' the housekeeper said in a broad Yorkshire accent. 'There's already a fine London gentleman with her.'

Desirée blanched. A *London* gentleman? But... surely Sebastian had not come back? Not after what had passed between them yesterday?

Her nerves in a flutter, Desirée quickly made her way downstairs. Perhaps Sebastian had called out of respect and Mrs Clyde had summoned her downstairs to remind her again of the impropriety of her actions. Certainly that seemed a more logical explanation.

Desirée nervously smoothed down the front of her ugly brown dress and then knocked on the drawing-room door. Upon being told to enter, she pushed it open and walked in. The first person she saw was Sebastian. He was immaculately dressed and was leaning nonchalantly against the mantle. It seemed to Desirée that his eyes were bright with merriment.

Mrs Clyde, on the other hand, was looking somewhat bewildered as she sat in her usual chair beside the fireplace, her gown of puce-coloured silk clashing hideously with her auburn hair.

'You wished to see me, Mrs Clyde.'

'Yes, Miss Nash, I did. We have been honoured by a visit from this fine gentleman, but you can imagine my surprise when he told me that he wished to see *you*.'

'Good morning, Miss Nash,' Sebastian said with a bow.

'Lord Buckworth.' Desirée greeted him politely.

'I was just explaining to Mrs Clyde the circumstances of our meeting yesterday,' he informed her. 'I assured her that the blame for it *and* for sending the children back unescorted was entirely mine and that you should not be held in any way responsible. Is that not so, Mrs Clyde?'

'It is, Lord Buckworth. And while I was most upset with Miss Nash for her conduct yesterday, I am willing to admit—now that I have met you—that I made a mistake. At the time, of course, I was most concerned for the welfare of my girls, and that is what Miss Nash is here for, after all.'

'Your concern for your daughters' welfare does you proud, Mrs Clyde,' Sebastian assured her. 'But now that you are more comfortable with my presence, perhaps you would be so good as to allow me a few moments alone with Miss Nash?'

The woman's smile slipped. 'Well, it is not entirely proper, Lord Buckworth—'

'I promise you that I shall be the soul of propriety, Mrs Clyde. You see, I come with news about a very dear friend of Miss Nash's, and it is of a somewhat...delicate and personal nature. As such, I would not wish to embarrass her by making it known in front of others. You understand.'

Not looking as though she did, but obviously unwilling to say so in front of this man, Mrs Clyde reluctantly got to her feet. 'Very well, Lord Buckworth. You may have a few moments alone with Miss Nash. But then I must return her to her duties. I am sure you understand that my girls require constant supervision. Especially my eldest daughter, Caroline,' she said pointedly. 'A pretty little thing, did you not think, Lord Buckworth?'

'I did indeed, Mrs Clyde. And no doubt she will be breaking hearts when she makes her come-out in four or five years time. No doubt just like her mama did when she made hers.'

Desirée pressed her lips together to keep from smiling. Truly, Sebastian was outrageous! Mrs Clyde was blushing like a schoolgirl. But his flattery was obviously achieving the desired results.

'You are too kind, my dear Lord Buckworth,' the woman said as she headed for the door. 'Pray, enjoy your visit with Miss Nash.'

As soon as the door closed behind her, Sebastian let out his breath. 'Good God, for a moment there I thought she was going to kiss me.'

'It would have served you right if she had,' Desirée replied tartly.

'Miss Nash, I am wounded that you would speak to me in such a manner,' Sebastian said, feigning injury. 'I came here today in an effort to clear your good name and to make sure you were not taken to task over what happened, and this is the thanks I receive?'

'Your good intentions are much appreciated, my

lord, but I am afraid they arrive somewhat late. I have already been chastised for my wanton behaviour.'

'Is that what she called it?'

'That was what she *would* have called it, had she bothered to put a name to it.'

Sebastian quickly smothered a smile. 'Dear me. Then what you're saying is that I needn't have been so ingratiating in my address today.'

'No, but I am sure it sent her off in a sweeter temper than she would have gone otherwise.' Uncertain of what to do next, Desirée walked towards the couch and sat down. 'But pray, what brings you back here this morning? I thought you would have been well on your way to London by now.'

'I could not go back to London and leave you here, Desirée. Surely you know that.'

His voice had lost its teasing quality and turned infinitely gentle—and Desirée hardened her heart against it. 'I know nothing of the sort, my lord. Why should I?'

'Because I was a fool,' Sebastian said as he sat down beside her. 'I owe you an apology, Desirée. I thought long and hard about what you told me yesterday. And I realised, in my heart, that I didn't believe Perry for a moment when he intimated that you and he had been involved.'

'That is not what you led me to believe yesterday.'

'No. Because it wasn't until last night that I realised my reaction to Lord Perry was motivated by jealousy rather than anger.'

Desirée gasped. 'You were…jealous?'

'Outrageously,' Sebastian admitted. 'Even the thought of him being that close to you disturbed me to such an extent that I lost the ability to see the situation rationally. You mean more to me than it is possible for me to express in words, Desirée, and I am so deeply sorry that I hurt you.'

His eyes were filled with such tenderness and compassion that Desirée felt tears well in her own. 'My lord, I—'

'No, let me finish. It was never my intention to hurt you, Desirée. After that day in the river, I never imagined that I would see you again. You were like…a beautiful dream; someone I could think about, but never have. And yes, when I got back to London, I did tell someone that I had met you. But what I said to him was not in any way improper or obscene. I did not tell him what you were wearing or suggest that you behaved in a loose or wanton manner. If he drew those conclusions from what I said, then all I can do is apologise for his misinterpretation. But I can assure you that I said nothing of the kind.'

'You did not say that I was naked?'

'No. In fact, I did not refer to your physical appearance at all, other than to say that you were an extremely beautiful young woman. And though I am not trying to assign blame for what happened, I think it only right to tell you that Lord Perry is actually the one who betrayed you.'

Desirée's eyes widened in dismay. 'How do you know?'

'He told me as much a few days ago. He said he knew that you were partial to swimming in the river, and that when he heard Lord Hutchings's version of the story, he assumed it had to be you. But if it is of any comfort at all, I do not think as many people know that you were my delightful water nymph as he might have led you to believe. I think that was part of his plan for making you agree to become his mistress.'

Desirée felt the blush creep up into her cheeks. 'I suppose, in all fairness, I should not be so quick to condemn you for telling a friend when I have already admitted to telling one of my own.'

'Ah yes, the young lady who shared her knowledge of my...reputation with you.'

Desirée's colour heightened. 'Perhaps. But it is *because* of what Helen said that I wrote to you in the first place.'

'And what I know now, that I didn't know then, was that you wrote that letter because of what Lord Perry had done to you,' Sebastian said gently, 'and what it necessitated you doing in return.'

'Yes. I did not see that I had any choice,' Desirée said, knowing there was little point in prevaricating now. 'Mrs Guarding was very sorry to have to dismiss me but she had no choice either. There was very little likelihood that word of what had happened would not make its way around the school. And if it were to reach the village and beyond, the reputation of the school might have suffered. So, I thought about my choices and realised there was no possibility of respectable employment in the villages, and, in my highly distraught state, I thought about you and...what you had offered that day in the pool.'

Sebastian looked down into her face and shook his head. 'It must have been terribly difficult for you to write such a letter.'

'It was. But when I considered all of my options, I truly could not see...any other way out,' Desirée admitted softly. 'I had to leave Steep Abbot, for I knew there would always be a stigma attached to my name. And Helen had told me that you were a good man, so I acted on impulse and sent you the letter.'

'So in a way, I have Helen to thank for all of this.'

'In a way.' Desirée glanced up at him and smiled. 'Had she told me you were a brute, I would certainly not have written it.'

'But you did, and it started us upon a journey that neither of us expected to end here.'

Desirée sighed. 'No, my lord, certainly *I* did not.'

Hesitating, Sebastian took her right hand in his and stared down at it. 'Something else became clear to me last night, Desirée. Something which has been on my mind for some time now. Indeed, since long before I went away to Hertfordshire.' He raised his eyes to hers and knew in his heart that what he was doing was right. 'I want you to come back to London with me, Desirée. My life has been so empty without you and I need you back in it. I want us to ride together in the park and to dance the night away. I want you in my life, Aphrodite.'

Desirée's smile abruptly faded. For one heart-stopping moment, she had thought that Sebastian was about to offer her marriage—until he had called her Aphrodite. Then, she'd known. That was the name he had used when they had first met and when she was to have been his mistress. Obviously, that was what he wanted again.

She slowly withdrew her hand and stood up. 'I am…sorry, Lord Buckworth, I cannot return to London with you.'

'But…why not?'

'I have already told you. Nothing would change. Everyone would look at me exactly the same way they do now. The only difference would be that the men would leave me alone knowing that I was your mistress—'

'My mistress!' Sebastian's face darkened as he also got to his feet. 'Is that what you think this is all about? That I am asking you to come back to London as my *mistress*?'

'Well, what else was I to think? You said that...you wanted me in your life, and that we should....ride together in the park and dance the night away. And then you called me Aphrodite.'

'Yes, and so you are and always shall be,' Sebastian said as he drew her close. 'But I want you beside me as my wife, Desirée, not as my mistress.'

'Your *wife*!' she gasped.

'Of course, you silly girl. I don't intend to have any man look at you in any way but with the respect due you as Viscountess Buckworth. I want them all to admire your beauty—but only from a distance. And I shall challenge *any* man who is foolish enough to think he can take liberties with you. I want you as my wife and my lady, Desirée Nash.' Sebastian took her chin in his hand and gently tipped it back. 'Please tell me that I have not lost any hope of one day hearing you say that you love me.'

'Love you? Oh, my dearest Sebastian, now it is you who are being foolish,' Desirée cried. 'For I have been in love with you for such a very long time.'

With a muffled cry of joy, Sebastian pulled her into his arms. His mouth came down on hers and Desirée knew that she had finally come home. Here, in this man's arms, was where she was meant to be.

At length, Sebastian raised his head to look down into her sparkling green eyes. 'My sweet Aphrodite. When I think how close I came to losing you.'

'It would not have happened. *Quos amor verus tenuit, tenebit*,' Desirée quoted softly. 'To whom true love has held, it will go on holding.'

Sebastian smiled and brushed his lips lightly against hers. 'What other things do you intend to teach me, my beautiful bluestocking?'

'Only this. *Amor vincit omnia*.'

This time, there was a sparkle in Sebastian's eyes as his lips closed over hers again. 'How very appropriate,' he murmured huskily. 'Love conquers all. Well, if that is to be the nature of the lesson, my darling Desirée, I think I shall be only too happy to be the pupil!'

* * * * *

A Noble Man
by
Anne Ashley

Anne Ashley was born and educated in Leicester. She lived for a time in Scotland, but now lives in the West Country with two cats, her two sons and a husband who has a wonderful and very necessary sense of humour. When not pounding away at her keyboard, she likes to relax in her garden, which she has opened to the public on more than one occasion in aid of the village church funds.

Chapter One

March 1812

The Earl of Yardley glared in frustrated silence at his daughter's lustrous blue-black curls. Anyone might be forgiven for supposing that Lady Sophia's bent head and clasped hands expressed contrition, but he was not fooled for a moment. Oh, most definitely not! Unless he much mistook the matter, his daughter's striking green eyes were twinkling while she was doing her level best to conceal that wickedly provocative smile of hers.

'So, you flatly refuse even to consider this latest proposal,' he reiterated, still somehow managing to keep a tight rein on his temper. Any other young woman would have been overjoyed to receive four offers for her hand since her arrival in town a mere two weeks ago. His Sophia, however, was a law unto herself!

Swinging round on his heels, he went across the room to stare sightlessly out of the library window. 'At least may I be permitted to know why you have taken Lord Vale in such dislike?'

'Oh, I do not dislike him, Papa,' his most undutiful offspring hurriedly assured him. 'The truth of the matter is I haven't known him long enough to form an opinion.'

'In that case, what can be your objection other than a need to know him a little better?'

Sophia, with a suspicion of wicked amusement still lingering in her eyes after learning of this latest offer for her hand, raised her head at last. 'Well, apart from the fact that he will never see forty again, he is the only gentleman of my acquaintance who could sit in a carriage and stare out of both windows at one and the same time.'

A noise sounding suspiciously like a suppressed chuckle reached her ears, and she looked across the room at her father's surprisingly straight back and silver-grey hair. For a gentleman who had celebrated his seventy-first birthday just a few short weeks before, he was still in fine physical condition. 'Papa, you don't seriously expect me to consider this offer from Lord Vale, do you?'

He didn't, but he had no intention of admitting to it. 'You seem to forget that I was several years older than Lord Vale is now when I proposed to your mother.'

'True, but you were such a distinguished-looking

gentleman...still are, for that matter. Besides which, you haven't a turn in your left eye.'

'Don't try those wheedling ways with me, my girl!' his lordship snapped, striving not to let his favourite child twist him round her little finger, which, sadly, she so often did. 'Very well, I can understand your reluctance in not wishing to consider Vale's offer, but what about the one from young Farley?'

Sophia's finely arched brows rose. 'Are you by any chance acquainted with the Honourable Cedric Farley? I don't think you possibly can be, sir...He's a moonling!'

Once again his lordship was forced to exercise the firmest control in order to conceal his amusement. His daughter was nothing if not brutally candid. 'And what were your objections to both Pelham and Neubert, may I ask?'

'A pair of tailor's dummies!'

'God in heaven!' His lordship clapped a hand over his eyes. 'Where in the world do you learn such expressions?'

The exaggerated raising of one brow was a clear indication that she considered the question totally unnecessary. 'From the male members of this household, who else?'

Not best pleased at suddenly finding himself at a disadvantage, the Earl went striding back across to his desk. 'I'll have a word with that brother of yours when next I see him. He must learn to put a guard on his tongue when you're about.'

'I'm reliably informed that Marcus should be arriving any time now, and intends to stay in town for a week or two. I must say though, Papa, I think you're being grossly unfair to take him to task,' she pointed out in her absent half-brother's defence, 'especially as you yourself use the most appalling cant when in my presence.'

He was about to refute this, but then thought better of it and, instead, scooped up and waved the letters he had received during the past two weeks from those four hapless suitors. 'Don't think that you can lead me away from the matter in hand, you cunning little minx!'

The only effect this mild rebuke had on his head-strong daughter was to make her smile more brilliantly, and his lordship's annoyance finally got the better of him. 'You appear to take a light view of marriage, Sophia. Well, permit me to point out that it is a very serious business. An ill-judged choice of partner only brings misery to all concerned, and I do not intend that you should make a mistake in your choice of husband if it is within my power to prevent it. So, I have come to a decision.'

He paused for a moment to ensure that he had her full attention. 'I have made no secret of the fact that I intend to settle a large sum of money upon you when you marry. There is, however, a condition attached to my generosity. If you choose to marry without my consent, then your future husband had better possess sufficient funds to support you, because you will receive not a penny from me.' Again he paused while he tossed the letters from the rejected suitors back on the desk. 'Now, do I make myself clear?'

'Perfectly, sir. What you are trying to tell me is that I may marry whomsoever I choose providing he has wealth and belongs to our social class.' An ominous glint replaced the teasing sparkle in her eyes, as Sophia rose gracefully from the chair nearest to the hearth. 'It would appear, then, that I am destined to lead a life of hardship, for I would far rather be poor and married to a man of real worth than riveted to some empty-headed fribble whose only concern is how best to tie his cravat.'

His lordship could be as determined as his headstrong daughter when he chose, and refused to give way on this issue. 'I would suggest that you go up to your room and think very seriously about this matter,' he remarked, unbending.

Obediently she moved across to the door, but turned back to add, eyes still glinting, though whether in anger or devilment or a mixture of both, his lordship wasn't perfectly sure. 'Of course I shall do as you wish, but not for any great length of time. Mama would not be best pleased if I were late in putting in an appearance at my very own ball.' And with that quite deliberately provocative remark she left the room, and her father wondering what he had ever done that the gods should have seen fit to curse him with such a headstrong chit of a girl.

The Countess, emerging from the front parlour in

time to see her daughter mount the stairs, was not
slow to notice the stubborn set of those lovely features, and knew even before she entered the library
to find her husband glowering out of the window that
the interview had not progressed quite as he might
have wished.

'I assume Vale's offer received the same contemptuous refusal as the other three,' she remarked, seating
herself in the chair recently vacated by Sophia.

'That daughter of yours is impossible!' his lordship
snapped. Which, of course, was answer enough.

'Why is it, Thomas, that she is always my daughter
whenever she has displeased you in some way, and
your darling little Sophie at all other times?'

Annoyed though he was, he could not help smiling
at this undeniable truth. He turned to look at the
woman who had brought real peace and contentment
to his life, and not for the first time blessed
Providence for ensuring that their paths had crossed
all those years ago out in India.

Unlike Danielle, his first wife, Marissa had never
possessed any real claim to beauty, not even in her
youth, and yet his lordship considered that her many
wonderful qualities had withstood the test of time,
whereas mere prettiness never could. She had proven
to be a devoted wife and loving mother to their own
offspring, and even though she had failed completely
to cement a maternal bond with Marcus, the only
child by his first marriage, his eldest son had never

made any secret of the fact that he held his stepmother in the highest esteem.

A sigh escaped him as he drew his mind back to the present, and seated himself in the chair on the opposite side of the hearth. 'I fear, my dear, that I have made a mull of it all. Sophia flatly refuses even to consider Vale's offer.'

Her ladyship smiled faintly. 'Can you honestly say that you're surprised? He is, after all, a good deal older than she. Apart from his wealth, he has little to commend him, and I'm afraid the size of a gentleman's fortune would have very little influence on our daughter.'

'She has made that abundantly clear.' The Earl's grey brows snapped together, clearly revealing his continuing displeasure. 'Of course, all this flagrant disregard for wealth and rank was instilled in her at that confounded school. She ought never to have gone there, Marissa! That Guarding creature is nothing short of a revolutionary, with her nonsensical notions of equality.'

Once again the Countess smiled that serene smile of hers. 'If you recall, Thomas, we both agreed that Sophia would benefit from a year or two away at school. It was, let me remind you, you who insisted that she should not be placed in any one of those superior seminaries in Bath, where she would be absent from home for weeks at a time. The Guarding Academy, being situated so close to home, and having such a good reputation, was the most obvious choice.

And as regards what she learnt there…' Her ladyship reached for her embroidery and began calmly to ply her needle. 'She learnt nothing from Mrs Guarding that you yourself did not instil in all your children. From an early age all four of them were taught to treat those less fortunate than themselves with fairness and civility. And that, my dear Thomas, is precisely why we rarely have a servant wishing to leave our employ.'

He found himself quite unable to argue with this. 'Very true, my dear,' he concurred. 'I do believe in treating good and loyal servants courteously, but that doesn't mean I'd be content to have a footman as a son-in-law.'

Her ladyship's brows rose at this. 'And what on earth makes you suppose that there is any likelihood of that occurring?'

'Because that confounded daughter of yours can be quite stubbornly headstrong when the mood takes her!' his lordship retorted, irritation surfacing again. 'She as good as informed me that nothing would induce her to marry a member of her own social class, and that she would far rather be poor and riveted to some impoverished nobody, would you believe?'

The Countess regarded her husband in silence for a moment, realising suddenly that far more had taken place between father and daughter than she had at first realised. 'Why should Sophia imagine that she will ever be poor? She is an heiress. You have agreed to settle a fortune on her.'

For the first time his lordship betrayed clear signs of unease. 'Only on condition she marries with my full approval,' he mumbled, already regretting having issued such a threat.

It was only to be expected that a girl accustomed to having most everything her own way almost from the day of her birth would kick over the traces when finding herself harnessed for the very first time. But what choice had he? He had only her best interests at heart. Why in heaven's name couldn't the headstrong chit see that!

Feeling suddenly weary, he leaned back in his chair. 'Oh, Marissa, I'm at a loss to know what to do for the best. I'm one-and-seventy. I can't live for ever. I do not doubt for a moment that the boys will go on very well without me, but who will take care of my little Sophia when I'm gone?'

Refusing to become depressed at discussing such a melancholy topic, her ladyship said, 'Marcus will, I'm certain, admirably fill your shoes when the time comes. Which I sincerely trust will not be for several years yet.' She clearly heard the faint derisive snort. 'You do Marcus a grave injustice, my dear, if you suppose for a moment that he would neglect his responsibilities. He has looked after your estate in the north superbly during these past years. I know that he sometimes seems hard and unapproachable, but beneath that prickly exterior he is a very considerate man. He is very fond of his twin brothers, and of Sophia in particular.'

Much to his intense regret, his lordship had never been able to deal well with his eldest child. None the less, he was fair-minded enough to admit that his wife was right. 'But remember, my dear, that Marcus will one day marry himself, and raise a family. He will not then wish to be saddled with the added burden of keeping his eye on his frequently wayward half-sister.'

'She might be wilful on occasions, Thomas,' her ladyship responded, once again finding herself coming to Sophia's defence, 'but she's no fool. She may still harbour some girlish romantic notions, but I believe she will think long and hard before she ties herself to any man.'

The Earl remained unconvinced, but the Countess had more faith in their daughter's judgement. 'Leave it to me, my dear,' she said in her placid way. 'I'll have a talk with her.'

Final arrangements for the ball kept the Countess occupied for the remainder of the afternoon. Even if this had not been the case she would still have refrained from searching out her daughter and raising the topic of marriage, simply because it could only make the situation worse if Sophia felt that both her parents were intent on her making a superb match before the Season was over.

In fact, nothing could have been further from the truth. Although the Countess could well understand her husband's concern over their only daughter's future, and could appreciate, too, even though he had not admitted to it in so many words, that he was eager to keep fortune-hunters at bay, she saw no earthly reason why Sophia should not relax and enjoy her first Season in London. If she did happen to make the acquaintance of some personable gentleman with whom she could happily spend the rest of her life, all well and good; if not…well, there was always next year.

It was in this very understanding mood that the Countess entered her daughter's bedchamber in time to see the skilful young abigail positioning a spray of silk flowers in Sophia's beautifully arranged black locks. Unlike her occasionally volatile daughter, her ladyship always kept a tight hold on her emotions, but there was definitely a hint of pride in her grey eyes as she studied her daughter's faultless appearance.

'My dear, you look utterly charming,' she announced in her quiet way, while nodding dismissal to the maid.

Although Mother Nature had been undoubtedly generous, blessing her with lovely face and figure to match, Sophia was singularly lacking in conceit, as she proved now by glancing at her reflection with scant enthusiasm. 'This is a very pretty gown, Mama, and I do like it very well, but I would have preferred to have it made up in dark blue or red. Madame Félice said that, with my colouring, vibrant shades would suit me best.'

'And Madame Félice has earned herself something of a reputation for never being wrong, I know,' the Countess responded. 'Nonetheless, I'm still old-fashioned enough to believe that only pastel shades are suitable for young ladies. After you're married, of course, the wearing of richer colours will be perfectly in order.'

She caught her daughter's suddenly assessing look in the dressing-table mirror, and smiled. No, she mused, there was precious little wrong with Sophia's understanding. Nor did she suppose for a moment that her daughter would disgrace herself by eloping with some penniless nobody, providing, of course, pressure was not brought to bear which might induce her to commit such folly.

'No, my dear, I didn't come to your room with the intention of discussing the subject of marriage,' she assured her, knowing precisely what was going through that pretty little head. 'I should imagine you've heard more than enough on that particular topic for one day.'

Sophia almost sighed with relief. Her mother, always remarkably composed, was unfailingly sympathetic to the feelings of others. How she wished she could be more like her! Sadly, though, she feared she had inherited the occasionally fiery and frequently stubborn Cleeve temperament.

'I've never known Papa to be so unreasonable before. He seems to suppose that only a person of rank and wealth will make me a good husband.'

The Countess, appreciating only too well her poor husband's dilemma, remained silent. How could a loving father explain to a much beloved daughter that her hand might be sought in marriage for her fortune alone, without hurting her feelings?

'And yet it was he who instilled in us all,' Sophia went on, 'that a servant can exhibit just as much nobility as a duke. Perhaps he taught me too well, for I would much rather be married to a good and worthy man, no matter what his position on the social ladder, than marry a titled gentleman simply because by doing so I could continue to live in luxury.' She cast her mother a look of entreaty. 'You can understand that, can't you, Mama?'

'Better than you think, my dear. What you are trying to say is that you wish to marry a man you can love and respect and, moreover, a man who will love and respect you in return.' Seating herself on the *chaise-longue*, she held out her hand and waited for her daughter to join her before adding, 'Your father wants that too. He is only concerned for your happiness, Sophia. He would do everything within his power to ensure that you do not make the mistake that he once made.'

The Earl's first marriage was a subject that was rarely mentioned—taboo, almost. Sophia had, none the less, learned enough over the years from elderly servants and friends of the family to be certain that her father bitterly regretted marrying the beautiful Danielle.

'Yes, I do understand,' she said softly. 'But I have yet to meet a man with whom I could happily spend the rest of my life. I'm afraid, Mama, that the Lord Vales of this world are not to my taste.'

'Middle-aged dandies were never to mine either, child,' the Countess confessed, giving her daughter's hand an affectionate pat. 'There is no earthly reason why you should accept a proposal of marriage if you do not wish to. Sooner or later I feel certain that you will meet some personable young gentleman who will succeed in capturing your heart, but until such time, do not worry your pretty head over it any more.'

This was easier said than done. Although slightly reassured by her mother's understanding attitude, Sophia remained decidedly troubled. She hated being at odds with her father, while at the same time she continued to resent the unreasonable stand he had adopted. Was it her fault that four gentlemen had proposed marriage to her since her arrival in town? She certainly hadn't offered any one of them the least encouragement, unless agreeing to partner someone in a dance was considered sufficient inducement for a gentleman to propose marriage.

It was all so ridiculous, she decided, rising to her feet and accompanying her mother from the room. She had barely exchanged more than a dozen words with any one of those rejected suitors, so what on earth had made them suppose that she would make an ideal wife?

She was not so small-minded as to suppose that

just because love at first sight was a phenomenon that she herself had failed to experience the event never took place. She was well aware, too, that gentlemen were frequently beguiled by a pretty face. She could not help wondering, though, whether she would appear quite so appealing to certain members of the opposite sex if it were not for the fifty thousand pounds her father had promised to settle upon her when she married.

A slow and wickedly calculating smile curled the corners of what one besotted young fop had been overheard to call the most kissable mouth in London, as Sophia caught sight of her father standing at the entrance to the ballroom in readiness to greet the first of the guests. His threat to disinherit her if she married without his approval might well be turned to her advantage. If it became common knowledge that she wasn't an heiress at all, those offers for her hand might swiftly lessen and, with any luck, cease altogether, leaving her free to enjoy her first Season in London without causing further friction between her and her sire.

The idea, once firmly embedded, quickly began to grow, and Sophia had little difficulty in putting her plan into effect by dropping a word here and there into a receptive ear. Although the Season had not officially begun, London was certainly not thin of company, and invitations to the Yardley ball had been eagerly accepted. Among the four hundred guests were many hopeful mamas whose daughters sadly possessed scant claim to beauty. It was only to be expected, therefore, that some doting parents would be only too willing to pass on unfavourable snippets concerning a dangerous rival, especially if it increased their own offspring's chances of achieving a suitable match.

Consequently, as the evening progressed, Sophia became increasingly satisfied with the many long and thoughtful glances cast in her direction. She was not so foolish as to suppose for a moment that everyone would believe the rumour which was circulating about her, nor did she consider that a supposed lack of fortune would deter every gentleman from making her an offer, and made allowances for this contingency by not standing up with the same gentleman more than once.

Nevertheless, she was never short of a partner, and the evening was well advanced before she managed to leave the dance floor and search out her good friend Robina Perceval, who also happened to be enjoying her first London Season.

'This is a truly magnificent ball,' Robina announced when Sophia had almost slumped, exhausted, in the vacant chair beside her. 'I do not think I've ever seen so many people crowded into one room before. The dances Aunt Eleanor organises at the Angel back home are nothing to it.'

Sophia was not so impressed. Unlike Robina, who lived a rather quiet life at the vicarage in Abbot Quincey, a small market town situated within easy walking distance of the Cleeves' country home, Sophia had attended many large parties since the age of sixteen. 'Yes, a dreadful squeeze, isn't it? You'll need to accustom yourself to such gatherings, Robin, because I'm reliably informed that a party isn't considered a success unless you're forever stepping on someone's toes.'

She took a moment to gaze about the crowded ballroom, trying to pick out the odd familiar face. 'I was sorry to learn that your cousin Hester would not be attending, but her brother Hugo is here. I danced with him earlier.'

'I understand that Aunt Eleanor and Hester will not be arriving in town until April.' Robina couldn't help but smile. 'I think if it was left to Hester she wouldn't be coming at all. Unlike Hugo, she has no taste for town life. She would much prefer to remain locked away in that attic room of hers. Though what she finds to keep her so occupied up there for hours at a time is anybody's guess. Who would believe a brother and sister could be so dissimilar!'

Her smile faded as she glanced at her friend's lovely profile. They had known each other most all their lives, and had always been the very best of friends, so Robina experienced no hesitation in saying, 'I think you should know that there is a rather unpleasant rumour circulating about you tonight.' It was then she noticed the betraying twitch at the corner of her friend's mouth. 'Never tell me that you put it about that you haven't a feather to fly with! What on earth possessed you?'

Well aware that the vicar's daughter would never betray a confidence, Sophia didn't hesitate in enlightening her. 'So you see,' she went on, after repeating the gist of the interview with her father earlier in the day, 'I was forced to do something to stem these ridiculous proposals of marriage. And it isn't as if the rumour is a lie. Papa has threatened to disinherit me if I marry against his wishes.' A defiant little gleam sprang into her eyes. 'And to be perfectly honest with you, at this precise moment in time I'm inclined to do precisely that.'

Robina sat silently digesting what she had learned. She had been taught to consider envy a sin, but couldn't help feeling a touch resentful over her friend's privileged position. Their circumstances were vastly contrasting. Sophia could reject suitors at will, whereas she herself would need to consider very carefully any offer of marriage that came her way. There was no fault to find with her lineage: both her parents came from noble stock. The Perceval name was an old and honoured one, but that did not alter the fact that she was little more than a country parson's daughter whose dowry was woefully small. Her parents, though comfortably circumstanced, were by no means wealthy, and they most certainly could not afford a second London Season for their eldest daughter with three younger ones eagerly waiting to be launched into society. So Robina felt it her duty to accept any reasonable offer of marriage. But how she wished that she too could marry just for love!

'I have been away from the steadying influence of the vicarage a few days only,' she remarked with a wry little smile, 'yet already I'm in danger of being corrupted by the dangerously frivolous lures and heady atmosphere of the metropolis.'

Sophia frankly laughed. 'My staid little friend being led astray…? By whom or what, may I ask?'

'I shall explain some other time, for unless I much mistake the matter, a gentleman is approaching, with every intention of asking you to dance.'

Lord Nicholas Risely was, indeed, heading in their direction. Tall, slim and very good-looking, he was a firm favourite with a great many of society's leading hostesses and, consequently, was invited everywhere. His attire was faultless, his address excellent, and as he just happened to be the son of a duke, albeit a younger one, he was looked upon as being a very eligible *parti*.

In the normal course of events these facts alone would have prompted Sophia to add his name to that list of gentlemen best avoided, but she had not. Instead, she had permitted him to add his name to her dance card, simply because she had been most reliably informed that Lord Nicholas Risely was not on the look-out for a wife.

Happily allowing him to lead her onto the dance floor, she couldn't help noticing the strange look he cast her as they prepared to join one of the sets.

'Something appears to be troubling you, my lord,' she remarked. 'I cannot imagine you are concerned over making a cake of yourself. You are such an excellent dancer.'

As luck would have it the steps of the dance separated them, which granted Lord Nicholas the opportunity of formulating a response. Having met her on two occasions before, he had already decided that he rather liked Sophia Cleeve. She was bright and witty, nothing like the majority of simpering misses who flooded the marriage mart every year. If he had not been quite content to continue with his bachelor existence for a few years longer, she would have been just the sort of girl that would have appealed to him.

She was immensely pleasing on the eye, too. Perhaps not a beauty in the true classical style, but certainly lovely enough to prompt many a spiteful tabby with a daughter of her own to launch to start spreading malicious gossip about lack of fortune in the hope of making the lovely Lady Sophia appear far less desirable. It was all so unfair, so underhanded, and he for one had no intention of aiding any match-making mama's cause by repeating what he had overheard that night.

'Nothing troubling me at all, my lady,' he assured her, as they came together again. 'Couldn't be happier. This is a wonderful ball, and I am honoured to be dancing with its belle.'

'How very gallant of you to say so, Lord Nicholas! Had any other gentleman said such a thing I would have been instantly on my guard, but with you I know I'm perfectly safe.'

Now what the deuce did she mean by that? he wondered, as they separated, and didn't hesitate to ask for an explanation when they came together again.

'Simply that your good friend Freddy Fortescue assures me that you're not about to relinquish your bachelor status quite yet and, therefore, I can accept your compliments without fear that you will be foolish enough to follow them up with a proposal of marriage.'

Nicholas blinked. This was plain-speaking of the highest order, and he wasn't certain that he cared for it very much. He might not have any intention of asking this chit, or any other for that matter, to marry him, but it was very lowering to be told that one's suit would never be welcomed anyway.

Sophia was not slow to notice the flicker of annoyance. 'I've offended you, my lord, and I never meant to do so,' she assured him, her dazzling smile going some way to soothe a young gentleman's bruised ego. 'It's just that I too am in no hurry to relinquish my single state either, and when I do it will never be to a member of the Ton.'

He thought for a moment that she couldn't possibly be serious, that she might well be indulging in some wicked jest. Then he recalled being informed earlier in the evening that Lord Vale's suit had not prospered. The gentleman himself was not present tonight to confirm this or not, though whether his absence stemmed from pique at having been rejected, or having a prior engagement, was anyone's guess.

'You see, Lord Nicholas, men of wealth and rank hold no appeal for me.' Sophia decided that it could only aid her cause to spread this about. 'I am determined to marry a worthy man, no matter how lowly his station in life.'

'A footman, rather than a marquis; a groom rather than a duke,' he suggested, half-joking. 'I rather think your father will have a thing or two to say about that, Lady Sophia.'

'Oh, he already has, believe me,' she didn't hesitate to disclose, 'but his threat to disinherit me is certainly no deterrent.'

Still doubtful whether to believe her or not, he returned her to her pretty friend's side once the dance came to an end, and promptly moved away in order to sample some of the excellent refreshments being served that evening. He had only just relieved a footman of a glass of champagne when he received a tap on the shoulder, and heard an imperious voice enquire, 'Well, Risely, is what I've learned true or not?'

He turned to discover that most feared patroness of Almack's regarding him with haughtily raised brows. Had it been anyone else he might have been tempted not to answer, but one ignored Sally Jersey at one's peril. 'Couldn't say for certain, ma'am, one way or t'other. Shouldn't imagine so, though, would you? The Earl of Yardley seems dashed too fond of his daughter to disinherit her.'

She dismissed this with a wave of one slender hand. 'I'm not talking about that piece of utter nonsense. I really don't know how these foolish rumours get started. No, it was to Sharnbrook I was referring. I ran into your sister the other day, paying one of her rare visits to town, and she mentioned that nothing had been heard from your brother in months.'

'Oh, aye, that's right enough,' he confirmed, betraying what some might consider a callous lack of concern. 'We received a letter from him six months ago, after he had learned of our father's death, stating his intention of returning to this country before the end of the year. Can only imagine that something must have detained him out there in Jamaica.'

'Well, you may tell him from me, when he does return, that he's not to hide himself away in that magnificent ancestral home of his. We hostesses need him here in London. Such a matrimonial prize! Why, all the young ladies will be eager to capture his interest.'

'Oh, no—not quite all,' he murmured, catching sight of a raven-haired beauty being led once again on to the dance floor.

Chapter Two

Lord Nicholas Risely was among the first guests to leave the ball. He certainly managed to raise a few startled brows when he took his gracious leave of the host and hostess, for he had gained the reputation, since entering society two years before, of being a very sociable young man whose energy seemed boundless. Rarely did he seek the comfort of his bed much before three in the morning, once the social rounds had begun. Tonight, however, he seemed to have lost his desire for company, enjoyable though the Yardley ball had been.

Without waiting for a servant to find him a hackney carriage, he stepped outside into the cool night air and, heedless of any possible footpad lurking in this fashionable part of the town, walked briskly in the direction of his small but comfortable London home.

Although he had managed to appear sublimely unconcerned at the time, his short conversation with Lady Jersey had renewed those feelings of disquiet over his brother's safety which had plagued him increasingly during these past weeks. In the last letter sent from Jamaica, Benedict had clearly stated his intention of returning to the land of his birth some time during the autumn. That was almost six months ago, and nothing had been heard from him since.

It was quite possible, of course, that he had been forced to change his plans and had delayed his departure. It was equally possible that a letter informing his family of his revised plans had gone astray. Nevertheless Nicholas could not wholly dismiss the possibility, no matter how hard he tried, that some accident had befallen the Seventh Duke of Sharnbrook.

Long sea voyages were dangerous undertakings at the best of times, and more so during these past troubled years. Britain's splendid navy might be master of the seas, but those gallant sailors could not guard every stretch of water, and an attack from a French vessel was an ever-present danger. More disturbing still was the memory of those vicious gales which had wreaked havoc along the coast during the winter months, whipping the seas into a frenzy and causing more than one vessel to come to grief. The Atlantic was a vast ocean; any sailing ship foundering out there miles from land might not be reported missing for some considerable time.

He tried not to dwell on this dreadful possibility as he arrived back at his house. Not only had he a sincere regard for the brother he had not seen for more

than half a decade, but he had no desire whatsoever
to step into Benedict's shoes as head of the family.
He was more than content with his carefree bachelor
existence, and although he didn't consider himself to
be in the least light-minded, he recoiled at the mere
thought of having to accept responsibility for the running of the family's vast estate in Hampshire, not to
mention the other sizeable properties dotted about the
land.

Extracting the key from his pocket, he let himself
inside the house. As he was never very sure of precisely when he would be returning home, he never
encouraged his worthy factotum to wait up for him,
and was faintly surprised to discover his butler-cum-
valet dozing in the comfortable leather-bound chair in
the hall.

'What's all this, Figgins? Why aren't you abed,
man?' he demanded, as the servant awoke with a start
at the closing of the door.

Having been in service most of his life, Figgins was
quite accustomed to the ways of the nobility, and was
not in the least offended by his young master's rather
impatient tone.

Although he had always considered himself to be
a very superior valet, he had not been averse, after
his previous master had passed away, to accepting a
position as general factotum in this small but fashionable household. He had worked for Lord Nicholas for
the past two years, and could say with a clear con-

science that not once had he ever committed the least solecism—never until tonight.

Rising to his feet, he cast a faintly concerned look in the direction of the parlour. 'I felt it my duty, sir, in the—er—circumstances, to await your return in order to apprise you.'

'Apprise me of what, may I ask?' Nicholas prompted when his very correct manservant cast a further glance in the direction of the parlour's closed door.

'Of the fact, sir, that there is someone else awaiting your return.'

Nicholas, having by this time divested himself of his outdoor garments, gave his servant his full attention. It was by no means unusual for him to return home in the early hours to discover one of his many friends sound asleep on the couch in the parlour, so he was at a loss to understand why Figgins should be making such an issue of the fact.

'Well, who is it? Harry Harmond?'

'No, sir. It is someone I've certainly never seen before.' Figgins, who rarely displayed the least emotion, permitted himself a thin smile of satisfaction. 'I have always prided myself on being an excellent judge of character, able to pinpoint very accurately a person's station in life. And I certainly know an encroaching individual when I see one.' His smile disappeared. 'But I am forced to admit that the person who called shortly after you had left the house, and who is now comfortably ensconced in the parlour, has me well and truly puzzled. His appearance leaves—er—much to be desired, as you might say, but his speech and manners are those of an undoubted gentleman. I have therefore formed the opinion, sir, although he stubbornly refused to give his name, that he must be an old acquaintance of yours who has, perhaps, fallen on hard times.'

For a few moments it was as much as Nicholas could do to gape in open-mouthed astonishment. 'And you let him in? Good gad, man, you must be all about in your head!'

Nicholas was by no means a hard-hearted person, and would willingly come to the aid of a friend, should the need arise, but he refused to be taken advantage of by some rascally individual he barely knew. 'What in the world prompted you to admit him? The rogue has probably taken himself off long since. And with all my best silver, if I know anything!'

'Oh no, sir. He hasn't done that,' Figgins responded, completely unruffled. 'And I can assure you, sir, that I would never have permitted him to set foot inside the house, let alone provide him with supper and a glass or two of wine, if it hadn't been for the fact that he informed me that he had news concerning your brother.'

'Oh, he has, has he?' Nicholas was decidedly sceptical. 'Well, his tidings had better be worth the food and drink he's consumed already at my expense,' he ground out, throwing wide the parlour door, and striding purposefully into the room to discover the shabbily dressed individual sprawled at his ease in the most comfortable chair in the house. 'Otherwise he'll find himself helped on his way by the toe of my boot!'

A slow and lazy smile tugged at the corners of the visitor's well-shaped mouth, but the eyes remained firmly closed as he said, 'I shall take leave to inform you that I consider that a most impolite greeting to offer someone you haven't seen for several years, dear brother.'

Nicholas stopped dead in his tracks, once again powerless to prevent his jaw from dropping perceptively when the lids of dazzling blue eyes finally opened and the visitor rose to his feet in one graceful movement. 'Benedict?' he murmured, taking a hesitant step forward. Then, 'Ben, by all that's wonderful!…It is you!'

Figgins, hovering in the open doorway, experienced a sense of pride as he watched the two men clasp each other warmly. It was comforting to know that his instincts had not played him false and that the very welcome visitor, taller than his brother by an inch or two, and noticeably broader, had turned out to be what he had suspected from the start—a gentleman of quality.

He coughed delicately, thereby indicating his continued presence, and the brothers loosened their hold. 'Do you wish me to fetch brandy, m'lord?'

'Yes. Yes, of course,' Nicholas answered, still

somewhat bemused by his sibling's unexpected arrival. 'And make sure it's the best brandy, Figgins. This calls for a celebration.'

After his servant had departed, Nicholas busied himself for a minute or two by going about the room lighting more candles, and then joined his brother by the hearth. He was quite unable to forbear a smile as he watched Benedict piling more logs on what was already a substantial fire. Evidently the British climate no longer agreed with him, which was hardly surprising after spending so many years abroad. This, however, was by no means the most obvious change in him.

No one viewing him now would ever have supposed for a moment that Benedict had once been considered a dandy, rivalling the famous Beau Brummell himself in dress. Nicholas recalled quite clearly watching his brother on numerous occasions, sitting before a dressing-table mirror, patiently tying intricate folds in a highly starched cravat until he had it just so. Yet here he sat, now, with a gaudy red kerchief tied about his throat, his long legs encased in a pair of rough homespun trousers, and a slightly soiled and heavily creased shirt encasing that broad expanse of chest. Why, he looked little better than a vagrant with that mass of golden-brown hair almost touching his shoulders. And the weeks of growth on and around his chin did absolutely nothing to improve his appearance!

'By that disapproving look,' Benedict remarked, after raising his striking blue eyes in time to catch his brother's frowning scrutiny, 'I assume my appearance does not meet with your approval.'

'Good gad, Ben! You resemble nothing so much as a rascally vagrant.'

'I am relieved the hard-working soul who gave me these clothes isn't present,' Benedict responded, with more than a hint of wryness. 'He would have been most offended. This shirt, I am assured, was his very best. Though it isn't strictly true, I suppose, to say that he gave me these clothes,' he corrected. 'We struck a bargain. I exchanged them for a suit of my own. And was heartily glad to do so! I was sick and tired of my own apparel after several weeks at sea.'

'Do you mean to say you exchanged all your clothes for those…those deplorable rags?' Nicholas did not believe a word of it. 'You must take me for a half-wit if you think I'll swallow that one.'

'True as I sit here, dear brother,' Benedict assured him. 'Except I only gave him the clothes I stood up in. They were all I had, you see. Pirates deprived me of the rest.'

Once again Nicholas found himself gaping. 'Pirates? What pirates?'

'The ones we unfortunately encountered two days after setting sail from Port Royal.' Benedict smiled at his young brother's decidedly sceptical look. 'Sailing through the Caribbean is not the same as taking a boat trip down the Thames, dear boy. It is still a dangerous place. Many people of varying nationalities, fleeing from the law, seek refuge there. Piracy is still quite common, believe me.'

'What happened?' Nicholas prompted, suddenly resembling an excited schoolboy, and Benedict was of a mind to be indulgent.

'The captain of our ship, being a Christian soul, could not find it within himself to blithely ignore what appeared to be a vessel in distress, and gave the order to heave-to. Grappling-hooks were thrown with remarkable speed, and before the captain and crew realised what was happening we were being boarded by a horde of cut-throats. The captain and crew of our ship gave a good account of themselves, as did a couple of the passengers, and we soon had the rogues returning to their own vessel, but not before they had deprived us of some of the food on board, and several other items of worth, including my trunk, which contained not only my clothes, but my valuables, too. Consequently all I was left with were the clothes I stood up in. And, as you can imagine, by the time we had docked in Liverpool, I was heartily glad to be rid of them, even to exchange them for the ones I'm wearing now.'

Nicholas could well understand this and smiled, until a thought suddenly occurred to him. 'How on earth did you manage to reach London without money? Surely you didn't walk?'

'Thankfully, I wasn't reduced to that, though it could hardly have been more uncomfortable than travelling by the common stage. I have grown accustomed to doing without many creature comforts during my time in Jamaica, but sitting for hours in a vehicle that smells of perspiration, onions, and various other unpleasant odours was almost more than I could bear.'

His pained expression almost had his young brother writhing in laughter. 'No, I still retained my pocket watch, which I was able to sell for half its real value. I swear the rogue who purchased it in Liverpool thought it had been stolen.'

'I can't say I'm surprised,' Nicholas responded when he had gained sufficient control of himself. 'No one would take you for a member of the peerage!'

'That isn't strictly true,' Ben corrected. 'Your estimable butler, unless I much mistake the matter, managed to penetrate the disguise.' He glanced round as the door opened, his face brightening. 'And here he is, and armed, I see, with more of that delicious apple tart.'

'I thought, perhaps, you could manage another mouthful, your grace,' Figgins said, placing the tray containing the food and brandy down on a convenient table near his master's chair. 'Will there be anything else you require, sir?'

'Yes, you'd best make the bed up in the spare room, and look out one of my night-shirts.' Nicholas turned his attention back to his brother as soon as Figgins had left the room. 'There's only a skeleton staff now at the house in Grosvenor Square. The place hasn't been used since Father died.'

He searched in vain for a sign of remorse on his brother's handsome face, and yet he knew how fond Benedict had been of their father. 'He passed away peacefully in his sleep. He didn't suffer,' he assured him, and this time Benedict responded with a softly spoken, 'I'm glad,' and then promptly changed the subject by enquiring after their sister.

'Oh, Connie's in fine fettle. Put on some weight since the last time you saw her. Still,' he shrugged, 'only to be expected at her age. Increased the progeny by three since you've been away. Five of the little blighters she's produced now. Which says something for Lansdown, I suppose. I have a deal of respect for our dear brother-in-law. Poor chap must possess the patience of a saint to put up with our bird-witted sister.'

Benedict, willingly accepting a further slice of the apple tart and a full measure of the brandy, could not suppress a smile. No doubt Constance continued to treat Nicholas as though he were still a mischievous schoolboy, and his evident resentment was quite understandable. He decided to make his own feelings known.

'I perceive a great change in you, Nick.' He took a moment to study the very fashionable attire. 'Apeing the dandy yourself now, I see.'

'One must dress, dear brother.' The pained expression returned as his attention was drawn to that gaudy neck decoration once more. 'Just as well you did come straight here. Wouldn't do to let people see you

looking like that, you know. There's the name to consider, and all that,' he remarked with quaint snobbery.
'We'll rise early tomorrow and pay a visit to a tailor…Or perhaps several.'

The following morning Benedict discovered that
his brother's idea of rising early was not quite the
same as his own. So, after he had consumed a hearty
breakfast of ham, eggs and buttered rolls, washed
down with several cups of freshly-brewed coffee, and
there were still no signs that Nicholas was ready to
leave the comfort of his bedchamber and face the new
day, Benedict decided to pass the time by exploring
the metropolis to see what changes had taken place
during his years away.

He stepped outside to discover a morning that was
both dry and bright, and blessedly free from the evil
choking fog that often shrouded the city even at this
time of year. His athletic, long-striding gait quickly
brought him to the end of the street and into a wider
thoroughfare, where hordes of people were now busily going about their daily work.

This was the part of the city that he knew best of
all, where pretty girls in white pinafores and black
taffeta bonnets were parading the fashionable streets
and squares dispensing milk from the buckets they
carried, their cries mingling with those of other hawk-
ers, eager to sell their wares. This was where he had
happily frittered away his time, and money, paying
visits to friends and enjoying the many pleasurable

activities the capital had to offer any young gentleman of wealth and rank. This was what, five years ago, he had very much resented being forced to leave behind.

He remembered clearly the bitterness he had felt when his father had insisted that he travel to Jamaica and learn to respect the value of money by taking charge of the family's plantation out there. Their parting had been an unpleasant one, with many biting recriminations uttered on both sides. Not many months had passed, however, before Benedict had come to realise that his father's actions had been totally justified, and he could only be thankful that the majority of letters exchanged during their years apart had been full of warmth and understanding; his only real regret now being that he had not returned to England in time to see his father one last time before his death.

Yes, those years in Jamaica had changed him completely. He was no longer that care-for-nobody, that frivolous, pleasure-seeking fribble whose only ambition was to cut a dash in society, and who squandered vast sums of money without a thought to whose hard work financed his pleasures or from whence the money had come. Older and, hopefully, wiser now, he believed he could take his father's place and carry out his duties as head of the family in a responsible and caring manner. The cut of a jacket, the set of a cravat and a looking-glass shine on a pair of boots were no longer important to him. A sigh escaped him. Nevertheless he supposed it behoved him to take his brother's advice, and attire himself as befitted his station in life before returning to the fashionable world, a world that, if the truth were known, he had little desire to re-enter.

The stink of rotting refuse and equally unpleasant odours suddenly assailing his nostrils induced him to take stock of his surroundings. Without being aware of it, he had walked ever eastwards into those areas of the capital where most people of his class rarely or never ventured. The distinction between rich and poor could not have been more marked. There were no fine mansions here, no crossing-boys to clear away the filth from the streets, and no ladies and gentlemen, dressed in their finery, taking the air. Which was hardly surprising, he decided, ripping the kerchief from his neck and putting it to good use by placing it over his nose and mouth.

The air was foul, polluted by filth and grime which oozed from the tightly-packed hovels, and half-starved children, dressed in rags, or nothing at all, were grubbing round in the dirt. What it must be like here when the weather became warmer he dreaded to think. Little wonder these areas of the city harboured the constant threat of typhus. To the poor wretches living here disease and starvation were commonplace, a way of life from which there was little hope of escape.

He knew, of course, that it was the height of folly to remain in these noisome streets, where vice and corruption abounded on every corner, and yet he found his interest well and truly captured. So engrossed did he become in the heart-rending wretchedness surrounding him that it was not until almost noon that he ventured back to the more affluent part of the city, and was greeted none too politely when he did eventually return to his brother's house.

'Where the deuce have you been?' Nicholas demanded to know. 'Figgins informed me that you left the house hours ago.'

'That is correct.' Benedict joined him at the table, and helped himself to a cup of fresh coffee. 'I decided to occupy my time while waiting for you to rise in exploring the capital.'

'Expect you discovered some changes, eh?'

'Can't say I took much notice of the area round here. Whitechapel, Bethnal Green, Shoreditch and Smithfield certainly proved most interesting, though.'

'Good gad, Benedict!' Nicholas was beginning to wonder whether those years spent under a tropical sun might not have had some adverse effect on his brother's mental state. 'What on earth possessed you to venture to those spots? They're all notorious havens for every form of low life. Even the Runners won't enter those places alone, not even in broad daylight.' A disturbing possibility suddenly occurred to him. 'Dear Lord! You didn't go there to find a woman, did you?'

One ducal brow arched. 'Credit me with some intelligence. Not that I didn't receive several offers, but I have far too much respect for my health.'

'Well, thank the Lord for that!' his graceless brother responded, audibly sighing with relief. 'Though I'm rather surprised you managed to return totally unscathed.'

'Dressed as I am, I no doubt appeared one of their own and, therefore, not worthy of accosting.'

This candid response returned Nicholas's thoughts to what for him was the most pressing problem besetting him at the moment and, after hurriedly finishing his meagre repast, he wasted no further time in taking the first steps in putting his brother's deplorable appearance to rights.

It rather amused him to see the appalled expressions on those famous Bond Street tailors' faces when his brother entered their superior establishments in his wake. Benedict did not appear to take offence at the unenthusiastic reception he received wherever he went, and certainly displayed praiseworthy self-control when he was pulled this way and that, and measured with ruthless efficiency. Nicholas soon discovered, however, that beneath that veneer of complacency was an iron strong will, for nothing would induce Benedict to have his coats made fashionably tight, nor tempt him to select anything other than the plainest of colours for his clothes.

'Damned unimaginative! That's what I call it,' Nicholas remonstrated, as they emerged into the sunlight once more. 'Yellow-and-black-striped waistcoats are all the fashion this Season.'

'I do not doubt you are correct, brother. But I have

no intention of going about the capital resembling something that spends most of its life collecting pollen.'

Nicholas was about to cast further aspersions on what he considered a deplorably unimaginative taste, when he caught sight of one of his degenerate friends on the opposite side of the street, and took evasive action by concealing himself in a doorway.

'I have no intention either of wearing coats so close-fitting that one cannot breathe, or breeches so tight that they're in danger of splitting every time one sits down,' Benedict announced before he realised he was conversing with fresh air and, glancing round in an attempt to locate his sibling's whereabouts, promptly collided with something soft, slender and totally feminine emerging from Hookham's Library.

Benedict was powerless to prevent several books cascading from slender hands and ending up on the pavement, but managed to prevent the lady herself suffering the same fate by reaching out a steadying arm to encircle a very trim waist. 'I'm so very sorry,' he apologised, silently cursing his clumsiness, and was about to relinquish his hold when the head beneath the fashionable bonnet was suddenly raised.

For several moments it was as much as Benedict could do to stop himself gaping like some lovelorn fool as thickly lashed eyes, with a spark of mischief in their beautiful green depths, twinkled up at him, and perfectly moulded lips curled into the sweetest of smiles. Beauties he'd known by the score, but never before had the sight of a lovely face and trim figure held him so totally captive, mind and body under some hypnotic spell, quite unable to function. The sights and sounds around him slowly began to fade, and he was conscious only of her, and the ever-increasing desire never to relinquish his hold.

Nicholas, on the other hand, stepping out from the convenient hiding-place, was instantly aware of the interest his clumsy brother was arousing in several passers-by, and promptly took command of the situation by treading none too gently on one roughly shod foot. 'Don't just stand there like a dolt!' he ordered, sublimely ignoring the flashing look of annoyance he perceived in a pair of masculine eyes. 'Help this lady's maid to pick up those books!'

Very reluctantly Benedict did as bidden, and Nicholas wasted no time in escorting the young lady in question to her waiting carriage. 'Can't apologise enough. The clumsy brute might have done you a serious mischief. I trust you're none the worse for the encounter?'

'No, not at all, sir,' she assured him, her gaze momentarily wandering in the tall man's direction as he handed her maid the books. 'And please do not blame your servant. It was as much my fault as his. I was not attending where I was going either.'

Out of the corner of his eye Nicholas saw Benedict approaching, and hurriedly helped the lovely damsel into the carriage. 'You are too kind, ma'am,' he responded, stepping to one side to enable the maid to enter, and then wasted no time in closing the door.

'Why in heaven's name didn't you introduce me?' Benedict demanded, aggrieved, as he watched the carriage move away.

'What!' Once again Nicholas very much feared those years spent beneath a Caribbean sun had taken their toll. 'When I've done everything humanly possible to keep your identity secret since we left the house? You might have no pride in the name you bear, brother, but I most certainly have. Do you imagine I'll permit London to see you going about looking like that? Why, it would be the talk of the clubs for months to come if your identity ever became known!'

Catching the eye of a passing jarvey, Nicholas hurriedly bundled his troublesome brother into the hired carriage before Benedict could draw more attention to himself. 'I don't understand what's come over you, Ben. You used to take such pride in your appearance, and yet now you don't seem to care a whit that you look more like a didicoi than a duke.'

More interested in the lovely image his mind's eye was conjuring up, Benedict had listened with only half an ear to his brother's strictures. 'Who was she? Do you know?'

Nicholas cast him an impatient glance, wondering anew what had come over him. No one would have believed his brother capable of fending off an attack from pirates, when a pair of green eyes could fell him with one glance!

'Of course I know her. I was dancing with her only last night. She's Lady Sophia Cleeve, the Earl of Yardley's daughter.' He raised his eyes heavenwards when his brother's besotted expression did not alter. 'Anyone would suppose you'd never seen a pretty face before.'

'Pretty? A totally inappropriate description!' Benedict scoffed. 'She's exquisite.'

Nicholas considered this for a moment or two. 'Opinions differ. Some consider her a beauty. However, blondes are all the fashion this Season.'

His brother appeared decidedly unimpressed. Evidently flaxen hair was not to his taste. 'My, my, the little minx appears to have you well and truly in her toils,' Nicholas remarked, highly amused now by the unfortunate encounter with the Earl's daughter. 'Not that I don't think it's high time you were leg-shackled, brother, but if you take my advice you'll look elsewhere for a wife.'

A heart-rending possibility occurred to Benedict. 'She isn't married already, is she? Or engaged?'

'No, nor likely to be, either.'

'Why? What do you mean?'

'She doesn't seem interested in marriage. At least,' Nicholas amended, memory stirring, 'certainly not a marriage to a member of our class. If what she tells me is true, she prefers the company of grooms to dukes.'

'Ha! She must have been teasing you,' Benedict scoffed, thinking his brother highly gullible.

'Perhaps,' Nicholas conceded. 'I'm only repeating what I was told last night. Furthermore, she's received four proposals of marriage to my certain knowledge since her arrival in town, and has refused them all. Which would suggest that she certainly isn't hankering after a husband, let alone a title.' His wicked sense of humour coming to the fore, he gave a shout of laughter. 'Why, she paid more attention to you out there in the street just now than she pays to most members of her own class.'

Evidently his brother did not share the joke, for he sat silently staring out of the window. 'Don't disturb yourself,' Nicholas advised. 'There'll be plenty of other pretty wenches gracing the Season once it officially gets under way.'

'I dare say you're right,' Benedict murmured, a decidedly calculating gleam springing into his striking blue eyes, 'but it's Lady Sophia Cleeve I intend to get to know. So perhaps, all things considered, it might serve me best if I remain incognito for a while longer.'

'How on earth can that benefit you?' Nicholas asked, totally at a loss.

Benedict transferred his gaze to his sibling's puzzled countenance. 'You said yourself that she prefers the company of grooms...And if there is one thing I do know...it's my way around a stable!'

Chapter Three

The Earl of Yardley was essentially a man of habit, and his sojourn in the capital had not altered his routine to any great extent. Consequently, Cardew knew precisely where his master was to be found at this time of day, and entered the library to discover his lordship, as expected, seated at his desk, carefully studying his correspondence.

'I regret having to disturb you, sir,' he said, as the Earl, pausing in the perusal of the letter in his hand, raised an enquiring brow, 'but the head groom is here, requesting an interview with you.'

Like all the other servants, Cardew held his master in high esteem. During the twenty years he had been employed as butler in the Cleeve household he could never recall even one occasion when the Earl had been too busy to spare one of his employees some of his time, and he knew what the response would be even before his lordship said, 'Of course. I shall see him at once.'

Certain that his most loyal henchman would not seek an interview on some trivial matter, the Earl set aside his correspondence and a moment later watched his head groom enter, cap in hand, looking totally ill-at-ease, just as he always did whenever in elegant surroundings. Trapp was never happy when away from the stables for any length of time. Horses were his life, and his lordship suspected that he much preferred their company to that of most people.

'Well, come in, Trapp,' his lordship ordered when the groom, who had been with him all those years ago out in India, continued to hover by the door. 'What can I do for you?'

'I'm here on young Clem's behalf, sir.' Looking and sounding nothing like the iron-handed ruler of the stables whose word was law, and whose barking commands kept the youngest stable-lads in a permanent state of terror, he moved hesitantly across to the desk.

'Seemingly Clem's been offered a post as head groom on some large estate in the south, sir. I 'ave to say I don't want to lose 'im. He's a good lad and he's been with us for a number of years, but there's no denying it would be a good move for 'im.' His weather-beaten face creased into a semblance of a smile. 'I ain't quite ready to hang up the harness yet, as yer might say, so I can't blame Clem for not wanting to wait around until I do.'

His lordship nodded his head in agreement. 'Do you know precisely who has made him this offer of employment, Trapp?'

'That I don't, sir. Don't know that Clem does neither, if it comes to that. Or if he does, he ain't saying.
Seemingly someone approached 'im when he were in
The Red Lion t'other evening. Said that if he wanted
the position, he'd 'ave to take it right away. He's been
given until this evening to make up 'is mind.'

The Earl's silver-grey brows snapped together,
clearly betraying his staunch disapproval. He considered this underhanded way of acquiring employees
totally unacceptable. Why, it smacked of nothing
short of poaching! Yet, at the same time, he could
quite understand Clem's wishing to improve his lot,
and felt it would be very mean-spirited on his part
not to let the young groom go simply because he and
Trapp would be put to the trouble of finding a suitable
replacement.

'If Clem wishes to leave us, then we must accept
the situation with a good grace,' he responded at
length, echoing his thoughts aloud. 'It's unlikely we'll
find a replacement at a moment's notice, so I'll arrange for one of the lads at Jaffrey House to come
here.'

'There may be no need to put yourself to the
bother, sir,' Trapp surprised his lordship by announcing. 'As luck would 'ave it, someone wandered into
the mews this morning in search of work. Seemingly,
he's been away in foreign parts for a number of years.
Brown as a nut he be, so I don't doubt the truth o'
that. Came back after his old master died, he told me.'

His lordship was not enthusiastic. 'Who was his

late employer, do you know? Can he supply a reference?'

'No, sir. Happen there were a spot o' bother on the boat journey home. Lost all his belongings, so he told me.'

'Mmm.' His lordship's brows once again met at the bridge of his thin, aristocratic nose. 'You know my views, Trapp. I'm never altogether happy about employing people who cannot provide a reference, especially strangers.'

'Aye, sir. I do know.' Trapp raised a hand to scratch his grizzled hair: a habit of his when pondering a ticklish problem. 'And, ordinarily, I'm of a similar mind. But I 'ave to say that this fellow knows a thing or two about beasts. It just so 'appens that Miss Sophie's filly was in one of her frisky moods when he wanders into the mews. Had her quietened down in a trice, so he did. Beasts, I reckon, 'ave a deal more sense than most folks. And what I always says is, if horses take to a cove, then he can't be all bad.'

There was perhaps more than a grain of truth in this simple philosophy, his lordship decided, and he took a moment or two more to consider the matter. 'Very well, Trapp. If you're willing to give this stranger a chance, that's good enough for me. If he doesn't prove suitable, I can, as I've already mentioned, send to Jaffrey House for a replacement.'

Although he had given his consent readily enough, his lordship was not completely happy with this unexpected turn of events. Was it mere coincidence, he wondered, watching his henchman leave the room, that soon after his groom had been offered a new position, someone should have turned up looking for work? A wry smile tugged at the corner of his thin-lipped mouth. Perhaps he was just getting too cynical in his old age, he decided, his mind returning to something else which had puzzled him during the past few days.

Why, he wondered, had there been a marked lack of interest of late shown by eligible young gentlemen in his daughter? Since the night of their ball he had not received one offer, verbal or otherwise, for Sophia's hand. He was not so foolish as to suppose that he would be likely to receive a proposal of marriage every single week for the duration of their stay in town. Nor was he such a doting father that he imagined for a moment that his daughter, lovely though she was, would be to every man's taste.

There was no denying, either, that Sophia could be troublesome on occasions, and any gentleman hoping for a quiet life would do well to consider long and hard before proposing matrimony to her. Only a gentleman with a stronger will than her own could ever hope to keep Sophia under control. Surely, though, somewhere in the length and breadth of this land existed a gentleman of good birth quite capable of keeping a tight rein on a troublesome filly? His lordship could only hope that this was so, and that it wouldn't be too long before this ideal mate crossed his daughter's path.

The door opened and the subject of his thoughts, looking perfectly charming in a lavender silk gown and matching bonnet, swept into the room. The sweetly angelic smile on her face, as she tripped lightly across to the desk, would fool most gentlemen into believing that by nature she was compliant. A grossly inaccurate supposition which any poor deluded fool might make, he decided, his suspicions surfacing anew.

'What on earth have I done to make you scowl so, Papa?' After placing a kiss on the soft, silver-grey hair, she perched herself, uninvited, on the edge of his desk. 'Anyone seeing that disapproving look of yours might suppose that I'd been up to some mischief.'

'It is not beyond the realms of possibility that you have been, my dear,' he responded drily, thereby igniting that gurgle of feminine laughter which never failed to bring a smile to his own lips. 'Where are you off to this morning, decked out in all your finery?'

'I'm going out with Mama in the carriage to visit Madame Félice. I'm due there in an hour for the final fitting of my new riding habit, and we mustn't be late, otherwise we might find ourselves having to return some other time.'

'My, my! How things have changed!' his lordship remarked, in the same dry tone. 'In my day no seamstress would dare to dictate what time a member of the aristocracy was to arrive at her shop.'

'Ah! But she's no ordinary dressmaker, Papa. Anyone who is anyone has a gown made by Madame Félice,' Sophia remarked, wickedly mimicking the élite hostess whose ball she had attended the previous night. 'Ordinarily, as you know, that wouldn't weigh with me, but I am desperate to have my new habit finished. I haven't ridden once since we arrived in town.'

This innocent admission jogged his lordship's memory, and he wasn't in the least surprised by Sophia's crestfallen expression when he apprised her of Clem's wishing to leave, and the reason behind the young groom's decision.

'I shall be very sorry to see him go, Papa. I always preferred Clem to accompany me whenever I went out riding.' Slipping lightly from the desk, she went over to the door, but turned back as a dreadful thought suddenly occurred to her. 'That doesn't mean I shall be forced to take Trapp with me for the duration of our stay in town, does it? I shan't be able to do a thing without his reporting my comings and goings straight back to you.'

'And wouldn't that be a good thing!' his lordship retorted, wickedly teasing, and then laughed outright as Sophia gave a haughty toss of her head before sweeping regally from the room.

No, it certainly would be no bad thing for someone to keep an eye on the little monkey, he reiterated, silently revising his own plans for the forthcoming weeks.

Although he enjoyed good health, he was no longer a young man, and had decided long before they had embarked on this visit to the metropolis that he would be leaving the supervision of his most trying offspring in his wife's very capable hands. He had adjusted reasonably well already to town hours, but was very well aware that he no longer possessed the stamina, or the inclination for that matter, to throw himself headlong into the social whirl. None the less, it would not do him a mite of harm, he decided, if just every once in a while he accompanied his wife and daughter out for an evening. His added presence would certainly ensure his daughter's good behaviour. Furthermore, it would not hurt to have a word with Trapp, just to ensure that this new man was well aware that he must keep a strict watch whenever he accompanied the daughter of the house out on what might very well turn out to be a daily ride, if the weather continued fair.

Although Sophia had said very little when she had learned of Clem's wishing to leave, she was very upset by the unexpected news. Clem had been her personal groom for more than ten years. Unfailingly vigilant, while at the same time allowing her free rein, he had proved to be the perfect bodyguard and companion during those innumerable rides they had taken across the Earl's Northamptonshire acres. Some would consider, she didn't doubt, that her manner towards the young groom had been far too free and easy, but Sophia had looked upon Clem more as a friend than a servant, and she felt that he would be very difficult to replace.

Consequently, when she entered the famous *modiste*'s premises in Bond Street, her mood was quite naturally subdued. Her mind locked in the past, recalling those numerous occasions when she and her trusty companion had explored far-afield areas of the Northamptonshire countryside, she hardly noticed the other customers sitting in the plush velvet chairs, nor did she realise that none other than the much coveted dressmaker herself had accompanied her into the fitting-room until a sweetly accented voice remarked, 'Your new habit does not please you, *mademoiselle*? Or is it, perhaps, something else that makes you unhappy this day?'

Drawing her mind back to the present, Sophia received something of a shock when she discovered the *modiste* studying her intently, the lovely blue eyes openly assessing. 'Oh, no, Madame, the habit is perfect.'

'Not quite,' the modiste countered, her professional eye quickly perceiving a slight fault. 'A little adjustment to the skirt is required. I hope then that you will look a little happier when you are wearing it, *petite*, otherwise my reputation *par excellence* will tumble, no?'

So the famous *modiste* had a sense of humour, had she? Sophia mused, quickly detecting the mischievous twinkle in the blue eyes. The dressmaker was possibly more amused than gratified by her meteoric rise to fame, and Sophia felt suddenly drawn to the woman who, she suspected, was not so many years older than herself.

'I assure you, madame, that the habit pleases me very much,' she assured her, taking care not to step on the soft velvet folds as she stepped out of the skirt. 'It is just that this morning I received some rather sad news. Someone who has worked for my family for many years is to leave us.'

The smile that curled the dressmaker's full lips appeared full of warmth and understanding. 'I think, perhaps, that the one that leaves you is something more than just a servant, *hein*?'

Sophia nodded. 'More a friend.'

'Then could you not, perhaps, persuade him to stay?' Madame suggested, helping Sophia to don the walking dress and matching pelisse which she herself had made for the Earl's daughter only the week before.

'I dare say I could, but I shan't make the attempt.' She caught the dressmaker's look of surprise in the large, oval mirror. 'He has been my personal groom for many years and, I believe, has been happy in his work, but now wishes to better himself. He has been offered the position of head groom on some country estate, though I know not which.' She moved one of her slender hands in a slight gesture of resignation. 'It would be selfish of me to try to stop him improving himself.'

The look that sprang into the *modiste*'s eyes was difficult to interpret, but Sophia thought she could detect a hint of respect in those striking blue depths.

'I do not think, *petite*, that you will have the least difficulty in finding a replacement,' the young dressmaker responded softly, as she held back the curtain for Sophia to pass into the elegant waiting-room.

'My, my, Sophia! You have been honoured this day,' her mother teased, after they had left the shop and had settled themselves in the carriage once more for the short journey back to Berkeley Square. 'Lady Strattan went quite pea-green with envy when Madame Félice selected to offer you her undivided attention. How does it make you feel to have eclipsed such a leading society hostess as the Marchioness of Strattan? The poor woman will never be able to hold her head up in public again!'

'You know full well, Mama, that I consider such things totally unimportant,' Sophia responded, chuckling at her mother's rather wicked sense of humour. 'I would have been just as content to have had one of the assistants attend to me, though I must confess, I did find the celebrated *modiste* most interesting,' she admitted, settling herself more comfortably on the seat. 'She isn't nearly so old as I had imagined. She's not many years older than myself, I shouldn't have thought. And she's extremely pretty too, though she does her level best to conceal the fact by wearing very plain gowns, and hiding her hair beneath a cap.'

'Perhaps she's still in mourning, dear,' her ladyship

suggested, memory stirring. 'I believe someone did mention that she's a widow.'

'Perhaps she is,' Sophia conceded, but remained doubtful. 'It wouldn't surprise me, though, if she had never been married at all. She wouldn't be the first female to feign the status of a married woman. Our very own housekeeper does precisely that.'

'Very true,' her ladyship concurred. 'I should imagine high-ranking female servants feel that adopting the status of a married woman adds to their respectability.'

'Just as dressmakers believe that pretending to be French will ensure their success.'

'Are you implying that you suspect Madame Félice is not a Frenchwoman, dear?'

Turning her head a little to one side, Sophia considered this. 'I'm not certain. That pretty accent of hers sounds genuine enough.'

'Well, you were certainly granted ample opportunity to form an opinion. You were in the fitting-room quite some considerable time,' her ladyship remarked. 'I trust there are not too many alterations needing to be made to your new habit.'

'No, just a slight adjustment to the skirt. Madame Félice promised faithfully before I left her that she would have it delivered to the house the day after tomorrow.'

'That must please you. I know how much you have been longing to ride since our arrival in town.'

'The prospect of doing so has suddenly lost much

of its appeal,' Sophia was not slow to admit, realising that her mother could not have heard the news. 'Clem is leaving us. Which means, of course, that until a replacement can be found I shall be forced to suffer Trapp's presence. And as we both know, Trapp is unfailingly loyal to the head of the family. Everything I say and do will be reported straight back to Papa.'

The Countess could not forbear a smile at the underlying note of pique in her daughter's voice, and turned her head momentarily to stare out of the window.

Like her husband, she too had not been slow to notice that fewer personable gentlemen were paying calls to the house these days, though she could hardly say this had come as any great surprise. She had had a fairly shrewd idea who had been behind those foolish rumours which had circulated on the evening of their very own ball, but which, thankfully, now were dying a natural death. She had noticed, too, during the subsequent days that her daughter's choice of dancing partners had undergone something of a change. There was still a smattering of eligible young men among the favoured few, but these, the Countess strongly suspected, were gentlemen who were not quite ready yet to exchange bachelorhood for wedded bliss.

More amused than annoyed by these rather childish tactics, her ladyship had decided to keep her own counsel, and not take her daughter to task over the mischievous stratagems that she had employed to keep any eligible *parti* at bay, but could not resist saying now, 'But, my dear, I'm certain that you would never do or say anything that might annoy your dear papa,' and then found it was as much as she could do to stop herself laughing outright when Sophia turned to stare resolutely out of the window.

Three days later a message was sent to the stables informing Trapp that Lady Sophia wished her horse to be saddled and brought round from the mews. The head groom received these instructions with mixed feelings: on the one hand he was pleased to learn that Lady Sophia's frisky filly would be receiving some regular exercise at last—she was always far easier to handle when she had been out for an airing; on the other hand, though, he wasn't at all easy in his mind over entrusting the care of the Earl's precious daughter to a virtual stranger. He frowned as he stared at the broad, straight back of his underling, busily engaged in grooming one of his lordship's fine carriage horses, and wondered anew just what to make of Master Benjamin Rudgely.

Trapp himself would have been the first to admit that he could be a hard taskmaster, quick to rebuke, slow to praise. The trouble was, though, he could find no fault with his new subordinate. Master Rudgely had proved to be surprisingly diligent, not once cutting corners in order to get his work over and done with quickly. His handling of horses was a joy to behold, and he tooled the master's town carriage with effortless ease. He had no fault to find with the young man's personal habits either, which had come as something of a relief as they shared the room above the stables, so Trapp could not quite understand why he should continue to have this niggling little doubt in the back of his mind about young Ben.

He scratched his grizzled hair, wondering whether he wasn't just a mite too cynical, just too suspicious of his fellow man. Until his subordinate betrayed the fact that he couldn't be trusted, he ought to be given the benefit of the doubt.

'You can stop what you're doing, lad, and saddle Lady Sophia's filly. The young mistress wishes to ride this morning,' he announced, and didn't notice a pair of blue eyes suddenly flicker with joyful expectation. Which was perhaps just as well, because he would certainly have had second thoughts about allowing the handsome groom to accompany the young mistress out on her ride.

'Now, lad, I want you to listen to what I 'ave to say,' he went on, sitting himself on one of the stools while momentarily pondering over how best to broach the topic of the young mistress's occasionally wayward behaviour. 'I want you to take excellent care of 'er, see. A firm but gentle hand on the reins is what's needed. The master's right fond of 'er, and he wouldn't be best pleased if she came to any harm. So you keep a watchful eye, understand? She can be a mite 'eadstrong on occasions.'

There was a suspicion of a twitch at the corner of

the younger man's mouth. 'I know that, Mr Trapp. I've handled her often enough during the three days I've been here.'

'Eh?' The head groom was startled for a moment, then enlightenment dawned. 'I ain't talking about the filly, you nincompoop!' he snapped testily. 'I knows you can 'andle 'er easy enough. It's Miss Sophia that may cause you problems if she 'appens to be in one of 'er troublesome moods.'

The sight of broad shoulders shaking with suppressed laughter did little for Trapp's peace of mind, and once again doubts assailed him. 'Now, lad, if you feels you ain't up to the job, then I'd rather you say so now, and I'll go with Lady Sophia m'self.'

'Oh, I'm up to it, right enough,' was the prompt response. 'I've had some experience of handling wayward females in my time.'

'Aye, I don't doubt that,' the older man muttered, as a further worrying possibility suddenly occurred to him, and he stared up in troubled silence, scrutinising the undeniably handsome face beneath the beard. 'Just you remember your station, boy, and don't be taking any foolish notions into that head of yours. Miss Sophia's a lady, and you'd best not forget it.'

There was a further moment's silence, then, 'I give you my solemn word that I shall not get ideas above my station, Mr Trapp. I shall treat Lady Sophia just as though she were...my very own sister whenever I accompany her out for a ride.'

'Oh, you will, will you?' The head groom was not

totally reassured and betrayed this fact by a suspicious frown. 'I can't recall your making mention of any sister.'

'Possibly not, but I have one all the same. I've a brother too, as it happens. I was staying with him here in London before I came to you.'

'Strikes me, young Ben, there's a great deal I don't know about you.' Trapp peered owlishly up at him again. 'Why, for instance, did you suddenly take it into your 'ead to leave Jamaica and come back 'ere?'

The answer came promptly enough. 'I'd been out there for five years, and I'd had enough. Homesick, as you might say. Sir Simon Fellows can confirm what I've told you. I can always write to him, and ask him to send a reference to his lordship.'

'Oh, so you can read and write, can you?' Trapp responded, swooping down on this surprising disclosure while at the same time committing the name of Fellows to memory, just in case his lordship should happen to choose at some point in the future to verify Rudgely's bona fides. 'And how came you to be so learned, may I ask?'

The response was not quite so swift in coming this time. 'My—er—old master was keen for me to learn.'

Strangely enough this in no way surprised Trapp, for it had been none other than the Earl who had given of his time when out in India to ensure that Trapp had learned to read and write. Something else, however, did occur to him as peculiar, and he wasn't slow to remark upon it. 'And, I suppose, it were your old master that got you to talk so genteel.'

Once again there was a suspicion of a twitch at the corners of those perfectly sculptured masculine lips. 'I thank you for the compliment, Mr Trapp, but I don't speak that genteel. The old master, though, wouldn't tolerate any cussing when his womenfolk were about, so I suppose I've sort of got out of the habit of using bad words.'

'Well, that ain't no bad thing,' the master of the stables responded fair-mindedly. 'You'll need to mind your tongue when Miss Sophia's about. She's always had the bad habit of remembering words she should never 'ave heard in the first place.' Feeling slightly easier in his mind after the brief talk, Trapp rose to his feet. 'Well, we can't stand about chattering all day. You'd best make haste, lad, and saddle those horses, otherwise the young mistress will be waiting for you.'

The new groom was not slow to obey the brusque command, and had just arrived at the front of the house when the door was thrown wide. A moment later Sophia herself came tripping lightly down the steps, only to stop dead in her tracks, a look of total astonishment on her lovely features.

'Great heavens!' she exclaimed, not attempting to hide her instant recognition. 'So you're my new groom!'

Chapter Four

For the second time in his life Benedict Risely, Seventh Duke of Sharnbrook, experienced that strange bittersweet longing, that intoxicating mixture of tenderness and desire that began somewhere in the region of his loins and spread rapidly through every part of him, sending his pulse rate soaring and his senses reeling. He wanted nothing more than to take her into his arms, and into his bed, to begin to satisfy this earthy powerful craving, and yet all he could do was touch his floppy, misshapen hat in polite acknowledgement, and cup his hands in order to help her into the saddle.

As he mounted the bay, and proceeded to follow at a discreet distance, he began to question, yet again, the wisdom of his actions and wonder what madness had possessed him even to contemplate indulging in such an absurd charade. As a groom his contact with this lovely young creature, who had captured his interest like no other woman had succeeded in doing before, would be frustratingly rare: a mere hour every day if he was lucky. However, given what his brother Nicholas had told him was true, would the Duke of Sharnbrook be better placed to win her regard? At least this way, he decided, he might be granted the opportunity to get to know her a little better without any outside interference or pressures from family and friends; would be given the opportunity to make certain himself whether what he had experienced during those memorable moments in Bond Street, and again now, was something rather more meaningful than mere searing physical attraction that would undoubtedly fade in the passage of time.

He remembered quite clearly that during that tedious sea voyage home he had been granted ample opportunity to think long and hard about the kind of woman he wished to marry. Fortunately the Risely family was a wealthy one, perhaps one of the most affluent in the land. Consequently marriage to an heiress was a consideration which need never weigh with him. His family, of course, would expect him to marry a female of unimpeachable breeding, someone who would know what was expected of her as the Duchess of Sharnbrook, and who would provide him with the sons to carry on the family name.

He, on the other hand, was looking for something rather more than a high-class brood mare in the female he eventually married. He wanted his Duchess to be a helpmate and friend, someone who would share his joys and sorrows, not merely a beautiful adornment to grace the ancestral home. Could Lady Sophia Cleeve turn out to be this perfect companion, this ideal woman whom he had feared he might never be blessed to find?

Glancing over her shoulder, the subject of his thoughts raised one slender hand and beckoned imperiously. 'Come,' she ordered, making the command sound sweetly inviting. 'Come and ride beside me. I wish to speak with you.'

Benedict needed no second prompting, and was beside her in a trice, thinking how magnificent she looked in the severely tailored bottle-green habit, with the cascade of delicate lace adorning her neck, and wondering anew if he were nothing more than a besotted fool to be so enraptured by a lovely face.

'What is your name?'

'Ben, my lady. Benjamin Rudgely,' he answered, repeating the name his resourceful young brother had invented for him.

'And how came you to seek employment with my family, Benjamin Rudgely?' There was a hint of something that sounded suspiciously like disapproval in her pleasant voice. 'Surely Lord Nicholas Risely did not turn you off simply because of that trifling incident in Bond Street the other day?'

Benedict's mind worked rapidly. Evidently she supposed that he had been Nicholas's servant. How his incorrigible young brother would laugh if he ever discovered that!

'Lord Nicholas who?' His feigned bewilderment was worthy of a Drury Lane actor.

'Oh, I see! He just happened along, did he?' Sophia responded, pleased to have this point cleared up. Poor Lord Nicholas had been on the point of plummeting in her estimation. And through no fault of his own either! Her mischievous smile faded as something else rather puzzling occurred to her. 'How came you to hear so quickly that we would be requiring the services of a groom?'

Benedict had decided, when planning this little subterfuge, that the nearer he stuck to the truth when questioned, the easier it would be to maintain his role. It had been a simple matter to persuade his brother's worthy factotum to approach the Earl's groom, and for Figgins to arrange to meet him again at an inn the following evening.

'I happened to be supping a tankard of ale in a tavern not far from here, and overheard a conversation taking place at the next table between your old groom and some other man.' He could sense those green eyes regarding him keenly as he continued to stare straight ahead. 'You see, my lady, I have only recently returned to this country, and have been looking for work, so I felt it couldn't do any harm to take advantage of the situation and ask at your father's stables, just in case the groom did accept the offer made to him.'

She appeared to accept this readily enough, and

after a moment said, 'So, you have been abroad, Ben. What prompted you to return?'

'My old master's death, my lady.' Which was no less than the truth, of course, though he did find it strange referring to his deceased father in that way. He shrugged. 'Besides, I'd been away in Jamaica for five years, and I was keen to see my family again.'

'And does your family reside in London?'

'My brother lives here,' Benedict responded, still determined to stick to the truth as far as possible. He cast a fleeting, sideways glance at his companion, noted the intelligence in striking green eyes, and realised he would be foolish to underestimate her.

He had up until now been very careful to keep his story consistent, but it would not do for him to become over-confident in the role he was playing. Already he had aroused the head groom's suspicions by admitting to the fact that he could read and write, and had foolishly divulged the name of a fellow plantation owner out in Jamaica, but there was little chance of trying to rectify those blunders now. It would not do, however, to drop his guard again, most especially when in this delightful creature's company.

'You must take the opportunity to visit your brother during the time my family remains in London, Ben,' Sophia suggested, after acknowledging the occupants of a passing carriage by raising her crop. 'I shall probably ride most days, weather permitting, but I'm certain you can slip away for an hour or so from time to time to visit members of your family, providing Trapp does not object, of course.'

Again she was betraying that sweet, considerate side to her nature. Benedict stared straight ahead, hiding the glint of admiration in his eyes. He had not forgotten that she had been willing to take her share of the blame after that unforgettable encounter in Bond Street. How many other young females of her class would have concerned themselves unduly over the welfare of a being whom they mistook for a mere servant? Not too many, he felt sure.

'You must not allow our formidable head groom to bully you, Ben,' she continued, an easily discernible hint of devilment in her eyes now. 'He can be a cross-grained old curmudgeon on occasions. The stable-lads back at Jaffrey House are terrified of him.'

'Jaffrey House?' he echoed. 'Is that your country home?'

Sophia nodded. 'The family home in Northamptonshire. My father had it built shortly after his return from India. I and my two younger brothers were born there. It's a lovely place.' Her smile was a trifle wistful. 'It's a great pity that it isn't the Cleeve family's ancestral home, although it is built on land which was once part of the late Earl's estate.'

Memory stirred, and Benedict vaguely recalled his own father mentioning something about the late Earl committing suicide after ruining himself at the gaming tables.

'And who owns the ancestral home now?' he

asked, hoping that for a mere groom he did not seem too inquisitive. Thankfully, she did not appear to think so, although he did note the sudden look of contempt on her face.

'The Marquis of Sywell, a detestable creature of low morals and disgusting habits, whose wanton neglect over the years has resulted in Steepwood Abbey deteriorating into almost a ruin. Papa has offered to buy the place on numerous occasions during the past twenty years, but without success. Fortunately, though, he has managed to regain most of the other properties which once belonged to the Cleeve family, including the town residence.'

They had by this time reached the park. Sophia drew her filly to a halt and gazed about her with scant enthusiasm. It was still more than two weeks before the Season officially began, and yet already the streets and parks were crowded with the rich and famous.

'Look about you, Ben! Isn't it wonderful the way society parades about in its finery for the edification of the populace?' Her sudden shout of laughter was certainly not lacking contempt. 'The Marquis of Sywell is a foul, disgusting member of the human race, but he is in no way unique. Many of those you see here are just as bad. I must remember in future to ride earlier in the day when the air is less contaminated.'

So Nicholas had not been exaggerating, after all, Benedict mused, as he proceeded to follow again at a discreet distance. Lady Sophia Cleeve truly harboured a deal of contempt for her own class. His task, it seemed, was going to prove to be far more formidable than he had at first supposed!

That evening the Earl, still determined to attend the occasional party, escorted his wife and daughter to the ball being held by the Marquis and Marchioness of Strattan. If the formidable matron harboured any ill-will at being passed over by a certain famous *modiste* a few days before, she certainly betrayed no sign of it as she graciously welcomed the young lady who had received preferential treatment, a circumstance which the Countess herself was not slow to remark upon once her husband had drifted away into the room set out for cards.

'But isn't it considered vulgar for women of our class to give vent to their feelings in public, Mama? I know some do, while others...' Sophia's eyes drifted towards a young woman whose husband had been quite openly indulging in an amorous affair with a notorious Cyprian since his arrival in town '...manage to hide their emotions quite remarkably well.'

Her ladyship followed the direction of her daughter's gaze. She too had heard rumours of Lord Rochford's torrid affair, and felt a great deal of sympathy for his pretty young wife, whose behaviour in public was faultless. 'Not all marriages turn out so badly, Sophia.'

'No, Mama. I know they do not. But I suspect a great many ladies here tonight have at some time or other been forced to suffer in silence over their husbands' peccadilloes. I rather fear that, my nature being what it is, I should not be so tolerant.'

The Countess thought it wisest to change the subject and, catching sight of her friend and neighbour, Lady Elizabeth Perceval, sitting with her daughter, guided Sophia towards them.

'I'm so pleased you accepted this invitation tonight,' Robina said, when her mother's attention was being held by the Countess. 'It seems ages since I last saw you. What have you been doing with yourself?'

'Oh, nothing particularly exciting,' Sophia responded, sublimely ignoring the fact that she had not spent a single evening at home since the night of her own ball.

'I do not believe that for a moment,' Robina countered, suddenly feeling much more relaxed, just as she always did whenever Sophia was about. 'Everywhere Mama and I go we hear your name mentioned. Why, only the other day we heard some silly rumour about you wishing to marry one of your papa's footmen.'

Robina's amusement faded the instant she detected a certain glint in a pair of green eyes, a look she had seen too many times in the past not to know precisely what it signified. 'Oh, Sophia! Surely you didn't start that silly rumour about yourself as well? Your father will be furious if he ever finds out.'

'Yes, I expect he probably would be,' Sophia agreed. There could be no denying that the Earl had always been very indulgent where she was concerned, far more so than with any one of her brothers, and yet she knew that even with her his patience was not limitless.

'Unfortunately, Robina, unlike you, I do not always behave as I ought. I'm very well aware that back home in the Abbey villages it is a commonly held belief that I've been thoroughly spoilt and indulged. Which is no less than the truth, of course,' she agreed, with the honesty that was so much a part of her charm. 'I hate being thwarted. It's a failing, I know, and one I really must try to overcome. My only excuse is that I didn't precisely say that I intended marrying a footman, merely that in general I prefer the company of servants to that of more privileged members of society.'

She paused for a moment while she considered the painted figures on her fan. 'Which, strangely enough, has turned out to be true. I went riding this afternoon in the company of my groom, and can honestly say that I felt perfectly contented for the first time since arriving in town.'

Robina didn't find this in the least surprising. 'Oh, well,' she shrugged. 'That's only to be expected. I know you look upon Clem as more of a friend than a servant.'

'It wasn't Clem who accompanied me,' Sophia informed her, staring sightlessly across the ballroom, her mind's eye conjuring up a clear image of a tall and powerfully built man, with his long mane of thick golden-brown hair and penetrating blue eyes. 'Clem, sadly, has left us to take charge of the stables at an estate somewhere in the south of England, I believe.'

Robina was shocked to learn this and hardly knew what to say. The inhabitants of the four Abbey villages had grown accustomed over the years to seeing the Earl of Yardley's daughter riding over the Northamptonshire countryside in the company of her trusty groom. For years Clem had been Sophia's loyal companion. It would seem most strange no longer seeing them riding about together.

'I know you must have been terribly upset at losing him,' she said at length, genuine sympathy edging her voice.

'Very,' Sophia agreed, smiling wryly. 'Spoilt I may be, Robin, but not so selfish as to try to prevent someone I like from bettering himself. It will be some years yet before our head groom is ready to retire, and Clem is more than capable of running a stable. I must confess, though, I was very favourably impressed with Clem's replacement,' she went on to divulge, after her attention had just for one moment been captured by two gentlemen sitting together on the opposite side of the room. She shook her head. 'It was so strange. At the time I wasn't aware of it, but when I arrived back at the house, and thought about the conversation we'd had during our ride, I realised that it hadn't seemed as if I'd been conversing with a servant at all.'

Again Robina wasn't unduly surprised. 'You always did chatter away quite happily to Clem,' she reminded her.

'Very true. Somehow, though, this seemed different. I found myself agreeing with almost everything he said, especially remarks he made about our own class.' She laughed at the absurdity of being instructed by a groom on the correct way to behave. 'Silly, really. Perhaps it was just that I felt totally relaxed in his company.'

Robina did not think it at all silly. 'I know what you mean. There are those, even servants, with whom you instantly experience a rapport.' She gave vent to a heartfelt sigh. 'I know Mama and Papa wish me to make a good match. Oh, but I would much rather marry someone with whom I felt comfortable, who didn't expect me to behave correctly all the time, and would accept me as I am!'

Sophia's gaze automatically strayed towards the lady sitting on her friend's right. She didn't doubt for a moment that Robina's upbringing at the vicarage in Abbot Quincey had been happy for the most part. It could not, however, have been easy living up to Lady Elizabeth Perceval's exacting standards of behaviour.

Lady Elizabeth was well respected in all four of the Abbey villages. She had proved the perfect companion and helpmate to Abbot Quincey's hard-working and kindly vicar. Her own efforts on behalf of the poor and needy were as tireless as her husband's, and she had never been too proud to enter the humblest of abodes in order to offer some comfort to the sick and dying. Yet there remained an imperious air about her that never failed to remind one and all of her noble birth and that they were in the presence of the daughter of a duke.

Sophia could only assume that Lady Elizabeth's upbringing had been a strict one, for the vicar's wife had certainly instilled rigid standards of behaviour in her daughters, most especially in Robina, who, being the eldest, had been expected to set an example to her three younger sisters. No easy task to be forced to conform to such high ideals, Sophia mused, her gaze once more travelling about the large and now well-filled ballroom, and she could not help wondering just how much of her sweet-natured friend's character had been suppressed over the years, and what surprising traits might surface if ever dear Robina was removed for any length of time from her strict mama's sphere.

'Tell me, Robin, do you happen to know who that dark-haired gentleman is sitting across the room with Lord Byron? I do not believe I've ever seen him before.'

Robina, having a remarkable memory for names and faces, was able to enlighten her at once. 'Sir Lucius Crawley. He has only recently arrived in town. Although,' she added in an undertone, 'I think there must be something quite unsavoury about him, for Mama said, after I had stood up with him just once at a party the other night, that on no account was I to do so again.'

'How very interesting!' The telltale glint which

preceded some outrageous utterance or action on Sophia's part appeared in her eyes. 'I expect he's a rake.'

Robina's spontaneous chortle earned her a look of mild reproof from her punctilious mama, but help was at hand in the form of her equally meticulous cousin, Hugo Perceval, who came across to request her as his partner in the next set of country dances.

As she followed their progress on to the floor, Sophia noticed the strikingly attractive Sir Lucius Crawley rise to his feet and begin to saunter across the room in her direction. If his intention had been to claim her for his partner he was destined to be disappointed, for Lord Nicholas Risely, appearing from nowhere, was suddenly standing before her, politely requesting that she partner him in the next dance.

As the young lord continued to rein supreme amongst that group of 'safe' admirers, Sophia did not hesitate. She always found him amusing, his witty remarks coming as a welcome relief after the studied politeness she was usually forced to endure from most other gentlemen. He was a fount of wisdom too, always able to regale her with the latest *on-dits*, and what he did not know about the famous and infamous who moved in the highest circles really wasn't worth knowing. Consequently she did not hesitate to tax him about the strikingly handsome man who had succeeded in capturing her interest.

'Has Crawley arrived in town?' Betraying faint surprise, Nicholas glanced about him and quickly caught sight of the Baronet, whose reputation was, to say the least, slightly unsavoury. 'Ah, yes! So he has. Doesn't usually arrive before the beginning of the Season. Can only assume that he must be contemplating matrimony again.'

'Again?' Sophia echoed, intrigued.

Nicholas was longing to discover how his brother went on, for he had not seen or heard from Benedict since he had adopted the guise of a groom. Realising, however, that a sudden change in the topic of conversation would appear most odd, and not quite knowing how to broach the subject of stable-hands anyway, he thought it wisest to satisfy the roguish Lady Sophia's curiosity with regard to Sir Lucius.

'Yes, he married some ''golden dolly'' a few years ago in order to save the ancestral home. Mortgaged up to the hilt, so I was led to believe. Still,' he shrugged, 'not surprising he got himself in high water. A bit of a loose screw is Sir Lucius, m'dear. Not a man to deprive himself of his pleasures, as you might say.'

Sophia had discovered over the years that one learned a great deal more if one refrained from prying too hard. She had also discovered that gentlemen were far less inhibited in their choice of language if not continually asked what they meant. So, committing Lord Nicholas's more colourful vocabulary to memory, she merely said, 'And I presume his first wife died.'

'Giving birth to a stillborn child within a year of

their marriage, if my memory serves me correctly. Lucky escape, if you ask me,' he remarked, with a tactless disregard for the poor young woman's tragic demise. 'Common knowledge that he only married her for the money. Made that plain enough by re-sorting to his old ways within weeks of the marriage taking place.'

Disappointed, but not unduly surprised, Sophia's interest swiftly began to wane. If what Lord Nicholas had told her was true, then it appeared that Sir Lucius, a profligate with no thought for anyone but himself, epitomised what she most despised in her class.

Ordinarily she wouldn't have given the Baronet an-other thought, but as the last strains of music died away, and the couples began to leave the floor, she discovered Sir Lucius, evidently not a man to be thwarted in his objectives a second time, standing be-fore her. Lord Nicholas had little choice but to make the introductions before he moved away, leaving Sophia to stare up into a pair of striking blue eyes, deeply set in a thin, but not unattractive, masculine countenance.

She could not help comparing the faintly mocking eyes that stared unblinkingly down at her with another pair of the same striking hue which had regarded her keenly from time to time earlier that day. She recalled quite clearly that there had been a directness in Ben Rudgely's gaze, but at least his blue orbs had left her fully clad, whereas now she felt as if she had just been divested of her chemise, and her charms were being ruthlessly scrutinised for any slight flaw.

She smiled to herself as, after a brief exchange of pleasantries, they took up their positions in the set. Undoubtedly a great many women would be attracted by Sir Lucius's darkly brooding good looks and provocative gaze, but Sophia could detect a distinct lack of warmth in the smiling, thin-lipped mouth, and a hint of something faintly sinister in his whole demeanour which made her very certain that any woman would be a fool to place her well-being into the hands of this man.

In this, at least, she and her father were in perfect accord. Although he had visited the capital rarely during the past few years, the Earl had kept abreast of society's comings and goings, and had learned something of Sir Lucius's tainted reputation. Consequently he was not best pleased, after paying his brief visit to the card-room, to discover his beloved daughter in the disreputable Baronet's company.

Quickly locating the whereabouts of his wife, he did not hesitate to draw her a little to one side and give voice to his displeasure by demanding to know what she was about in allowing their daughter to stand up with a man of Sir Lucius Crawley's stamp.

'My dear, I was hardly in a position to do much about it,' she responded in her calm way, while suspecting that he had been keeping a watchful eye on proceedings from the first. 'He approached Sophia before she had left the floor with Lord Nicholas Risely.'

Momentarily diverted, he said, 'Risely?' He had thought that there had been something vaguely familiar in the tall, blond-haired young man who had danced with Sophia first. 'What, one of old Sharnbrook's brood, is he?'

'Yes, the younger son. Sophia is quite fond of him.'

'Is she indeed?' Hope stirred, but was quickly dashed by his Countess's assurance that friendship was all that Sophia felt for the late duke's younger son.

'He's an endearing young scamp. I'm very fond of him myself,' she went on to confess, 'but he wouldn't suit Sophia at all. He's far too young. So I would be most obliged if you did not try to promote a union between them.'

'I wouldn't dream of interfering, my love,' he assured her, but she was not wholly convinced, and betrayed the fact by raising a decidedly sceptical brow.

'Then why, pray, did you suddenly take it into your head to accompany us this evening, if it was not to keep an eye on our daughter? If you consider me an inadequate chaperon, Thomas, then I would suggest that you employ a suitable duenna,' she suggested bluntly, but without rancour. None the less his lordship took note of the mild reproof.

'Now, now, dear,' he said soothingly. 'You know full well that there is no one I would trust more with the care of our daughter than you. It's just...it's just...'

'It's just that you are concerned for our only daughter's well-being,' she finished for him, smiling in spite of the fact that she considered he worried unnecessarily. 'I love Sophia no less than you do, Thomas, but unlike you I have far more faith in our daughter's judgement. Sooner or later I believe that she will meet a gentleman whom she would be happy to marry, and, moreover, a gentleman whom we shall find perfectly acceptable. But until such time, if you take my advice, you will let well alone, and permit our far from obtuse daughter to enjoy her first Season.'

Chapter Five

Resolved to take her exercise long before the park became congested with fops and dandies, and sporting-mad gentlemen bent on displaying their skills on horseback or in their racing carriages, Sophia rose early the following morning and was pleased to discover, as her maid threw back the drapes, that the day looked set to remain fair.

She was convinced that the mounting excitement bubbling up inside, as she broke her fast and then hurriedly scrambled into her habit, stemmed purely and simply from the pleasure she would attain from having the park virtually to herself. So she was at a loss to understand why her spirits should suddenly plummet when, a short while later, her new groom's only response to her bright smile and cheerful good morning was the merest nod of his head.

Being singularly lacking in conceit, Sophia would never have supposed for a moment that the mere sight of her could reduce a self-possessed gentleman into little more than a languishing dolt who seemed to spend half his time these days staring into space, longing for that moment when he could call her his own, and his nights dreaming that she was lying in his arms, a willing recipient of his lovemaking, only to wake and find himself frustratingly alone.

She would never have supposed, either, that the man bending before her, hands cupped in readiness to toss her into the saddle, was doing his utmost to keep an iron control over his emotions and frustrations. She only knew that she was feeling unaccountably hurt by her new groom's seeming indifference to her presence, and stared down at the bent head, wondering how her perfect companion of yesterday could turn overnight into some surly dullard who could not bring himself even to pass the time of day.

After a few moments, when she made not the least attempt to place her slender foot in his hands, Ben raised his head, a question in his eyes. 'Have you changed your mind, my lady? Do you not wish to go riding this morning?'

'Now, is that not strange!' she remarked, with more than just a hint of sarcasm coating her every word. 'I was about to ask you the same question.'

He straightened to tower above her, his expression guarded. 'I do not perfectly understand you, m'lady.'

'No?' Sophia wasn't at all convinced that this was true, for the intelligence she could easily perceive in those striking blue eyes told a different story.

Imps of mischief began to dance in her own. 'Then

let me make myself perfectly clear. I believe I'm generally held to be a most unexacting mistress, but even I'm not above dealing a sound box round the ear to any servant who shows reluctance in carrying out the few services I might demand of him.'

It was at this precise moment that the filly chose to demonstrate her impatience to be off. Ben's muttered, 'Unruly little baggage!' had her calmed in a trice, but Sophia wasn't at all certain that the mild admonition had been directed at her horse. She decided to give him the benefit of the doubt over this, but wasn't feeling generous enough to permit his subdued state to pass without explanation and demanded, as they rode out of the square, why he appeared to be out of sorts that morning.

'And please do not insult my intelligence by telling me that there's nothing wrong,' she went on. 'You've a face like a wet Friday.'

Benedict could not prevent a smile. His little darling evidently was not one to mince words. But how on earth could he tell her that she was the cause of all his present troubles, and that he was simply a frustrated man?

'If I appear a little—er—diffident, my lady, then you must forgive me and put it down to inexperience, and my desire not to be found wanting. I have not always been a groom, you see,' he admitted, consoling himself with the knowledge that at least this much was true.

'What kind of work were you engaged in before?'

she asked and, prepared, he was ready with the answer.

'I have performed many duties in my time, my lady. I was born in the country, and am quite accustomed to working with various animals, not just horses.'

'A farm boy, eh?'

'Er—no, not quite, my lady. I was born on a large estate in Hampshire, and worked from time to time on the home farm when I was much younger.'

How very interesting! Sophia mused, eyes narrowing as she studied the handsome profile, with its high, intelligent forehead, the faintly aquiline nose and the strong line of the square jaw. He might dress and vaguely sound like a yokel, but he was certainly no country bumpkin. Rustics didn't use words like 'accustomed' and 'diffident'. There was far more to Master Benjamin Rudgely than met the eye!

'So, what prompted you to go to the West Indies, Ben?' Her voice was light, pleasantly conversational, yet Benedict could easily detect the note of keen interest barely concealed. Her curiosity, quite understandably, was well and truly roused, and he had every intention of satisfying her inquisitiveness with the truth as far as he dared.

'My old master ordered me to go, my lady. I cannot in truth say that I wished to leave England,' he divulged, recalling his resentment quite clearly, 'but I have to own that my time in Jamaica taught me a lot.'

Although continuing to stare straight ahead,

Benedict was well aware that he was being regarded
rather closely. He waited for the next searching question, and was faintly surprised when she merely remarked that he must have observed many changes
since his return.

'Some here in the capital, certainly. Many new
buildings have been erected since I was last here.
And, of course, you have the new gas lighting in this
part of the city.' He swiftly glimpsed a less impressive sight. 'Some things, however, have not improved
in the least.'

Sophia followed the direction of his gaze in time
to see a beadle chasing two poverty-stricken children
round a corner into a side street. There were poor
everywhere, but one tended to notice them particularly here in London, where the gap between the
classes seemed even more marked. The authorities did
their best to keep the streets in this part of the city
free from beggars, but they were fighting a losing
battle; there were just too many of them.

'London's shame,' she murmured, experiencing a
surge of sympathy.

'Mankind's shame,' he corrected. 'And mankind
has a great deal of which it need be ashamed.'

They had by this time reached the entrance to the
park, and Benedict changed the subject by remarking
how pleasant it was to have the place almost to themselves. His delightful companion wholeheartedly
agreed, and he could easily detect the wistful note in

her voice, and knew precisely what was passing through that delightfully wilful little head of hers.

'How unfortunate that it isn't permitted to enjoy a good gallop in the park!' He slanted a mocking glance as she turned startled eyes in his direction. 'Oh, yes, my lady. Lowly groom I may be, but even I know that ladies are permitted to ride only at a sedate trot while in the capital.'

'A timely reminder!' she exclaimed, gurgling with laughter. 'How very glad I am that I have you to instruct me in how to go on.' Those imps of mischief, always lurking beneath the surface, added a distinct sparkle to her eyes. 'You missed your vocation in life, Benjamin Rudgely. You ought to have been a duenna.'

He almost choked. How dared she suggest that he ally himself to that species which he had found an utter bane in his younger days! Her gurgle of laughter at his affronted expression quickly faded, and he turned his head in the direction of her suddenly perturbed gaze.

In the years he had spent abroad many of society's lesser personages had faded from his memory, but Benedict had little difficulty in recognising the lone figure approaching on a showy chestnut gelding.

He would have been the first to admit that he had never been, and possibly never would be, a paragon of all the virtues. He'd certainly been no angel in his younger days. Long sessions of drinking and gambling had not been, he was ashamed to say, rare occurrences. Nor had it been unusual to see him about the town with a ravishing beauty on his arm. His liaisons, if not precisely discreetly conducted, had without exception been with women of his own class or with those who knew the rules. He had never tampered with innocence, nor had any one of the ladies with whom he had enjoyed more intimate relations suffered as a consequence of her association with him. Which was a great deal more than could be said for several young women whose names had been linked with that of Sir Lucius Crawley.

One particularly unsavoury tale involving the Baronet instantly sprang into Benedict's mind. The young lady involved in the affair had come from a good family, and rumour had had it at the time that she was destined to come into a considerable sum of money upon her marriage. Soon after her arrival in town the poor girl had fallen under the destructive spell of Sir Lucius and had agreed to an elopement. Fortunately the young woman had not been without male protectors. Her uncle, in hot pursuit, had managed to overtake the runaways some twenty miles north of London and, certain that Sir Lucius had been nothing more than a fortune-hunter, had not hesitated to inform the Baronet that his niece would not inherit a penny unless she married with her family's consent. This, of course, had changed everything. Sir Lucius had returned to town, and the poor broken-hearted young woman had cast herself from an upper-storey window at her uncle's home a few days later and had died instantly.

Unfortunately that poor deluded girl was by no means the only fair damsel to suffer as a consequence of trusting the self-seeking Baronet. So it came as something of a relief to Benedict, as he fell back a few paces to allow Sir Lucius to manoeuvre his mount alongside Sophia's filly, to discover that his darling girl did not appear in the least susceptible to Sir Lucius's darkly brooding good looks, though she managed to greet him cordially enough by remarking that she was rather surprised to see him out and about at this time of day.

'Truth to tell, my lady, I do not make a habit of rising at this ungodly hour when residing in town,' he admitted, his dark gaze devouring her every curve, and making Sophia thankful that she was wearing extra layers of clothing that morning. 'But I was fortunate enough to overhear you mention to that pretty little friend of yours that you intended riding early this morning, and could not let such a golden opportunity of furthering our acquaintance slip through my fingers.'

So he was not above doing a spot of eavesdropping when it suited his purposes. And what was his intention? Sophia couldn't help wondering. Seduction? No, she doubted that very much. A womaniser he undoubtedly was, but he would not risk being ostracised by society by foolishly attempting to ruin the daughter of an earl.

She regarded him in silence for a moment, her gaze far less flattering than his own. Perhaps Lord Nicholas had been correct in his assumption, and Sir Lucius was once again contemplating matrimony. Perhaps he was even considering her as a possible candidate for the future Lady Crawley. If so, she would swiftly disabuse him. Not for the world would she ally herself to a person who would, she didn't doubt, in the years to come turn out to be a mirror image of that debauched roué the Marquis of Sywell!

'You flatter me, sir, but you should have saved yourself the trouble. I'm certain that our paths will cross from time to time during the forthcoming weeks.'

This was not precisely the reaction to which he had grown accustomed over the years when paying a certain lady particular attention, but Sir Lucius was not deterred. Experience told him that Lady Sophia, for all her self-possessed air, was a complete innocent when it came to the gentle art of dalliance. Added to which, he had always found the chase far more exciting than the inevitable surrender, and knew that he would attain the utmost pleasure in taming this spirited little minx and bending her to his will.

'And I would consider it a great favour,' Sophia continued, disliking the way he continued to regard her, like some ravenous dog drooling over a bone, 'if you did not make it generally known that I prefer to take my exercise at this time of day, sir. My morning rides are sacrosanct periods when I can enjoy a little solitude.'

A deep masculine rumble, only partially suppressed, reached her ears, and it took every ounce of self-control Sophia possessed not to laugh outright herself when Sir Lucius swung round in the saddle to cast her highly amused groom a darkling look. She knew she ought to take Ben roundly to task for riding so close and shamelessly listening to every word of the conversation, but she had no intention of doing so, now or later, for she sensed that as long as Benjamin Rudgely was at hand she need never fear a man of Sir Lucius Crawley's stamp.

'I sincerely trust that you do not consider my presence this morning an intrusion, my lady,' the Baronet said smoothly, though he couldn't quite disguise his lingering annoyance at the insulting servant's behaviour. 'You were certainly not averse to my company last night, as I recall.'

Sophia silently cursed herself for every kind of fool for paying Sir Lucius particular attention at the Strattans' ball. She had known that it would be a mistake to dance with him a second time, and yet she had foolishly done so, simply because earlier in the evening she had glimpsed an expression on her father's face that informed her clearly enough that he did not approve.

Although her experience of men most certainly was not vast, some inner feminine wisdom warned her that Sir Lucius could be a dangerous man if crossed, and one, moreover, who would not take kindly to being made to look a fool. So it would be far better, surely, she decided quickly, to make her feelings clear now, rather than allow further misunderstandings to occur in the future. Yet, for some obscure reason, and for the life of her she couldn't understand why, she just didn't want Ben to know how very foolish she had been to offer a man of Sir Lucius's reputation encouragement, minimal though it had been.

They had by this time reached a very secluded area of the park. 'Shall we stroll for a while?' she suggested, drawing rein by a clump of trees, and slipping lightly to the ground before either Ben or Sir Lucius could assist her.

She did not notice the disapproving look that flickered in a pair of alert blue eyes as she wandered beneath the canopy of branches, but Sir Lucius most certainly did, and it gave him a deal of satisfaction to order the groom to remain with the horses.

Coming to a halt by a sturdy elm, Sophia waited for Sir Lucius to join her. 'I believe I owe you an apology, sir,' she announced, coming straight to the point and sounding far more composed than she was in fact feeling. She had not meant to walk quite so far, and Ben seemed a disturbingly long way away.

'Apologise, my dear?' Sir Lucius, his eyes glinting with satisfaction, and with something far more disturbing that Sophia didn't choose to define, took a step closer. 'Apologise for what, pray? You have done me no disservice,' he purred silkily. 'Quite the contrary, I assure you.'

Sophia instinctively took a step away, only to find her back pressed against the trunk of the elm. What had seemed quite a simple task a few minutes ago had assumed alarming proportions. Sir Lucius was no easily managed callow youth whose desires could be suppressed by a few well-chosen words. He was a master at the art of dalliance; undoubtedly a man whose success with women over the years prompted him to pursue a particular quarry remorselessly if given sufficient reason to suppose that his attentions would not in the end be wholly unwelcome. And hadn't she foolishly offered him sufficient encouragement already by leading him to this secluded spot?

He confirmed her worst fears by moving a step nearer and placing one shapely hand on the trunk by her head. Faint-hearted she had never been, not even as a child, and it would have afforded her the utmost satisfaction to administer a resounding box round the ears when he lowered his eyes and unashamedly contemplated the bodice of her habit. She didn't suppose for a moment that an assurance from her that she was completely indifferent to him would be believed, and she began to wonder just how she could manage to extricate herself from this embarrassing predicament when she clearly detected the sound of a twig snapping nearby.

Sir Lucius heard it too, and swung round sharply. Unlike Sophia, it was not profound relief that he was experiencing at discovering the groom standing a matter of three feet away, as he betrayed clearly enough by his rasping demand to know what he thought he was doing. 'I believe I told you to remain with the horses,' he growled between clenched teeth.

'You did,' Benedict confirmed smoothly and, as far as Sophia could detect, completely unperturbed by the Baronet's display of hostility. If he betrayed anything at all, it was a trace of exasperation when he glanced briefly in her direction. 'But might I remind you that I'm not your lackey and, therefore, am not prepared to take orders from you.'

Then everything happened so quickly that Sophia could only utter a startled gasp in dismay. Sir Lucius, cursing under his breath, raised his crop, but Ben easily warded off the blow aimed at his shoulder, and a second later delivered a powerful hit to the jaw which had the Baronet sprawling on the ground.

'What the devil's going on here?' an authoritative and very familiar voice demanded to know, and Sophia, utterly stunned by what had taken place, was unable to believe the evidence of her own eyes as she saw her elder brother stalking purposefully towards them.

If she had possessed the power to make herself invisible she most certainly would have made good use of it. She didn't suppose for a moment that Marcus honestly required an explanation, and as her tongue seemed to have decided to attach itself to the roof of her mouth, she found herself completely unequal to the task of offering any.

She watched as her brother's astute gaze went from Ben, who looked ready, and more than willing, to repeat his actions of a few moments before, to Sir Lucius who, still appearing slightly dazed, was making an attempt to rise.

'Allow me to assist you, Crawley,' he said, only to have his helping hand thrust irritably aside.

'You'll permit me to inform you, Angmering,' Sir Lucius remarked, when he was at last on his feet again, and doing his best to repair his slightly dishevelled appearance by brushing the leaves from his jacket, 'that your father's choice of servants leaves much to be desired.'

'So it would seem,' Marcus responded, glancing once again in the groom's direction. 'None the less, you'll allow me to point out, Crawley, that we are not in the habit of whipping our people. From what I observed, this man reacted in self-defence. So might I suggest that we forget the whole unfortunate incident and go our separate ways before we attract the attention of the vulgarly curious.'

Sophia realised by Sir Lucius's suddenly alert expression as he gazed about him that her shrewd brother had said precisely the right thing. The Baronet's temper might be hasty, he might even enjoy the notoriety his amorous exploits had brought him over the years, but she doubted very much that he would risk being ostracised by the Ton by making a

vulgar spectacle of himself in a public place. There
had been no one in sight a few minutes before. This,
however, was no longer the case, for a small cluster
of riders was now heading down the path in their
direction.

'You are quite right, of course, Angmering.'
Swooping to retrieve his hat, which still lay among
the leaves, Crawley cast an unmistakably vindictive
glance in the groom's direction. 'I just hope my memory proves as amenable as yours,' and with that, and
the briefest of nods, he was gone.

'Now perhaps you'll be good enough to inform me
what the deuce that was all about!' Marcus demanded, easily detecting his sister's faint sigh of relief.

Ten years her senior he may have been, but Sophia
had never been in awe of her frequently abrupt elder
brother. Flashing him a look from beneath her lashes,
which informed him clearly enough that she was beginning to regain her equilibrium and was not best
pleased with his cavalier attitude, she turned to Ben,
who continued to appear quite remarkably unconcerned in the circumstances. 'You return to Berkeley
Square now. My brother, I'm sure, will see me safely
home. And, Ben,' she added softly, when he turned
to go. 'Thank you.'

'Who the deuce is that fellow, Sophie?' Marcus
was not slow to enquire once Ben was safely out of
earshot. 'Strangely enough he reminds me of someone, but for the life of me I cannot think who it can

be.' He shook his head as though dismissing it from his mind. 'And why wasn't Clem with you?'

'Clem has left us to work for someone else. My new groom's name is Benjamin Rudgely.'

'Is it by gad!' The name meant absolutely nothing to Marcus. 'Well, Benjamin Rudgely will not be your groom for very much longer if he continues to conduct himself in such a fashion,' he warned. 'A menial cannot go round flooring his betters and expect to retain his position.'

Sophia couldn't understand why, but she took great exception to having her new groom labelled a menial and was not slow to voice her displeasure. 'Furthermore, Marcus, I shall not hear of Ben being dismissed because of this morning's unfortunate occurrence. You saw yourself what happened.'

'I saw, right enough,' he confirmed, as they returned to the horses, 'but I cannot understand for the life of me why it should have occurred.'

'It happened because I was foolish enough to pay Crawley attention last night. I certainly didn't invite him to come riding with me this morning,' she hurriedly assured him, accepting his help to get into the saddle, and easily detecting the reproachful glint in his dark eyes as he mounted his own fine bay, 'but evidently he must have supposed that his presence would not be unwelcome. I was trying to think of some delicate way of informing him that rakes were not to my taste when Ben suddenly appeared.'

She decided to be fair and give Sir Lucius the benefit of the doubt. 'I don't suppose for a moment that Crawley would contemplate a seduction scene here in the park, but I cannot deny that I was very glad that Ben was with me. And now, Marcus, all I wish to do is forget the whole unfortunate episode.'

He looked as if he was about to say something in response, but then, evidently, thought better of it, and they rode towards the park gates in silence, until Sophia asked him when he had arrived in town.

'Late yesterday evening. I'm staying with my friend Lawrence Petersham. We'll be here for a few days, and then we're travelling to his country home in Hampshire to do a spot of shooting and fishing.'

Disappointed, but not unduly surprised, Sophia cast her brother a thoughtful glance. Marcus never attempted to make use of the town house in Berkeley Square when the Earl was in residence, preferring instead to put up at a hotel or stay with friends. During the past few years his visits to Jaffrey House had been less frequent too, and she could not help feeling that as long as he continued to avoid their father's company whenever possible, any resentment he might continue to harbour with regard to the ill-treatment he considered his mother had received at the Earl's hands would continue to fester deep inside.

As the Earl had always flatly refused to discuss anything about his first marriage, and the Countess, loyal to the last, had not betrayed his trust by divulging any of the details, Sophia had never been in possession of all the facts and she doubted very much that Marcus had either.

Childhood memories began to filter through her mind, and she recalled vividly that lovely summer day, almost eleven years ago, when she had peered out of one of the upper-floor windows at Jaffrey House and had spotted her brother heading across the park in the direction of Steepwood Abbey. The grounds especially had always held a certain fascination for him, and he had frequently gone there to be private with his thoughts.

Sophia herself had never been similarly drawn to either the Abbey or its grounds, not even as a child. Many eerie stories about the place had been passed down through the centuries. In more recent years the Marquis of Sywell's debauched activities had been sufficient to dissuade most young females from venturing there alone, and Sophia, not always the most obedient of children, had for once adhered to her parents' strict command and had never once attempted to venture into the Abbey grounds on her own. Having her elder brother's protection, however, had made a visit perfectly in order, and she had not hesitated on that long-ago summer's day in escaping from her governess in order to follow him.

Marcus, having been something of a taciturn youth, had not been best pleased to discover his young sister racing across the park in his direction. When she had finally reached his side, he had made his feelings brutally clear by ordering her to return home in no uncertain terms and, her nature being what it was, she had flatly refused. A heated argument had ensued, which had culminated in Marcus saying some rather unkind things about their father, and she retaliating by flying at him, small fists making contact with any part of his anatomy she could reach, while screaming insults about his mother. Marcus had swiftly captured her flailing arms, and when eventually she had grown calmer they had made a pact: never again would he say unkind things about their father and in return Sophia had promised never to pass a derogatory remark about his mother.

During the ensuing years they had both kept to the bargain. Sophia had no intention of breaking her promise now by informing him that she considered his continued avoidance of their father's company very foolish, and merely voiced the hope that she would be seeing something of him during his short sojourn in town.

'I should imagine that highly likely,' he announced, and then promptly lessened her delight by adding, 'It's quite obvious that you need someone to keep an eye on you, my girl.'

Sophia could feel her occasionally ungovernable temper begin to stir. She was still feeling very guilty, but steadfastly refused to be held entirely responsible for what had occurred. 'I shall take leave to inform you, Marcus, that I neither desire nor require your services as a chaperon,' she hissed, putting him in mind of a pettish kitten. 'I should go on a great deal better if the male members of my family ceased to meddle in my affairs.'

'Ha!' Marcus barked, not slow to understand. 'So Father's been laying down the law, has he? High time too!'

'I might have expected some such tactless response from you!' she retorted, thoroughly nettled now. 'I only hope that when you finally decide that it's time for you to settle down and marry he'll lay down the law in your choice of partner too!'

'So, that's the way of it, is it?' Wicked though his smile undoubtedly was, it did contain a trace of sympathy. 'Come on, Sophie, be fair,' he urged gently. 'I would be the first to admit that I haven't always agreed with everything he's ever done or said, but I'm sure Father has only your best interests at heart. The last thing he would want is for you to fall prey to some fortune-hunter.'

'I'm not a complete widgeon, Marcus. I do realise that. What you and Papa fail to realise, however, is that I'm no longer a child, and am quite capable of making the reasoned choice when it comes to selecting a husband.'

He seemed decidedly unconvinced, as his next words proved. 'You may consider yourself up to snuff, my girl, but I'm afraid your behaviour this morning rather refutes that. No female in her right mind would ever offer a man of Crawley's stamp a h'a'porth of encouragement.'

They had by this time reached Berkeley Square,

and Sophia, not waiting for assistance, slipped down from the saddle. The fact that there was more than an element of truth in what he had just said only succeeded in annoying her further, and she could not resist wiping away his smugly satisfied smile by announcing, 'You may be certain of one thing, Marcus, a green girl I still might be on occasions, but not so foolish as ever to become tied for life to an overbearing, arrogant bore such as you!'

Half amused, half annoyed by what he considered a totally inaccurate assessment of his character, Marcus walked the horses round to the mews. His little sister, it seemed, had not yet learned to curb that temper of hers, nor had she completely abandoned her wilful ways.

'What she needs, of course, is a firm hand. I sincerely hope her future husband will be a man who won't be afraid to school her when necessary,' he muttered, with a certain grim satisfaction, only half aware that he had spoken his thoughts aloud.

'The right sort of man could handle her easily enough, sir,' an amused voice remarked.

'You may be right, but I for one will pity the poor devil, whoever he may be,' Marcus responded, automatically handing over the reins to the new groom. 'She can be an unruly little madam when the mood takes her.'

'Can't say I'm surprised. It's quite obvious she was spoilt as a child. The Earl's fault, I suspect.'

'There you have the right of it! If he had been

firmer in his dealings with Sophie years ago, she wouldn't have turned out to be such a—' Marcus caught himself up abruptly, suddenly realising to whom he was speaking, and cast Ben a frowning glance. 'I'd advise you to keep your opinions to yourself, my man!' he snapped, but was unable to prevent a smile as he stalked into the house. Impertinent the groom might be, but he was certainly no fool and already had Sophia's measure.

He discovered his father alone in the library, and as he had certain details he wished to discuss concerning the estate he managed in the north, it suited his purpose admirably to spend some time alone with the Earl.

Without any display of real warmth on either side, they greeted each other cordially enough. For his part, his lordship certainly wished it could be otherwise, that he could freely exhibit the deep affection in which he held his eldest son, but he doubted very much that Marcus would appreciate any display of emotion. And who could blame him for that? His lordship most certainly did not, for he was very well aware that if he had been more open about his disastrous first marriage, if he had not tried to spare Marcus more hurt by steadfastly refusing to tell him the truth about his mother, he himself would not have figured all these years as the villain of the piece in his son's eyes.

Well, perhaps it was too late now to attempt to set the record straight, he thought, handing his son a glass of wine, but if the opportunity ever arose in the future, he would not allow the chance to try to win his son's affection slip through his fingers. In the meantime he must be content with the respect Marcus always showed, and returned the compliment by listening intently to his son's proposed plans for the northern estate.

After nodding his head in agreement, and informing Marcus to put into effect the changes he wished to make, his lordship expected his son to bring the interview to a close. When he made no attempt to leave, and furthermore went over to the decanter to refill his glass, he knew at once that his son must have some other topic he wished to discuss, and waited patiently for him to resume his seat.

Marcus took a fortifying sip of the rich red liquid, while casting his father an uneasy glance above the rim of his glass. 'I'm no tale-bearer, sir, as I hope you know, nor am I one to interfere in something which really is none of my concern, but I think it only right that you are aware of something that happened in the park earlier, as it concerns Sophia. Or perhaps it would be more accurate to say an incident involving one of your servants.'

Marcus could see at once that he had his father's full attention. 'My friend Petersham is wishing to sell his bay, and as I'm in need of a new hack I decided to put the horse through its places. Quite by chance I came upon Sophie in a quiet area of the park. She was in the company of Sir Lucius Crawley.'

His lordship was not best pleased to learn this and wasn't slow to betray the fact. 'The devil she was!'

'She informed me that she didn't arrange to meet Crawley there,' Marcus assured him. It was not his intention to cause trouble for his sister, merely to put the Earl on his guard. 'And I believe her, sir. Sophia may have her faults, but she's certainly no liar. I honestly believe that she doesn't even like Crawley.'

The Earl grunted. 'That wasn't the impression I gained last night. The little minx danced with him twice. And I suspect it was simply because she knew I wouldn't approve.'

Marcus could not help smiling at this. His father might have turned seventy, but there was absolutely nothing lacking in his upper storey. 'I think you may possibly be right. Anyway, getting back to what I have to tell you, I arrived on the scene in time to see Crawley raise his crop to your new stable-hand, and to see the groom floor the Baronet with one flush hit to the jaw.'

'Did he, by gad!' There was more than just a hint of excitement in the Earl's grey eyes.

'Believe me, sir, I couldn't help but admire the way he did it myself. I wouldn't be at all surprised to learn that he's done some sparring in his time. There was no bluster about it. Excellent science!' The glint of admiration in Marcus's dark eyes faded. 'Still, I'm not suggesting for a moment that he should have done it, though I have to say he reacted in self-defence.'

The Earl looked across at his son steadily. 'Are you

suggesting that I should dismiss him because of the incident?'

'No, sir. I'm not.' A further wry smile tugged at the corner of his mouth. 'He may be an insolent dog, but he was only doing his duty by guarding Sophia. I understand he hasn't been with you for very long, but unless I much mistake the matter he already has my sister's measure. She would not find it easy to escape from him, and I believe he'd always guard her well.'

'I respect your judgement,' his lordship responded softly, 'and find that very reassuring to hear.' He regarded his son in silence for a moment, and noted the look of concern that remained in his eyes. 'So what precisely is troubling you, Marcus?'

'I'm not certain. I don't suppose for a moment that Crawley will bring charges of assault against the groom, not when there were witnesses to the incident, and he would probably be made to look a fool. But he's a vindictive devil...And I just didn't care for that look in his eyes before he left.'

Chapter Six

Marcus was by no means the only one to have noticed that malevolent gleam in a pair of hard, blue eyes. Benedict had not been slow to recognise that vengeful glint either and, given Sir Lucius's somewhat unsavoury character, had well expected the Baronet, at the very least, to write to the Earl of Yardley complaining bitterly, and demanding the instant dismissal of the perpetrator of the attack upon him. When, however, several days had passed and he had not even received the mildest reprimand for his behaviour in the park, Benedict began to wonder whether Sir Lucius might not be quite the black-hearted rogue he had been painted. Then something occurred to restore his former opinion of the malicious Baronet.

He had been taking one of his lordship's fine coach-horses to the blacksmith when he had first suspected that he had become the object of attention. Turning suddenly, he had caught sight of a thickset individual in a frieze coat darting down a side alley. Then, as he had sat himself down on a rough wooden bench outside the smithy, waiting for the horse to be shod, he had glimpsed the same scoundrel across the street, staring directly at the blacksmith's premises. Later that same day he had noticed him yet again loitering near the entrance to the mews; only this time he had a companion with him of equally villainous appearance.

There was little doubt in Benedict's mind that he was being watched, and his movements noted, so the following evening when Trapp, in a surprisingly sociable mood, suddenly suggested that he might like to accompany him to The Red Lion inn, and enjoy a tankard or two of ale, Benedict accepted the unexpected invitation eagerly, realising that it would offer the opportunity to confirm beyond doubt that he was, indeed, the object of someone's interest.

Dusk had almost fallen when he and Trapp left their room above the stable, but even so there remained sufficient light for Benedict to be fairly certain that there were no shadowy figures lurking in the mews. It was impossible to tell whether someone was dogging their footsteps when they turned on to the main street and walked in an easterly direction towards the tavern favoured by a great number of grooms and coach-drivers. London never slept, certainly not at this time of year, and there were just too many people abroad to be sure whether he was once again being followed.

As things turned out, it was the eagle-eyed Trapp who, once comfortably seated in the friendly inn, tankard of well-earned ale in his hand, first noticed that Benedict appeared to be the object of a certain someone's attention.

''Ere, lad,' he remarked, after swallowing a mouthful of ale and wiping his mouth on the back of his hand, 'that cove standing over there seems to be eyeing you quite a bit.' He gestured towards an ill-favoured rascal leaning against the end of the counter. 'I noticed he came in not long after us. A friend of yours, is he?'

Benedict glanced across the tap in time to see the man turn his back towards them. Even though he could not see his face clearly, he felt certain in his own mind that it was neither of the two who had been skulking at the entrance to the mews the day before, and was therefore able to say with total honesty that he'd never seen the fellow before in his life.

Trapp appeared to lose interest, and changed the subject by remarking that Lady Sophia would be requiring Ben's services again in the morning. 'That seems to have cheered you up, lad,' he remarked, noting the gleam which just for one unguarded moment flickered in his companion's eyes.

Benedict didn't attempt to deny it. 'To be honest with you, Mr Trapp. I've found it a mite wearisome these past days with so little to do. I'm a man who likes to keep himself occupied.'

The head groom found nothing amiss with this attitude. 'I know what you mean, lad. I'm of a similar bent m'self. Her ladyship gave up riding a horse a decade or more ago. His lordship will still climb into the saddle from time to time, but never when residing in town. It's only Lady Sophia that takes regular exercise. Still,' he shrugged, 'I suppose we oughtn't to complain. I can tell you now, while we remain in town, we won't get too many evenings like this one, when the family remains at home, so we'd best make the most of it.'

Benedict agreed, and in the normal course of events didn't doubt for a moment that he would have enjoyed this novel experience, for never before could he recall ever having spent an evening in a common tavern, supping ale, with only a groom for company. His pleasure in the occasion, however, was totally marred by the presence of the man leaning against the counter, who, he had noted by this time, had already glanced in his direction on several occasions.

There wasn't a doubt in his mind now that he was certainly the object of someone's interest. The question was whose? Who would interest himself in the movements of a common groom? It was not beyond the realms of possibility of course that, while he had been out and about exercising one of the Earl of Yardley's fine horses, someone from his past, a friend perhaps, had penetrated his disguise. Surely, though, if that were the case, it would be a simple matter for this friend to approach him directly. Why have him watched? he asked himself, peering down at his tankard before fortifying himself from its contents. No, there was more to it than that, instinct told him, something distinctly sinister.

'Of course, when we return to Jaffrey House we'll be kept busy enough,' Trapp continued, and Benedict, thrusting aside his disturbing thoughts, paid him the compliment of listening. 'The boys will be home from school in the summer. Then we'll certainly have our hands full! The stables is a favourite haunt of theirs.'

Benedict had gained the distinct impression from their conversation a few days before that Sophia was very fond of her twin younger brothers, and he himself was very much looking forward to making their acquaintance. The meeting, however, would not take place whilst he was still in the guise of a groom, if he could possibly avoid it. It was bad enough having been brought into contact with the eldest brother. Lord Angmering was no fool, and Benedict didn't doubt for a moment that Marcus would have little difficulty in recognising the Duke of Sharnbrook when they met in the not too distant future. He would need to cross that bridge when he came to it. In the meantime he had more than enough to concern him.

Once again he found himself glancing across at the counter in time to catch a pair of decidedly unfriendly eyes staring fixedly back across at him. Surly and unkempt, the rogue bore all the appearance of someone who would do virtually anything for money, perhaps even murder. But who on earth disliked him so much, bore him such a grudge, that he was prepared

to hire ruffians in order, perhaps, to attain his ends?
He smiled grimly as one name, and one name only,
sprang to mind.

If his suspicions were correct, and Sir Lucius
Crawley had hired a pack of ruffians to satisfy his lust
for revenge, then Benedict did not want Trapp involved in the inevitable confrontation. He had quickly
come to respect this frequently gruff, hard-working
man, and although he didn't doubt for a moment that
he would give a good account of himself if set upon,
Benedict had no intention of allowing this to happen
if he could possibly avoid it.

So, after tossing the remaining ale down his throat,
he carried the empty tankards across to the counter.
Trapp glanced up, surprised, when Benedict returned,
setting just the one refilled vessel down on their table,
and then did not offer to resume his seat.

'What's this then? Ain't you joining me, lad?' he
asked, not attempting to conceal his disappointment.

'No, Mr Trapp. One is more than enough for me,'
he lied. It was the best home-brewed he'd tasted in
many a long year, and in normal circumstance he
would have been quite content to have remained all
evening. 'I'll get back and check on the horses. You
stay here and enjoy your ale.'

Trapp did not attempt to argue and, being unsocia-
ble by nature, would have been more than happy to
sit by himself supping his ale had he not happened to
notice the rat-eyed rogue who had been propping up
the counter follow Ben from the inn.

He had no reason to suppose for a moment that Ben had lied, that he did, in fact, know the man, and he began to feel decidedly uneasy. Some sixth sense warned him that all was not as it should be. He just hadn't liked the look of that fellow—a villain if ever there was one!—and it seemed just too much of a coincidence that he should have chosen to leave when young Ben had.

Abandoning his tankard, he wasted no time in following. Fortunately Ben had chosen to take the same route back to the stables by which they had come, and Trapp quickly caught sight of his tall, long-striding figure some distance ahead. Unfortunately he could also see the stranger following, and closing fast.

He increased his own pace, and was certainly gaining on his quarry, when what he had feared happened: two men suddenly appeared from nowhere and, aided and abetted by the stalker, hauled Ben into a side alley. The street was busy, crowded with carriages, but there were very few people about on foot and, seemingly, no one except himself had seen the incident, or if someone else had, he or she was disinclined to become involved.

Galvanised, Trapp ran with surprising speed for a man who would not see fifty again, and arrived at the entrance to the narrow alley in time to witness Ben, still manfully attempting to grapple with the three stocky attackers, suddenly tumble to the ground.

Slightly stunned by the heavy fall, Benedict was forced to sustain a volley of merciless kicks and

blows before one of the attackers was blessedly
hauled from the fray. Out of his rapidly swelling left
eye he caught sight of his valiant rescuer delivering
a punishing blow to the villain who had followed him
from the inn and, summoning up his last reserves of
strength, took immediate action by smashing a sizeable stone against a well-muscled leg. The assailant
fell back, groaning in agony, too badly injured to be
a further threat.

Marcus had been correct when he had supposed
that his father's newest employee had sparred in his
time. Benedict was indeed a keen exponent of the art,
and he had little difficulty in dealing effectively with
the third and last assailant. Quickly scrambling to his
feet, he delivered one powerful blow which sent the
man in the frieze coat sprawling to the ground, and a
merciless clasp on a grubby neckcloth kept him there,
gasping for air.

'Who paid you to kill me?' Benedict hissed, piti-
lessly maintaining his constricting hold.

'Not kill,' the man croaked, ineffectually clawing
at the powerful fingers while fighting for breath.
'Only—only rough you up a bit.'

'Who was it?'

'Swear I don't know, guv'nor. Never seen 'im
afore. Came in The Three Ferrets a day or so back
looking for someone who'd do a job for 'im.'

It would have afforded Benedict supreme satisfaction to squeeze the very life out of the rogue, but

sense prevailed, and he released his hold. 'Describe him! What did he look like?'

'A weedy cove in black clothes.'

This was hardly a description of Sir Lucius, but then, Benedict reminded himself, Crawley was unlikely to have gone about hiring thugs himself. 'A servant?'

'Aye. Looked like it to me.' The hired thug raised a hand to his throat, but wisely refrained from attempting to escape. 'Told me where to find you, told me what you looked like too. Wanted you followed, see? Then, when the time were right, we were to give you a good 'iding. But we weren't to take our time about it, not if we wanted the rest of the money. The cove wanted the job done quick, like.'

With lips bruised and bleeding, Benedict managed a twisted smile as he hauled his captive to his feet by the lapels of the worn frieze coat. 'Well, it would seem you've earned your full reward, you rogue.'

'Eh?' The man looked bewildered, suspicious and hopeful in equal measures. 'Ain't yer going to turn us over to the Runners?'

Benedict didn't answer, but glanced up the deserted alley. Some detached part of his brain had registered that the man with the injured knee had limped away long since, quickly followed by the second partner-in-crime, with the doggedly determined Trapp hard on their heels.

'If I did that then you'd be quite unable to collect the remainder of your ill-gotten gains, now, wouldn't you?' he responded at last. 'Not that I think you'll have an easy time of collecting your—er—blood money.'

'No 'ard feelings, guv'nor, eh?' The small but sturdy villain looked even more unprepossessing when he smiled. He had several teeth missing, undoubtedly the result of his nefarious activities, and what few remained were black and decayed. 'These be 'ard times, and work be 'ard to come by. A man must take what 'e can get.'

'Work?' Benedict echoed, totally unmoved. 'Yes, and there are those who aren't too particular what they do so long as they get their reward. Which brings me back quite nicely to what I was saying earlier... Are you quite certain that you shall receive your dues?'

It was quite obvious from his expression that the villain wasn't at all sure. 'Told me he'd be in The Three Ferrets the day after tomorrow. And he'd better be there!'

'Take it from me, he won't be,' Benedict assured him with a certain grim satisfaction. 'But you will be paid in full if you do precisely what I tell you...'

The following morning Sophia left the house just before noon. Since the unfortunate encounter with Sir Lucius Crawley she had made a point of never taking exercise at the same time each day, in the hope that in this way she could avoid any further confrontations with would-be suitors. Her brother's escort, of course, had ensured that there had been no repetition of the unfortunate incident in Hyde Park, and she had very much enjoyed having Marcus with her for the past few days, for he could be the most amusing companion when he set his mind to it. Nevertheless she couldn't deny that she was very much looking forward to furthering her acquaintance with her enigmatic groom.

Consequently she was most disappointed to see her father's trusty henchman awaiting her arrival outside the house, and demanded to know why Ben was not to escort her.

If Trapp felt aggrieved by this total lack of enthusiasm for his company, he certainly betrayed no sign of it. 'Had a bit of a mishap, as yer might say, m'lady, and so I've relieved 'im of his dooties.'

Sophia was not slow to notice that the head groom himself was sporting a fine black eye. 'You also appear to have sustained an injury yourself, Trapp. What on earth has been happening? You look as if you've been in a mill.'

'A mill, m'lady?' he echoed, trying to appear the picture of innocence. 'Now, what on earth makes you suppose that I'd indulge in a bout of fisticuffs? I'm a peaceable man, I am.'

Raising a decidedly sceptical brow, Sophia allowed him to help her into the saddle. 'No one would think you peaceable, Trapp, if they'd ever heard you rant and rage at the stable-boys back at Jaffrey House.' She didn't quite catch his muttered response, but didn't trouble to ask him to repeat himself, and merely demanded to know what, precisely, had occurred to render Ben incapable of escorting her out that morning.

'Oh, he were more than ready to do so, m'lady, but I thought he ought to rest.'

Sophia succeeded in maintaining her temper, but it was an effort. 'And still I'm waiting for an answer, Trapp. No doubt you'll oblige me in your own good time.'

The sarcasm was not wasted on him, and he could not forebear a smile. His master's only daughter always put him in mind of a little terrier dog—inquisitive and determined, never willing to release its hold once it had its teeth into something.

'Titus decided to take exception to a rat visiting his stall, and lashed out. Unfortunately young Ben just 'appened to be standing behind him at the time and copped the hoof full in the chest, poor lad!'

As Titus, the most placid of all her father's fine carriage horses, had never been known so much as to draw his ears back when pestered by a yapping dog, Sophia found this explanation very hard to believe. 'And I suppose Ben caught you in the eye with his elbow while he was reeling from the impact.'

'Aye, that's the way of it, my lady,' Trapp confirmed, the derisive note in her voice having gone completely undetected this time, and Sophia, faintly smiling, decided to say no more for the present, thereby successfully lulling her father's minion into a false sense of security.

She maintained quite beautifully an air of sublime unconcern, not once attempting to raise the subject again, not even to enquire into the extent of her personal groom's injuries. After a sedately ridden circuit of the park, during which she stopped from time to time to exchange a few words with several acquaintances, including Lady Elizabeth and Robina, she returned to Berkeley Square and, still maintaining the innocently complaisant air, accompanied the groom round to the mews.

'I could quite easily have led your horse, my lady,' Trapp informed her while helping her to dismount.

'I know you could easily have done so,' she responded, smiling with deceptive sweetness, the period of feigned docility having well and truly come to an end. 'What you seem quite incapable of doing, however, is satisfying my curiosity over precisely why Ben was unable to accompany me today,' and before he could do or say anything to deter her, she was already halfway up the staircase leading to the room above the stables.

She discovered Ben lying down on his narrow bed, which seemed totally inadequate for a man of his size, browsing through an old edition of the *Morning Post*. The fact that he could evidently read never occurred to her as being in any way out of the ordinary, for she had come to the conclusion days before that she had acquired a personal groom with quite exceptional talents.

Benedict was very well aware that someone had entered. Quite naturally assuming it was Trapp, he made no attempt to rise, nor did he attempt to speak either, for although Trapp was becoming less taciturn with each passing day, there were still lengthy periods when he made not the least attempt to converse. It was only when Benedict detected the unmistakable foreign aroma of feminine perfume in the room that he troubled to lower the printed sheets in his hands, and glance round.

'My lady!' The joy at seeing her so unexpectedly induced him momentarily to forget his hurts. He tried to stand and received a painful reminder when several ribs groaned in protest.

Sophia was beside him in an instant, hand gently placed on one broad shoulder for a moment or two, urging him to remain seated. She could see clearly enough the evidence that he had been in a fight: the gash above the left eye, the cut and swollen bottom lip and the grazed knuckles.

She did not suppose for a moment that the head groom had been responsible for inflicting these injuries. Trapp, she knew, could be difficult on occasions, hard to please. Nevertheless she had never known him resort to physical violence before in order to maintain his high standards, except on one or two occasions when he had been caught administering a sound box round the ear to a certain work-shy stable-boy back at Jaffrey House. Ben, however, was no idle lad. With his superior height and strength, not to mention the added advantage of age, he could overpower Trapp in a trice.

'What happened to you?' Gentle yet determined, she was intent on knowing the truth. 'And please do not insult my intelligence by repeating that farrago of nonsense concerning Titus.'

What in heaven's name had the inventive Trapp been telling her? Benedict wondered, detecting the sound of a heavy tread on the stairs, and wishing fervently that the crowned head of the stables would hurry and offer some guidance on how to proceed.

When they had eventually returned to their room the previous evening, and Mr Trapp, his work-roughened hands surprisingly gentle, had tended to both their hurts, Benedict had not hesitated in confiding in the man who had so gallantly come to his aid. The name Sir Lucius Crawley had meant nothing to Trapp, and although he had voiced in no uncertain terms his wish to see the vindictive Baronet receive his just desserts, he had agreed wholeheartedly with Benedict's dictum that the fewer people who knew about the incident, the better. In return Benedict had reluctantly agreed that he ought to remain out of sight as much as possible, at least until the evidence of the confrontation had begun to fade. Their carefully considered stratagems, however, had been made without taking into account the unpredictable behaviour of the very determined daughter of the house.

'I'm waiting for an explanation,' the subject of his thoughts announced, tapping her crop impatiently against the folds of her skirt, and Benedict wasn't certain whether he wished to kiss her or shake her, or both.

Trapp's eventual arrival was of little help either. In response to Benedict's enquiring glance, he merely raised his hands in a helpless gesture, proof enough that he had had little experience in dealing with unruly females, at least the two-legged kind. So Benedict had little choice but to take command of the situation, and swiftly came to the conclusion that, all things considered, only honesty would serve.

With considerable discomfort he rose to his feet, the better to face her. 'It pains me to tell you, in more ways than one, that both Mr Trapp and I were involved in a fight last night.'

'That much is abundantly obvious,' she responded, not in the least amused by his obvious attempt to make light of it all, and Trapp, feeling that it behoved him to say something, experienced a sudden flash of inspiration.

'Set upon by three ruffians. After our purses, they were. They didn't get 'em though, 'cause young Ben 'ere and me, we gave a good account of ourselves, and soon had 'em scurrying away like whipped pups.'

Ben's expression of comical dismay only succeeded in increasing Sophia's scepticism. 'Although one must deplore such behaviour, one cannot help but feel a degree of sympathy for those ruffians' plight,

Trapp,' she remarked, her tone as dry as kindling. 'They must have been desperate men indeed to have chosen you two as their victims...Desperate, or just plain stupid! Had they succeeded in their aim, they would have been woefully disappointed with their ill-gotten gains. After all, two grooms out enjoying an evening tipple hardly present rich pickings.'

Trapp looked helplessly across at his subordinate. If it was guidance he sought, then none was forth-coming, for Benedict was staring directly at Sophia, his eyes alight with amusement, and more than just a hint of admiration too.

'What really induced those men to set upon you?' she asked, directing the question at him.

'The inducement was money, my lady,' he assured her. 'They were paid to do so.'

'But why? Does someone bear you a grudge?' She found this difficult to believe, and would have dis-missed it in a trice if he hadn't appeared quite so sincere as he nodded his head. 'I would be the first to admit that I do not know you very well, but I wouldn't have supposed for a moment that you were the kind of man to go out of his way to make enemies. Do you know who instigated the attack upon you?'

He did not attempt to answer.

'Whoever hired those men must surely have pos-sessed sufficient funds to do so,' she persisted. 'Have you truly no idea who it might have been?'

Again he did not answer, but suddenly there was no need for him to do so, for all at once she realised who it must have been, and was assailed by a veritable torrent of conflicting emotions. Foremost among them was a searing sense of shame, knowing that but for her none of this would have happened, realising that her childish behaviour in trying to thwart her father's plans to marry her to some eligible *parti* had resulted in an innocent man becoming hurt.

'Crawley,' she muttered, anger coming to the fore. 'It must have been he. Rot his black heart!'

'I dare say in time he will go the way of all flesh,' Benedict responded with a flash of wry humour, but Sophia refused to be diverted.

'I do not believe that I can wait that long,' she announced, determination hardening her voice. 'Crawley's an utter blackguard, and I shall personally ensure that he pays dearly for what he has done to you.'

There was a moment's silence, then, 'Let be, my lady!'

It was undoubtedly a command, and one which had Trapp gaping in astonishment and Sophia regarding her suddenly authoritative groom in a mixture of anger and surprise. It was evident that she was unaccustomed to being spoken to in such a fashion, least of all by a servant. Nevertheless Benedict was not deterred.

'I do not require a female to fight my battles for me,' he went on in the same resolute tone. 'I may not, at this present moment in time, be in a position to extract due penance, but I have a long memory and shall not forget Sir Lucius Crawley's behaviour in a hurry. In the meantime it would be in our own best interests, both yours and mine, to let the matter rest.'

It was easy to detect both anger and resentment in her expression. Benedict, regarding her keenly, could discern a flicker of admiration too, and finally he detected the reluctant acceptance before Sophia swung away and walked the few paces to the head of the stairs.

'Very well, Benjamin Rudgely, it shall be as you wish,' she flung over her shoulder. Then she was gone without uttering another word, leaving Trapp gaping in utter astonishment once again.

'Well, I'll be damned!' he announced, when at last he had found his voice. 'If I hadn't witnessed it with me own eyes, I'd never 'ave believed it.' He glanced in Ben's direction, a look of dawning wonder in his eyes. 'You're a marvel, my boy! Miss Sophia's always been a headstrong chit, wanting her own way in all things, and yet she agreed to let well alone without so much as a blink.'

'Not quite, Mr Trapp,' Benedict countered. 'Unless I much mistake the matter, she didn't find the decision an easy one to make.' He smiled softly as he eased his aching body back down on the bed. 'Headstrong and spoilt she might be, but I for one do not doubt for a moment that she will keep her word.'

Chapter Seven

Benedict's faith in the young woman who had succeeded in capturing his interest like no other female has done before was not misplaced, as he discovered for himself two days later when he received an unexpected summons to present himself at the house promptly at midday.

As Trapp had driven the Earl and Countess out in the light town carriage half an hour earlier, Benedict had a fairly shrewd idea of precisely who wished to see him. Prepared though he was, he still found his pulse rate soaring when he entered the library at the appointed time to discover the raven-haired darling who continued to bewitch him seated at the mahogany desk, busily engaged in writing a letter.

Disappointingly there was no smile of welcome this time, as she instructed him to be seated in the chair on the opposite side of the desk, but Benedict refused to be too downcast. She appeared totally absorbed in the letter she was writing, so he made no

attempt to interrupt her, and merely occupied himself
by taking stock of the book-lined room.

Unlike Trapp, Benedict quite understandably felt
not in the least out of place in the elegant surroundings. The well-stocked shelves, and the unmistakable
aroma of leather and fine old brandy, put him vividly
in mind of the library at Sharnbrook. He didn't doubt
for a moment that during his long absence the dedicated servants had taken excellent care of the house,
and its contents. No doubt most of the rooms were
swathed in holland covers, and he was very much
looking forward to that day when he could order their
removal and take up the many duties for which he
had been groomed from birth.

Drawing his mind back to the present, he glanced
across the desk to discover that the being who had
been instrumental in delaying his return to the ancestral pile had finished writing and was studying him
rather intently.

'Your injuries appear to be healing fast,' Sophia
remarked, having observed that his lips were no
longer swollen, though the gash above his left eye
was still very noticeable. 'I trust, in the circumstances,
Trapp has not been working you too hard.'

Benedict wasn't slow to assure her that the opposite
was true, and that he had been given only the lightest
of tasks. 'In fact, my lady, the sooner I'm allowed to
resume all my duties, the better I shall like it.'

'In that case you may accompany me out tomorrow. My brother leaves London today, so I shall require your services from now on.'

This was music to Benedict's ears. It was not that he disliked Lord Angmering; far from it, in fact. The Viscount had often paid a visit to the stables when he had called at Berkeley Square, and his frequent caustic remarks had never failed to amuse Benedict. He could not deny, though, that the Viscount's presence in the capital had succeeded in obstructing his wooing of the Earl's delightful daughter, and he couldn't in all honesty say that he was sorry to learn of Marcus's imminent departure.

'In the meantime, however, I do not think you should be in too much of a hurry to resume all your duties,' Sophia advised softly, experiencing yet again that searing stab of guilt as she detected the clear outline of the bandages beneath the rough cotton shirt. 'I do not wish to be instrumental in causing you yet more pain.'

It was a moment or two before Benedict realised that she was referring to his physical injuries, not his present emotional state, and almost sighed with relief, for he didn't doubt for a moment that his days as the Yardleys' stable-hand would be well and truly numbered if it ever became known that he had serious designs on the daughter of the house.

'You are not to blame for what occurred the other evening, my lady,' he assured her gently, but she refused to be so nobly exonerated.

'Yes, I am, Ben,' she countered. 'I'm totally to

blame. It was my foolishness in offering encouragement to a man of Crawley's stamp that resulted in your being attacked.' She couldn't prevent a wry little smile. 'You must allow me to suffer a guilty conscience, and feel thoroughly ashamed of myself. I don't suppose for a moment that, my nature being what it is, I shall suffer this lowliness of spirits for very much longer,' she said lightly, unaware herself just how much the experience had begun to change her attitude towards a great many things.

The change in her expression, however, was instantly noticeable, and there was more than a hint of resentment in the look she flashed him. 'Of course, it certainly didn't improve my state of mind when I saw Crawley yesterday evening, and was forced to keep a civil tongue in my head because of that ridiculous promise I had made to you.'

'You spoke to him?'

'Briefly, yes,' she disclosed, not finding his evident interest in the least strange. 'Thankfully, though, he never asked me to dance.' She frowned suddenly. 'Now I come to think about it, I cannot recall seeing him dance at all. He seemed rather preoccupied, and left the party early, as I recall.' This seemed to afford Ben a great deal of amusement, and she was curious to know why.

'Because, my darling girl, I strongly suspect that Crawley's preoccupation was due entirely to my little stratagem,' he admitted and, ignoring her evident surprise at the familiarity, he went on to explain the steps he had taken to attain a modest revenge.

Sophia thoroughly approved, and it went some way to lessen her lingering feelings of guilt. 'I just hope those rascals who set upon you continue to press for payment. And attain it too!'

'I suspect that he will be forced to meet their demands in the end, if only to ensure their silence. A man like Crawley might enjoy a degree of notoriety, but engaging known felons to attain his nefarious ends would not be tolerated. He would lose face, might even be branded a coward, and that spells disaster for any member of the Ton.'

As always, what he had said was no less than the truth, and Sophia couldn't help wondering from where he had acquired this extensive knowledge of her class. Curiosity got the better of her and she found herself saying, 'You never cease to surprise me, Ben. You're quite familiar with the rules laid down by polite society. How did you acquire this wisdom, I wonder? From scanning the gossip-columns in the newspapers, perhaps?'

He would have been most surprised if sooner or later she hadn't passed some remark about his ability to read and, prepared, wasn't in the least disturbed by the half-mocking enquiry. 'Mr Trapp isn't one to indulge in unnecessary small talk, as perhaps you are aware, so reading does help to pass the time.'

Sophia digested this reply in silence for a moment. It was quite the norm for higher-ranking servants to read and write, but a stable-hand was quite another matter, and yet she could not in all honesty say that she had been at all surprised to discover that Ben had acquired these skills. 'No doubt your old master insisted that you learn.'

'He most certainly did, my lady.' Again Benedict found it not in the least difficult to return that level feminine gaze, though he continued to find it most strange referring to his late father as 'the old master'. 'He believed that a man could never hope to better himself without acquiring a little education.'

'Mmm.' Sophia regarded him in silence again, not totally satisfied with the explanation, but deciding not to press for more details at the present time, and merely waved one slender hand in the general direction of the small table near the door. 'You'll find some recent copies of the *Morning Post* over there. And if you are so inclined you may cast your eyes over the shelves before you go, and borrow any book which happens to take your fancy.'

Touched by the generous offer, Benedict was in the process of voicing his grateful thanks when the door opened and the butler entered to inform his young mistress that Miss Perceval had called and was awaiting her in the drawing-room, which effectively brought the interview to an abrupt end to the intense disappointment of at least one of the room's occupants.

Assuring Ben that he might feel free to take all the time he needed to make his selection, Sophia hurriedly left the library and went across the hall. 'It quite slipped my mind that I had invited you here this morning,' she freely admitted, entering the elegantly appointed salon in time to see her friend removing a pretty powder-blue silk bonnet from her dusky locks.

Robina wasn't in the least offended, but couldn't resist saying, 'And I suppose you've also forgotten the reason why you invited me here.'

'Oh, no, I haven't forgotten that,' Sophia assured her, smiling at the half-teasing tone. 'Although, as things have turned out, you may as well have saved yourself the trouble of calling. When I issued the invitation, I expected Marcus to be here, but he has decided to leave London today. You know what a gadfly he is, Robin.' She raised her hands in a helpless gesture. 'One just never knows where he'll be from one day to the next. Unfortunately, without his assistance I really cannot demonstrate the waltz very well, unless...'

A thought suddenly occurred to her, and she turned to the butler who had entered in her wake, bearing a tray containing ratafia and a plate of sweet almond biscuits. 'Cardew, be good enough to see if Ben is still in the library, and if he is, request him to come in here.'

The butler expressed his disapproval by giving vent to a loud sniff. He objected most strongly to outside workers having free run of the house, even those who took the trouble to titivate a little before presenting themselves at the door, but knew better than to remonstrate with the master's daughter, and went away to do as he was bid.

Although Sophia had spoken of her new groom on several occasions, she had failed completely to mention how very handsome he was, and Robina found herself almost gaping when the door opened a short while later and a tall man, his golden-brown hair easily reaching the base of his neck, walked smoothly into the room. She found herself quite unable to draw her eyes away from him. It wasn't his superior height or breadth of shoulder which struck her most forcibly, but the fact that, even dressed in rough workman's clothes, he didn't look in the least out of place in the elegant surroundings.

'Ah, good!' Sophia remarked, glancing briefly at the book and papers in his hand. 'I see you've made your selection. Lay your reading matter to one side, Ben, because I need your help.'

Betraying faint surprise, he obeyed the command. 'How may I be of service, my lady?'

Although rapidly losing the last vestiges of childish immaturity, there remained an element of roguery in her nature. 'I'm certain that such an accomplished person as yourself, at some point in his life, learned to dance.'

'Dance, my lady?' he echoed, casting a wary glance across the room in Robina's direction.

'Yes, dance, Ben. You know—that silly pastime we lesser mortals engage in when we've nothing better to do with our time.'

A suppressed chuckle from behind reminded Sophia of her friend's presence, and that she was forgetting her manners. She immediately rectified this lapse on her part by formerly making the introductions, just as though Ben had been a gentleman caller to the house, and then persuaded a slightly bemused Robina to take the seat at the pianoforte.

Robina was more than willing to oblige. Nowhere near as gifted as her sister Frederica, she could none the less play very creditably when called upon to do so, though her fingers did stumble slightly when she saw Sophia quite brazenly place one masculine hand lightly on her waist, while retaining his other in her own slender fingers.

Benedict was no less surprised. Naturally he had heard of this new dance, which was rapidly gaining in popularity, but had never performed it himself before. Nevertheless he was very willing to learn, especially if it meant that he could maintain some physical contact, frustratingly slight though it might be, with the woman who he was daily becoming more convinced would make him the perfect wife.

Sophia was not as indifferent to that light masculine touch as she tried to appear, either. She recalled clearly that evening at Christmas when Marcus, after a little persuasion, had taken the trouble to teach her the dance which was still considered by many to be extremely improper, but she couldn't recall feeling in the least conscious of her brother's touch when he had swirled her round the drawing-room at Jaffrey

House, and it took a monumental effort on her part to marshal her thoughts and concentrate on the task in hand.

She swiftly discovered that either she was an excellent teacher, or Ben was a remarkably apt pupil. After one or two minor lapses in concentration, when they neatly avoided stepping on each other's toes, they were soon swirling about the large drawing-room in perfect harmony, until Sophia inadvertently caught the toe of her slipper under the edge of the carpet. Only her partner's lightning reflexes prevented her from falling. One strong arm snaked round her slender waist, and she was held protectively against a stone hard chest for a moment before being set gently back on her feet.

The contact was brief, moments only, and yet every inch of her body was left tingling with a wealth of sensations which brought colour rushing to her face. She instinctively took a step away, and risked a fleeting glance up at the man whose touch had wreaked such havoc with her senses, only to discover that he wasn't even looking at her, but across at the instrument in the corner of the room. It was only then that she realised that the music had stopped.

'My, my! What an energetic dance the waltz is!' she exclaimed, striving to control her erratic breathing as she followed the direction of his half-amused gaze to discover Robina, fingers poised above the keys, looking decidedly thoughtful. 'I think we'll end the first lesson there, don't you? I feel quite exhausted.'

This was no less than the truth, but it didn't account for the sudden feeling of shyness which assailed her, and she discovered that it was as much as she could do to nod dismissal to Ben, before moving across to the sofa.

Robina joined her the instant the door had closed behind him. 'You appear to have acquired a most accomplished groom.'

The quietly spoken observation in no way struck Sophia as odd. In fact, she would have been most surprised if her very observant friend had not noticed that there was something very singular about Benjamin Rudgely.

'More accomplished than you realise,' she responded, having swiftly regained much of her composure, and wondering why she had come to lose it in the first place. 'Every time I'm in his company, I learn something new about him. Why, only the other day I discovered that he can read and write.'

'Good heavens!' Robina did not attempt to hide her surprise. 'Unusual, don't you think?'

'Very,' Sophia agreed. 'But then Benjamin Rudgely is a most unusual man.'

Reaching for the ratafia, conveniently placed on the nearby table, she poured out two glasses, handing one to Robina before leaning back against the sofa to sip hers meditatively. 'It wouldn't surprise me to discover that he was some rich man's by-blow.'

A vicar's daughter she may have been, but Robina was neither naïve nor easily shocked. She merely gazed at some distant spot, as though conjuring up a vision of a handsome face with undeniably aristocratic features, and after a moment or two nodded in agreement.

'He always refers to his late employer as "the old master",' Sophia explained. 'I have a strong feeling, though, that the relationship between them was rather more than that of master and servant. After all, how many people would take the trouble to ensure that their servants received an education? I know my father did just that with Trapp, but it is unusual, you must admit.'

Again her friend nodded in agreement. 'So you think that his old employer might well have been his father?'

'It's a possibility, certainly.'

'But you don't know his name?'

'No, I don't,' Sophia freely admitted. 'Furthermore, I have no intention of trying to discover it, either. If Ben wishes me to know, he'll tell me—if not, then I'm certain he has his reasons for not doing so.'

Robina's regard turned from merely interested to downright penetrating in a matter of seconds. 'You have evidently taken a keen interest in your groom, Sophia,' she remarked softly.

'Yes, I suppose I have.'

'You have grown fond of him, I think.'

'Yes,' she admitted, seeing no earthly reason to lie. 'But I was also very fond of Clem, remember?'

'Yes you were...But Clem, let me remind you, was

short, slightly on the portly side, and certainly no Adonis, whereas Benjamin Rudgely...'

'Is excessively handsome,' Sophia finished for her, for the first time hearing a tiny alarm bell ringing, but steadfastly refusing to heed its warning. 'Yes, I had noticed that myself, Robin. I'm not blind. But if you are trying to imply that there is anything improper going on between—'

'I'm not suggesting anything of the sort,' Robina hurriedly assured her. 'It's just that...' there was more than a flicker of concern in her soft blue eyes '...you have never been one to hide your feelings. Everybody knew how fond you were of your old groom, and no one living in the four Abbey villages thought anything of that friendship. But this is London, Sophia, a veritable hotbed of scandal and malicious gossip. If you display the same affection for this new groom as you did for Clem, then I dread to think of the vicious rumours which might begin to circulate.'

Sophia sat silently digesting what Robina had said for a few moments, then, reaching for a sweet almond biscuit, gave a tiny dismissive wave of her hand. Her friend was making far too much of it!

As things turned out, Robina's fears were well-founded. Before too many days had passed, Sophia and her handsome groom had become a regular sight in the park, and gossip and speculation had not been slow to follow. A great many people, of course, saw nothing amiss in a young lady and her groom riding side by side, deep in conversation; while others, most especially those who had attended the Yardley ball the previous month, could not help wondering if there might be some truth in the gossip which had been circulating at the time. After all, Lady Sophia Cleeve had paid precious little attention to any gentleman of the Ton since her arrival in town, and yet here she was quite brazenly displaying the keenest interest in a lowly groom!

Sophia remained oblivious to the many surreptitious winks and malicious whispers exchanged behind her back. She was conscious only of the fact that London had become excessively crowded, its population seeming to have doubled overnight. No matter what time she chose to take her daily ride, it was impossible to find a street that was not teeming with traffic, or a spot in the park that was not peppered with gossiping couples, a circumstance that prompted her to complain bitterly to her parents at the breakfast table one morning, a little over a week after Marcus's departure from town.

The Countess cast her daughter an understanding smile. 'I'm afraid, my dear, you must grow accustomed to it. The Season has begun, and the majority will remain until its conclusion.'

'I realise that, Mama, but it seems to me that everyone has descended on the capital during the past few days.' She was struck by a wicked possibility. 'In fact, to be precise, the influx has occurred since Marcus's departure. Perhaps we ought to summon him back, and see if his presence cannot induce some to return to their estates.'

His lordship, absently browsing through the pile of correspondence by his plate, found himself quite unable to suppress a chuckle at this impish sally. 'Anyone listening to you, my girl, might be forgiven for supposing that you hold your brother in very low esteem, whereas in fact the opposite is—'

He broke off, his face turning such a sickly hue that the Countess was prompted to ask if he were feeling quite the thing.

'W-what...?' He gazed wide-eyed across the table at her, just as though she were a complete stranger. Then he seemed to collect himself and hurriedly rose to his feet, gathering together all his correspondence as he did so. 'I'm fine, dear...Yes, I'm fine. If you'll excuse me, I shall finish reading these in the library.'

'I do hope he hasn't received bad news,' Sophia remarked the instant he had left them.

'Something certainly seems to have disturbed him,' the Countess was forced to concede, but flatly refused to speculate on what might have caused her husband's momentary distress, and promptly changed the subject by voicing the hope that her daughter's letter did not contain bad tidings.

'Quite the contrary,' Sophia assured her. 'It's from Olivia Roade Burton. I wrote to her last week, but it would appear she hasn't received my letter as yet, for she writes that she considers me the biggest beast in nature for having forgotten her so quickly.'

'That young lady,' her ladyship responded, her tone suddenly clipped, 'has no right to criticise anyone, not after the way she behaved.'

Sophia could not help smiling at this rare display of staunch disapproval on her mother's part. 'I am well aware that you do not think too highly of Olivia, Mama. Perhaps she is a trifle selfish and spoiled. But then so am I.'

'Very true, my dear,' her ladyship agreed, not attempting to spare her daughter's feelings. 'I am persuaded, however, that you would never play fast and loose with a gentleman's feelings by promising to marry him in one breath, then changing your mind in the next. And before you come to Miss Roade Burton's defence,' she went on, interrupting her daughter's attempt to do just that, 'I shall tell you plainly that I never for one moment believed that farrago of nonsense dear Lord Ravensden put about, suggesting that they had never been officially engaged and that the announcement which appeared in the newspaper had been a dreadful mistake.'

What her mother had said happened to be no less than the truth, and Sophia felt it would be quite useless attempting to show her friend Olivia in a more favourable light by suggesting that the events which had taken place several months before had been quite otherwise. So she merely said, 'A gentleman to the last, then, Mama! That is perhaps why you like Lord Ravensden so much, and why you were so very glad when he decided to marry Beatrice. You have always much preferred Beatrice to her sister...Come, confess it!'

The Countess, truthful to the last, never attempted a denial. 'And I, for one, feel that Ravensden had a lucky escape when Olivia took it into her head to jilt him.'

'You are perfectly right,' Sophia agreed. 'I might not approve Olivia's methods, but the outcome of her actions was to the benefit of all concerned. Furthermore,' she added, with a little knowing smile, 'I do not truly believe you blame Olivia for refusing to marry a man who did not love her.'

'Perhaps not, dear,' her ladyship answered, but flatly refused to concede more than this, and changed the subject by asking if the letter contained any interesting gossip.

'Not very much, no.' Sophia quickly scanned the single sheet. 'She mentions that the Abbey villages seem deserted. Which is hardly surprising since I swear that most of the inhabitants have descended on the capital. I'm certain I spied Beatrice herself driving out with Ravensden yesterday, and I feel sure I saw Lord Isham, looking as grim as a thundercloud, riding in the park the other day, though I cannot say that I noticed whether or not India was with him. And, of course, you know yourself that the Percevals have at last arrived in town.'

'Yes, I did.' Her ladyship found herself quite unable to suppress a smile. 'From what dear Hugo was saying the other day, it would seem his mama is not best pleased with me for holding your ball before she and Hester had arrived in town. He, the darling boy, fully understood my reasons for having done so. With the hectic social calendar it would have been quite hopeless trying to squeeze in our little event once the Season had officially got under way. Which reminds me,' she went on, after fortifying herself from the contents of her coffee cup. 'You haven't forgotten that dear Hugo is to escort us to Lady Sefton's soirée next week?'

'No, I hadn't forgotten,' Sophia assured her, smiling at her mother's habit of always adding a mild endearment when mentioning the name of someone she particularly liked.

'I cannot help wondering, Mama,' an imp of mischief prompted her to add, 'why you have never attempted to promote a match between *dear* Hugo and myself, as you quite evidently hold him in such high esteem.'

Her ladyship's eyes began to twinkle. 'It is for precisely that reason that I have never done so, child. I should never dream of foisting such a mischievous little minx on the dear boy. You would never give him a moment's peace, and he is far too much of a gentleman to deal with you as you so frequently deserve.'

Sophia could not help laughing at this candid, though unflattering, assessment of her character. 'Yes, you may possibly be right. Hugo's brother would be a far better choice.'

'On the contrary, he most certainly would not!' Her ladyship countered, shuddering at the mere thought. 'Lowell's as harum-scarum as you are, besides being far, far too young. Oh, no, my dear. You must marry a man whose views you respect and whose decisions you'll accept without question. And I assure you that if and when I meet such a person, I shall do everything within my power to promote a match between you.'

Sophia fixed her attention on an imaginary spot on the opposite wall as, unbidden, a vision of a tall man with long golden-brown hair and intelligent blue eyes sprang before her mind's eye. Ben had never been slow to issue a mild reproof if she ever uttered something unladylike whenever they had ridden out together, and not once had she come remotely close to bridling at his mild strictures. How very strange that was!

Suddenly aware that her mother was regarding her closely, she hurriedly rose to her feet. 'Well, no doubt, Mama, I should be happy to marry such a man, if ever we should meet. In the meantime, I mustn't delay in replying to Olivia's letter.'

Completely forgetting that her father had sought solace in the library, she entered the room to discover him standing at the window. Staring out at the square, his shoulders stooped, his expression grave, he looked for the first time, Sophia thought, very much the elderly gentleman.

He appeared lost in his own private gloom, oblivious to her presence, and she was just debating whether to slip quietly away when he suddenly demanded to know what she wanted.

'I'm sorry I disturbed you, Papa.' Having rarely been on the receiving end of his sharp tongue, she was startled by his brusque tone, but didn't allow it to upset her. Anyone could tell just by looking at his haggard features that he was deeply upset over something. 'I had forgotten that you were in here. I wished to write a letter, but I can come back later.'

'There's no need.' He merely sounded weary now, and the customary spring was singularly lacking from his step, too, as he moved across to the desk to pick up a single sheet of paper and thrust it into his pocket. 'I shall be going out for a short while, so you may stay to write your letter.'

Concerned, Sophia moved to one side to allow him to pass and thought how grey he looked, the lines in his face seeming far more pronounced. She recalled that several years ago, when he had learned that one of his sailing vessels had sunk during the passage home from India, his face had worn just such a grave expression for several weeks. It was not the loss of a fine ship or its cargo which had upset him so much, but the loss of life, and she could not help wondering if just such a catastrophe had occurred again.

Praying that this was not the case, she seated herself at his desk and reached into the top left-hand drawer for a sheet of paper, dislodging the lid of a small box as she did so. In the normal course of events she would merely have replaced the lid, but what she saw so captured her attention that she took out the box to study its contents more closely.

She vaguely recalled that Cardew had placed a package with the letters by her father's plate at the breakfast table earlier, and could not help wondering if this was what the package had contained, for she felt certain that she had never seen this pretty box before, nor its strange contents. The lock of silky black hair might well have been her father's, for Sophia was well aware that his lordship's locks had been as dusky as hers in his youth. There was not the slightest possibility, however, that the tiny ring lying beside the silken strands had ever been worn on his hand. Its setting was delicate, undoubtedly old, and had been fashioned for a finger as slender as her own.

Sophia shook her head in wonder, unable to comprehend why anyone should send such things to her father, for they were surely someone's treasured mementoes…Love tokens, perhaps…

Chapter Eight

The Earl of Yardley left London by hired carriage early the following morning, the twenty-second of April, without informing any member of his household, not even the Countess, where he was bound, or the reason behind his sudden departure. It so happened that he remained away from town one night only and appeared, if anything, more perturbed than ever on his return.

Sophia grew increasingly concerned, for as the days passed her father seemed to withdraw more and more within himself. He rarely attempted to indulge in any form of conversation when they did happen to meet, and remained for the most part alone in his library, with the door firmly locked against intruders.

As he never once attempted to offer any kind of explanation for his continuing depressed state of mind, and both Sophia and her mother were disinclined to pry, the reason behind the drastic change in him remained a complete mystery until Sophia received information from a most unexpected quarter which, although offering no explanation regarding his present mental state, at least disclosed his lordship's whereabouts during his brief absence from town.

Sitting in the sunny front parlour with her mother in readiness to receive morning callers, Sophia was surprised to see her father enter the room with a letter in his hand.

'Cardew inadvertently placed this among my correspondence,' he explained, handing her the missive, before unexpectedly seating himself on one of the spindle-legged chairs.

His actions ignited a spark of hope in Sophia, for although he didn't attempt to indulge in small talk, at least he seemed inclined to bear her and her mother company for a while, something which he had certainly avoided doing in recent days. She glanced briefly at her mother, sitting on the sofa beside her, quietly plying her needle. The Countess didn't attempt to make conversation either. So, following this example, Sophia remained silent, and turned her attention to the letter.

She recognised the handwriting at once, and knew even before she broke the seal precisely who had written. After quickly digesting its contents, her eyes became riveted to the hurriedly scrawled postscript, where her friend Olivia clearly stated that she had been astounded the previous week to see the Earl on horseback riding in the direction of Steepwood Abbey.

'Good heavens, Papa!' Sophia exclaimed, not thinking twice about voicing her own astonishment. 'What on earth prompted you to return to Jaffrey House last week?'

She realised her mistake the instant she had spoken. The Earl, his complexion acquiring an alarming purple hue, rose so abruptly that he almost sent his chair toppling to the floor. 'Where I go, and what I do, is purely my affair, Sophia!' he ground out. 'You would do better to concentrate on finding yourself a suitable husband, instead of interfering in matters that are none of your concern!'

Masterfully concealing her distress at what she considered an unwarranted outburst, the Countess reached across the sofa to grasp her daughter's hand the instant her husband had stormed from the room, slamming the door behind him with quite unnecessary violence. 'There, there, child,' she soothed. 'Do not look so injured. Your father is not himself, otherwise he would never have spoken to you in such a fashion.'

Sophia was not a female easily brought to tears, and she wasn't remotely close to weeping now, but she couldn't disguise her distress as she said, 'I know, Mama.' Her faint sigh was clearly audible too. 'It would be easier to bear if I had some idea what was causing Papa such concern. At first I thought he might have received some tragic news about one of his sailing vessels, but I don't imagine for a moment that that can be the reason for his deep depression, otherwise I'm certain he would have confided in us by now.'

Her ladyship nodded her head in agreement, at a complete loss herself to understand what had wrought this drastic change in her husband. 'I'm afraid, my dear, that your father has always been a man to keep his own counsel over many things. He is not a man, however, to brood unnecessarily, so I'm afraid that until such time that he overcomes his present melancholy state of mind, or perhaps takes us into his confidence, we must bear with his moods as best we can.'

Sighing again, Sophia reluctantly agreed. 'I sincerely trust, though, Mama, that we are not forced to bear with this situation for too much longer. The atmosphere in this house is becoming daily more strained. Why, even poor Cardew has taken to tiptoeing past the library door whenever he crosses the hall.'

The butler, not noticeably tiptoeing, entered the room just then to announce the arrival of the first callers to the house that day, and a moment later Lady Elizabeth Perceval, accompanied by her daughter, came tripping lightly into the room.

Sophia, for some reason which escaped her completely, was growing increasingly more sensitive to the moods of others these days, and sensed at once that something was troubling her friend. So, as soon as the Countess had engaged Lady Elizabeth in conversation, she drew her friend over to the window embrasure, asking outright what was wrong.

Robina couldn't forbear a smile. 'I didn't realise I was quite so transparent.' The brief attempt at a lighter mood soon over, she went on to divulge, 'There's no easy way of telling you this, Sophia, and I know you're not going to like it one little bit, but I think you ought to be aware of what a few very nasty-minded people are saying about you...about you and your new groom, that is.'

Robina was not slow to notice the slender body, clad in the pretty pale green morning dress, stiffen slightly, but didn't allow this to deter her from relating what she felt she must. 'Mother and I attended a small and rather informal party last night at the house of Lord Exmouth. He and his mother arrived in town only last week, and the Dowager, for some reason, appears to have taken quite a liking to me. She's a charming lady,' Robina continued, digressing slightly, 'certainly something of a character, full of life and not afraid to speak her mind, but she isn't in the least spiteful, and it was she who first mentioned this nasty rumour concerning you.'

'And what precisely did Lady Exmouth tell you?' Sophia prompted in an undertone, after casting her eyes briefly in her mother's direction.

There was a moment's silence, then, 'Because you have shown no preference for any particular gentleman's company since your arrival in town, there are those who are only too willing to believe that there

might be some truth in the rumours that were circulating on the night of your own ball, that you do,
indeed, prefer the company of a—er—rougher type
of person.'

'Oh no,' Sophia murmured, the muscles in her
stomach twisting themselves into painful knots of anger, and bitter regrets. For the second time in the
space of two short weeks she was being made to suffer the consequences of her own folly. There was no
denying the fact that she herself was wholly responsible for this current gossip. She didn't mind so much
for herself, but she had no wish for the rumours to
reach her dear mother's ears, especially not now.

'You are certainly not without your champions,'
Robina assured her in an attempt to lessen her friend's
evident distress. 'Mama dismissed the talk with an
impatient wave of her hand, saying that you had been
reared to show consideration to servants, no matter
how lowly their place in the Earl's household.' A sudden glint in her eyes betrayed the sportive element in
her nature which very few had been privileged to experience. 'And Lord Nicholas Risely was overheard
to say he wasn't in the least surprised that you betray
a marked partiality for your personal groom, since he
happened to know for a fact that the servant was responsible for saving you from falling beneath the
wheels of a carriage one morning in Bond Street.'

'Lord Nicholas said that?' A reminiscent smile
curled up the corners of her mouth. 'A slight exag-

geration,' she admitted, 'but I'm grateful to him, all
the same.'

'To be sure, I didn't know whether to believe him
or not, for I felt certain you would have told me if
anything of that nature had happened to you.' That
sportive gleam flickered once again. 'But that didn't
prevent me from assuring any one who asked for con-
firmation that it was perfectly true.'

Sophia could feel the tension in her slowly ebbing.
'You're a good friend, Robin. One of the best,' she
told her, bringing a rush of colour to delicate cheek-
bones.

Although it would have afforded her much pleasure
to show her utter contempt for the gossips by ignoring
the rumours about her and continuing to behave as
usual, Sophia knew that for her mother's sake she
could not. The Countess had done everything humanly possible to make their stay in town a happy
one. Even during the past trying days, when she had
been forced to contend with the Earl's almost reclu-
sive behaviour, she had continued to be an unfailing
source of comfort and support, and the least Sophia
could do in return was to try to avoid causing her
mother further anxiety.

So when she left the house early in the afternoon
to enjoy her customary daily ride, she was determined
to behave with the utmost propriety, as befitted her
station in life. Unfortunately the resolve, unselfishly
motivated though it was, had been made without tak-

ing into account the feelings of someone whose companionship had come to mean rather more to her than she yet realised.

The instant Benedict saw her emerge from the house, and noted the tense set of those delicate features, he suspected that something had occurred to disturb the calm waters of her mind. The faint, well-bred nod in response to his greeting succeeded in confirming this belief, and the lack of invitation to ride beside her put the suspicion that all was not as it should be beyond doubt.

Racking his brains to think of what he might have said or done to upset her, Benedict followed out of the square, keeping a discreet distance. Nothing very obvious sprang to mind. In fact, he remembered quite clearly that they had parted very amicably after their ride the previous afternoon, during which they had discussed a variety of topics ranging from the war with France to the appalling conditions endured by the London poor. So he was fairly certain that he was not responsible for her present decidedly frosty mood.

Having worked in the Earl of Yardley's stables for over a month, he had by this time acquired a fair knowledge of Sophia's character, and infatuated though he still might be, he certainly wasn't blind to her faults. She could still be disturbingly impetuous on occasions, and was frequently outspoken, but these slight flaws only seemed to enhance her charm. Added to which, it was very much to her credit that she wasn't in the least missish, nor prone to take a pet over mere trifles. He was forced to conclude, therefore, that she must have a sound reason for treating him with complete indifference.

He couldn't prevent a wry smile from curling his lips as he considered his present unenviable situation. Had he truly been a groom, born and bred to the life, he would probably have accepted his young mistress's indifference to his presence without so much as a blink. But he was Sharnbrook, with proud aristocratic blood flowing through his veins, and he'd be damned if he would tolerate being ignored by the young woman who was destined to become his Duchess!

The instant she glimpsed that tall figure looming alongside Sophia could feel the tension in her steadily mounting, but the command for him to fall back a pace which rose in her throat lacked the conviction to reach her lips. How could she now begin to treat this man like a servant when she had never done so before? Impossible to tell him to remember his station in life when she herself was finding it increasingly difficult not to think of him as an equal!

She risked a sideways glance in his direction, noted that those strikingly clear blue eyes regarding her in turn totally lacked even the smallest degree of deference, and could not help wondering if she had been slightly at fault to allow him so much licence. Yet, she reminded herself, it was quite understandable in the circumstances why she had done so.

Without having really been aware of it she had, she

supposed, instinctively turned to Ben for that wholly masculine companionship which she had enjoyed with her father over the years, but which had been denied her during recent days. It had not seemed in the least odd to do so either, for Ben was an attentive listener, and an interesting conversationalist whose frequent pithy remarks had never failed to make her laugh. Strangely enough, his views on many topics were not dissimilar to her father's, and she couldn't help thinking that if he lost that rich country burr, and was dressed appropriately, he would not seem in the least out of place at either White's or Boodle's, depending on his political views, of course. She felt certain, too, that many of the famous society hostesses would not object to his gracing their elegant drawing-rooms, either.

The thought made her chuckle, and she turned her head to discover the object of her thoughts regarding her with a faint look of surprise.

'Well, thank heavens for that!' he announced in a distinctly half-mocking tone. 'I was beginning to think you'd suffered a death in the family. Or, worse still, that I had fallen from favour.'

'Oh, no. That would never happen,' she assured him softly.

Her smile faded as they rode side by side into the overcrowded park, and she noticed a certain notorious gossip in an open carriage snickering behind her hand as she glanced in their direction. 'It's hateful tabbies like Lady Tockington, over there, who put me out of temper. Is her life so empty, so grossly uninteresting, that she can find nothing better to do than spread malicious untruths about people?'

Having always kept half an eye open for any old friends who, although not having seen him for more than five years, might quite easily penetrate his disguise, Benedict had been aware for several days that he and Sophia had been the object of no little attention, and could guess precisely what was being said about them. The best way of dealing with the situation, of course, was simply to ignore it, for sooner or later the gossips would find a new object on which to vent their spite. Unfortunately, his position was, to say the least, slightly precarious. Although he felt fairly certain that his disguise had not been penetrated thus far, he wasn't so very confident that it could withstand too close a scrutiny, and being discovered now just might result in his losing completely what he had been striving so hard to attain.

He returned his gaze to his future wife's lovely profile, slightly marred now by a very disgruntled expression. 'Perhaps it might be wise in the circumstances, my lady, to engage Mr Trapp as your escort, at least until the gossips have turned to a new source with which to ply their despicable trade,' he suggested, and was faintly surprised when she immediately nodded her head in agreement.

'Ordinarily, Ben, I wouldn't care a jot what was being said about me,' she admitted. Upset and annoyed though she was, she could not prevent a tiny rueful smile tugging at the corners of her mouth. 'The fact of the matter is I do like you, and I really do not care who knows it.'

She glanced at him then, but a little too late to see the gleam of satisfaction her admission had brought momentarily to his eyes. 'But for once, I'm not thinking of myself. My poor mother has enough to contend with at the moment without having to concern herself with nasty rumours about me.'

Sophia did notice his slightly puzzled frown, and without a second thought decided to confide in him. 'The Earl has been behaving very strangely of late. I've never known him act this way before. He's almost in an enclosed world of his own, shutting both Mama and me out. If he were ill, I could understand it, and make allowances, but I do not believe his health is the issue here.'

Although he had never had any personal dealings with the Earl, Benedict had discovered from Trapp that his lordship was in remarkably good health for a man of his advanced years. He also knew about his lordship's unexpected short absence from town the previous week, and suggested that something might have happened while the Earl had been away to cause him some concern.

Sophia considered this for a moment, then shook her head. 'I remember quite clearly that something had upset him the day before he left the capital. Besides,' she shrugged, 'I discovered only this morning that he paid a visit to our country home when he left London.'

'And what do you suppose prompted him to visit there?' Benedict asked, not so much interested in the Earl's activities as concerned over Sophia's peace of mind. She was evidently worried about her father, and anything that troubled her was of immense importance to him now.

'He was seen riding towards Steepwood Abbey,' she confided, 'so one can only assume that he had every intention of visiting Sywell. But just why Papa should suddenly take it into his head to do so, and at such a time, remains a mystery.'

Benedict thought it rather odd too. Then memory stirred. 'I recall your mentioning once that your father was intent on buying the Abbey. Perhaps he had learned that Sywell is at last considering selling the place, and was determined to put in his bid before any one else was given the chance. After all, Sywell has no near relatives to whom he could bequeath the property.'

'That isn't strictly true,' she corrected, smiling faintly. 'There's always his Marchioness.'

Stunned, Benedict almost found himself gaping. When on earth had Sywell taken the matrimonial plunge? It must have been during the time that he himself had been away in the Caribbean. However, he was more inclined to think that his darling girl, possessing something of a teasing nature, was hoaxing him.

'It's true,' she assured him, having no difficulty whatsoever in following his train of thought. 'He married his bailiff's ward, a young woman of about my own age. Young enough to be Sywell's granddaughter!'

'Good gad!' he said faintly, no longer doubting her word.

'One can only suppose that after years of producing illegitimate offspring, he felt inclined to produce a legitimate one.' She shrugged. 'Though whether he succeeded or not is anyone's guess.'

'Highly unlikely, I should say. He's left it rather late to consider producing an heir.'

'Well, I wouldn't know about such things,' she freely admitted. 'Though I dare say you might be able to enlighten me,' she added, when broad shoulders distinctly shook with suppressed laughter.

'I dare say I could, and might well do so when I consider you old enough to know about such things.'

Such familiarity was deserving of a severe reprimand, but Sophia found herself laughing, something which she had not done in several days. 'You are an impudent rogue, Benjamin Rudgely, and I really don't know why I bear with you. It will be a relief to have the respectful Trapp escorting me from now on.' But nothing could have been further from the truth, and she suspected that the tall man riding beside her knew that perfectly well.

With the possible exception of her father, there was no one whose company she preferred more than

Benjamin Rudgely's. Unlike a great many gentlemen with whom she associated during the evenings, Benedict was never dull, nor ever at a loss to introduce a new and interesting topic on which to converse, and, most important of all, he never required an explanation if she ever ventured a mild witticism or slightly provocative remark. He was quite simply exceptionally good company, and possibly one of the most interesting members of his sex she had ever met. Which made her ponder anew on why he was working in a situation that was far, far beneath his capabilities.

Casting a further sideways glance, she caught him staring about, those intelligent, clear blue eyes of his scanning the other occupants of the park in a way that was anything but respectful. Yes, she mused, there was certainly something proud in his bearing; one might even go so far as to say haughty. It was almost as if he did not consider those wealthy members of society who were now parading in their finery in any way superior to himself, and she truly felt that if he ever did manage to lose the countrified burr, and was dressed appropriately, he certainly would not seem in the least out of place in the most fashionable London salons.

She shook her head at the thought, wondering if she were not allowing her sincere regard for the man riding beside her to cloud her judgement. Yet, at the same time, although Ben had never once attempted to confide in her, she could not rid herself of the feeling that he had at some time in the not too distant past enjoyed a far more comfortable existence than he did now living with Trapp above the stables. She strongly suspected too that he had held a far more responsible position, one where he had issued the orders, not taken them. So why in heaven's name, she wondered, had he accepted work in a stable, when he was capable of doing so very much more? Was it simply that he had been unable to find a more responsible position since his return to England, or was there, perhaps, some underlying reason for his doing what he was doing now?

Benedict, turning his head suddenly, caught the pensive look, and completely misjudging the reason behind the expression, said, 'If you take my advice, my lady, you will not worry too much over your father. No one can possibly go through life without being troubled over something from time to time. The Earl, it sounds to me, is the kind of man who will confide in others only when he's ready to do so, and not before.'

And he is by no means the only one, Sophia decided, surprisingly realising that her father and the man at her side were not so very dissimilar. Which was most strange, because they could not possibly have very much in common...Or could they?

'My lady, you mentioned when first I came to work for your family that I might take some time off to visit my relatives,' he remarked, breaking into her perplexing thoughts, 'and I was wondering whether you'd permit me to pay a visit to my brother later this afternoon?'

She didn't take even a moment to consider the matter. 'Of course you may. I'm sure Trapp can manage quite well without you for an hour or so. In fact, I wish I could accompany you. The atmosphere in the house at the moment is strained to say the least.' There was an element of recklessness in her sudden laughter. 'Why, if my father's mood doesn't improve soon, I shall be very tempted to accept the very next gentleman who offers for me, if only as a means to get away from Berkeley Square!'

Benedict certainly did not find this in the least amusing, and his high intelligent forehead was noticeably marred by a deeply troubled frown as he fell back a few paces in order to allow one of her many admirers to draw alongside.

Chapter Nine

Before embarking on what he had once considered nothing more than a harmless little subterfuge, Benedict had arranged with his brother that, unless something arose urgently requiring his attention, there should be little or no contact between them.

Nicholas had wholeheartedly agreed, for there was always the chance that some observant devil seeing them together just might perceive the slight family resemblance, and even he, inveterate prankster that he was, balked at the mere thought of trying to explain to the world at large just why his estimable brother, whose return to fashionable society had been eagerly awaited for some little time, was masquerading as a common groom.

So he was a little surprised when, later that same day, the parlour door opened, and his brother unexpectedly came striding into the room. 'Good gad!' Nicholas exclaimed, abruptly losing interest in *the* novel which was causing no little sensation in fashionable circles. 'Taking something of a risk coming here, weren't you? Supposing you were seen?'

'I took the precaution of not attempting to gain admittance by way of the front entrance.' Swiftly realising that he would wait in vain for an invitation, Benedict lowered his tall frame into the chair opposite. 'It's surprising how quickly one grows accustomed to behaving like a servant. It's almost second nature to me now.'

'I'll take your word for that,' Nicholas responded, with an acute feeling of distaste, the mere thought of entering a dwelling by way of the area steps making him shudder. 'Evidently the novelty of playing the lowly groom has not diminished quite yet?'

Benedict's expression betrayed his feelings clearly enough even before he said, 'On the contrary, I'm heartily sick of it!'

Nicholas's sudden shout of laughter held an unmistakable note of triumph. 'I knew it would be only a matter of time before you lost interest in the delectable Sophia and turned your eyes in quite a different direction. Who's the filly that's taken your fancy now?'

Hardly the most flattering testament to one's constancy, Benedict decided, but he couldn't find it within himself to be in the least annoyed with his brother for thinking so poorly of him. If he were honest, he would be forced to admit that, when he had been Nicholas's age, he had been something of a feckless fribble, faithful to no female for any length of time.

Unable to suppress a self-deprecating half-smile, he gazed across the short distance which separated them. 'When I embarked on this somewhat shameful escapade—yes, I did say shameful, brother,' he reiterated, when Nicholas betrayed surprise, 'my reasons for doing so were purely selfish. I wished to know Sophia Cleeve a good deal better before committing myself to any lasting attachment. Ashamed though I am to admit to it, it is true none the less that in the past I have not infrequently fallen victim to a pretty face, and know full well that infatuation is a flame which may burn brightly for a time, but is seldom lasting.'

'And has the short period working in the Yardley stables extinguished the flame of desire altogether?' Nicholas prompted when Benedict, his expression completely unreadable now, fell silent and fixed his attention on the empty grate.

'No, it has not. If anything it burns brighter than ever…But, then, what I feel for the Earl of Yardley's only daughter has little to do with infatuation.'

He raised his eyes to meet his brother's interested gaze. 'I am very much in love with her,' he freely admitted, in a voice that, although lacking any vestige of emotion, sounded totally sincere. 'If I had searched the length and breadth of the land I do not believe I could have found a woman who would have suited me better. And I can only thank Providence for ensuring that our paths crossed that morning in Bond Street.'

Approval was the last thing Benedict had sought, for he considered that his choice of Duchess was his and his alone, and yet he found himself experiencing no little annoyance at the look of mild concern which momentarily flickered across his sibling's boyish features.

'Evidently you do not wholeheartedly approve my choice.'

'Oh, no, no! It isn't that exactly,' Nicholas hurriedly assured him, easily detecting the sudden steely element in the deep voice. 'I like Sophia. She's a grand girl—one of the best. In all the weeks I've known her, I've never once heard her utter a spiteful remark about any other young woman making her London début. What's more,' he continued, warming to the subject, 'she's the sort of girl a chap can talk to without his having to mind what he says all the time. She enjoys a good joke, and never needs things explained twice. Which is a great deal more than can be said for most of the little darlings gracing the town this Season.'

This was high praise indeed, but Benedict was not slow to notice that the faintly troubled look still lingered in young eyes. 'So you harbour slight reservations as to whether she would make a suitable Duchess, is that it?' he remarked, reading his brother's thoughts with uncanny accuracy, and Nicholas didn't attempt to deny it.

'Well, she ain't anything like our dear departed mama, now, is she?'

Reared from the cradle never to demean herself by the smallest display of emotion, their mother had been a cold, unapproachable woman. Not once, not even during his childhood, could Benedict recall receiving a loving word or gesture from his mother. It was little wonder that their father had not infrequently sought certain necessary comforts elsewhere, and Benedict, for one, had never thought any the worse of him for those frequent lapses.

'No, thank God!' he responded with feeling.

'Aye, she was an iceberg, right enough,' Nicholas was forced to concede. 'But you cannot deny, Ben, she knew her duty. She may not have been universally liked, not even by the members of her own family, but I lay a monkey that you've never heard it said that she ever behaved in a way which brought disgrace to the Risely name. Not that I think dear little Sophia would intentionally behave in a less than dignified manner,' he hurriedly continued, fearing that he had expressed himself rather badly. 'She's an earl's daughter, after all, and knows quite well how to conduct herself. The trouble is though, brother, she doesn't always behave as she ought, and she frequently utters the most outrageous things.'

Benedict didn't attempt to come to his future Duchess's defence, simply because his brother had spoken no less than the truth. 'I would be the first to admit that Sophia is not without her faults. Yes,' he agreed, 'she can be thoughtlessly impulsive on occasions. Disturbingly so!' he added, recalling clearly the little episode involving a certain unscrupulous Baronet. 'She doesn't always consider carefully before she speaks, either.' These to him were trifling flaws in what was otherwise an utterly charming character, consequently he didn't choose to dwell on them. 'You must remember, though, that she's still very young, not yet one-and-twenty, and in some ways remains her doting papa's pampered darling. But I rather think that she is slowly beginning to free herself from the last of those paternal ties, and leave her girlhood behind.'

He paused for a moment to study the filled decanters standing temptingly within easy reach on a nearby table and, suspecting that his abominably casual host would continue to forget his duties, decided to help himself to a large measure of brandy; the first he had sampled in many a long day.

'My life in recent weeks has not been without its enforced privations,' he admitted, after tossing half the contents of the glass down his throat and savouring its taste. 'Although I dare say my overall health has not suffered because of it, as I mentioned a little earlier, I shall not be sorry to return to my hitherto privileged existence.'

This was something Nicholas could quite easily understand, and he was not slow to voice his wholehearted approval. 'Well, thank the Lord for that! As far as I'm concerned the sooner you effect the transformation the better. All your new clothes have been delivered. They're upstairs in the spare bedchamber, just waiting for you. I'll ring for Figgins. He'll have you looking the part in a—'

'My purpose in coming here today was not to don my ducal robes,' Benedict interrupted, his voice soft but determined.

'Then why the deuce did you come?' Nicholas was at a complete loss to understand his brother's reasoning. 'You've just told me that Sophia is everything you could wish for in your future wife. You're quite obviously head-over-ears in love with the chit, so why continue any longer with the deception?'

A moment's silence, then, 'Because I believe there is a very real possibility that I might lose her altogether if I reveal my identity too soon.'

The deep lines which suddenly furrowed his brow were clear evidence of a troubled mind. 'I have had sufficient experience of the fair sex over the years, Nick, to be sure that Sophia Cleeve is not indifferent to me. What I am not quite so certain of at this point in time is whether her evident regard is strong enough to withstand the knowledge that the man of whom she is daily growing more fond is nothing more than a pompous inveigler whose actions during the past few weeks were motivated by pure self-interest.'

Managing a faint smile at his brother's astounded expression, Benedict tossed the remaining brandy down his throat before replenishing his glass from the slowly diminishing contents of the decanter at his elbow. He didn't doubt for a moment that Nicholas's astonishment stemmed from his inability to believe that any female in her right mind would ever consider for a moment refusing an alliance with the head of the noble Risely family. It was possibly true that most would not, but Sophia Cleeve belonged to that rare breed whose affections and loyalty could never be bought.

'Weeks ago,' he continued meditatively, 'when Sophia informed you that, in general, she preferred the companionship of servants, she wasn't being totally frivolous, you know,' he remarked, in an attempt to help Nicholas understand. 'She does feel a deal of contempt for the majority of her own kind, especially towards those who take flagrant advantage of their privileged positions to the detriment of less fortunate souls. And I cannot say I blame her for feeling as she does,' he went on as the names Crawley and Sywell, together with those of several other unsavoury characters, flashed through his mind. 'But, at the same time, I cannot help wondering, Nick, what makes me suppose that I am in any way superior to those she holds in such low esteem. After all, have I not lied and deceived, and made use of those less fortunate than myself in order to attain my selfish ends?' There was little humour in his sudden shout of laughter. 'For rank self-interest and arrant conceit Benedict Risely, Seventh Duke of Sharnbrook, would, I very much fear, feature very near the top of darling Sophia's list of contemptuous peers of the realm.'

He attempted to wash the bitter taste from his mouth with a further mouthful of amber liquid, but with little success. 'My main objective during these past weeks has been to determine whether or not the Earl of Yardley's lovely daughter would make me a suitable wife. It never once crossed my mind to wonder whether I would make her a suitable husband. She is not likely to overlook that piece of crass arrogance on my part. Nor the fact that I have continually lied to her almost from the moment we met.'

Nicholas, ever the optimist, voiced the belief that Sophia was not the kind of girl to take a pet over mere trifles, and was sure to forgive and forget once matters had been explained to her, but Benedict was not so certain.

'Perhaps,' he conceded, after a few moments intense thought. 'A great deal will depend, of course, upon choosing just the right moment to make a clean breast of everything. I can tell you now, brother, that I've been offered numerous opportunities to confide in her. Young, Sophia may be, but she's certainly no fool, and she has, unless I much mistake the matter, known from the start that I am not quite what I seem.'

'Do you mean she suspects that you're Sharnbrook?'

Troubled though he was, Benedict could not help smiling at this. 'No, she most certainly doesn't suspect that. In fact, I believe she's under the distinct impression that I'm some rich man's by-blow.'

Nicholas almost choked. 'Good gad!' he managed faintly, much to his brother's intense amusement.

'Yes, these past few weeks have certainly not lacked their lighter moments,' Benedict admitted, before the reminiscent smile faded and he became serious again. 'But time is no longer on my side. The last thing I want is for Sophia to discover my true identity from someone else. Which is not beyond the realms of possibility. Unfortunately I'm attaining a deal of unwanted attention at the moment.'

No further explanations were necessary. 'Ah, so you've heard what the tabbies have been saying about you both, have you?'

'Yes, I've heard. The gossip in itself doesn't worry me unduly, Nick, but the fact that I'm now being regarded with keen interest most certainly does. Sooner or later someone is going to recognise me.'

Nicholas nodded, for once in complete agreement. 'I saw your old friend Carstairs the other day, tooling his curricle along Piccadilly. And I know for certain that both Halstead and Melcham have arrived in town.'

It was inevitable that sooner or later certain of his very close friends would descend on the capital, but this did not stop Benedict from cursing long and fluently under his breath. 'If any one of those old reprobates catches a glimpse of me, I'm dished. Is our sister also in the capital, by any chance?'

'No, and isn't likely to be either, unless it's just for a day or two. I think I've mentioned before that dar-

ling Constance has lost her taste for town life.'
Nicholas took a moment or two to ponder over their
sister's surprising bent for country living, before
bringing his mind back to the present and discovering
that Benedict now appeared to have relapsed into a
world of his own, where he seemed quite content to
remain until he took his leave a few minutes later.

When the door had closed behind his caller
Nicholas stared across at the empty chair, which still
bore the imprint of his brother's well-muscled frame,
and wondered just why he had been honoured with
that unexpected visit.

Perhaps Benedict had simply wished to talk to
someone, he mused, share his hopes and fears for the
future. His big brother certainly hadn't come for the
express purpose of seeking consent for his choice of
Duchess. That much was certain! Benedict had made
up his mind that he wanted Sophia Cleeve, and
Nicholas didn't suppose for a moment that his brother
would care a jot if any member of the family disap-
proved of his choice. No, he reiterated silently, what
appeared to concern Benedict at the moment was that
Sophia herself might not want him. Could there truly
be any foundation for this fear?

He would have been the first to admit that, although
he had been acquainted with the Earl's daughter for
longer than his brother had, he didn't really know her
that well. True, they had danced together on numerous occasions, and had occasionally exchanged views
on the latest *on dits*, but not once, as far as he could

recall, had they ever indulged in any meaningful discussions.

Beautiful simpletons, Nicholas reminded himself, had never been very much to Benedict's taste; but there again neither had bluestockings. So he could only assume that the lovely Sophia fell somewhere between the two.

Reaching for the pile of gilt-edged cards on the nearby table, he began to study with interest those invitations he had received for that very evening. Surely his future sister-in-law would be attending one of these very fashionable gatherings? Perhaps if he succeeded in running her to earth, he might be able to uncover just what it was about her that had succeeded in capturing totally the interests of a man of Benedict's wide experience. More importantly, he just might be able to discover if there truly was any reason to suppose that the Earl's daughter would turn down the opportunity of becoming the next Duchess of Sharnbrook. If there was, he doubted there was very much he could do to alter the situation. But one never knew.

There were perhaps no more than a hundred guests present in the handsomely decorated salon. A very insignificant affair when compared to the several grand balls taking place that evening, Sophia reflected, as she moved about the room, automatically performing the steps of the dance.

Initially she had been delighted to discover that her

mother had accepted this invitation to Lady Carlisle's small, informal party; happier still when she had been informed, just before setting out, that the Earl had decided to escort them. That, of course, she reminded herself, was before she had realised that her father's decision had stemmed not from a desire to begin socialising again, but merely from a stubborn determination to keep an eye on his daughter's activities.

Irritated though she was, she couldn't help smiling to herself. It had taken no time at all to see through her father's little stratagem, so she could only wonder at herself for failing completely to notice that she had become the butt of some malicious gossip in recent days. Part of the reason, of course, was simply that whenever she was in Ben's company she became far too engrossed in what he was saying to take very much notice of anything else. Unlike now, when she was finding it increasingly difficult to concentrate on her young partner's conversation, and was very well aware of what was taking place around her. Even the sudden appearance in the room of a late arrival did not escape her notice.

Now what in the world had prompted Lord Nicholas Risely, of all people, to attend such an insignificant gathering as this one? she wondered, happy to let her mind wander again. Although he was not considered one of the richest prizes on the *Marriage Mart*, he was nevertheless judged to be extremely eligible, and consequently was invited everywhere. He was always to be seen at the most lavish events, and there were plenty of those taking place this night, so why had he chosen to grace this rather mediocre affair?

Intrigued, and with precious little else to occupy her, Sophia found herself following his progress into the room. She saw him relieve one of the waiters of a glass of champagne, before looking about him, as though searching for someone in particular. Their eyes met, and he raised his glass in a silent toast, before moving on and stopping from time to time to exchange a few words with various other guests.

It might have been her imagination, but he appeared disinclined to remain with any particular acquaintance for very long, and seemed intent on reaching the corner of the room where her own mother stood amid an animated little group.

The instant the set came to an end, Sophia wasted no time in returning to her mother's side in time to hear the Countess politely enquire whether there was any likelihood of seeing the Duke of Sharnbrook in town that Season.

'Not if the man possesses a ha'p'orth of sense,' Sophia could not resist saying, and found herself on the receiving end of an appreciative masculine stare.

'And why do you suppose my brother would be foolish to set foot in town?'

She suspected he knew the answer to that without being told, but had a mind to indulge him. 'Because the poor man won't be given a moment's peace, that's why. He'll have every matchmaking mama for miles around descending on him, vying to bring her daughter to his notice.'

The Countess's eyes gleamed every bit as brightly as her daughter's. 'Not quite every mother.'

'No, perhaps not every one,' Sophia agreed, casting her own a look of approval. 'But certainly most would be.'

Nicholas's gaze, openly assessing, went from mother to daughter. 'I assure you my brother is not faint-hearted. He's also quite accustomed to receiving a deal of attention, welcome or otherwise. I'm certain he'll show his face in town when he feels himself ready to do so.'

It was Sophia and her mother who now exchanged glances before the Countess said, 'Am I correct in assuming from what you have just said that the Duke has at last returned to our shores, and that you have had the felicity of seeing him again after your long separation?'

It was quite evident from his expression that Lord Nicholas was annoyed with himself for divulging as much as he had, but he did not foolishly attempt to deny the truth of what he had inadvertently disclosed. 'Yes, ma'am, I have seen him,' he admitted. 'It just so happens that I received a visit from him this very day. However, he doesn't wish his return to this country to become common knowledge quite yet. He requires a little time to—er—accustom himself to his new role in life.'

'Quite understandable,' the Countess responded,

before an acquaintance of long standing suddenly appeared at her side, demanding her attention, and it was left to Sophia to assure his lordship that neither she nor her mother was prone to gossiping, and that society would not hear of the Duke's return from either of them.

'That's a relief to know,' he answered, and sounded totally sincere. 'Benedict certainly needs some time to adjust.' He took a moment to finish the contents of his glass. 'He isn't the same person who went out to the West Indies five years ago.'

'In what way has he changed?' Sophia asked, more out of politeness than any real interest.

'Just about in every possible way,' he surprised her by divulging. 'Before he left England he was considered a leader of fashion.' He chuckled. 'To look at him now you'd never believe that! He doesn't seem to care a jot about his well-being either. Do you know that on his very first day back in town he went about exploring the slums?'

This succeeded in capturing Sophia's attention. 'What on earth prompted him to do that?'

He shrugged. 'Curiosity, I imagine. I remember he was utterly appalled by what he saw. Said that our slaves live in far better conditions than those poor wretched in the East End.'

'Ah, yes,' Sophia responded softly, and with more than just a hint of disapproval in her voice. 'I was forgetting you owned a plantation.'

'Wouldn't if Benedict had his way,' his lordship

disclosed, and noticed at once the change in her expression. 'My brother believes that no man has the right to own a fellow human being. He would free his slaves tomorrow, but fears the consequences of such an action. They're sitting on a powder keg out there. If he freed his slaves, it would undoubtedly lead to great unrest on the other plantations, and Benedict doesn't want that. He's a staunch supporter of the Abolitionists, and believes it's only a matter of time before there is an end to such an inhuman practice as owning slaves.'

Sophia found herself sharing Nicholas's noble brother's hopes, while at the same time remembering something her groom had said to her only the other day. 'You are too quick to condemn your own class, my lady. There are good and bad in every walk of life. You only have to open your eyes and ears to discover that for yourself.' And as usual he was right.

'I should very much like to meet your brother, Lord Nicholas. I believe we might discover we have much in common.'

A moment's silence, then: 'I think it could be arranged without too much difficulty.'

Suspecting that his lordship, for reasons best known to himself, was disposed to remaining at her side, Sophia took the opportunity to thank him for coming so gallantly to her defence by attempting to stem the foolish gossip presently circulating about her. 'I must say it comes to something when one cannot even hold a conversation with one's groom in public without some idiotic person starting silly rumours!'

'Think nothing of it, m'dear. Spoke out as much for my own amusement as anything else. Can't remember precisely what I said now, or to whom, but I do recall silencing a few viperous tongues.'

'So I've been reliably informed, and I'm grateful,' she responded, before changing the subject again by openly admitting how astonished she had been earlier to see him walk into the room.

He appeared nonplussed for a moment. 'Now why should you have been surprised, I ask myself? Did you suppose I consider myself too high in the instep to be seen at such a small party as this one?'

Sophia turned her head on one side, as though considering this. 'Now, how am I to answer that, I wonder...with candour or studied politeness?'

His shout of appreciative laughter resulted in more than one glance being slanted in their direction. 'So that's it!' he exclaimed somewhat enigmatically. 'Now I understand, and wholeheartedly approve. You'll suit very nicely, I do not doubt.' Then, suddenly seeming to collect himself, he changed the subject by enquiring whether she was still enjoying her first season in town.

'To be perfectly truthful, Lord Risely, it has lost much of its appeal of late,' she admitted, catching sight of her father emerging from the card-room. 'In fact there are times when I feel like suggesting an early return to Northamptonshire,' she disclosed, and did not notice the very troubled look which for one unguarded moment suddenly took possession of his lordship's handsome features.

Chapter Ten

Raising her head to glance out of the parlour window, the Countess just happened to catch sight of her daughter returning to the house. No violent slamming of the front door immediately followed her entry. Which was a great pity in the circumstances, she decided. Although in general no advocate of childish displays of temper, she couldn't help feeling that her daughter might benefit from venting any frustrations she might possibly be experiencing at the moment out on something or, better still, on someone—ideally the person solely responsible for the very unpleasant atmosphere pervading the house these days!

Returning her attention to her sewing, she began absently to ply the needle while her mind commenced to dwell, as it so often did of late, on her husband's uncharacteristic behaviour. Fanciful though it might be, she was none the less beginning to feel increasingly that she was married to a complete stranger. Gone was the kind and tolerant man whom she had known for a score of years and more, and in his place was an ill-tempered bore who appeared to delight in making himself as disagreeable as possible for much of the time.

Unable to suppress a wry smile, the Countess recalled clearly the delight she had experienced a few days before when the Earl had unexpectedly announced his intention of attending Lady Carlisle's informal party. Foolishly, as things had turned out, she had supposed that at long last he was beginning to recover from whatever it was that had caused him such distress, and that he was now, once again, ready to enjoy the numerous pleasures London had to offer. Thankfully she had not foolishly deluded herself for very long. Even before they had left the party that night, she had come to the conclusion that her husband's only reason for putting an end to the period of self-imposed isolation was simply that he had every intention of ensuring that his daughter returned to Northamptonshire at the end of the season betrothed. And unless she was very much mistaken, she suspected that their daughter was very well aware of this too!

Poor Sophia! Her ladyship experienced a surge of sympathy. The dear child must surely feel that her life was not her own any more, with her father demanding to know where she was going every hour of the day, and with whom. The evenings were worse, of course, when he made not the slightest attempt to hide the fact that he was watching her every move.

He was never slow to take her roundly to task if she stood up more than once with any gentleman whom he considered unworthy of attention. And woe betide the poor child if she refused to stand up with a gentleman whom he considered was worthy!

Her ladyship could only silently applaud her daughter's forbearance, for not once had Sophia attempted to remonstrate with her father for his unreasonable, not to say eccentric, behaviour of late. Which was a most strange circumstance in itself, she decided, after giving the matter a moment's consideration. Sophia's temperament could never have been described as placid. Even as a child she could be roused to anger with little difficulty, and had never been afraid to speak her mind. Yet not once, the Countess reminded herself, had her daughter displayed the least sign of losing her composure, handling herself with praiseworthy self-control whenever in her father's presence.

She shook her head, wondering why it had taken her until now to appreciate these subtle yet definite changes in her daughter's character which had undoubtedly taken place since their arrival in town. She didn't suppose for a moment that it was she herself who had succeeded in influencing Sophia's behaviour. Yet, someone, somewhere, was most definitely having a highly beneficial effect on the girl, changing her from an occasionally unruly and thoughtless child into a poised and gracious young woman, the

Countess decided, wondering who on earth it could possibly be.

The parlour door opened and the object of her ladyship's silent approval entered the room. Sophia had changed her habit for a simple muslin day dress and looked, if not precisely glowing with happiness, contented enough, as she seated herself at the other end of the sofa.

'Did you enjoy your ride?' she enquired, and was surprised to see a look of comical dismay bent in her direction.

'To be perfectly truthful, Mama, no, I did not. I cannot in all honesty say that I've ever found Trapp's company particularly stimulating. And it seems to me that the older he's getting the more taciturn he becomes. Or maybe,' she added, generously giving the loyal retainer the benefit of the doubt 'he isn't changing at all, and it's just that I've grown accustomed to a more stimulating companion of late.'

'By that, I assume you're referring to Clem's replacement.' Focusing her attention on her embroidery, the Countess didn't notice a faintly wary look flit over her daughter's delicate features. 'I haven't once heard you complain about him, so I assume he meets with your approval?'

'I have no fault to find with him whatsoever.'

'That is a relief to hear. I must say I had my doubts that you would ever find anyone whom you could grow to like half so well as Clem.'

'Oh, yes, Mama, I certainly…like him. I like Ben very well.'

Her ladyship noted the slight hesitation, but chose not to remark upon it and merely said, 'I cannot recall that I've ever spoken to him, apart from acknowledging his presence on the rare occasion he has been called upon to tool the town carriage, that is. Do you think he's content working for the family, or do you suspect that he might seek employment elsewhere once the Season is over? After all, residing in the country is not to every person's taste. He might prefer to remain in town.'

Receiving no response to this, her ladyship raised her eyes and was not slow to note the sudden disappearance of her daughter's normally healthy bloom. 'Why, my dear! Are you feeling quite the thing? You look as if you've just received the most severe shock.'

The laughing denial that anything was wrong sounded false even to Sophia's own ears. The fact of the matter was she felt as if she had just received a punishing blow to the pit of her stomach, and for the first time in her life experienced blind panic. If the mere suggestion that Ben might take it into his head to move on to pastures new was sufficient to make her feel physically sick, how would she feel if the suggestion became a reality?

Conscious of her mother's intense scrutiny, she turned her head to stare out of the window, lest her expression betray something that, as yet, she was not prepared to admit even to herself.

'Great heavens!' she exclaimed, relieved to be granted a legitimate reason for changing the subject abruptly. 'Lord Nicholas Risely has just entered the square...And, yes, I do believe he is heading this way! Now why, I wonder, are we being honoured with a visit from him?'

This was precisely what was passing through the Countess's mind, though she was careful not to betray the fact, when the butler showed the charmingly irresponsible young lord into the sunny front parlour a minute or so later. Although he had never failed to request Sophia to stand up with him if they happened to be attending the same function during an evening, her ladyship had never looked upon him as a serious contender for her daughter's hand, and she doubted very much that he wished to be considered a suitable *parti* by paying this unexpected visit now.

'What a very pleasant surprise, Lord Nicholas,' she greeted him, before bidding him to be seated. 'I do not believe I have seen you since our paths crossed the other evening at Lady Carlisle's party.'

'No, ma'am, you haven't. I've been out of town for the past few days, visiting a good friend of mine, Toby Alderman. He's—er—rusticating at the moment, as you might say.'

'His pockets are to let, you mean,' Sophia put in, clearly betraying the fact that, although she was increasingly growing more dignified, she still was not above passing some ribald comment when the mood should take her. 'I met him once when we first arrived in town. If my memory serves me correctly, he was forced to depart the capital very soon afterwards because of mounting debts.'

'There you have it in a nutshell, my lady! He's been playing deep of late, and Lord Alderman has flatly refused to honour his grandson's debts unless Toby proves that he is willing to mend his ways. Consequently, he's been blackmailed into remaining in the country, taking care of the estate, while the rest of the family are on a protracted visit to Scotland. I dare say, though, he'll take a bolt to town from time to time, just to relieve the tedium of country life, don't you know.'

'Before you betray any more of your friend's secrets, I think I should point out that young Mr Alderman's grandfather happens to be a close friend of my husband's,' the Countess warned, striving not to smile at the young lord's artless disclosures. 'As I'm sure you're aware, neither my daughter nor I am prone to gossiping, but we're only human, and do from time to time let fall snippets we have learned.'

'Oh, don't concern yourself, ma'am,' Nicholas responded with a dismissive wave of one shapely hand. 'Society has far more interesting things to gossip about at the moment. What with the continuing saga of Lady ''C'' and her poet friend, and all the speculation surrounding *The Wicked Marquis*, no one is likely to take much interest in Toby's comings and goings.'

'Yes, I've been hearing one or two things about

this book,' Sophia admitted, recalling something rather amusing that her friend Robina had disclosed the previous evening. 'It's commonly believed that certain characters have been drawn from real life.' It took a monumental effort, but she managed to refrain from divulging to her mother that 'dear' Hugo Perceval was believed to hold a prominent place between the book's covers, and that the author's vitriolic pen had been less than kind to him. 'I do not know how true it is, but I have also been told that the villain of the piece is based on none other than our oh, so charming neighbour.'

Her ladyship betrayed more than a faint interest on hearing this. 'Sywell…? Really…? Well, one cannot deny that he would admirably meet the requirements of the title.'

'He's certainly supposed to be the odds-on favourite,' Nicholas informed them. 'I cannot recall ever having met the chap myself. Something of a mad recluse, so I've been led to believe. Still,' he shrugged, 'I've always maintained that living in the country is grossly overrated, and that spending too much time watching the grass grow is bound to have an adverse effect on one in time. Why, you only have to look at m'sister to appreciate the truth of that. Gone peculiar in the attic since she turned her back on town life, and no mistake!'

'Which reminds me of the reason for my visit today,' he continued, after his listeners had with some success managed to suppress their chuckles. 'My sister's home is less than ten miles from Toby Alderman's place, so I decided I'd best pay a call, otherwise I'd never hear the end of it if she ever discovered I'd been so close and hadn't taken the trouble to pay her a visit. While I was there she reminded me that it's our aunt Tabatha's birthday on Friday and that I had foolishly promised to represent the family by attending, as Constance herself will be unable to do so this year owing to the fact that she'll be paying a visit to Bath.

'Well, the truth of the matter is I'd clean forgotten about the wretched party, and that I'd foolishly offered to bring some friends along to stay the night and help celebrate the event. I've been racking my brains since returning to town trying to think of suitable people to ask.' He looked distinctly hopeful as he gazed across at Sophia. 'And I was wondering whether you would make up one of the small party I'm taking from town?'

Although slightly surprised by Lord Risely's unexpected invitation, the Countess was not in the least offended that she had not been included. Ordinarily, of course, she would never have considered permitting her daughter to leave the capital in the middle of the Season, and remain overnight in the house of a woman who was to all intents and purposes a virtual stranger, but given the strained atmosphere in the house of late, she was not prepared to dismiss the idea out of hand. After all, a little time away from the

Earl's all-seeing eye could do Sophia nothing but good, she decided, smiling warmly at their visitor.

'As you can imagine, the invitation has come as something of a surprise to us both, Lord Risely,' she announced while Sophia was silently rehearsing her polite refusal. 'As I'm sure you can appreciate, too, we shall need a little time to consider the matter. However, I think I should point out at the outset that I would never permit Sophia to travel to your aunt's home without a chaperon.'

'Certainly not,' his lordship agreed. 'I'm assured that my aunt intends to put her carriage at my disposal, and will ensure that all the young female guests are adequately chaperoned at all times.'

Lady Yardley could find no fault with these arrangements and, in turn, assured him that she would send a message to his lodgings informing him of her decision before the end of the day. Sophia was frankly astonished that her mother would even consider permitting her to go, and was not slow to voice her feelings once his lordship had taken his leave.

'But, Mama, you cannot have forgotten that it's the Meechams' ball on Friday. It is held to be one of the events of the Season, and not to be missed.'

'No, I hadn't forgotten, dear,' she responded, turning to her embroidery once more. 'And if you are set on going, then of course you must refuse the invitation.'

Rising to her feet, Sophia moved over to the window in time to see their unexpected visitor walking out of the square. 'Strange,' she said, frowning slightly, 'that the invitation didn't include you, Mama.'

'No, I do not think so, dear,' she countered. 'Lady Tabatha Risely has always had a reputation for being slightly eccentric. She lives fairly comfortably, but if my memory serves me correctly her house is not large, so she's possibly restricted in the number of people she can invite to stay at any one time.'

'Are you acquainted with her, Mama?'

'Slightly, yes, but I haven't seen her for a number of years. She has turned seventy now, and rarely comes to town.'

A dreadful possibility having taken possession of her mind, Sophia was only vaguely aware of her mother's response. 'You don't suppose Lord Nicholas has developed a *tendre* for me, do you, Mama?' she asked, sharing her fears, 'and a desire to introduce me to his family is what really lies behind this unexpected invitation?'

'Would you be offended if I said most certainly not?' Her ladyship cast her daughter a reassuring smile. 'Rest easy, child. He likes you well enough, but he's certainly not in love with you.'

Sophia almost sighed with relief as she rejoined her mother on the sofa. 'In that case I shouldn't mind getting away from the capital, if only for one night. It has become quite warm, quite oppressive of late. The country air will do me good.'

'Precisely what I thought myself,' the Countess

agreed. 'So I shall write informing Lord Nicholas that you accept, shall I?'

If Sophia's initial reaction to the unexpected invitation had been less than enthusiastic, by the time Friday had arrived, and she was standing at the parlour window awaiting the arrival of Lady Tabatha's carriage, she had begun to view the impending short sojourn away from town as nothing short of a godsend.

She was finding the changes in her father's personality increasingly difficult to accept and his continued presence in the evenings increasingly claustrophobic. Whenever she turned round, she would discover him hovering nearby, watching, scrutinising her every reaction to the different gentlemen who paid her varying degrees of attention. If he was hoping to see a sudden lovelorn expression take possession of her features, he would wait in vain, for although there were several personable young men in whose company she was more than content to while away an hour or so, no immaculately attired gentleman with whom she could happily spend the rest of her life had yet crossed her path.

And why this sudden urgency to see her married, anyway? she wondered, pondering anew on the question which had plagued her frequently during these past days. She recalled clearly enough that, when they had first arrived in town, the Earl's main concern had seemed to be a determination to protect her from fortune-hunters. Perhaps, in part, this was still the case, but she couldn't help feeling that at some point during the recent past the Earl had, for reasons known only to himself, developed an almost obsessive desire to see her married, or at the very least betrothed, before the Season was over.

She shook her head, still quite unable to account for this drastic change in him. But life was not all doom and gloom, she reminded herself, flatly refusing to allow her father's continuing unreasonable behaviour to mar totally the pleasure she was surprisingly still managing to attain from this, her first Season in the capital. After all, she could still rely on her mother's unfailing support. Thank goodness! How lucky she was too to have friends like Robina Perceval about her to confide in...And then, of course, she now had Ben...

How she had missed him during this past week! she was forced silently to concede. At least, though, they had managed to exchange a few words whenever she had returned to the stables after her daily ride. That wonderful, spontaneous, wide smile of his, always preceding a few reassuring words, never failed to raise her flagging spirits.

Ben continued to be firmly convinced that her father's present melancholy state would not last indefinitely. And one never knew, perhaps he was right, she decided, absently watching a very smart curricle and pair turn into the square. Ben's judgement had most certainly not been at fault when he had predicted that the gossips would swiftly forget about a young lady's seeming infatuation with her groom once they had been provided with tastier morsels to drool over. Lady Caroline Lamb's scandalous exploits, together with those of another high-ranking female personage whose name was being linked these days with a certain member of the royal household, had definitely kept the tattle-mongers' tongues busy of late. Not once during the past two or three days could Sophia recall observing any sly glances cast in her direction. So perhaps it was safe now to resume her daily rides with Ben once she had returned to town, she thought, watching the curricle which had driven into the square a few moments before pull up outside the house.

Sophia had little difficulty in recognising the tall figure jumping down from the smart equipage, once a servant had rushed from the house to hold the horses' heads, and felt her spirits begin to flag a little when Lord Nicholas, not looking too happy himself, entered the room a few moments later. 'Has the party been cancelled?' she asked, deciding that this must be the reason for his visit.

'No, no! Nothing like that,' he hurriedly assured her, casting a furtive glance over his shoulder at Cardew, who remained standing sentinel-like by the door, determined it seemed to protect his young mistress from the unwholesome attentions of young men. 'Thing is my aunt's carriage hasn't turned up. Should have arrived over an hour ago. Can only imagine it must have met with an accident.'

Sophia considered the matter for a moment before proposing that she make the journey in her father's own well-sprung travelling-carriage, but she could discern by his expression that his lordship was not precisely in favour of this, even before he said, 'No need for that. Old Freddy Fortescue and his sister are taking a bolt to the country today. Their grandmother lives only a stone's throw away from my aunt's place, so we can beg a lift with them.' He took a moment to glance at the clock. 'Chances are they won't have left town yet. With any luck we'll catch them before they set off if we hurry.'

He turned, about to retrace his steps into the hall, only to discover his way blocked by the solid figure of the butler. 'I think it behoves me to remind you, my lady,' Cardew remarked at his most haughty, 'that her ladyship gave strict instructions before she left the house earlier that I was to hand you personally into Lady Tabatha Risely's carriage, and no other.'

'Yes, but as you've already heard, Cardew, for some reason Lady Tabatha's carriage hasn't arrived, so stop creating unnecessary difficulties by delaying me further and have my overnight bag taken out to his lordship's curricle at once.'

'You know, this man of yours has a point, there. Must think of the proprieties,' Nicholas put in, earning himself a faint look of approval from the punctilious retainer. 'It's all very well for you to travel with me as far as the Fortescues' place, no harm in that at all. But supposing Freddy and his sister have already left? Can't go careering after them with you sitting beside me, unchaperoned, now can I?'

He appeared to ponder over the problem for a moment. 'I tell you what, we'll take that groom of yours along with us. Then, if someone does observe us leaving the capital, it'll not cause a stir.'

Having anticipated a relatively peaceful afternoon, Ben was mildly surprised when he received the summons to present himself at the front entrance without delay. He knew for a fact that the Earl and Countess were at that very moment being conveyed about the town by the dutiful Trapp in the light town carriage. Sophia, he had been reliably informed, was spending the afternoon and evening out of the capital, so he was hardly expecting to see her, as he rounded the corner from the mews, being assisted into a curricle by an instantly recognisable figure in an expertly tailored bottle-green coat.

Benedict's suspicions were instantly aroused. His brother, as far as he could recall, had never betrayed the least inclination to join the sporting-mad Corinthian set. Feather-edging a corner with less than an inch to spare simply wasn't Nicholas's style at all. So what, he asked himself, was his young brother doing in charge of such a bang-up-to-date turnout which was almost certainly not his own? More importantly, what was the young reprobate doing with the future Duchess of Sharnbrook, when the darling girl ought to have been away from the city long since, enjoying the sweet country air? he wondered, his suspicions increasing alarmingly when he noticed that Nicholas seemed very reluctant to meet his eye.

Sophia experienced no such reservations, and smiled brightly down at him. 'You are here to lend me countenance, Ben,' she told him when he at last stood beside the carriage and had cast her an enquiring glance. 'Lord Nicholas and Cardew, here,' she added, as the butler placed her overnight bag beneath the seat himself, 'seem to think that my reputation will suffer if I am seen leaving town in an open carriage. Silly, don't you think?'

'No, I do not,' Benedict responded with the brutal honesty to which Sophia had grown quite accustomed. 'And might I point out that I am a groom and not a duenna. Furthermore, my lady, you should not be contemplating leaving town in this equipage at all!'

In any other circumstances Cardew might have taken the groom roundly to task for daring to answer his young mistress in such a disrespectful fashion. The fact of the matter was, however, he wholeheartedly agreed, and couldn't bring himself to play the hypocrite by administering a strong reprimand.

Nicholas, on the other hand, experienced no such qualms, and gained a deal of perverse pleasure in ordering his big brother to mind his tongue before commanding him in the same brusque manner to climb up on the back of the curricle. He gave him only sufficient time to do so before picking up the reins and giving the splendid pair of matched greys the office to start.

They swept out of the square, a silent trio, each absorbed in his or her own thoughts, but it was not very long before Benedict's curiosity got the better of him and, swallowing his ire, forced himself to enquire where they were bound.

'Curzon Street,' Nicholas answered, secretly smiling at the clipped tones. Unless he very much mistook the matter, big brother would dearly love to strangle him. 'And with any luck we'll get there in time.'

'In time for what, dare I ask?'

'It appears to me, my good man,' Nicholas responded, mimicking quite beautifully the haughty disapproval shown by the Yardleys' very correct butler a short while earlier, 'that you have the gall to dare anything. I shall take leave to inform you that you are an impertinent devil!' He caught what sounded suspiciously like a suppressed feminine chuckle. 'I wonder that you bear with such insolence, Lady Sophia,' he continued, enjoying himself hugely, though at the same time well aware he would probably pay dearly later if his brother managed to get him alone. 'I certainly would not. The rogue would not last five minutes in my household. Or any other, come to that!'

'Ben is not in the common way, certainly,' Sophia was forced to concede, glancing over her shoulder in time to see her groom casting the gentleman on the seat beside her a dagger-look. 'We are hoping to catch some friends of Lord Nicholas before they leave town, Ben. Then I shall be suitably chaperoned, and you can return to Berkeley Square.'

'And if you are not in time, my lady?'

Ben's question was not an unreasonable one, but Sophia found herself quite unable to answer it, and turned to his lordship for guidance. 'Oh, there'll be no problem,' Nicholas announced, sounding sublimely unconcerned. 'Even if they have already left the house, I dare swear we'll catch up with them long before they've reached the outskirts of the capital.'

Unfortunately this did not turn out to be the case. Which certainly did not surprise Benedict in the least, for the perfectly matched greys were not once encouraged to go above a very moderate pace.

Of course his brother might have an excellent reason for maintaining such a slow speed, Benedict decided, as they left the last of the straggling dwellings on the outskirts of the capital behind. The turn-out, he strongly suspected, belonged to one of his brother's friends, and Nicholas was no doubt taking extra care to ensure that neither carriage nor horses sustained any damage at his hands. Or maybe he was hoping to cover as many miles as possible with the same team, and was therefore not overtaxing the greys. Both explanations were plausible, and yet he could not rid himself of the ever-growing conviction that his brother was bent on some mischief.

He turned his attention to the other occupant of the seat, and realised suddenly that during the last few miles Sophia had grown increasingly quiet, and was now looking rather thoughtful. His brother might, indeed, be indulging in some wicked prank, but Benedict doubted very much that his future bride was a party to it. No, unless he much mistook the matter, she was as puzzled as he was himself as to why Nicholas had made no attempt whatsoever to catch up with his friends the Fortescues.

They continued at the same monotonous snail's pace for a further twenty minutes or so, during which time they were overtaken by a variety of carriages including a lumbering coach. Then Nicholas, quite without warning, announced his intention of putting up for a change and, betraying an element of skill, turned the curricle with a flourish into the yard of a very busy posting house.

'Might I be permitted to know where we are bound, my lady?' Benedict asked while his brother, who had swiftly alighted, was busily engaged in issuing orders to an ostler.

'To the home of Lady Tabatha Risely, a relative of his lordship's,' she enlightened him, not finding his curiosity remotely suspicious. 'If we ever manage to get there, that is.'

Not even by the raising of one of his expressive brows did Benedict betray the least surprise at their intended destination, though he found it impossible not to chuckle at his beloved's hint of sarcasm.

Sophia found the deep masculine rumble immensely reassuring and turned in the seat to look directly at the man whom she had never been able to view in the light of a servant. 'I'm so very glad you're here, Ben,' she told him, unashamedly betraying her thoughts. 'I should feel distinctly uneasy if you were not.'

Out of the corner of her eye she noticed Nicholas slinking away to disappear into the inn. 'Does it seem to you that his lordship has made no attempt whatsoever to overtake his friend's carriage? The Fortescues' servants assured us that the carriage left not half an hour before we arrived at the house. We ought to have caught up with them long since. Most certainly would have done so if you'd held the ribbons!' She was struck by a sudden thought. 'I've a mind to suggest that you do take over. And where in heaven's name has Lord Nicholas got to now!' she snapped, allowing mounting irritation to surface.

Something in her expression must have betrayed her feelings of pique, for Nicholas apologised for keeping her waiting the instant he returned. 'Just popped inside to ascertain whether or not my friend Freddy has already passed this way.'

'It must have been so long ago that I'm surprised the landlord could remember,' she retorted, and it took a monumental effort but Nicholas did somehow manage to preserve his countenance.

'The Fortescues do keep fine cattle, so perhaps I was slightly foolish to attempt to overtake them,' he acknowledged in a voice which shook only very slightly. 'I shan't, however, continue the attempt. Nor shall I delay further in the hope of seeing Aunt Tabatha's carriage come bowling towards us. Instead, I'll try to make up for lost time by taking a little short cut I know,' and so saying he turned off the post road.

They continued for several miles down a series of narrow, twisting lanes. As far as Sophia was concerned, the county of Surrey might have been a foreign land. She had no idea of where they were, nor did she even know in which direction they were heading, now that the sun had disappeared behind a thick blanket of cloud. Benedict, too, was not familiar with this route, for although he had paid numerous visits to the home of his elderly maiden aunt in the distant past, he had invariably travelled along the main post roads whenever making the journey.

'I don't think it would be a bad idea at all if we took the time to stop for a short while in order to refresh ourselves,' Nicholas suggested as they reached a sleepy little village where a rambling thatched inn, nestling among some trees, stood opposite the church. 'I've been here before, and can assure you the fare is excellent. I might even be persuaded to treat that impertinent groom of yours to a tankard,' he could not resist adding before bringing his horses to a halt and, ignoring his brother's loud, derisive snort, escorted Sophia into the spotlessly clean, low-ceilinged building.

When his brother, having seen to the comfort of the horses, sauntered in a few minutes later, Nicholas decided that he might as well have been invisible for all the notice that was taken of him. Over the rim of his tankard he studied his companions, and for the second time in the space of a few hours found himself having to exert a monumental effort to maintain his countenance. How his brother had managed to remain employed for this length of time eluded him completely. Benedict was not remotely deferential. In fact, for a 'servant' he was appallingly rude! Yet it was quite evident that Sophia didn't appear to mind, or didn't appear to notice, one or the other.

He shook his head. They certainly made an unconventional couple—the Earl's daughter and her golden-haired groom. At least he didn't doubt that they would make a perfect couple, providing nothing went wrong with his well-laid plans!

Chapter Eleven

When it happened he really ought to have been prepared, ought to have been expecting something to occur sooner or later, and yet Benedict would have been the first to admit that at the time he was taken completely by surprise. One moment they were bowling along the narrow, twisting country lane, hoping against hope that they could manage to reach their destination before that threatening dark bank of clouds, which had been slowly gathering from the west, released its moisture; the next moment they were in the ditch, viewing the landscape from a very peculiar angle, all helplessly watching the offside wheel rolling away along the road ahead of them.

Fortunately none of them was hurt. One of the bays, however, had not been so lucky, and had sustained a slightly strained hock. Although the injury was not serious, the animal could no longer be expected to pull the carriage, even if the equipage were roadworthy. Which it most definitely was not!

At the time Benedict considered that his young brother had had no choice but to take such swift and drastic action in order to avoid a collision with the oncoming carriage, which had been travelling far too swiftly for safety along such narrow lanes. It was only a short time later, after Nicholas had suggested that he journey back to the inn with the horses, and Benedict and Sophia seek shelter until his return at the cottage which stood a little further along the road, that Benedict's suspicions were first aroused, and he began seriously to consider the possibility that the unfortunate occurrence might not have been the innocent accident which it had first appeared.

He glanced over his shoulder in time to see Nicholas, mounted on the healthy bay, and carefully leading the injured animal, disappear round the bend in the road, and decided that it was a stroke of great good fortune that they had met the other carriage along that particular stretch of road, for it was the only place, for some considerable distance, wide enough for two vehicles to pass with care. Chance, or pure contrivance? he couldn't help asking himself. Was it a happy coincidence also that there just happened to be a cottage nearby where shelter might be sought? His eyes narrowed. It was all beginning to appear rather smoky, he decided, blithely entering the cottage after receiving no response to his second knock.

Sophia, having little experience of the conditions endured by the unfortunate poor, cast an interested glance round the one-roomed dwelling and was favourably impressed. 'Well, I must say, this is all very clean and cosy.'

Yes, a little too clean and cosy, Benedict decided, his suspicions increasing with every passing second. Not even at Sharnbrook did the estate workers live in such comfort. White linen sheets, feather pillows and what felt suspiciously like a horsehair mattress were not the usual trappings of cottage-dwellers. And how many working men, he wondered, unable to suppress a wry grin as he turned his attention to the foodstuffs placed on the wooden table, could afford the luxury of a fine claret to wash down their bread and cheese? Really, Nicholas was stretching things a little too far for authenticity!

He shook his head. Undoubtedly these items had been carried here from some large house nearby, solely for his and Sophia's comfort. Furthermore, he considered it pretty safe to assume that whoever it was who had so thoughtfully catered for their needs had not contemplated that their stay would be of short duration.

'We may as well make ourselves comfortable while we await his lordship's return,' Benedict suggested, adding a log to the sizeable fire some considerate soul had prepared in readiness for their arrival. He didn't add that he would be amazed if they saw any sign of Nicholas before morning, or anybody else, come to that. No, unless he was very much mistaken, he was supposed to take advantage of a night spent alone here with Sophia. Strangely enough he had never once considered the possibility of seduction as a means by which he might attain his ends. He watched her seat herself in the rocking chair by the hearth. But he was only human, and she was a very lovely young woman...

'Are you contemplating a drastic drop in temperature, Ben?' Sophia enquired as he absently added a further sizeable log to the blaze. She edged the rocking chair a little further away from the hearth. 'Though perhaps you're wise,' she added as the first spots of rain began to trickle their way down the small window. 'Lord Nicholas is likely to arrive at the inn soaked to the skin, poor man.'

Poor Nicholas? Benedict silently echoed, unable to suppress a further wry grin. Would she be quite so concerned over the young lord's well-being if she began to suspect the truth? There was not a doubt in his own mind now that Nicholas, no doubt aided and abetted by some close friend living not so very far from here, had planned this escapade down to the finest detail.

Suddenly experiencing his first pangs of conscience, Benedict did not find it at all easy to meet that trustful green-eyed gaze. 'There's no guarantee,' he warned in an attempt to prepare her, 'that his lordship will be able to hire another carriage. In fact, it is most unlikely that he shall. That place we stopped at is just a village inn, remember, not a posting-house. He's unlikely to attain much joy there.'

'True, but might not the innkeeper own a gig?' she suggested, after giving the matter a moment's thought.

'It's possible, certainly. But whether or not he'd be willing to hire it out to a perfect stranger is quite another matter.'

Sophia regarded him in mild surprise. 'I do not believe that his lordship is a stranger to that particular innkeeper or his wife. Didn't you notice the friendly terms on which they appeared to be?'

He had, but he could have wished that she had been less observant, for it was quite obvious that she was expecting Nicholas to attain all the help he needed with little difficulty. Which was possibly no less than the truth, though Benedict strongly suspected that his young brother had already attained all the aid he required with the deliberate sabotaging of the curricle, and would require no further assistance until morning.

Fixing his eyes on an imaginary spot on the floor, he began to ponder over how best to voice his suspicions, and swiftly discovered that he could not bring himself to be the one to crush those childlike beliefs she still managed to retain. He didn't wish to be the one to tell her that people whom she liked and admired could and perhaps often did behave in a less than honourable way on occasions; that people were not simply good or evil, but a complex mixture of both. She had, he knew, suspected all along that Nicholas had deliberately tooled the curricle at a very slow pace, but it would never cross her mind to suppose for a moment that the accident which had resulted in their being alone together here had been anything other than an unfortunate mishap; it would never cross her mind to suppose for a moment that everything that had happened to her since she left Berkeley Square had been carefully planned down to the finest detail and that the honourable young lord whom she liked so much had never had the least intention of taking her to his Aunt Tabatha's home.

'I'm not in the least familiar with this part of the country, are you, Ben?'

Drawing his eyes away from the imaginary spot on the floor, and his mind back to the present, Benedict searched in vain for a hint of concern in that lovely face of hers. She appeared, as she slowly began to untie the ribbons of her fashionable bonnet, completely undisturbed by her present unfortunate predicament, accepting her lot with a quaint and dignified resignation.

'I haven't any real idea of exactly where we are, no,' he admitted. 'This place is undoubtedly an estate-worker's cottage, so there's bound to be a big house somewhere nearby. When the rain eases off a little, I'll see if I can locate its whereabouts, and get help.'

Once again she made no attempt to hide her surprise. 'Do you think that's wise? Supposing his lordship returns while we're away. Yes, I did say we,' she added, smiling at the sudden raising of those expressive masculine brows, a trait which she had come to consider most endearing. 'You don't suppose that

I'd calmly stay here on my own, and permit you to go wandering off to heaven knows where? Besides, the tenant might well return while you're away. There's no saying what sort of person I'd find myself having to deal with.' She glanced about her, as something at last occurred to her as odd. 'Though I must say, whoever lives here does keep the place very clean and tidy. Are all cottages kept this well, Ben? I must confess to being quite ignorant about such things.'

'In my experience, no,' he answered, smiling in spite of the fact that he was rapidly becoming annoyed by the situation in which he now found himself through no fault of his own.

He moved over to the window, and was appalled to discover that the rain, far from abating, was increasing. Confound his brother for an interfering young cub! he cursed silently. If Nicholas had been standing beside him, he would quite cheerfully have throttled him. He didn't doubt for a moment that Nicholas's actions had been prompted by nothing more than deep brotherly concern. But hadn't the headstrong young fool even taken the time to consider the very real possibility that Sophia just might not care for his big brother enough to want to marry him? Worse still, that she might consider a ruined reputation favourable to being tied for life to someone she could never respect?

It was a heart-rending possibility, but one that was much better faced, if not by Nicholas, then certainly by himself. Just as it was better to face the fact that some deep and wholly dishonourable part of him was not sorry to have been granted this golden opportunity to attain what his heart most desired. Nor could he deny the fact that he was not totally unwilling to listen to that demon of temptation urging him to take advantage of this situation, goading him to seduce her now and to the devil with the consequences! He had managed to resist thus far the prompting of his baser instincts…But for how much longer could he continue to do so?

By the time Ben had lit the tallow candles on the mantelshelf, and they had eaten their fill of the simple yet wholesome fare, Sophia was well and truly resigned to spending her very first night in a humble cottage, and a part of her was determined to enjoy the novel experience, too. Although the rain had begun to abate some little time ago, it was far too dark now to contemplate an expedition outside in order to discover some larger dwelling where they might attain aid in reaching their destination, and she had sensibly abandoned all hope of seeing his lordship again until morning.

Drawing her eyes away from the flames dancing in the hearth, she looked across at Ben, seated opposite on the wooden settle. It might have been pure imagination, but she sensed a suppressed tension about him now that had not been apparent when they had first arrived at the cottage. Concern over her reputation might well be the cause, she decided, unable to suppress a smile. How strange that she was not in the least perturbed; had not once experienced the least trepidation throughout the entire eventful afternoon and evening, simply because that particular man had been with her.

She didn't even attempt to analyse this rather startling truth; instead, she merely echoed her initial thoughts by remarking quite casually, 'I think we must face the fact, Ben, that his lordship might be unable to rescue us until morning.'

He paused in the act of adding a further log to the blaze, his blue eyes penetrating, and glinting with some emotion that was difficult to interpret, as he turned them momentarily in her direction. 'You do not appear unduly disturbed. Doesn't it trouble you being alone here with me, Sophia?'

What made her start, caught her completely off guard, was not the bluntness of the question—she had grown accustomed to this directness quite early in their association—but the fact that he had deliberately made free with her given name, and that it had sounded so natural coming from his lips.

'No, of course it does not,' she assured him, forcing the words through a mouth that for some inexplicable reason had suddenly grown uncomfortably dry.

Rising from the chair, she went across the small room and swiftly eased the slight discomfort by helping herself from what remained of the bottle of wine resting on the table. She knew she really ought to reprimand him for such familiarity, but instead found herself asking, 'Why do you suppose that I might be troubled?'

An unmistakable challenging gleam sprang into blue eyes. 'Because I'm a man…a groom, perhaps, but no less a man than—shall we say—a marquis or a duke. And because we'll be spending the whole night together…and quite alone.' In one lithe movement he had risen from the settle and was slowly coming towards her. 'It might be wise for you to take a moment or two to consider the consequences.'

'Consequences?' she echoed, wondering why her heart had suddenly decided to attempt to beat its way through her ribcage when she remained quite unafraid, and steadfastly refused to move even though he had come to stand so close behind her that she could feel his warm breath fanning the tiny curls feathering the nape of her neck.

'If you imagine my father is likely to come after you brandishing a pistol and demanding you do the honourable thing, you may rest easy,' she assured him, astonished herself at the unmistakable note of disappointment which had found its way quite without design into her voice. 'Had you been a marquis now…well, that would be a different matter entirely.'

'To your father, perhaps, but not to you.' His fingers were on her upper arms, turning her round gently yet firmly to face him squarely. 'It is the man you would care about, not his wealth or his social position.' The glinting devilment in his eyes had disappeared completely, leaving a gaze so intense that she found it impossible to draw her own away. 'But supposing your father, for whatever reason, did insist on a match between us, Sophia, would you try to dissuade him?'

No, never! her heart responded with such vehemence that her mind refused even to attempt to deny the truth of it. It was madness, perhaps, but she could think of no one with whom she would rather spend the rest of her days than this tall enigmatic stranger who had unexpectedly come into her life, and who by degrees so subtle that she had hardly been aware of it had become totally indispensable to her happiness. Quite simply she loved him, and had for some little time.

The realisation, sudden though it was, in no way surprised her. Her lips parted, but the assurances that her heart longed to make were smothered by the firm mouth which suddenly covered her own.

No thought of resistance crossed her mind, then or moments later, when she found herself being pressed inexorably back against the softness of the horsehair mattress, one powerful, muscular leg moving across her thighs keeping her a very willing prisoner, while masculine lips and fingers were working a particular kind of intoxicating magic on her highly responsive body. The chaste salutes she had permitted a few honoured members of the opposite sex to place upon her fingers and proffered cheek in the past had in no way prepared her for this peerless display of masculine passion. And her reaction to it was no less shocking. Instead of striving to attempt at least a token display of maidenly modesty, she was actively encouraging him to take further liberties by easing her body into a position whereby he was better able to reach the tiny buttons at the neckline of her dress and ease the restricting garment down over her shoulders.

She found herself quite unable to control the shivers of pleasure rippling through her as Ben's right hand began to explore the fine bones of her shoulder, and then moved lower to trace the rounded contour of her breast. She would never have believed it possible that the feather-light touch of masculine fingers could create such a wealth of wholly pleasurable physical sensations, blocking the mind, suppressing all rational thoughts save one.

'I love you,' she murmured, so softly that she was hardly aware that she had spoken, but instantly aware of the change in him. She felt him stiffen, felt those magical fingers still, before he raised his head to stare down into her face, his eyes glinting with a strange mixture of triumph and hard determination. Then he was on his feet and, easily avoiding the tentative hand she stretched out towards him, was moving out of reach, muttering words which made little sense at the time, but which she was to remember very well in the weeks, months, and years to come.

'No, not this way,' he said again, as though desperately striving to convince himself. 'Perhaps I'm mad. No doubt my enterprising young brother will think me mad...but, no matter. I cannot allow it to happen...not this way.'

Sophia regarded him in silence as he reached out to grasp the mantelshelf with those fingers that had wrought such havoc on her senses only moments before. 'Ben, I don't understand you.' She felt like a child, hurt and confused, being punished for doing something, though it knew not what. 'Have I done something wrong?'

He did not attempt to answer, and she couldn't help wondering whether her immodest lack of restraint might not be at the root of this sudden change in him. Instinctively she reached for the neckline of her dress, and tried to set the garment to rights as unobtrusively and swiftly as possible, which was certainly no easy task as all her fingers seemed to have been replaced by thumbs.

'I do love you, Ben,' she assured him when she felt more able to face him again. 'I would never have allowed you...I mean, I would not have permitted you...'

'I know what you mean.' He did take the trouble to look at her then, and although she could not be perfectly certain of precisely what he was thinking, or feeling, she could detect no hint of disgust or revulsion in his eyes. 'That is precisely why I'm not prepared to let it happen this way. I must approach your father in the accepted manner. I want him...and you to be given the choice.'

'What!' Sophia gaped across at him, unable to believe that such an intelligent man had uttered anything so foolish. 'Ben, you must be all about in your head…Or I am!' Which was highly likely, as her poor temples had begun to throb. 'Papa will never give his consent. Never, do you hear!'

'No?' He appeared not in the least convinced, nor, it had to be said, very concerned, either. In fact, if anything, he looked merely highly amused. 'Well, I hope you're wrong, but if not, we must just trust that sense will prevail and that he'll come round given time.'

'He won't!' A simpleton could not have mistaken the conviction in her voice. 'You don't know my father. Where do you suppose I inherited my stubborn, determined streak? I've told you before what it's been like at home during these past two or three weeks,' she reminded him, wondering why those broad shoulders appeared to be shaking with suppressed laughter. 'It's been a constant battle of wills. I have through various stratagems remained the victor thus far, but there's no saying that that state of affairs will continue for very much longer. For some reason Papa seems determined to see me suitably settled before the Season comes to an end, and he isn't a man to accept defeat easily.'

'That being the case, he ought to be delighted when I approach him with my offer.'

Her ludicrously crestfallen expression was almost his undoing. He knew precisely what was passing through that pretty little head of hers, and wanted nothing more than to assure her that everything would be all right when he did eventually approach the Earl to ask for her hand, but he remained firm. The lovely Sophia, spoilt and indulged from birth, needed to be taught that she could not have everything she wanted in life, that she must be prepared to make concessions, and, most important of all, she had to be persuaded to abandon those few remaining girlish fancies which she was trying to take with her into womanhood and accept the reality of who she was and what she was.

'Of course I do realise there is always the possibility that he may take me in dislike, may not approve of me, in which case when we do marry we must be prepared to forfeit your dowry.'

For the first time there was a faint hint of uncertainty in her eyes, and in her voice, too, as she asked, 'Would that matter to you so very much? It certainly would not to me.'

'It wouldn't, eh?'

'No, it wouldn't. I would willingly forfeit my inheritance in order to marry the man I love.'

'Very affecting!' He didn't spare her feelings, couldn't spare her feelings if he wanted to be certain of winning her, and raised his eyes ceilingwards. 'So, you suppose that love is the only thing that's important, eh?'

'Ben, what's wrong?' Her evident anxiety was almost more than he could bear. 'Don't you wish to marry me?'

'More than you realise, my darling, but we'll leave

that for the moment. Let us discuss instead just how good a wife you'd make for a hard-working groom.'

Planting his feet firmly apart, he folded his arms across his chest, and looked her over, just as though she were some prize filly up for sale at Tattersall's. 'You're pleasing on the eye, and there's no mistaking that air of breeding. But a sensible man wouldn't purchase a thoroughbred to pull a plough.'

He could easily detect the first stirring of her temper, even before she advised him in no uncertain terms to keep a civil tongue in his head.

'I doubt you can cook,' he continued, just as though she had not spoken, 'and I doubt you've ever held so much as a broom in your hand, either. I would be astonished if you've ever attempted to starch a cravat, or wash an item of clothing, come to that. All in all you'd be of precious little use to a poor man, my darling, and I think any would do well to consider very carefully before contemplating taking you to wife.'

To Sophia the implication seemed perfectly plain: the man whom she had just discovered that she loved, the man for whom she would quite happily have sacrificed everything in order to be with, was himself having second thoughts about her!

She felt bitterly hurt, especially after the loving exchange which had taken place between them only a short time before, and thoroughly humiliated by the catalogue of what he evidently perceived as her shortcomings. She had never considered herself to be a vindictive person, but she found she was totally unable to suppress the overwhelming need to hurt and humiliate him in return.

Tapping into that deep well of feminine pride, she rose from the bed and faced him squarely. 'I think, all things considered, we would both do well to think long and hard before making a decision which in the future we might come to regret,' she announced, sounding every inch the haughty aristocrat. 'You most especially, because it must be perfectly plain that you cannot possibly continue as my groom, not after what has taken place between us.'

'I could not agree more,' he obligingly concurred. 'Furthermore, I have no intention of spending the night with you in this cottage, but shall relieve you of one of your blankets and await the arrival of dawn on the porch.' And so saying, he did no more than whisk one of the covers off the bed and move over to the door, remaining only to murmur what sounded suspiciously like, 'Goodnight, Duchess.'

Several times before she eventually fell asleep Sophia was on the point of calling out to him to come back inside and spend the night on the settle before the fire, but stubborn pride prevented her. Long before she awoke to find bright sunlight filtering through the cottage window, she had come to regret hasty words spoken in anger, and was determined to persuade him to stay, certain that they could find some way out of their difficulties. But it was already too late. Although she wasn't to know it as she threw off the covers and hurriedly scrambled into her crumpled gown, Benjamin Rudgely was already heading off down the road on a borrowed mount and out of her life for ever.

Chapter Twelve

'Flagrant ingratitude!' One or two of the breakfast dishes came perilously close to ending on the floor as the Earl of Yardley gave vent to his annoyance by bringing the flat of his hand down rather hard on the table. 'What else can you call it, pray? I knew at the time I was being less than sensible to consider taking the fellow on without so much as a reference, but, kind-hearted fool that I am, I did so against my better judgement. And how does the rogue repay my generosity?' he demanded of neither of his listeners in particular. 'I'll tell you how—by taking himself off without so much as a by your leave, and leaving us short-handed! Ungrateful scoundrel!'

The Countess, having listened with a sympathetic ear to her husband's justifiable grievances against the errant groom, Benjamin Rudgely, could not forbear a smile. It was a pleasure to have her husband's company at breakfast again, even if he did on this particular occasion happen to be bemoaning life's iniquities. At least, she reminded herself, these instances of ill-humour were becoming far less frequent of late, and although she could hardly say that he was anywhere near back to his normally even-tempered self quite yet, there had been a noticeable improvement in his attitude during the past few days.

'His actions might have been, shall we say, a trifle thoughtless, dear, but I think it's unjust to brand him a scoundrel,' she pointed out, fair-minded as always. 'It was inconsiderate of Master Rudgely, I'll own, not to take the trouble to work his notice, but at least he did not help himself to the family's silver, or anyone else's as far as we're aware, before he disappeared.'

'True enough,' his lordship conceded, his frown of disapproval marginally fading. 'But it's still deuced odd.' His eyes moved from his wife to the third occupant of the table. 'And you can shed no more light on the matter, Sophia?'

'She's already told us all she can, dear,' her ladyship put in, instantly coming to her daughter's aid. 'If anyone should bemoan the disappearance of Benjamin Rudgely, then it is our daughter.' She cast a sympathetic smile across the table. 'You had grown fond of him, hadn't you dear?'

'Very,' Sophia responded, marvelling at her continuing self-control and—yes—feeling more than just a little proud of herself too.

Not once since she had woken that morning to discover not Ben sitting on the veranda outside the cottage, but Lord Nicholas Risely and the wife of the innkeeper whose hostelry they had patronised briefly the previous afternoon, had she betrayed to anyone the searing heartache which never left her for a moment. She recalled clearly that Ben had always considered ladies of her class who indulged in forceful displays of emotion in public faintly vulgar. She had always listened with interest to his opinions and, quite surprisingly, had very nearly always agreed with his point of view.

She was fast coming to accept too, painfully hard though it was, that everything he had said during the unforgettable night spent in that cottage just one short week ago, one week which seemed more like a year, had been no less than the truth. Only in fairy tales did princesses marry frogs. Only foolish childish fantasies could permit ladies of quality to marry their grooms and live happily ever after. Oh, yes, he had been painfully all too right, she reminded herself silently. She could only hope that one day she might be granted the opportunity to tell him so—tell him that although she loved him still, and perhaps always would, a match between them could never have taken place.

'I do not believe there is anything I can add to what I've already told you,' Sophia confirmed, abruptly abandoning her reverie when she became aware of two pairs of eyes firmly turned in her direction. 'I've already explained the reason why I decided to take Ben with me. Although,' she amended 'to be perfectly honest with you, I do believe it was Lord Nicholas's suggestion. When his aunt's carriage failed to turn up, he felt I couldn't possibly accompany him about town without even a groom to lend me countenance.'

His lordship tutted. 'Lady Tabatha Risely always

was an idiotish female. Fancy forgetting to send the carriage for one of her guests when she'd promised faithfully to do so!'

'Perhaps there is some excuse,' his wife pointed out. 'After all, she has turned seventy, dear.'

His lordship's grey brows rose sharply. 'Well? And what of it? So have I turned seventy, and there's nothing wrong with my memory.'

'No, dear,' the Countess thankfully agreed. 'But you are rather exceptional. And as you've already remarked, Lady Tabatha has always had a tendency to be—er—slightly scatty. Thank heavens it doesn't run in the family! Lord Nicholas, the dear boy, showed great presence of mind insisting on taking our groom along, although I could have wished he had not taken it into his head to travel the whole distance to his aunt's house in an open carriage when he failed to catch up with his friends.'

'No, perhaps that wasn't the wisest course of action,' Sophia was forced to concede, 'but as I've already explained, Mama, by the time we'd stopped at that inn to change horses, it would have taken us just as much time to return here to collect the travelling-carriage as it would to travel on to Lady Tabatha's home.'

Sophia had considered the explanation a reasonable one, and both her parents seemed to have accepted it as such. 'I didn't realise that his lordship hadn't intended staying the night at his aunt's home, but had arranged to stay with his friend Toby Alderman who resides nearby,' she went on to explain, remembering clearly what Lord Nicholas had advised her to say in the event her parents should ever enquire further.

Somehow her numbed brain had managed to assimilate everything he had said to her during the short journey back to town in Toby Alderman's carriage, with the landlady of that small inn acting as chaperon. Their return to town could not have appeared more proper, and he had had every intention of its remaining so by the wonderful tale he had concocted.

Sophia had accepted his suggestion at the time without question, Ben's unexpected disappearance having left her so numbed that she had been in no fit state to do otherwise. It was only during the past day or so that she had begun to wonder why Lord Nicholas had been so set against her offering the true account of what had taken place. After all, nothing very improper had occurred. Ben had spent the entire night out on the veranda. Nevertheless she had given her word to Nicholas, and she had no intention of breaking it now.

'When his lordship suggested that he take Ben along with him to spend the night at the Aldermans' place, I never thought anything of it. As you remarked yourself, Mama, Lady Tabatha's house isn't large, and she really didn't want to be troubled with the added burden of having to cater for unnecessary servants. Of course it came as a shock when I discovered Ben had taken himself off without telling a soul where he was bound.'

'Yes, I'm sure it must have, dear. Most odd of him!' Her ladyship, looking decidedly thoughtful, took a moment to finish the contents of her cup before enquiring, 'I do not suppose Lord Nicholas has managed to discover anything further?'

'Not as far as I am aware, Mama. He knows that part of the country very well, and has promised to make enquiries. As you know, the whole town is now talking of his brother's return, and I believe Lord Nicholas has gone into Hampshire to spend a few days with the Duke at Sharnbrook. I'll see him when he returns to town, and find out if he's discovered anything further then.'

'It's a great pity young Rudgely did take it into his head to leave us,' his lordship unexpectedly remarked. 'I wish now I'd taken the trouble to get to know him a little. Apart from passing the time of day on one or two occasions, I don't believe we exchanged more than half a dozen words during the whole time he was here. Trapp came to see me the other morning,' he went on to divulge. 'Very concerned he was that the lad hadn't even bothered to return to collect his few belongings.'

Dry-eyed and remaining remarkably composed, Sophia looked directly at the Earl. 'I must admit, Papa, that that concerns me too. I'm not suggesting for a moment that if Ben did return we ought to take him back.' That she knew would be just too much for her to bear. 'But I should like to set my mind at rest and be sure that nothing dreadful has happened to him.'

'Very well, child,' his lordship responded gently, betraying once again that he was making a steady recovery from whatever it was that had upset him so much. 'If young Risely is unable to discover anything,

I'll perhaps take a little stroll along to Bow Street.'
He glanced up as the door unexpectedly opened. 'Yes,
what is it, Cardew?'

The butler came forward bearing a single letter on
a silver tray. 'Delivered by hand, my lord, a few
minutes ago. The messenger is at this present moment
happily refreshing himself in the kitchen, awaiting
any response.'

His lordship's grey brows rose as he broke the impressive seal. 'Great heavens!' he exclaimed, after digesting the contents of the brief missive. 'What do
you make of that, m'dear?'

Her ladyship cast her eyes over the single sheet
written in a bold, elegant hand. 'Perfectly clear,' she
answered, betraying none of the evident shock her
husband was experiencing. 'His grace the Duke of
Sharnbrook has kindly invited us to spend a few days
with him at his ancestral home.'

'Yes, but why?' His lordship made a gesture with
his hands which betrayed clearly his continuing astonishment. 'The last time I saw young Benedict Risely
he was in short coats. Why should he suddenly take
it into his head to invite me and my family to
Sharnbrook, may I ask?'

The Countess shrugged her shoulders. 'I really
have no idea. I can only imagine that Lord Nicholas
might possibly have mentioned his friendship with
Sophia, and of her kindness in attending their aged
aunt's birthday party. Perhaps his grace wishes to
thank her in person.'

'Well, I hope that's all it is, and that he ain't taken
some foolish notion into his head that our little Sophie

would make him the ideal wife.' Far from annoyed, his lordship appeared genuinely amused. 'He'll quickly discover his mistake, if I do take it into my head to accept, and he finds himself having to play host to perhaps the only young filly in the country who has an aversion for titled gentlemen!'

'Do I infer correctly from that that you are undecided whether to accept or not, Papa?' Sophia remarked, her own sense of humour surprisingly rising to the surface. 'You do surprise me! I would have thought you would have grasped such a golden opportunity with both hands. After all, I rather like Lord Nicholas, so there's every chance I should like the brother equally well. Stranger things have happened, you know.'

Rising to her feet, she went over to the door. 'I should accept if I were you. Even if the Duke and I take each other in dislike on sight, a brief spell away from the stale town air will undoubtedly do us all the world of good,' and with that she left the room, and her father gaping after her in open-mouthed astonishment.

No matter what the underlying reason for encouraging her father to accept the unexpected invitation, and she wasn't so very certain herself what it had been, Sophia experienced no regrets whatsoever when Trapp, three days later, tooled the carriage expertly round the sweep of the drive, and she caught her first glimpse of the Duke of Sharnbrook's ancestral home.

Set amid acres of unspoiled parkland, and bathed in mellow late afternoon sunshine, the Restoration mansion, designed by none other than Inigo Jones's famous disciple, was a truly awe-inspiring sight. Sophia could not recall ever having seen anything quite so perfectly situated, and could only wonder at the present head of the family remaining away from such a beautiful spot for such a long time. If it were hers she would never wish to leave the place for five weeks, let alone five years, she felt sure, alighting with the assistance of the liveried footman who had emerged from the eastern entrance of the house the instant Trapp had brought the carriage to a halt.

The interior was no less impressive; at least what she could glimpse of it swiftly earned Sophia's full approval as she, together with her mother and father, followed the elderly housekeeper up an ornately carved oak staircase. At the top they turned left and went along a passageway which led to the recently added east wing. Here Sophia was shown into a bright, airy bedchamber, where hand-painted Chinese paper decorated the walls, and rich green silk hangings adorned both windows and four-poster bed.

She took a moment to stare about her in wonder, from ornately plasterworked ceiling to richly carpeted floor. For more than two centuries, according to the Earl, some of the very best architects and designers had been employed to work on the house and its grounds, creating a place of timeless beauty which rivalled, many considered, the very best in the land.

No mansion she had ever visited before had succeeded in capturing her interest in quite the same way. She did not know what it was about the place that enthralled her so, but she suddenly experienced an overwhelming desire to see it all, to explore every last nook and cranny and uncover its every hidden secret. Consequently, she wasted no time in changing from her travel-creased garments into one of her pretty light muslin day dresses, snatching up a light fringed shawl, and going along to her mother's room.

One glance at the Countess, relaxing on the *chaise-longue* by the open window, was sufficient to inform her that for the present her mother did not share her enthusiasm. 'Oh, I'm sorry, Mama, for barging in this way. Were you asleep?'

'No, child, merely resting my eyes.' She held out her hand, inviting her daughter to sit beside her, and could see at once that there appeared an extra sparkle in those green eyes, something which, she suddenly realised, had been singularly lacking in recent days. 'You seem excited, child. Is it the prospect of meeting our host which has touched your cheeks with added colour, I wonder?' she quizzed. 'He is reputed to be very handsome, you know.'

'Yes, so I'm reliably informed,' Sophia responded drily, thereby betraying her total lack of interest. 'I'm in far more danger of becoming entranced with this glorious house than with its master, I assure you. Have you ever seen a place so perfectly situated?'

'No, I do not believe so.' The Countess, watching her daughter move across to the window, was reminded of something which had occurred to her as rather strange a few days before and, after nodding dismissal to the maid, did not hesitate in attempting to have her curiosity satisfied now.

'Why did I encourage Papa to accept the invitation

to visit here?' Sophia echoed. 'I suppose I considered it would benefit him to get away from town for a few days. I hope the change will do him good. He seems so much better of late, don't you think?'

'Yes, child, I do.' A moment's silence, then, 'Are you sure there was no other reason?'

Sophia closed her eyes, successfully checking the threat of tears which she only ever permitted to fall at night in the privacy of her bedchamber, where she would sob long and silently into her pillow and wake in the morning feeling not a whit the better for having done so. The bouts of weeping might be gradually diminishing; the heartache remained precisely the same, a painful reminder that life could be cruel, and Fate a vicious tormentor for ensuring her path would cross that of a man whom she could not fail to love, but whom she could never hope to marry.

'There were several, Mama,' she admitted softly. 'I was secretly hoping that Lord Nicholas would still be here. Unfortunately, as you probably heard the housekeeper remark after I had enquired, his lordship returned to London this morning.' She shrugged. 'But, no matter. I can see him on our return to town. In the meantime I am determined to enjoy the fresh country air. It will be pleasant to be away from the capital's noise and smells.'

Her ladyship did not doubt that her daughter was being perfectly truthful as far as it went, but she suspected that there was much Sophia was keeping to herself. She refrained from probing further, however, and merely said, 'I sincerely trust we all benefit from this short sojourn in the country, child. But I think I should point out that by encouraging your father to accept Sharnbrook's totally unexpected invitation, you have in all probability put the notion of you achieving a truly splendid match into his head.'

There was a faint reckless quality in Sophia's shout of laughter. 'Well, and why not?'

'Because by your own admission you prefer footmen to marquises.' Her ladyship could not resist reminding her, and then smiled at the astounded expression. 'Yes, I did hear the rumour on the evening of our very own ball,' she admitted, 'and had a fairly shrewd idea from where it had sprung.'

'That I could ever have uttered anything so idiotic!' Sophia exclaimed, utterly ashamed. 'How you have put up with my foolishness all these years, Mama, I shall never know.' A wistful smile tugged at the corner of her mouth. 'Perhaps it has all been a judgement on me, then,' she murmured, hardly aware that she was speaking aloud. 'No more than I deserved.'

The Countess, suddenly alert, detected a look in her daughter's eyes that she had never seen there before. 'What is it, child?' She began to fear the worse. 'Is there something wrong?'

'When we first arrived in London, Mama,' Sophia answered, turning away to stare out of the window at the vast area of parkland, as though seeking solace there, 'I recall Papa was concerned that I should not fall prey to some fortune-hunter. I don't suppose that he ever considered for a moment that his precious daughter might turn out to be the one found wanting, the one who could not quite meet the necessary requirements to make her the perfect wife.'

Turning her back on the magnificent view, she moved swiftly across to the door, fearing that that iron self-control was beginning to show signs of strain. 'Oh, if only frogs could turn into princes!' she cried. 'Well, I cannot have my frog, Mama, so I must be prepared to settle for second best. A duke would suit me as well as any, I suppose.' And before her mother could gather her scattered wits together sufficiently to enquire what on earth she had meant, Sophia had left the room.

For several minutes her ladyship, prey to tumult of conjecture, sat perfectly still, staring in dawning wonder at the closed door, then she flew into the adjoining room to discover her husband, himself standing before one of the tall windows, hands clasped behind his back, contemplating the magnificent views.

'Thomas, we must leave here at once!' she announced, not mincing words.

'Eh…?' Startled out of his reverie, the Earl turned to see his normally placid wife pacing the room like some demented creature. 'Deuce take it, we've only just arrived! What ails you, Marissa?'

'Nothing. But I very much fear Sophia is ailing. And I also very much fear that if Sharnbrook makes her an offer, she'll accept him!'

This was music to his lordship's ears. 'Well, and what of it? It would be a splendid match.'

'Not if she's breaking her heart over her frog, it won't.'

'Frog…?' His lordship's jaw dropped perceptively. 'What the deuce are you talking about, Marissa?' He cast her a sympathetic smile. 'I tell you what it is, old girl. All that gadding about in London has over-tired you, has been a bit of a strain. You need a rest.'

'There's nothing at all the matter with me!' she snapped, for perhaps the first time ever coming perilously close to losing her temper. 'It's Sophia you should be concerned about.' She ceased her pacing. 'I should have realised. I detected the changes in her…knew someone was exerting a beneficial influence…But I never imagined for a moment that she was falling in love…God, what a fool I've been!'

'Fallen in love? Sophia…? With whom, pray?' His lordship was utterly bewildered now. 'With the possible exception of young Risely, she ain't shown a ha'p'orth of interest in any man since we arrived in town, as far as I'm aware.'

'No, I know she hasn't,' her ladyship agreed, concern clearly writ across her pale features. 'And that is precisely what worries me, for I very much fear she has lost her heart to—to someone you would find totally unacceptable.'

'Ha! So that's the way of it, is it!' His lordship bellowed, bringing his fist down none too gently on a conveniently positioned occasional table. 'I might have guessed the little minx would do something like this just to annoy me.'

'If you truly believe that, Thomas, then you do our daughter a grave injustice,' her ladyship countered, surprising her husband out of his ill-humour, and swiftly gaining his full attention. 'If you had not been so wrapped up in your own misery, so uninterested in most everything that was going on about you of late, except your own private concerns, you could not have failed to perceive the changes in Sophia. She has dealt with your megrims and unreasonable behaviour with such a wealth of patience and understanding that I have felt proud to be her mother. Not once did she come even remotely close to losing her temper when you foolishly paraded every buck and dandy you could find before her. And little wonder the poor child remained totally unimpressed with all those candidates you found for her hand, when her feelings were engaged already!'

'Yes, but who is this man, may I ask?' the Earl demanded, not unreasonably.

'I don't know!' Striving to maintain her composure, the Countess seated herself in the nearest chair, and took a moment or two to try to make some sense of her disordered thoughts. 'If I had not been so concerned about you in recent weeks, I might have been more observant where Sophia was concerned. Evidently she's taken great pains to keep the truth from me. Perhaps, in her heart of hearts, she has known all along that by marrying this man she would be making a great *mésalliance*.'

Raising her head, she looked across the room at the Earl who was looking no longer angry, just merely thoughtful. 'In truth, Thomas, I do not know what has been taking place right under our very noses during these past weeks. The only thing I'm certain of is that our only daughter is desperately unhappy and striving not to betray her feelings to anyone. If there is a possibility that a marriage to this unknown man who has won our daughter's affections could take place, are you prepared to sit back and permit her to marry someone whom she could never love merely to please you?'

A long silence, then, 'No, Marissa I am not.' There was no mistaking the old steely determination in his voice. 'Come, let us find our daughter, and discover precisely what has been going on!'

Sophia, blissfully unaware that both her parents were in hot pursuit, was at that present moment walking along the gravel paths at the back of the mansion, and rapidly coming to the conclusion that the strain of the past few days was finally beginning to take its toll. Not only had she come perilously close to breaking down in front of her mother, but now she was convinced her eyes were playing tricks on her, for she had just seen someone who, had she not known better, she could have sworn was none other than her old groom Clem Claypole, mounted on the most magnificent black, heading in the direction of the stable block.

'Unutterable madness!' she muttered, entering a huge conservatory and finding herself amid garlands of fragrant blooms, most of which she did not recognise.

Finding the humidity a little oppressive, but the heady scent quite delightful, she stood for a moment gazing in wonder at the wonderful exotic collection, before focusing her attention on a tall specimen in a huge terracotta pot just a few feet away.'

'Be careful with that,' a beautifully modulated and startlingly familiar voice warned, as Sophia stretched out tentative fingers to touch one leathery, ovate leaf.

'It has travelled a very long way. From the Carolinas to be precise. It is the only specimen on the estate, and so is being treated with the utmost care.'

'Quite understandable,' Sophia responded, quickly withdrawing her hand as though she feared it might get burned, and then turning sharply to see a tall, immaculately attired figure emerge from between the dense foliage. The fact that some detached part of her brain had instantly recognised something achingly familiar in the deep voice should have been sufficient warning, and yet she still found herself gaping like a half-wit when she raised her eyes to see that beloved face, now clean-shaven, and with its crowning golden mane cut to a more acceptable length, smiling down at her.

'Ben!' she gasped, still reluctant to believe the evidence of her own eyes, as she took in every detail of the faultless attire: the well-starched cravat, which despite the humidity managed to retain its crispness, the expensive linen shirt tucked into the waistband of tight-fitting breeches, and the black-leather top-boots with their looking-glass shine. What he was doing here and dressed like a gentleman were the first of many questions amassing in her poor throbbing head, but before she could begin her inquiry an interruption occurred, and she found herself gaping yet again at the equally familiar figure who suddenly appeared in the doorway.

'Clem,' she murmured faintly, wondering if she were truly running mad.

'Hello, my lady. It is good to see you again.' Her ex-groom's lopsided grin faded as he turned to his

new master standing directly behind her. 'I'm sorry
for the intrusion, your grace, but would you be wanting Sultan saddled again today?'

'No, not today, Clem. I envisage my time will be
fully occupied with—er—other and more important
matters.'

Even in her hopelessly confused state, where she
refused to face the one fact that was becoming pat-
ently obvious, Sophia could not fail to detect the note
of amusement in that well-remembered, beloved
voice.

'By the by, has Trapp recovered from the shock of
coming face to face with me yet? I hope you've taken
good care of him.'

'He's sharing my room above the stable, your
grace. We'll perhaps have a tankard or two of ale later
and talk over old times.' Clem chuckled. 'Never fear,
your grace, he'll be as right as rain by morning.'

Somehow managing to respond to her ex-groom's
farewell, Sophia remained staring fixedly at the spot
he had just vacated. 'I know this is going to sound
incredibly foolish,' she said with dangerous restraint,
'but why did Clem refer to you as your grace?'

A brief silence, then: 'All my employees grant me
that courtesy,' Benedict responded softly. He could
almost hear those tiny white teeth grinding together,
and wanted nothing more than to take her into his
arms and kiss away the rising anger before there was
the understandable explosion of wrath, but he remained resolutely standing those few feet away.

'I know how you must be feeling at this precise
moment—hurt, angry, perhaps a little foolish for not

having guessed the truth long ago. Maybe even bitterly resentful because you believe I've been playing some May game at your expense.'

All those things and more, she thought, but said, somehow still maintaining that admirable self-control of which her mother had become so justifiably proud, 'Well...and haven't you?'

'No, my darling. From the start I've been in deadly earnest, wanting only to get to know you a good deal better.'

She did turn to look at him then, and he held the openly sceptical gaze levelly, instinctively knowing what she must be thinking and feeling, and not blaming her in the least for the contempt he saw mirrored in those lovely green eyes. 'I'll own, I did not go about achieving my objective in the most sensible way. In fact, it was damnably foolish of me to pose as a groom.'

'So why did you do it?' she put in, nowhere near ready to believe him yet, nor forgive him, either, for that matter.

'Because of something Nicholas had mentioned about you—about your aversion to titled gentlemen, and because...Oh, I don't know!' He ran impatient fingers through his hair, still annoyed with himself, if the truth were known, for embarking on such tomfoolery in the first place. 'I suppose because I gave way to a moment's sheer irresponsibility, a desire to enjoy just one last madcap venture before I took upon my shoulders the huge responsibility of becoming the head of the noble Risely family. God only knows what madness possessed me! I knew I couldn't hope to maintain the pretence for very long.'

His sigh was so heartfelt that she could not fail to be moved by it. She regarded him in silence, realising in those moments what ought to have been abundantly clear to her from the start—that he was every bit as much in love with her as she was with him. Did anything else really matter?

'I love you, Sophia Cleeve—have done so from the first moment I set eyes on you that morning in Bond Street,' he freely admitted, which merely confirmed what she now knew in her heart of hearts to be true. There was a great deal more she needed to know, but she was prepared to wait. All that mattered was that he was here now.

Something in her expression gave her away, and he was not slow to hold out his hand. 'Will you be my Duchess?'

'Yes,' she answered, willingly surrendering her fingers. 'But only because I intend to spend the rest of my life making you suffer unimaginable torments for the abominable trick you have played upon me!'

His triumphant shout of laughter was muffled in a tender embrace that dispensed with the need for further explanations. They clung to each other, exchanging kiss for kiss, caress for caress, until a staunchly disapproving voice demanding to know what the deuce was going on brought them down from the heady heights of their mutual passion with a jolt, and they fell apart half amused, half shamefaced to see the Earl glowering at them from the doorway, and the Countess looking not just a little confused as well.

'Loath though I am to contradict you on anything, Marissa, but I feel your reading of the situation in this instance is grossly inaccurate,' said his lordship ominously. 'Far from suffering a broken heart, it would seem our daughter is fast becoming a trollop!'

Sophia's only response to this unflattering assessment of her morals was to burst out laughing, and it was left to Benedict to take charge of the delicate situation. Suggesting that his future wife escort her mother back to the house, and arrange for a tea-tray to be brought to the yellow salon, he set about soothing his future father-in-law's ruffled feathers which he did so successfully that his lordship's laughing comment on first rejoining the ladies was, 'My dear Marissa, does it all not make you feel incredibly old? Our groom of all things!'

'Not at all,' she responded, bubbling with mirth herself. 'My only concern is that the gossips will get to learn about it all.'

'I took great pains to ensure that I wasn't recognised,' Benedict assured her. 'But in the unlikely event that someone did penetrate my disguise, I suggest a quiet engagement here at Sharnbrook, which can easily be arranged in a very few days. The Ton will then believe that it was a clear case of love at first sight...Which, of course, is no less than the truth.' He went across to Sophia. 'Are you agreeable to a swift engagement, my love?'

Her glowing smile was answer enough. She was more than happy to fall in with any plans he wished to make, which included a Christmas wedding to be held in the tiny church at Abbot Giles. The Countess was slightly disappointed, for she had dreamed of a truly magnificent wedding for her only daughter.

'It is what they both want, my dear,' his lordship remarked, watching the happy couple wander out on to the terrace a short time later. 'They can, as Sophia suggested, do all the lavish celebrating and entertaining they wish to when they go to London next spring.'

'Yes, of course they can. And I mustn't forget that dear Beatrice and Harry's wedding was a truly charming affair. I see no reason why Sophia's shouldn't be too. They're very much in love, that's plain to see.' She drew her attention away from the glowingly happy couple to glance up at her husband's profile. 'You must be overjoyed by the turn of events.'

'Very,' he assured her, then with an abrupt change of subject said, 'I shall return to London after the party, and arrange for a notice of the engagement to be placed in the newspapers. I see little point in remaining in town until the end of the Season, so I shall return to Jaffrey House at the beginning of June.'

'You mean you won't be returning here?' She was both surprised and disappointed. 'But you heard me promise Benedict that I would remain here with Sophia for several weeks.'

'And so you shall, my dear.' The Earl drew her arm through his. 'It is just that there are one or two matters requiring my attention which I have left unresolved for far too long. Nothing for you to concern yourself about.'

Her ladyship was not so certain, but kept this reflection to herself, and merely allowed him to lead her out on to the terrace to rejoin their daughter and future son-in-law…

The drama continues!

*Look out for more Regency drama, intrigue,
mischief…and marriage in*

The Steepwood Scandals Volume 4

featuring An Unreasonable Match
by Sylvia Andrew & An Unconventional Duenna
by Paula Marshall.

Available next month, from all good booksellers.

THE STEEPWOOD

Scandals

Regency drama, intrigue, mischief...
and marriage

VOLUME FOUR

An Unreasonable Match by Sylvia Andrew

Hester has learnt the hard way that men look for pretty
faces, not stirring debate. Accepting of her life as a
spinster, the last thing Hester wants is to accompany her
family to London for another Season.

❧

An Unconventional Duenna by Paula Marshall

Athene Filmer seizes the opportunity to act as a
companion to her decidedly timid friend when she
enters the *ton*. Could this be Athene's chance to
make a rich marriage?

On sale 2nd February 2007

Available at WHSmith, Tesco, ASDA,
and all good bookshops

M&B

A young woman disappears.
A husband is suspected of murder.
Stirring times for all the neighbourhood in

THE STEEPWOOD
Scandals

Volume 1 – November 2006
Lord Ravensden's Marriage by Anne Herries
An Innocent Miss by Elizabeth Bailey

Volume 2 – December 2006
The Reluctant Bride by Meg Alexander
A Companion of Quality by Nicola Cornick

Volume 3 – January 2007
A Most Improper Proposal by Gail Whitiker
A Noble Man by Anne Ashley

Volume 4 – February 2007
An Unreasonable Match by Sylvia Andrew
An Unconventional Duenna by Paula Marshall

Also available from M&B™ by *New York Times* bestselling author Stephanie Laurens

A superb 2-in-1 anthology of linked Regency stories

Featuring

Tangled Reins

Miss Dorothea Darent has no intention of ever getting married, but the disreputable Marquis of Hazelmere is captivated when they meet — and determined to win her heart…

Fair Juno

The Earl of Merton's days as a notorious rake are numbered when he finds himself rescuing a damsel in distress. But the lady flees the scene without revealing her name, leaving the Earl in pursuit of his mysterious *fair Juno.*

M&B™

Enjoy the dazzling glamour of Vienna on the eve of the First World War…

Rebellious Alex Faversham dreams of escaping her stifling upper-class Victorian background. She yearns to be like her long-lost Aunt Alicia, the beautiful black sheep of the family who lives a glamorous life abroad.

Inspired, Alex is soon drawn to the city her aunt calls home – Vienna. Its heady glitter and seemingly everlasting round of balls and parties in the years before WW1 is as alluring as she had imagined, and Alex finds romance at last with Karl von Winkler, a hussar in the Emperor's guard. But, like the Hapsburg Empire, her fledgling love affair cannot last. Away from home and on the brink of war, will Alex ever see England or her family again?

On sale 3rd November 2006

Set in 1940s London during the Blitz, this is a moving tale about family, love and courage

Queenie McLaren and her daughter Laura have long had to protect each other from Jock Mclaren's violent temper. In 1940, the evacuation of women and children from their homeland in Gibraltar is the perfect chance to escape, and Queenie and Laura eventually find themselves in London during the height of the Blitz.

During the darkest of war years, mother and daughter find courage in friendships formed in hardship, and the joy of new romances. But neither of them has yet heard that Jock is in England — and he won't rest until he's found them...

On sale 20th October 2006

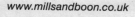

www.millsandboon.co.uk

M&B

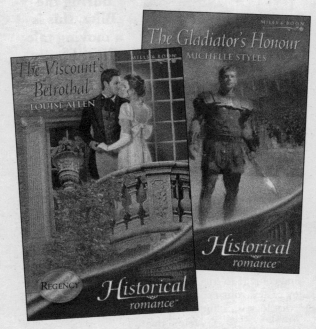

MILLS & BOON®

Live the emotion

Look out for next month's
Super Historical Romance

THE CAPTAIN'S WOMAN
by Merline Lovelace

She followed her heart…and found her destiny!

Victoria Parker has two passions: her journalism, which has
been confined to the society page, and Captain Sam Garrett,
whose heart belongs to another woman. But everything is
about to change.

As American soldiers take arms against the Spanish,
Victoria follows her captain to Cuba. There, instead of a
joyous reunion with the man to whom she has surrendered
body and soul, she finds chaos and heartache.

As Victoria grows from novice reporter to dedicated
journalist, she becomes a proud, courageous woman
– unafraid to fight for her country, her ideals, and her heart!

"…a story of great courage, friendship, loyalty, tenacity
and hope in the face of the horrors of war."
—*Romantic Times BOOKclub*

On sale 2nd February 2007

Available at WHSmith, Tesco, ASDA,
and all good bookshops
www.millsandboon.co.uk